BY DANIELLE TRUSSONI

THE
PUZZLE
BOX

THE
PUZZLE
BOX

A Novel

Danielle Trussoni

RANDOM HOUSE

NEW YORK

The Puzzle Box is a work of fiction. All incidents and dialogue, and all characters with the exception of some well-known historical figures, are products of the author's imagination and are not to be construed as real. Where real-life historical persons appear, the situations, incidents, and dialogues concerning those persons are entirely fictional and are not intended to depict actual events or to change the entirely fictional nature of the work. In all other respects, any resemblance to persons living or dead is entirely coincidental.

Published in the United States by Random House, an imprint and division of Penguin Random House LLC, New York.

RANDOM HOUSE and the HOUSE colophon are registered trademarks of Penguin Random House LLC.

Hardback ISBN 9780593595329
Ebook ISBN 9780593595336

Printed in the United States of America on acid-free paper

randomhousebooks.com

2 4 6 8 9 7 5 3 1

First Edition

Book design by Caroline Cunningham
Title and part-title background image: Adobe Stock /agsandrew

For my son, Alexander,

born in Japan the year of the Gold Dragon

PUZZLE TWO

The Dragon Box

Acquired savant syndrome is a rare, but real, medical condition in which a normal person acquires extraordinary cognitive abilities after a traumatic brain injury. There are fewer than fifty documented cases of acquired savant syndrome in the world.

I

ISE GRAND SHRINE, JAPAN
FEBRUARY 23, 2024
THE YEAR OF THE WOOD DRAGON

The Shinto priest runs to the temple, lifting the hem of his robes to keep from tripping. There isn't time to waste. The first light of dawn is falling through the trees, casting long shadows over fresh-fallen snow. Soon, his brothers will enter the sanctuary and sit before the shrine in prayer. Soon, the most important day of his life will begin, and with it the sacred duty he's spent years preparing to fulfill.

The priest shakes the snow from his robe, bows, and steps into the temple. Incense, thick and fragrant, fills the air. Beyond the shoji doors, candles flicker at the altar, their light bending over copper vessels and pooling over the tatami, leaving him with an impulse to fall to his knees and pray.

It's instinctual. Ingrained. Every day for the past twelve years he's arrived at the temple before sunrise to sit in meditation before the altar. He's never questioned his duty—not why he's there, not what would happen if he failed. None of them did.

And yet, over the years he'd gathered fragments of information about the precious object he guarded, whispers of the lore surrounding the emperor's Dragon Box. He heard that, during the war, the emperor hid the box to protect it from American bombs. In the years since, it had moved to shrines across Japan—Ise Grand Shrine, Atsuta Shrine, the Three Shrines Sanctuary at the Imperial Palace—where priests kept watch day and night, guarding it with their lives.

He'd heard rumors that the box hid a treasure, perhaps an ancient text, maybe even an artifact belonging to the imperial family itself. He'd heard of its dangers: *One look will blind you; one touch will burn your fingers to the bone.* He believed the warnings. Some decades before, a young priest had died cleaning the altar, and no doctor could explain why. The truth was not meant for men like the priest. And so he hadn't asked questions. One indiscretion, the slightest capitulation to curiosity, could be disastrous.

Bells ring in the distance, calling the priests to prayer. The first ray of sunlight falls through the shrine and spills over the floor, illuminating the altar. The seconds rush past, faster and faster, outpacing him. He must hurry before the others arrive. Now is the moment.

Kneeling before the altar, he opens the doors of the tabernacle and there it is: the Dragon Box. Large, the size of two outstretched hands, the box is made of bands of hardwood expertly cut and joined to create a single block. On its surface, composed of curls of inlaid wood, is the twisting shape of a dragon.

The priest sees only the surface, but inside the box, wrapped in layers of deadly traps, lies an ancient enigma, one that has waited thousands of years to be solved.

His instructions are clear. He must wrap the box in a square of silk and carry it to Tokyo. He must not touch it; he must not even look at it. He knows this as well as he knows his norito. And yet, as he gazes down at the Dragon Box, his resolve wavers. Could it be true what they say?

One look will blind you; one touch will burn your fingers to the bone.

He runs a finger over the surface of the wood, feeling the subtle ridges of the jointing, seeking out an opening, slipping a fingernail into a groove, applying the slightest pressure. The razor cuts quick, the blade hot and bright as fire, and draws blood.

Wiping the blood away, the priest wraps the box in silk, ties the ceremonial knot, and tucks it under his arm. Bowing to the altar, to the growing sunlight, to all that he serves—the kami, the emperor, the mountains, the seas—he turns and rushes away.

But already, a seed of poison has dropped roots in his bloodstream. Before the sun will set over the shrine, before the priest fully understands the terrible mistake he's made, he will be dead.

2

NEW YORK CITY
FEBRUARY 22, 2024
THE YEAR OF THE WOOD DRAGON

Mike Brink held his dachshund, Conundrum—Connie for short—tight by the leash. It was a freezing Thursday morning in February, and yet Columbus Park was packed with dogs—Dobermans and collies, golden retrievers and labradoodles, pugs and poodles. Connie strained against her leash, desperate to join the other dogs. Brink understood her impulse to run wild, that exuberant momentum that pulled her toward the melee of dogs racing and jumping through the fresh-fallen snow. Bending to her, he unclipped the leash and she bounded away, leaping and yelping, filled with the ebullient energy of a creature on a scent.

Brink took a deep breath, exhaled, and watched the air freeze around him. It felt good to walk through the snow, a cup of hot coffee in hand, a morning paper under his arm. Good to be alive at a moment in time when, despite everything wrong with the world—and he couldn't read the news without finding a thousand things wrong—he could rely on good coffee, the daily crossword, and a park where his dog could run free.

Opening *The New York Times*, he riffled through the sections until he found the Games page. His puzzle was front and center, his by-line in bold. His editor, Will Shortz, had asked him to make a moderately challenging number puzzle, and he'd delivered a Triangulum.

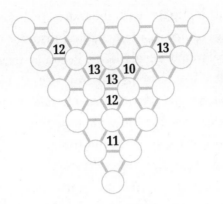

To solve it, one put a number from one to six into each circle. Identical numbers could not be put on the same gray line. He'd put a few sums in the circles, and the solutions touching each circle had to add up to that sum.

His gig as a regular contributor to the Games page was only one of Mike Brink's distinctions. He was considered by and large to be one of the most talented puzzle masters in the world. Six months before, he'd been featured on *60 Minutes*. The interview dug into his past and the traumatic brain injury that had transformed him from a teenaged football star to a mathematical genius with a seemingly endless ability to solve impossible puzzles. He was described as having "nuclear brainpower," and embarrassing memes of explosions ended up all over social media. Since then, he'd stopped giving interviews.

Brink found the attention disconcerting. He preferred the private pursuit of making puzzles to being in the public eye. And yet, after he'd solved what came to be known as "the God Puzzle"—a cipher that was the key to a murder in upstate New York—his name was everywhere. His refusal to discuss what happened—not on any of the morning shows, not even with Colbert, his favorite talk-show host—only made him more mysterious. He was called an eccentric, a reclusive genius *damaged*. And, if he was honest, that assessment wasn't far from the truth.

Damaged. The word resonated with Mike Brink. He'd spent the past decades learning to live with the traumatic brain injury that left him with savant syndrome, a rare medical disorder in which the injured brain, in a frenzy of plasticity, becomes overdeveloped. For Brink, the result was an astonishing gift—he could solve the most difficult, elaborate problems with ease. He saw the world as a series of interlocking patterns. He had a photographic memory, an astonishing facility to learn and retain information, and could untangle the most impossible puzzles without trying.

His gift was a superpower, but it was also his biggest obstacle. He struggled to live a normal life and to feel good in his own skin. While there was no outward sign of damage—he was charming, athletic, and popular with his friends and colleagues—under the surface, Mike Brink was filled with anxiety. The injury had left him with a damaged nervous system, insomnia, and synesthesia, a condition in which his senses mixed, causing a distortion of colors and sounds. Dr. Trevers, a neuroscientist who had worked with Brink from the beginning and had even relocated his practice from the Midwest to New York City to be nearby, speculated that synesthesia was responsible for his mathematical and mnemonic gifts.

"Your brain experiences patterns the way a normal brain experiences danger," Dr. Trevers had once told him. "When you encounter a challenge, there's a release of chemicals similar to those released when one is threatened. Or when one falls in love. The result is a super-salience that feels like connection, like everything makes sense. But these chemicals wear off. Your need to engage with obstacles is a way of getting more of them. Your brain is like a thrill seeker forever raising the bar. You need more-difficult, more-dangerous challenges just to feel normal. You need to put yourself in psychic danger to feel alive."

And it was true. Brink craved strenuous acts of solving. Ten-, twelve-, fourteen-hour contests that exhausted him physically and mentally brought a day or two of peace, sometimes more. But then the cycle would begin again.

With Dr. Trevers's assistance, he'd found ways to manage his condition. Meditation, diet, and exercise all helped to a certain extent, but only momentarily. Like taking an aspirin to mask a headache, the effects wore off, often leaving Brink feeling everything he'd felt before.

Making it all even harder was the fact that his internal struggle wasn't visible to other people. He was regarded as a great success, a handsome and boyish genius, a man who had everything. And while his high profile and his unrelenting schedule of international puzzle competitions created a bubble around him, he found himself longing for the simple things of a normal existence. Friends. Family. The comfort of being just a regular guy living a regular life. This longing would have seemed absurd to the outside world. Everyone believed that success and fame made him happy. In reality, the physical and psychological effects of his injury were a slow, ever-present form of torture. Coming to terms with his gift was the hardest challenge Mike Brink would ever face.

Your brain is a labyrinth, Dr. Trevers had once said. *The most challenging puzzle you will ever confront is yourself.*

Brink took the final sip of his coffee and was folding the newspaper under his arm when he noticed a woman watching from the edge of the park. There were dozens of people at the dog run—it was a popular time at the park, seven-thirty on a Thursday morning. But for some reason this woman stood out. When he met her eye, she didn't blink but watched him, her gaze tracking him. Something about the equanimity of her expression, the way she seemed to recognize him but made no sign of approach, made him feel uncomfortable.

As did her attire. It was frigid, the wind sharpened to a point, and yet she wore nothing more than a black blazer over a hot-pink T-shirt. Her hair was windswept, with a thick strand dyed bright blue. She was Asian, young, and wore no hat, no gloves, not even a scarf. It was as though she didn't feel the subzero wind at all.

Brink pulled a rubber ball from his jacket pocket and threw it to Connie. His fingers stung with cold. He rubbed them together and glanced back at the woman. The wind didn't even faze her. *What did she want? Why was she looking at him like that?*

It was possible that she'd recognized him. It didn't happen often—people knew Mike Brink's puzzles, not his face. Still, occasionally someone would approach him, one of his puzzles in hand, and ask for an autograph or a selfie. But this woman wasn't holding one of his puzzle books, and she didn't seem like the type of person to pose for pictures. Deciding to ignore her, he threw the ball to Connie a few more times, then clipped the leash onto her collar and headed home.

He'd completely forgotten about the woman from the park until he walked up the five flights of stairs to his loft and found her waiting at his front door. Her skin was raw from the cold, her cheeks bright pink, her black leather Doc Martens covered in salt and snow from the sidewalks. Clearly, she'd run from the park. That explained how she beat him to his apartment. It didn't explain how she knew where he lived.

"Hey there," she said, looking him over. "Didn't mean to startle you." She offered her hand. "I'm Sakura. Sakura Nakamoto. Can you talk a minute?"

Her name was Japanese, but she spoke to him in colloquial, unaccented English. He shook her hand. "Mike Brink."

"I know who you are."

Before he could respond, she reached into the pocket of her blazer and, like a magician conjuring a dove from a hat, removed a small wooden box and placed it in the palm of his hand. She stepped away carefully, as if the box were dangerous, a delicate thing wired with explosives. Brink stared at it, amazed. There, light as a pack of cards in his palm, was a Japanese puzzle box.

Turning the box over, he examined it from all sides. It was simple, elegant, the wood surface glossy and smooth. He glanced back at Sakura. Why in the world had she followed him from the park to give him a puzzle box?

She bowed, a formal gesture that seemed out of place in the dingy vestibule outside his loft. "In the name of the emperor of Japan, please accept this challenge."

Brink caught his breath as her meaning became clear. The woman was not an intrepid fan. She hadn't followed him home looking for an autograph. She'd brought an invitation to solve the most challenging and mysterious puzzle in the world: the Dragon Puzzle Box.

3

Mike Brink punched in his door code—his birth date and Social Security number added together, divided in half, and rearranged in a series of ascending numbers. He hadn't memorized the numbers but saw them as a scale of color at the edge of his vision, a byproduct of his synesthesia. Brink didn't know how it worked, only that the colors guided him to solutions, and they were always right.

He led Sakura into an apartment crammed full of his puzzle collection. Stacks of spiral-bound books of crosswords, sudoku, number puzzles, and mazes; a collection of rare books about puzzles; a glass case filled with Rubik's Cubes, nearly five hundred of them, solved and gleaming like cut gems. His cryptic jigsaws hung on the walls, each intricate square puzzle glued and framed like abstract art. And at the far side of the loft, displayed on custom-built shelves, were his Japanese puzzle boxes.

Japanese puzzle boxes were intricate devices filled with secret compartments, trick openings, false walls, and other diversionary tactics meant to confuse and frustrate a solver. In reality, they weren't one box but many—a box within a box within a box. To solve one, you had to arrange its pieces, step by step, in a way that changed the entire structure of the object. One wrong move and the thing closed like a fist. Rubik's Cubes, tangrams, burr puzzles, mazes, entanglement puzzles—all were examples of mechanical puzzles. They were his favorite kind of puzzle, but they could be maniacally difficult.

He'd bought his first puzzle box over a decade ago. He'd sought out a distributor that exported traditional Japanese boxes and ordered them by the dozens. He experimented with elaborate and perplexing boxes, trick boxes designed to turn a solver in circles. He met an innovative American puzzle-box designer who showed him his designs, demonstrating what—with a wicked imagination and a sharp sense of the mischievous—a puzzle-box constructor could do. With their precision and difficulty, their iron-tight sequences, puzzle boxes were like solving a tangible code.

Most people felt their way through the maze of sliding pieces, using trial and error to guide them. Not Brink. He had a sixth sense for puzzle boxes. He intuited each move, felt it in the way a pianist felt the next key or a sprinter the next step. He understood a box's secret language, responded to the slightest pop and click of a mechanism, knew the meaning when a piece slid easily or with resistance. A puzzle box had its own language, and Mike Brink spoke it.

Looking at the box in his hand, he felt an overwhelming urge to open it. "Is this what I think it is?"

Sakura held his gaze, as if enjoying his discomfort, then nodded, a terse gesture that made his heart leap. "Inside that box is an invitation to solve the Dragon Box," Sakura said. "It's yours, if you can get it."

Of course, this small box wasn't the puzzle itself. The Dragon Box would never have been taken from Japan. This was the riddle before the riddle. That was how a puzzle box worked: puzzles within puzzles, patterns within patterns, a nest of infuriating enigmas whose complexity was meant to confuse even the most expert solvers. The Dragon Box was the most complicated of all. It was legendary, as mythic as the riddle of the Sphinx. An invitation to solve it arrived once in a lifetime. He still couldn't quite believe it was real.

He turned the puzzle box in his hand, examining the surfaces. He felt its solidity, the expert construction, the ruthless economy of it.

Despite its size, it was a masterful puzzle box, one he couldn't approach lightly.

"How many moves?"

"This is a three-sun box," she said. "And it requires twenty-four moves to open."

A sun, Brink knew, was a Japanese form of measurement. It equaled roughly an inch. "Seems awfully small for twenty-four moves."

"Size has nothing to do with difficulty." She crossed her arms over her chest, assessing him. "Or the value of the treasure waiting within."

Big things come in little packages. He smiled, acknowledging this truth. "Any special design elements I should know about?"

"There are nothing *but* special design elements. A puzzle box is never quite what it seems. It's a master of illusion. Don't let your guard down, even for a second."

She glanced at his wall of puzzle boxes. He could feel her assessing him, wondering if he was good enough. Did she doubt his abilities? There was no one better. He'd spent years cracking these things. "Ready when you are."

"Good," she said, turning her wrist to reveal an Apple Watch with a black leather band. She tapped the reflective screen, calling up a glowing stopwatch. "You have sixty seconds."

She didn't wait for him to respond. With a tap, the countdown began.

Brink had one minute to solve the puzzle box. But he didn't need a minute. Not nearly. Without fully thinking, without even knowing what he was doing, his mind circled the box, assessing it, tearing at the surface, searching for a way in. That is how it always happened. His mind absorbed a puzzle the way his tongue absorbed taste or his nose scent—effortlessly, as if it were made for that singular purpose. His gift, that inexplicable genius left in the wake of trauma, took over. The first move came to him. Then the second. The solution appeared in his mind like a hologram, the slide of panels, the order of moves, clear and distinct, until the box lay open on the table, solved.

"Impressive," Sakura said, her eyes wide with admiration as she stopped her watch. "You opened it in twelve seconds."

He felt a wave of pleasure, a rush of triumph, a delicious release of chemicals in his bloodstream. That was it. *That* was what he loved about solving, right there—the moment the pieces came together. The moment it all made sense.

"But you're not done yet," Sakura said. "You may use the remaining forty-eight seconds to solve this. . . ."

Inside the box was a piece of crisply folded origami, the paper petals forming a bright yellow-orange chrysanthemum.

"The chrysanthemum is the symbol of the emperor of Japan," Sakura said. "He sends you his sincere hope that you will solve my puzzle."

"*You* designed this?" he asked, realizing that there was more to the origami than an artfully folded paper sculpture.

Sakura nodded, and Brink picked up the origami flower, turning it to examine the edges and shadows, its depths and volumes. It was incredibly light, a thing spun of air. One of the petals was slightly longer than the others, and when Brink pulled it, the flower unfolded into a flat sheet. The paper shifted. There was something underneath. He slid a fingernail along the edge, and the top layer of the chrysanthemum peeled away, revealing a puzzle. A grid had been drawn on one side of the paper and a series of written clues on the other. It was a crossword puzzle, a puzzle within a puzzle, a delicious temptation custom-made for Mike Brink.

Sakura tapped her watch, starting the clock, and Brink went to work.

CLOCKWISE
1 Lower-leg areas • 2 Window parts • 3 For-profit university of Naperville, Illinois • 4 Big houses? • 5 Beginning of many website addresses • 6 Sudden outpouring • 7 Eager to get started • 8 Miracle worker? • 9 Sought the love of • 10 Orthopedic surgeon's focus • 11 It's a little over a yard in Scotland Yard • 12 Leatherman collection • 13 Dwarf's name • 14 Island republic between Italy and Libya • 15___-mouthed • 16 In a clever, deceptive, or unscrupulous way

COUNTER CLOCKWISE
1 Gray-colored • 2 Taxonomic ranks between kingdoms and classes • 3 Every 24 hours • 4 Female donkey • 5 Those with plenty • 6 Mixes things (up) • 7 In an appropriate way • 8 Photographs, briefly • 9 Neighborhood of southern Los Angeles • 10 Idaho's capital • 11 Crescent-shaped • 12 You'd better believe it • 13 Lavished love (on) • 14 Rolling tracts of marshy land • 15 ___ syrup • 16 Tennis great Monica

4

Sakura Nakamoto knew that the opening moves of a game of skill were the most important, and the most difficult. From the outside, they might seem like guesswork—a series of random choices—but they weren't. One must know the right moves without knowing them. One must trust the phosphorescence of intuition, the wisdom of accumulated experience, that subtle, unquantifiable *something* that shows the way like a lantern on a darkened pathway. It was like answering a question that hadn't been asked. Or solving an equation that hasn't been formulated. It was a moment of pure imagination, all possibilities spread before you, beckoning. Some people just jumped in; others were careful, moving into the darkness slowly, one step at a time. Whatever method you used, nailing the opening was essential. One wrong move at the beginning and the whole thing would topple.

Mike Brink was famous for his opening moves. Sakura first heard of him a decade before, when she was thirteen and preparing for her first speed-cubing competition in New York City. Brink was considered the gold standard, the solver everyone wanted to be, so she'd looked him up on YouTube and watched him in action. His style, his speed, his intuitive grasp of solving had changed her way of seeing the game.

Since then, she'd watched hundreds of videos of Mike Brink and read everything she could find about him. The flesh-and-blood man matched what she'd seen online. He was tall, with blue eyes and pale skin and a Roman nose that gave him a strong profile. His sandy-blond hair was stylishly messy, and his three-day stubble made him both disheveled and handsome. His clothes were unassuming, almost plain. He wore red low-top Chuckies, soaked with melted snow, black jeans, and a T-shirt that read MIT PUZZLE HUNT 2015.

Sakura was born in Japan, moved to New York at nine years old, and was completely bilingual. Her intimate knowledge of the United States would be useful in dealing with Mike Brink. As would her training. She was born with a gift for strategy, her father said, and he'd taught her to play Go before she knew how to write complex characters. She'd won her first regional tournament at eight years old, in the adult category, a feat that had brought unwanted attention but fueled a passion for games of skill that never left her.

After she came to live in New York City, her training intensified. She played Go tournaments, won chess competitions, traveled across the United States for all variety of competitions. For fun, she began to participate in competitive video gaming. She won often and became one of the few influential teenaged-girl gamers. Videos of her playing Fortnite had been viewed millions of times. She inspired girls of a certain age to dye a streak of their hair bright aquamarine blue. Even now, years after she'd stopped playing, fans wrote to her.

But few people knew the real purpose of her training. Her skills were, as her aunt always said, a secret weapon. *Acquiring knowledge is good but can also be perilous,* her aunt said, quoting the priest Kōnan Oshō. A heroic warrior, a *kusemono,* must expect that knowledge, even when one has the best intentions, can be dangerous. Become too smart, and you will be become arrogant. Too strong, and you will be challenged. Too kind, and you will be exploited. And so, Sakura hid her skills. Now, at last, it was time to use them.

The teenaged Sakura would have been in awe of Mike Brink, but the twenty-three-year-old woman couldn't afford to be impressed. Too much was at stake. She'd been given the responsibility to oversee every element of the emperor's invitation: delivery of the box; assessment of Mike Brink's capacity to solve it; construction of a second puzzle and securing it inside the box. She'd been told to be ready to answer Brink's questions before escorting him to Tokyo. She didn't anticipate surprises—it was a rare moment when anything surprised her—but all of this had happened so quickly.

Two days before, on a visit to Tokyo, she'd been invited to the Fukiage Palace. She'd been ushered into the private quarters of the emperor, a modern room with plush white carpets and sleek contemporary furniture. An ikebana arrangement on a marble coffee table and a few pieces of traditional art were the only Japanese elements of the room. The emperor and empress sat side by side on a large white couch, waiting. Her aunt Akemi, their private secretary, sat nearby. Sakura hesitated, unsure of why she was there, but her aunt gave her a look and she entered the room, bowed low, her back stiff, her gaze turned to the ground, and waited to be addressed.

"Thank you for coming, Nakamoto-san," the empress said, calling Sakura by her last name, a formal gesture. Sakura felt a stab of unease. She looked to her aunt for some hint at what was happening, but Akemi only nodded, signaling that she should sit. Sakura sat.

"We need your assistance," the emperor said, staring directly at her. As she met his eye, a chill went through her. For thousands of years, the emperor of Japan was revered as a divinity, a direct descendant of the goddess Amaterasu. Sakura was a modern woman, with modern beliefs, and yet there it was, an instinctual need to turn her eyes away. "We require a person who is discreet, fluent in English, and absolutely loyal."

On a table between them sat a small box with an intricate wooden design—the very box she would place in Mike Brink's hands in New York. The emperor had explained what they wanted her to do, and she'd agreed.

"Officially, this invitation does not exist," the emperor had said. "Nor does this trip. If it is discovered, we will deny that it happened at all. As will you."

"Sakura will accomplish this without trouble," her aunt said. Akemi met her eye, and Sakura understood that this had been her doing, that years and years of planning had gone into that single moment. Her aunt had laid the groundwork. Now Sakura must do her part.

"The American man you will be meeting . . ." her aunt Akemi had said before Sakura boarded the imperial jet for New York. "Observe him closely. We have been watching him and believe he is what he seems. But you must confirm this. As you know, there are those waiting for the opportunity to harm us. If you have any doubts, even the slightest, you must inform me. Please be cautious."

Sakura bowed to her aunt, accepting the responsibility of the mission. She felt the weight of her task settle upon her. She was not just a simple emissary. Everything rested upon her expertise, her judgment, her skills. It was only now, after years of training, that she fully understood. The Dragon Puzzle Box had been waiting for her. She'd been preparing her whole life to open it.

5

B rink glanced at Sakura's watch. He had forty-eight seconds to solve the puzzle, not much time. He fumbled in his pocket for his favorite pen, a four-color Bic, and began working out the answers. The solutions came quickly—as soon as he read the clue, the answer was there. He wasn't sure how it happened, but solving word puzzles was more like remembering the answers than searching for them. Like déjà vu, only clear and present and accessible.

Not that this puzzle was easy. Not by a long shot. Sakura had designed a Saturday crossword, as they'd call it at the *Times,* the hardest of the week. But despite the elaborate design of the grid and the challenge of the clues, he blew through it. Some alchemy between his eidetic memory and his vast vocabulary had made solving as easy as breathing: Take the clue in; exhale the answer.

The Dragon Puzzle Box would be different, a challenge beyond any he'd encountered. When he first heard about it as a student at MIT, he'd been instantly intrigued. He'd searched everywhere for more information, hoping to find a photograph of the box, an academic paper, some bit of evidence that it actually existed.

But there was nothing to be found—not online, not in libraries. Nowhere.

The only people who'd ever heard of it were his nerdy puzzle-constructor friends. When he posted a thread on Reddit, the responses were all conspiracy theories—that the box held a map to Yamashita's treasure, the looted gold stolen from Southeast Asian countries by imperial forces during World War II; that it held a *yokai*, or demon, trapped inside by a curse; that the Dragon Box was just a tall tale told to distract American occupying forces after the war. That it never existed at all. Part of him preferred this explanation. If it didn't exist and was just a rumor invented by conspiracy theorists and puzzlers, it couldn't torture him.

Real or not, he'd heard rumors that the last contest, held in 2012, ended in failure. Online puzzle groups claimed that an Australian puzzle solver, a World Puzzle champion many times over who specialized in number puzzles, had been summoned to Japan to open the puzzle box. He'd boarded a plane to Tokyo and was never seen again.

Which only caused the rumors to multiply. Some of Brink's friends in the puzzle world believed the Dragon Box itself was deadly and the guy had died trying to solve it. Others speculated that, having failed to crack the box but knowing too much about it, the puzzle solver was murdered. Others said the puzzle box caused the guy to go mad and that he was wandering the streets of Tokyo, raving.

There was no way to know what the truth might be, but Brink understood that this contest was not any ordinary challenge. It was a life-or-death gamble. One Mike Brink was drawn to in ways he couldn't fully explain.

The truth was: *He didn't have a choice.* After his injury, such challenges became essential. They took on a deep and necessary role in his life. He saw consistencies and patterns everywhere, found elegant, mathematical arrangement in the seemingly chaotic flow of life. He solved impossible equations effortlessly, arranged massively complex systems of information with ease, and remembered thousands and thousands of number sequences without quite trying. But it was the way it made him feel that kept him going. Solving had become his identity. He needed it like air or water or love or shelter.

When he solved something, everything made sense. The universe configured, for a moment, into gorgeous artistic symmetry. It was an illusion, he knew that, but it was his illusion.

The flower crossword puzzle before him, for example, solved itself. When he looked back at the chrysanthemum puzzle, it was complete.

Brink put his pen down. His eye fell over the puzzle, and he saw, amid the chaos of letters, a message. Sixteen letters were highlighted. A solution within the solution. It resolved itself before him, the letters moving clockwise around the flower: *Invitation to Play.*

"Excellent, Mr. Brink," Sakura said, tapping her watch to stop the clock. "You solved my puzzle with fourteen seconds to spare. The emperor will be pleased to hear that you're as good as everyone says you are."

"That was some puzzle," he said, realizing that Sakura Nakamoto was a puzzle master in her own right, one of his own kind.

"Thank you," Sakura said, accepting the compliment lightly. "Now if you don't mind, we need to get going. There is a car waiting downstairs."

"Hold on," he said. "I passed the test, but that doesn't mean I've accepted the invitation."

She stared at him with the same unnerving look he'd noticed at the park. Clearly, she hadn't expected him to resist. No questions. No delays. She wanted him to leave that minute. Which was utterly crazy and yet utterly in line with everything he'd heard about the contest.

"Is this about the reward?" she asked. "I assure you it's substantial. If you succeed, you will be given the Dragon Box itself. It is, as I'm sure you're aware, a priceless artifact, one that many private collectors would be eager to purchase. A conservative estimate of its value is in the millions of dollars."

Sakura glanced at the wall of puzzle boxes, assessing Brink's collection.

"But I have a feeling that the real prize for a man like you isn't money or fame. For someone like you, solving the most difficult, most mysterious puzzle in the world would be reward enough."

She was right, of course; the prize Brink wanted most was the challenge and triumph of solving something no one had solved before. But he couldn't take this lightly. He knew from experience that an enigma could lead to unexpected and dangerous places. If the rumors were true, there was too much at stake. "Before I accept, I need to know the truth about a few things. For example, the Australian solver . . ."

"You are referring to the man who attempted to open the Dragon Puzzle in 2012?"

Brink nodded. "He never made it back home."

She stared at him, refusing to confirm or deny that the Australian solver had gone missing.

"And the solver before that," Brink said. "There's no record of him making it back, either."

She sighed and, weighing her words, said, "Every puzzle master who has attempted to open the Dragon Puzzle Box has died trying. It is dangerous, probably the most dangerous thing you'll do in your life. There is a real chance you will not come back from Japan."

"Reassuring." Without thinking, Brink picked up the puzzle box and, his fingers working it in reverse, retraced his steps, sliding the wooden slats until they clicked into place. He set it on the counter before Sakura. An offering. "Most people wouldn't even consider it."

"You're not most people." Sakura leveled her gaze at him. "And the Dragon Box is not an ordinary enigma. It was created to protect a secret, one that is important to many powerful people. Such a secret is invaluable, especially to you."

Invaluable to him? "I'm sorry, I don't understand what that's supposed to mean—"

"You have more to gain than the glory of winning," Sakura said. "I'm giving you the chance to understand the meaning, and purpose, of your extraordinary gift."

Brink took in this astonishing turn of the conversation. This woman barely knew him—she'd walked into this loft less than twenty minutes before—and now she was offering him the answers to his most profound questions. He didn't know what to think. "That's an awfully big promise."

"I wouldn't say this to just anyone, but you're not just anyone. You're the best solver I've ever seen. I know you're capable of winning. But you need to know that you have a reason to do it. And I'm here to tell you, Mike Brink, that you do."

6

The Hanwha IR motion-activated security camera detected a human presence at the southeast entrance of the Kōkyo. The live-stream feed tripped, the camera's arm swiveled right, the lens dilated, retracted, then focused on a man stumbling through the wide central corridor of the palace. He wore light-blue *jōsō* priest's robes, signaling his rank, and plain black boots that streaked snow over the marble floor. He carried an object tucked tightly under his right arm, a package wrapped in a white cloth. The Dragon Box, most certainly.

The priest swayed as he navigated the wide central corridor, his gait haphazard, causing the arm of the camera to track him in a dizzying sequence of movement, until he fell to the ground, heavy as a marionette cut from its strings. The camera's position became fixed, taking everything in. It recorded the robes that spread, blue as pooling water. It saw the still fingers, the inexpressive face, the motionless boots. Nothing moved. The infrared monitor flashed his body temperature as it declined. The priest was dead.

Akemi Saito, private secretary to the imperial family, entered the purview of the camera and squatted next to the man. She placed two fingers on his neck, feeling for a pulse. The camera took in her expression of shock. It recorded the careful urgency with which she stood, walked around the body, and examined it from every angle. But it could not record her thoughts. It could not see the frantic interior monologue that materialized, one that threatened her self-control.

There were many possible complications that could've arisen, she thought, but this was not one she'd imagined. *What on earth was she going to do?* She would have to remove the body. She would have to inform the emperor. She knew exactly what the empress would say: *A death before the contest is a very bad omen.*

As the private secretary to the emperor and empress, Akemi was privy to information unknown to the general population and even to the other members of the imperial family. There were small, personal secrets she must protect, anything that might reveal that the imperial family was as human as every other. And then there were the darker secrets, the ones that must be guarded at all costs. The Dragon Puzzle Box was one such secret.

Now was not the time for indecision. There was a body lying at the entrance of the Imperial Palace. It needed to be removed immediately. Akemi composed a list in her mind, a series of action points as she struggled to put her thoughts in order. First, and most important, she needed to clean this up. But how did one dispose of a corpse? It wasn't a problem she'd encountered before. She couldn't very well call the monastery and arrange for the priest's body to be returned, and she most definitely couldn't inform the Tokyo police. The priest was a small man, but she couldn't move him alone. Even the Imperial Household Agency, whose building was one hundred yards from the Kōkyo, couldn't be trusted with this.

She took her phone and sent a message to the only person who could be absolutely trusted. *The messenger is dead. Send someone here now.*

As she waited, she stood over the priest, transfixed. She studied his features, trying to read his expression. What could have inspired him to disobey such important orders? What had he felt in those last moments of life? Regret that he'd betrayed the emperor? Relief that he'd died knowing something, however minute, about the Dragon Box? Had he realized, as his limbs became heavy and each step became labored, that the very object he'd spent so many years protecting had betrayed him? It was incredible. The priest's curiosity had been more powerful than his faith, stronger than honor. It had corroded decades of loyalty, thousands of hours of veneration. But it shouldn't surprise Akemi. It was human nature to be curious. She herself was curious about the contents of this box. Only she would never, never allow curiosity to betray her.

She sighed, putting an end to such frivolous thoughts, and bowed to the body of the priest, the lowest, most formal bow she could manage. Then, using the silk cloth to protect herself, she lifted the box from the priest's hands. It was remarkably heavy, a brick of steel encased in wood. She imagined the maze of puzzles inside, the intricate and cruel tests. Its contents had the power to change everything. And in a few hours, she would know its secrets.

Stepping away from the body, she knelt and wrapped the box in the square of white silk. As she fastened it, tying the corners tight in a knot, she noticed a drop of blood, the priest's blood, in the fibers. It had expanded to a diffuse circle, a perfect red sun in the white fabric. If she needed proof that the priest had tried to open the box, it was right there before her—the cut on his finger, the bloodstained silk. He'd betrayed the emperor. There was no question that he deserved to die.

And yet she felt pity, not for the priest exactly but for all humankind. Pandora wasn't evil, after all. She hadn't intended to unleash suffering into the world. She'd simply needed to know what was inside the box.

7

Mike Brink caught the Q train at Canal Street. His appointment with Dr. Trevers was in less than half an hour at New York Presbyterian, all the way up at 68th and York, and even on the express train, he'd be late. He took a seat near the door. Connie settled at his feet, her nose angling toward a bag of Chinese takeout, then a guy's sweaty gym socks, then a woman wearing a wood-and-citrus perfume. A dog's sense of smell was acute and overpowering, the singular organizing principle of its experience of the world, much like patterns and puzzles were for Mike Brink. While Connie couldn't escape the smorgasbord of scents on the subway, Brink couldn't help but see the weave of hexagons on a sign advertising a dating app, the perfect cylinders of the metal poles stationed throughout the car, the delicate checked pattern of a silk tie that he knew, without quite knowing how, had 749 tiny squares.

He closed his eyes to block out the stimuli, and the extraordinary events of that morning filled his mind. He saw the puzzle box, the origami flower, the intricate crossword: *Invitation to Play*. He heard Sakura telling him that the contest would teach him something about himself, something he needed to know. But most of all, he considered the choice he must make about the Dragon Box. He'd proven himself worthy. He'd been invited to Japan to solve the most elusive and challenging puzzle in the world. But was it worth the risk?

He needed to talk to Dr. Trevers. He would help him think it all through. Over the past decade and a half, Brink had come to trust Trevers's judgment. Trevers knew which competitions he should enter and which ones would send him over the edge. He helped him understand what he called Brink's "reckless impulses": his restlessness, his anxiety, his constant need to—as Dr. Trevers said—rebalance the chemicals in his brain. Dr. Trevers believed Brink was addicted to the cycle of risk and reward that solving gave, forever pushing himself to more-difficult challenges, but that there was a way to get off the roller coaster. A way to stop it. And when he was with Dr. Trevers, Mike Brink believed it, too.

Trevers was more than a doctor. He'd become, over the past sixteen years, like a father. Brink's dad had died over a decade before, when Mike was at MIT. His mother was French and moved back to Paris. Brink had no other family. Dr. Trevers filled the void, inviting him for Sunday lunches at his apartment, stopping by Brink's loft to check in, going on long walks through Central Park with Brink and Connie. He'd become a friend, a mentor, his only family.

Dr. Trevers would be happy to hear how Brink had handled the invitation to solve the Dragon Puzzle Box. While his first reaction had been to accept it, he'd played it cool. He told Sakura he needed time to think it over. He told her he'd call her later with his answer. He'd behaved, in other words, less like an addict and more like a rational human being.

And yet even now, on the train to see Dr. Trevers, he trembled at the idea of it. *Puzzles within puzzles, patterns within patterns, a nest of infuriating enigmas.* It was the most tempting opportunity of his life.

He picked up Connie and exited at the 72nd Street station, emerging onto Second Avenue. It was cold, the wind bitter, and he zipped his jacket to his chin and hurried east. Glancing at his watch, he saw that he was ten minutes late. Trevers wouldn't be happy, but he was used to Brink by now and understood that his timing, speed-cubing aside, could be imperfect.

It wasn't a great day to be late. Aside from the Dragon Puzzle, they had a lot to talk about. For the past year, Dr. Trevers had been developing a new treatment. Brink knew very little about it, only that Trevers had been experimenting with a cocktail of medications to regulate the chemicals in his brain. The right doses of the right drugs, Trevers believed, would diminish the side effects of his traumatic brain injury and allow Brink to live a more normal life.

Not that he'd ever be normal. Dr. Trevers made it clear that medication could diminish his symptoms but never change what Brink had become. The damage was irreversible. Still, the treatment would help him sleep more than three hours at a time, allow him to reduce his grueling schedule of exercise, diminish the onslaught of synesthesia, and stop the incessant patterns and equations that made his daily life such a challenge. It would, in short, allow him to live the life his injury had stolen.

When Brink first learned of the treatment, he'd been stunned. The possibility of controlling his brain filled him with both hope and fear. If Dr. Trevers had developed such a treatment, Mike Brink could have something he'd never imagined: *a choice*. He could choose to be the most talented puzzleist in the world, or he could choose to be a normal person, living a normal life.

Running up the hospital steps, Brink pushed into the warmth of the lobby, took the elevator up to NEUROLOGY, and stepped into the reception area of Dr. Trevers's office. After years of regular appointments, the place felt like a second home—he'd been through every test imaginable in that office, had his weekly check-ins with Trevers in that office, knew where they kept the MRI and Nespresso machines, and had become friendly with April, the receptionist, a woman in her fifties for whom Brink designed custom crosswords. And so Brink knew, the second he walked into the reception area, that something was wrong.

April stood in the waiting area, her eyes swollen. "You didn't get my messages?"

Brink felt a burst of panic. *Her messages?* He hadn't had a second to look at his phone. He glanced past her and saw three men standing in the hallway outside Dr. Trevers's office. Between them was a gurney holding a body bag.

He shook his head, trying to understand what he was seeing. "There wasn't reception in the subway," he said. "What's going on?"

"Mike," April said, stepping close and placing a hand on his arm, a gesture of comfort. "The cleaning crew found him this morning."

Conundrum was wagging her tail, filled with excitement. Dr. Trevers always had a bag of treats in his desk drawer. A series of emotions flooded through Brink—confusion, denial, a mad scrambling to understand what she meant. What on earth was she talking about? "*Found* him?"

"He must've come in last night to finish entering some of his notes into the system. I know this is going to be hard on you. I'm so sorry."

Brink studied the shape of the body bag. It was short, stocky, roughly the size of Dr. Trevers. He knew, suddenly, that Dr. Trevers was gone. His body felt hot, cold, then numb. He needed to sit down.

"Come over here, honey." April took Brink by the arm and led him to a couch. He sat and stared at her, trying to take it in. It struck him that her eyes were swollen from crying. April had known that Dr. Trevers was dead for a while, even as Brink had traveled on the Q train.

"What happened?" he asked finally. He could hardly speak. It was as though he'd been punched, hard. Even breathing hurt.

April sighed. "They don't know yet. The door to his office was locked from the inside. They found him at his desk, slumped over the keyboard. The medical examiner is here, and they're going to make a report, but it sounds to me like a heart attack."

"We had an appointment today," he said, as if it mattered. He knew there was nothing he could do, but he couldn't get his mind around what was happening—the one person in the world who could help him was dead.

April stared at him, clearly concerned. "I'll let you know as soon as the medical examiner finishes his report. It could take a day or two."

He leaned against the back of the couch, feeling weak. He couldn't begin to think through what this meant. Dr. Trevers was his lifeline, the one person who'd guided him through the confusing nature of his disorder. His mentor. His friend. After his father died, it was Dr. Trevers Brink went to for support. He'd spoken to him just a few days before. They'd gone through the repercussions of moving forward with the treatment. Brink had told Dr. Trevers that he needed time to think about it. It was an impossible position—he could feel good and in control, or he could feel bad and do the one thing that made him utterly extraordinary. *Damned if I do, damned if I don't,* he'd said.

"Listen," April said, squeezing Brink's hand. "I probably shouldn't have touched anything in there before the medical examiner signed off, but I took this for you." She gave him a framed picture of the two of them, Dr. Trevers and Mike Brink, standing together at the World Puzzle Championship in 2018. It had been a moment of glory for Brink, one that Dr. Trevers shared. The men were arm in arm, Brink holding a trophy for the camera as Trevers smiled with the pride of a father for an ingenious son.

8

Mike Brink left the hospital in a daze, and forty-five minutes later he found himself on the Upper West Side, shivering outside Rachel Appel's apartment building. The doorman knew Brink, nodded as he approached, and handed him a package that had been left earlier that morning for Rachel. The doorman probably thought they were dating—Brink came over a few times a week and was on his list of visitors who were welcome anytime. Anyone watching closely might have thought the same thing. Rachel was his close friend, someone who knew his history, both medical and personal, and one of the only people he could tell something as serious as what had happened that morning. He needed to talk to her right away and hoped she was home.

They'd met nearly two years before, when Rachel was a world-class scholar and the director of an institute that housed and preserved religious manuscripts. He'd needed help understanding the complexities of a cipher made by a thirteenth-century mystic, and she'd come to the rescue.

Since then Rachel had become a regular presence in his life, a trusted confidant, and someone who never let him down. They spoke almost daily about everything from Rachel's research into feminine mystery cults to Brink's obsession with breaking his own Guinness

Record in reciting pi places. Their interests couldn't have been more different. Rachel was a historian of ancient religious texts, and her work on the history of the role of women in mystical traditions had made her famous—and controversial—in certain circles. Brink, on the other hand, had no interest in academics, mysticism, or anything that might keep him in a library for more than five minutes.

And yet they'd become close. They had dinner together a few times a week. She'd show up at Brink's loft with takeout, and he would push aside the stacks of papers on his kitchen table—his puzzles-in-progress were all drawn by hand with his Bic four-color ink pen on yellow legal pads—and they would eat and talk until late in the night. Rachel was an ally, sympathetic to the ongoing drama caused by his abilities, and his closest friend.

Deep down, he suspected that her interest in him wasn't only because of his humor and good looks. He knew Rachel was curious about savant syndrome, and many of their conversations revolved around her theories on his cognitive abilities. She believed that his gifts were connected to certain strains of mystical experience in the ancient world, and although she'd never come out and said it, Brink was sure she wanted to write about him in some capacity.

Just after they'd met, Rachel broadened the scope of her research, incorporating areas of study that might explain what she called his "miraculous gifts." She created a database of information that included anything that might illuminate Brink's cognitive abilities— religious experiences, parapsychology, liminal meditative trances, psychedelic practices that created ecstatic experiences. She believed his acquired savantism to be more than a neurological disorder, more than a simple empirical phenomenon. She'd once described his brain as a "crack in the wall between the human and the divine." His condition made him, in her words, "a conduit of the gods."

It wasn't lost on Brink that Rachel's views about his brain were exactly the opposite of the theories held by Dr. Trevers. He believed that what happened to Brink was a purely neurological event. His brain was altered by acute trauma; to adapt, the brain entered a period of intense plasticity that enabled certain abnormal traits: a photographic memory, an ability to solve highly complex mathematical problems, and an automatic response to patterns and puzzles of all kinds. An exceedingly rare but wholly explicable medical phenomenon. End of story.

"Maybe the brain injury explains *how* it happened," Rachel said whenever Brink argued Dr. Trevers's point. "But it doesn't explain why you're accessing information that you've never encountered before or where this information is coming from. You have access to stuff that you couldn't have possibly learned. For centuries, philosophers have argued that the universe is filled with information and that certain people can access it. And somehow, through your injury, *you can.*"

While Brink didn't share Rachel's faith—he was agnostic at best—he was willing to consider Rachel's theories, at least as much as he considered Dr. Trevers's ideas. These two doctors—one of philosophy, the other of medicine—created opposite poles in his life: the spiritual and the empirical. None of their theories helped him sleep at night.

But while her ideas about his injury didn't do much for him, Rachel's friendship did. With Rachel, he could talk about everything, however weird it might be.

That morning, Brink knocked on her door, holding her package in one hand and Connie's leash in the other. As always, Rachel was put together perfectly. She wore a pretty brown dress, one that highlighted her blue eyes and long dark hair, and a hint of gloss on her lips.

"Good morning," she said cheerfully, but didn't give Brink a second glance as she scooped Conundrum into her arms like a baby, rubbing her ears and kissing the top of her head. Connie let out a high-pitched yelp, her tail swishing with pleasure.

"Hello, you," she said, hugging Connie as she walked down a hallway filled with framed black-and-white photographs of Greek goddesses—Athena and Aphrodite and Hera. "Come with me, you sweet thing, do I have a treat for you!"

Brink put the package on a table and followed Rachel into her apartment, a spacious prewar with wood paneling, elegant wallpaper, and built-in bookshelves at every turn. He didn't know much about New York City real estate, but he knew this was a building with a years-long waiting list and a ruthless co-op board that was impossible to impress. But the apartment had been in Rachel's family since the building was constructed in 1887, which meant Rachel never had to worry about her co-op board.

Brink heard classical music playing—a Brahms string quartet—and he followed the music to her office at the end of the hallway. He walked into a spacious room with a wall of windows that gave a sweeping view of Central Park. Her gorgeous mahogany attorney desk was stacked with books and papers. A laptop was open. She'd been working.

She gave him a curious look. "Aren't you supposed to be at New York Presbyterian?"

"Yeah, I'm just coming from there," he said, feeling his chest tighten as he remembered why he'd come. "There was—"

Rachel held up a finger. "Hold that thought," she said, giving him a smile. "I made coffee."

As Rachel made noise in the kitchen, Brink sat on a tufted leather sofa and took out his phone. He opened his email app and scrolled through the messages, half-hoping that April would have more information for him. If the cause of death was a heart attack, surely they would know that by now. His pulse quickened as he saw a message not from April but from Dr. Trevers himself. He glanced at the time stamp. It had arrived in his inbox at 2:36 that morning.

The door to his office was locked from the inside. They found him at his desk, slumped over the keyboard.

Brink tapped on the message, opening it. The body of the email was completely blank, containing nothing but an image:

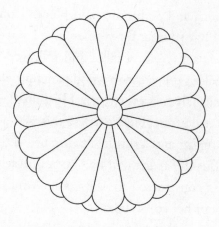

"What the hell . . ."

He saw the puzzle box, the origami flower, the swirl of numbers and letters of the puzzle. *An Invitation to Play*. Dr. Trevers's message had been sent a full five hours before Brink met Sakura Nakamoto. The doctor had most likely been dead when Brink opened the puzzle box and solved Sakura's word puzzle. And yet, somehow, he had known about the invitation. For reasons Brink couldn't explain, Dr. Trevers had sent him the imperial chrysanthemum.

9

Rachel felt a rush of pleasure as she put coffee cups on a tray, one for her and one for Mike. There were cinnamon buns in the oven, and she pulled them out and carefully arranged them on a plate. She loved that Mike stopped over unannounced. It was something that would annoy her had it been anyone but him. But she was always happy to see him and Connie. She'd felt that way since the day he stormed into her life nearly two years before. Since then, Mike had become important to her, a friend, someone whose very existence changed the way she saw the world.

Aside from their friendship, the most significant shift was professional. After seeing Mike's incredible abilities firsthand, she found herself deeply drawn to the mystery of his mind. She needed to understand it. Rachel was a smart woman. She had degrees from prestigious universities; she was practical, hardworking, creative, a woman at the top of her field. But she was aware that there were limits to research. Mike proved that to her again and again. He showed her that the miraculous could arrive in our lives at any moment, that it existed in the here and now, not in books. Someone extraordinary had arrived in her life, and she wasn't going to let him go.

Since the death of her husband, Isaac, nearly five years before, she'd made a decision to experience everything she could, to accept what life brought her. She was thirty-four years old, widowed and childless, independently wealthy, and quite aware that life could change quickly, violently, without warning. Isaac had been only thirty-five when he died of lung cancer, a nonsmoker with no family history of cancer. It had been so sudden, so shattering, that there was a time she believed she would never recover. There were moments when she wondered about the value of her life. Why was she still here when Isaac was gone? What was her purpose? After meeting Mike Brink, she knew.

Her goal now was to spend time with Mike Brink himself. In the past months, she'd accompanied him to his competitions, recording them, interviewing him about what he experienced, charting his best times. She took care of Connie, learning all the details of her special diet, where she went for her morning walk, and how Mike cared for her. He trusted her with Connie, which essentially was like trusting her with his child. When they'd gone to a pi competition in Amsterdam the month before, Rachel babysat Connie, which put Mike at ease and allowed him to break the world record. Brink needed the routine and reliability of his relationship with Connie to stay even, especially when he was doing up to six competitions a month, in addition to his work as a puzzle constructor for various magazines and newspapers.

All variety of practical matters were challenging for Mike. After realizing that he was living on coffee and potato chips, Rachel helped him set up a recurring grocery delivery, so he had real food coming regularly. One afternoon she stopped by his apartment, only to find that his electricity had been turned off. She found a pile of mail overflowing from a shoebox. It turned out there were months' worth of unpaid bills—the electricity bill included—but also over fifty thousand dollars in uncashed checks: prizes from various competitions he'd won. She asked him to log into his bank account, which she found was overdrawn. She had him sign the checks and deposit them electronically, then she introduced him to her accountant.

Mike also struggled with women, a situation that she found somewhat baffling. He was handsome, kind, and emotionally tuned in. After his injury, he'd spent years learning the cartography of his emotional world, exploring how his perceptions had been altered, refining his ability to communicate feelings until he was as perceptive about people as he was about puzzles. And yet women came into his life and faded away. He'd never had a girlfriend for more than three or four months. She guessed that the intensity of his routine—necessary to ward off the demons of savantism—left little room for romance. Mike worked out twice a day, jogging miles and lifting weights, spent the interim hours in a state of deep concentration as he constructed and solved, and hung out with Connie in his downtime. Heavy drinking and late nights were out of the question, as they disrupted his routine.

One woman, a writer named Jess Price, had seemed a promising match. She'd been erroneously convicted of murder, and Mike had proven her innocence by solving a cipher—the same cipher that had brought Mike to Rachel for help. The incident had become widely known as the God Puzzle and had created more attention than Mike wanted. He'd gone into hiding after the news broke and stopped seeing Jess, who courted the press, selling a memoir about the experience and, after the rights had been bought by Netflix, moving to Los Angeles to work on the adaptation.

Although he never spoke of it, Mike had been hurt by Jess. Watching him suffer made Rachel want to act as a shield between him and the rest of the world. She was suspicious of this impulse—it was such a typical female reaction to nurture and protect those in need, and as a feminist scholar and an expert in representations of women in ancient religions, she shouldn't be falling into the same old trap women had fallen into since the beginning of time. But she knew that this was different. Mike Brink was different. She observed the chemical imbalances that made the simple act of living—eating, sleeping, *being*—painful for Mike, and she wanted him to find relief.

"You have a thing for this guy," her friend Cullen Withers, director of the Morgan Library, said one afternoon when Rachel met him for lunch. "I get it. He's handsome. Smart. Damaged. I haven't heard you talk about anyone like this since Isaac passed. Don't try to tell me he's just a friend."

"I don't have a *thing*," Rachel said. "At least, not *that* kind of thing."

But Cullen was right. There was something about Mike Brink that exhilarated her. He was more than a friend and more than the subject of her work. He inspired her. He made her believe in things that she hadn't believed in for a long time. He made her see that the here and now was awe-inspiring, magnificent. That there was a place in the world for her. He gave her faith. She believed, with all her heart, that Mike Brink had come into her life for a reason. He was her friend and collaborator, the focus of her work. Their relationship was unique, a once-in-a-lifetime connection, and she wanted to protect it from anything that might alter or taint it. Including love.

10

As Rachel returned with a tray of coffee and cinnamon rolls, Brink took a deep breath, trying to find the right words to explain what he'd experienced that morning.

She's never going to believe this.

He stood, took the tray from Rachel, put it on a table, poured her a cup of coffee, then one for himself. She handed him a plate with a cinnamon roll, which he ate as he sat on the leather couch. The moment was so perfect, the taste of cinnamon and icing and raisins so good, that it made the news ever harder to deliver. *Impossible.* It was impossible that Dr. Trevers was dead. Part of him believed that if he didn't talk about it, it wasn't real.

"Something's on your mind," Rachel said, giving him a look. That was all it took. He broke down and explained everything—the woman in the park, her surprising arrival at his loft, the Japanese puzzle box, and the invitation to Tokyo from the emperor. He opened his messenger bag, removed the puzzle box and the chrysanthemum word puzzle, and placed them on the couch. Then he explained Dr. Trevers's death, feeling, suddenly, his eyes burning.

Rachel stared at him, wide-eyed with surprise. She got up from her chair and came to the couch to sit next to him. "Mike . . . I'm so sorry."

He'd held back tears for the past hour, but he felt himself on the verge of losing it. Taking a sip of coffee, he steadied himself. "April thinks it was a heart attack."

Rachel shook her head, stricken. "And that happened *this morning*? After the invitation to Japan?"

Brink nodded. It wasn't even noon, and already it was one hell of a day.

"So, what you're telling me is that the *same morning* Dr. Trevers passes away, you get an invitation to solve one of the most difficult puzzles in the world."

"*The* most difficult puzzle."

"Odd, don't you think?"

"It gets even weirder." Brink opened his phone and showed her Dr. Trevers's message with the chrysanthemum. She looked from the piece of origami to the screen, astonished.

Rachel took a deep breath. "Did you ever discuss this contest with Dr. Trevers?"

Brink shook his head. "I've never discussed it with anyone. Until a few hours ago, I thought it was just some crazy legend. But it's starting to look like there's some connection between this contest and Dr. Trevers."

"Could he have known the woman who delivered this invitation?"

Brink took the paper and folded it until it returned to the original origami shape—a crisp orange flower—then placed it lightly on the leather couch, before Rachel. A perplexing gift. "I mean, look at this. Who flies halfway around the world to deliver an invitation like this?"

Rachel raised an eyebrow and shook her head in disbelief. "I have to agree—this is very strange. And while you tend to attract these kinds of bizarre experiences, this is extraordinary. I mean: *the imperial family of Japan?*"

"What do you know about them?" Brink asked, drinking the last of his coffee.

"Well, I know that they are the longest-consecutive-reigning monarchy in the world. And that the emperor of Japan is the symbolic head of the Japanese religion—Shinto. It's a religion that I find interesting for many reasons but especially because there is also a strong feminist element to it. It was founded by a female deity, a sun goddess. That's about all I know, but I could certainly get more information if it will help you make a decision about this invitation."

Brink picked up the puzzle box and opened it, his fingers sliding over the pieces with ease. Solving helped him think. "This morning, I wasn't sure if I would go," he said. "But now I know that I don't have a choice."

Rachel watched him, picked up her coffee, noticed the cup was empty, and put it back down. "You always have a choice."

"How can I possibly refuse?"

"It's pretty darn easy. You say *no*."

"After *that*?" He glanced at his phone, where the chrysanthemum image glowed orange on the screen. "There's no way I could live without knowing why Trevers sent that message. After all he's done for me . . ." Brink felt tears collecting, and he turned away. He wasn't going to break down in front of Rachel. "I owe him at least that."

"Whatever you find out in Japan isn't going to change the fact that he's gone," Rachel said softly. "If he were here, he'd want you to protect yourself. *I* want you to protect yourself."

Brink knew Rachel was right. The risk he took in accepting the challenge was wildly irresponsible. The danger was clear: Every solver who had attempted to open the Dragon Puzzle Box had failed. And yet he couldn't walk away. He needed to go, not only because this was the biggest challenge of his life, but because the answer to Dr. Trevers's death was in Japan.

He took his phone, found the number Sakura had given him that morning, and typed out a text message: *Send me the flight information. I'll meet you at the airport.*

"I've accepted the invitation," he said, looking up at Rachel. "But I don't know who to trust. There must be a connection between Sakura and Trevers."

"You think she's involved?"

"I don't know, but I can't trust her—or anyone, actually—until I know what Dr. Trevers was trying to communicate with that symbol. I need someone there I can rely on."

He met Rachel's eye and felt an overwhelming warmth. When he needed someone, it was Rachel he turned to first.

"Please come with me."

Rachel stood, collected their coffee cups, and placed them on the tray. "I would never dream of letting you go alone."

11

Sakura bought a grande caramel macchiato and parked herself at a café table facing the entrance of Teterboro Airport. Mike Brink should be here any minute, and she didn't want to miss him.

She leaned back in her chair, pushed the strand of blue hair out of her eyes, and felt a wave of caffeine and sugar wash through her. She wasn't sure Mike would show up. The contest had spooked him, that much was obvious. He could change his mind, ghost her, disappear without a word, leaving her to return to Tokyo ashamed and alone. If she could just get him on the plane, if she could present him to the emperor, there would be no going back.

Glancing at her watch, she saw that it was nearly two in the afternoon. They needed to leave soon. She was doing the math—calculating the fourteen-hour flight minus the time difference between New York and Tokyo—when a message arrived from her aunt Akemi, asking for an update on behalf of the emperor and empress. Sakura responded with the good news: They'd be leaving within the hour. Her aunt replied immediately, and Sakura imagined Akemi walking in triumph through the halls of the Fukiage Palace to the private quarters of the emperor. *Her niece had come through.*

Sakura sighed, filled with anxiety. *What if he doesn't show?* Akemi would never forgive Sakura. As the personal secretary to the imperial family, Akemi's priority was to protect the emperor and empress from disappointment. She accompanied them to events and dinners, smoothing the way as they engaged with the real world, anything outside the protective bubble of the Imperial Palace. But if Mike Brink didn't walk through that door and get on the emperor's plane, it would be catastrophic. A disappointment even Akemi's incredible diplomacy could never alleviate.

Sakura had met the emperor Naruhito and the empress Masako for the first time eighteen years before, when they were the crown prince and princess. She'd been only five years old but remembered the day vividly. Aiko, the only child of the emperor and empress, who was almost the same age as Sakura, needed a playmate. Akemi suggested Sakura and brought her to the imperial residence to meet Aiko. The girls became instant friends, the way children do, without understanding the strictures of protocol. They fought over toys, laughed uncontrollably at silly jokes, and shared their bento boxes.

From the instant Sakura met Aiko, whose official name was Princess Toshi, she knew there was something special about her, something deeper and more unique than having been born into the oldest consecutive monarchy in the world. Sakura was precocious, but Aiko was even more so. Once, when the girls were six years old, Sakura watched in amazement as Aiko solved a complicated burr mechanical puzzle, disentangling the pieces with ease. Sakura had been deeply impressed and worked to match Aiko's skill. Aiko was also smart, funny, and humble, never lording her status over Sakura. But even more than these qualities, Sakura felt an aura around Aiko, something magnetic. She couldn't explain it, but at times Aiko seemed to be filled with light, her manner both of this world and another. It wasn't an exaggeration to say that there was something profound, even magical, about the princess Toshi.

Over time, duty and circumstance created distance between them, but Sakura still considered Aiko to be one of her closest friends.

Aiko's parents saw Sakura as their daughter's playmate and in some ways treated her like part of their family, calling her Sakura-chan, a playful term of endearment. The empress had always used the term with affection, denoting that she felt a maternal regard for Sakura.

The only time they'd addressed her formally was when they asked her to deliver the invitation to Mike Brink. She shouldn't have been surprised that they asked such an important request—they'd known her most of her life and trusted her—and yet she was. They'd given her access to one of their most important secrets. But what did they really know about her, or about Akemi?

At the far end of the terminal, Mike Brink walked through the glass doors. Sakura stood, grabbed her coffee, and walked to meet him. There was a problem; she saw it immediately.

He wasn't alone.

Mike approached with a tall white woman with long dark hair. Sakura hadn't anticipated having to deal with another person, just as she hadn't anticipated that Mike might refuse the invitation. Two surprises in one day. Not her finest moment.

Hurrying to him, she greeted Mike and nodded to the woman. He introduced her as Rachel Appel. She seemed to be about Mike's age, wore an elegant trench coat and leather boots, pulled a leather Louis Vuitton suitcase, and had an expensive watch on her wrist. She extended her hand, but Sakura didn't take it.

"I'm sorry, but this invitation is for one." Sakura glanced at Connie. "And a half."

"I accepted the invitation, but I have one condition: Rachel's part of the package," Brink said. "I need her assistance during the contest."

Sakura considered this, wondering what, exactly, this woman would do to assist during the contest. *Was she his girlfriend? A coach?* Whatever she was, she wasn't joining them. The imperial jet was the emperor's private plane; she couldn't bring just anyone along for the ride.

"I'm part of his process," Rachel said, giving Sakura a conciliatory look, as if being nice would change anything. "If you want him to perform to the very best of his abilities, I need to be there."

Sakura looked at Rachel, filled with skepticism. "Are you some kind of performance coach?"

"More like a thought partner," Rachel said. "Half of winning is finding the right mindset, and I am instrumental in that element of his performance. He needs me there, and you do, too, if you want him to win."

Sakura tried to imagine what her aunt Akemi would do. An uninvited guest who could increase Brink's chances of winning versus the repercussions of breaking the rules. Akemi always played by the rules. Her own rules, true, but rules nonetheless.

Sakura shook her head definitively. There was no way she could let this woman on the plane. "I can't allow it. I have clear instructions to bring Mike Brink alone. There's nothing stopping you from traveling to Japan, but you're not coming with us."

Brink and Rachel exchanged a look. From that one exchange, Sakura could see that they were close. His girlfriend, or potential girlfriend. The question was: Did he really need this woman by his side to win?

"Here," Rachel said, handing Brink Connie's leash and the bag with dog food. "There's got to be a flight to Tokyo leaving Newark soon. I'll be on it. Don't worry. I'll be there."

Brink turned to Sakura. "Are you sure you can't make an exception—"

"Come on, it's time." Sakura glanced out an enormous plate-glass window at the private plane waiting beyond, a white jet with a bright red sun painted on the stabilizer.

"Call Dr. Gupta," Brink said over his shoulder to Rachel as Sakura led him down a set of stairs to the tarmac. "He'll know what to do."

12

They flew out of Teterboro on the imperial jet, a midsize Cessna, its luxurious wooden cabin fitted with wide leather seats and an island of tatami mats. After the plane stabilized at 35,000 feet, Sakura invited Brink to join her at a low table at the center of the tatami, where a flight attendant laid out dozens of tiny lacquerware dishes filled with fish, pickled vegetables, fried meat, tofu. He was starving. He looked over the feast, realizing that in his rush to get to the airport, he'd missed lunch.

After pouring out two glasses of cold sake, Sakura picked up her chopsticks and nodded that he should, too. Maneuvering his chopsticks the best he could, he lifted a piece of sushi, buttery salmon on warm rice, dipped it in soy sauce, and ate it. He had sushi often but nothing like this. It was delicious.

Connie huddled next to Brink on the tatami. She didn't dislike Sakura, but she didn't warm to her, either. Connie had excellent instincts. When she hated someone, Brink knew there was a problem. When she loved someone, that person could be trusted. Connie's assessment of Sakura was a solid neutral, which made Brink watch her with care. He could sense that something was off about Sakura. Dr. Trevers's message made him wary. He hadn't sent the chrysanthemum for no reason. But how did these elements fit together?

While it was usually his nature to get to the point, he couldn't ask Sakura about Dr. Trevers. He needed to get to know her better. He needed to be cautious. Safer to watch and wait.

"It's a long flight," she said, selecting a piece of pickled radish. "Fourteen hours from New Jersey to Tokyo. But that leaves plenty of time to answer any questions you might have."

Brink adjusted his long legs on the tatami. He had so many questions; he didn't know where to begin. "I've tried to find information about the Dragon Puzzle Box for years and come up with almost nothing. Just rumors online that seem more like conspiracy theories than facts."

"That's by design. The imperial family has made sure that nothing concrete is known about the box or the contest."

"But *you're* aware of it. How did you get involved?"

"I've heard talk of the Dragon Puzzle my entire life. My aunt is part of the Imperial Household Agency, serving as private secretary to the imperial family. She knows every custom, every tradition, every family secret. But to give you an idea of how important this is: My aunt has never seen the Dragon Box."

Sakura bent to Connie and scratched her ears, then rubbed the soft spot between her eyes. Connie didn't object, but she didn't go closer, either. Still a solid neutral.

"My job was to deliver the invitation but also to help you understand the rules of the contest. They are quite particular, and you need to know them."

Of course there were rules. There were always rules and, Brink knew, the clearer the rules, the better chance he had at solving a puzzle.

"The first rule is: absolute discretion. You must not speak of the contest to anyone. Everything you will witness while you are in Japan—anything you discover about the imperial family, their history, or the puzzle box itself—is confidential. The second rule: What is inside the box belongs to the emperor. If you succeed in opening it, you have no claim to what you find inside."

It made sense. The contest could remain a secret only if everyone involved agreed to absolute silence. And he had no interest in keeping the contents of the box.

"Opening this thing will be enough for me," he said, feeling his pulse spike at the very thought of it. It had been days since he'd worked on anything really challenging. "What can you tell me about the puzzle box itself?"

"Everything I know, I'll tell you. But, unfortunately, that's not much. The Dragon Puzzle Box is the most closely guarded secret of the most closely guarded institution in Japan. It is so confidential that the current emperor himself saw the box only on the day of his coronation, in 2019, when it was presented alongside the customary ancestral treasures."

Sakura folded her hands in her lap, and Brink noticed her electric-blue fingernails, the exact color of her bangs. She wore a wide silver band on the middle finger of her right hand that he recognized as an Ōura Ring, a piece of wearable technology that tracked heart rate and created EKG-level reports. Lots of athletes, including professional gamers, wore them to track and optimize their performance. Dr. Trevers had suggested Brink wear one, but he didn't like weight on his fingers. Sakura turned the ring once, twice, three times as she thought.

"What I *do* know about the Dragon Box is that it's a puzzle of unimaginable difficulty, as intricate as a Swiss watch and as impossible to breach as a fortress. The basic facts are these: It was constructed in 1868, the Year of the Earth Dragon, a time of unimaginable upheaval in Japan. I'm not sure how much Japanese history you know, Mr. Brink, but that was the year the Tokugawa shogun renounced his control of Japan and returned power to the emperor. The fate of Japan changed that year. In the chaos, Emperor Meiji commissioned a puzzle constructor named Ogawa Ryuichi, a mastermind of mechanical construction who also happened to be blind, to make an unbreachable safe box. It is believed that the emperor locked something of great value inside, something with the power to change the imperial family, perhaps all of Japan, if it were to be discovered. Only two people knew the solution to the puzzle: Meiji and the man who made it, Ogawa. Ogawa died with this secret. And the emperor never told a soul."

Brink felt a tingle at the base of his neck. Something didn't make sense. If the object inside was as precious as Sakura said, and the emperor wanted to *protect* it, he must have intended for it to be opened eventually. That's how a mechanical puzzle works. It's like a coded telegram, constructed so that the right person will uncover its meaning at the right time.

"It's weird, don't you think, that the emperor left no information about the box for his heirs? Nothing about why he constructed it? Nothing at all about how to open it or even the significance of what's inside? Clearly he meant to protect this treasure, not bury it forever."

Sakura sighed, and he saw that the mystery around the Dragon Box frustrated her, as well. "Your questions are the same ones I've asked myself. Meiji left no explanation, making it impossible to know what he intended to be done with it. Emperor Meiji was a mysterious man. We know very little about him. Few images were ever created of him, and almost none of his personal letters remain. What he left to posterity was his poetry, thousands of small *waka* verses. And while these poems hint at a rich inner life, they are mostly as opaque as a mirror, reflecting all curiosity back at the observer. What is in that box has become the most profound, the most enigmatic question in the history of the imperial family."

Listening to Sakura, Brink felt a rush of adrenaline. Everything he'd heard was true: The Dragon Box was a total and complete mystery, utterly inscrutable. The impossibility of it made him want to go at it with everything he had, even as he wanted to abandon hope. That was the emotional and physical dilemma of being Mike Brink—he was forever caught between the two extremes: Pleasure and pain. Desire and fulfillment. "So you're saying it's a black box."

"Essentially, yes. And while his descendants have worked ceaselessly to understand Meiji's intentions regarding this legacy, they have no illusions. The Dragon Box is an utter mystery. Which is why *you* are so important to them."

Brink wasn't used to sitting on tatami. He rearranged his legs, trying to get comfortable, but his feet were falling asleep. "There must be something you know about it," he said, reaching for another piece of sushi. "Something like this generates rumors, at the very least."

"Of course, there are stories and superstitions that my aunt has told me. There was the empress Teimei—mother of Hirohito, Emperor Shōwa, for example—who claimed that the Dragon Box was cursed. She hid whenever it was brought to the Imperial Palace and, it is said, tried to have it destroyed. There were servants who claimed to see a *yokai* spirit wandering the Imperial Palace every twelve years, during the time of the contest. But *yokai* sightings are rather common in old Japanese structures. And there is an account about a visit made by Nicholas Alexandrovich, the czarevitch of Russia, to Japan in 1891. Somehow, he'd heard about the puzzle box and requested to see it. At first, the emperor refused. But then there was an unfortunate act of violence—during a parade, the czarevitch was attacked and wounded by an anti-Russian nationalist. Meiji, hoping to mend the relationship, agreed to show the future czar the puzzle box. He brought the Dragon Box aboard a Russian warship. They dined, looked at the box, talked about its ingenious design, and that was that. The czarevitch didn't attempt to open it. He didn't even touch it. But by all accounts, he was utterly changed. It was believed, at least by some in the imperial family, that everything tragic that happened to Nicholas and his family arose from his contact with the puzzle box."

Now we're really getting into conspiracy theories, Brink thought. "Do you actually believe this stuff?"

Sakura gave him a hard look, then shrugged. "They're just rumors, of course. As I said, I don't have hard facts about the Dragon Box. While I've heard stories from my aunt, it wasn't until two days ago, when I was asked to bring you the invitation, that I had any proof that it exists at all. In fact," she said, angling over a piece of sashimi, "until I see it myself, I still don't."

Two days ago. The whole world had been different two days ago.

"There is another thing you need to know," Sakura said. "The box must be opened during the first full moon of the Year of the Dragon. It is the one solid piece of information that was passed down from the Meiji period. If the solver takes too long and misses this window, the box cannot be opened. And so your time to solve the puzzle is limited."

"I'd wondered if there was a concrete reason that the contest takes place every twelve years."

"Very concrete," she said. "That is why the box is named as it was. And, of course, the Year of the Dragon had great significance in Japan when this box was constructed. Before the Meiji Restoration, we celebrated the lunar New Year, and the Dragon was considered the luckiest, most propitious year. But, like so much else, the lunar New Year was abandoned when Japan opened to the West. Meiji adopted the Gregorian calendar in 1873 and suppressed a beloved custom. But the box, like a time capsule, retains it. Every Year of the Dragon, during the hours of the full moon, the treasure can be won."

13

Brink needed to sleep—the contest would be hours of grueling mental spelunking, and he couldn't afford to be tired. But while the dimly lit cabin of the jet, with its gentle rocking and the wide, comfortable leather seat, should've knocked him out cold, his conversation with Sakura left him anxious. *What in the hell had he gotten himself into?*

In the lounge area of the plane, Brink found a library of books on the history, culture, and geography of Japan. Most of these books were in Japanese, but a few were in English. He pulled out the Japanese–English dictionary, a dense book containing the two Japanese syllabaries—katakana and hiragana—and the ten thousand kanji that formed the basis of Japanese literacy. He opened the dictionary and flipped through the pages.

One of the qualities of spatial and mechanical savantism—the variety he had acquired after the accident—was a photographic memory. He read quickly and remembered everything that passed before his eyes. Dr. Trevers had once measured his reading and found that he read 18,000 words per minute with a 100 percent retention rate. Accuracy in a foreign language wasn't as perfect, but soon, after a few hours of reading the dictionary, he'd memorized the basics of the Japanese language.

Leaning back into the soft leather seat, he stared out the jet's porthole window, taking in the vastness of the atmosphere. It was in moments like this, when he was forced into inaction—no work to distract him, no puzzles to solve—that he had to confront himself. It was never an easy encounter. He couldn't remember what it was like to be the person he'd been before his accident, but he was sure that guy wouldn't be flying around the world to risk his life for a complicated hunk of wood. Whoever he'd once been, the man he was now had no choice. Despite the risk, he couldn't stop himself. He needed this contest.

He could only imagine what Dr. Trevers would have to say about all this. If Trevers had left Brink one thing, it was an understanding of the medical causes of his compulsion. Brink recalled how, a few years ago, Dr. Trevers had called him into his office to show Mike an MRI scan of his damaged brain, a dark walnut hovering in a square of white.

"When we experience danger, the healthy brain produces chemicals that create feelings of elation, exuberance, even grandiosity. These chemicals help protect us, preparing us to face danger. Our world of relative safety has not diminished the human response to these chemicals. We crave the high that danger and risk bring us. Extreme sports, drugs, financial risk, sex, extreme behaviors of every kind. It's a merry-go-round of desire and fulfillment, fear and release, danger and safety, risk and reward. It's *human* to feel this way. But you, Mike, are different. Your need is more acute. The merry-go-round is moving faster. You need to get off the merry-go-round or eventually you will go too far."

Closing his eyes, he pictured Dr. Trevers the way he'd looked the last time they met. They'd talked about what the treatment would do—slow his brain function, reduce the intensity of his synesthesia, regulate his levels of dopamine. After Dr. Trevers revealed that the new treatment would allow Brink to experience the world as he had before his injury, the doctor asked if he was ready to give up his gift.

Your abilities have become your identity, Mike. They are what make you special. Are you prepared to lose that? Brink was suddenly faced with a question he never imagined he would need to answer. Was he ready to trade who he was—*was he ready to walk away from being extraordinary*—to live a regular, normal life?

14

Ume sat at the center of the dojo, legs crossed, eyes open, taking in the changing pattern of sunlight on the tatami. The sunrise brought a sheet of pale illumination through the dojo, ashen winter light that softened the hard edges of the room. She struggled to hold the light in her mind, watching it bend and waver over the planes of her consciousness as if on the surface of a pond. How beautiful it was, that light, always the same, yet always new. Like her breathing as she sat each morning. Like the enemies waiting beyond the dojo.

Ume's gaze fell to a photograph of Nakano Takeko mounted on the far wall. It was Ume's touchstone, the point of focus she went back to when her mind wandered. Her inspiration. The photo showed a young woman in a plain kimono, her hair pulled severely back, her expression serious, befitting someone trained in the traditions of Bushido. The photograph had been taken shortly before her death, in 1868, when she was twenty-one years old. Ume always detected something particular in her gaze, a kind of wisdom, as if she somehow knew she would inspire generations of women samurai.

She inspired Ume every day. When Ume took in Nakano Takeko's features, her bold eyes, the startling expression of determination, she understood herself. There was something about her gaze, so steadfast, that reassured her. One would never know from seeing the photograph that she was Japan's most famous female samurai, the ideal of an *onna-bugeisha*.

Ume turned her eyes from Nakano Takeko and focused on a linen banner hanging nearby. Black calligraphy swept down the vertical cream cloth, displaying four large characters: *wind, forest, fire, mountain*. The Furinkazan, taken from Sun Tzu, was a directive for Ume and all who trained in that dojo: *One must aspire to be as swift as wind, as gentle as a forest, as fierce as fire, as unshakable as a mountain*. As a girl of four, she had copied the *yojijukugo* of these four characters over and over, her brush inexpert on the rice paper. No matter how messy her attempts, she didn't stop trying. It was as if each imperfect stroke brought her closer to the ideals of her teachers, as if the ink staining her fingers were the ideals themselves.

A sharp beep signaled the end of the hour. Ume stood, walked to the *genkan*, and shut off the alarm. It was seven in the morning and, like every other day, her students would soon be there. She glanced through the window and out over Chiyoda City, a dense collection of buildings that bordered the Imperial Palace. In the glass, her reflection coalesced before her: the compact body, the long black hair, the wide-set eyes, the triangle tattoo branded on her right forearm. She glanced down at it, studying the arrangements of ten dots. She'd worn the tattoo for years, a badge of her loyalty. A reminder of her duty.

The dojo occupied the top floor of a glass tower. From that height, she could see the entire scope of Chiyoda. The palace grounds formed a green hexagon with a thick dark border—the moat that encased the palace's perimeter. Ume had never been inside the Imperial Palace, but her family had been close at hand for generations. Indeed, her great-great-grandfather had been given this very land because of its proximity to Edo Castle. As a Tokugawa samurai, his presence at the palace was mandatory. He was called to regular assemblies and ceremonies, fulfilling the endless duties of a samurai. She'd heard stories of his endurance, but what most intrigued her were the weaknesses: how the long ceremonies had tried his patience; how his uni-

form was so elaborate that he'd once suffered sunstroke; how he'd
abstained from water for hours before, so that he wouldn't need to
urinate. The tedious ceremonies were shows of loyalty, and he, like
Ume, was a loyal servant.

When Emperor Meiji relieved the samurais of their positions, her
great-great-grandfather had killed himself. After his death, his son,
Ume's great-grandfather, went into business. He built their first
commercial property on the back plot of the samurai mansion, a
two-story wooden shop. The structure was destroyed by fire in 1917,
rebuilt, and burned to ashes—along with the family home—during
the Greater East Asia War. From the ruins, her grandparents had
built a twenty-five-story concrete high-rise. Her father knocked it
down and built a glass tower of sixty stories in the 1980s. Ume and
her sister had inherited the building when their parents died.

Memories of her inheritance drew Ume to a table near the *genkan*. On its surface lay her weapons: a katana, a *wakizashi, bo-shuriken*
and *hira-shuriken,* iron darts, and three throwing stars. The weapons
were her heritage as much as the name and the land and the duty
she'd inherited. She ran her finger over the cold blade of the *wakizashi.* Ume remembered the day her grandfather placed it—a dagger
lighter and smaller than the katana—in her hand, on her fifth birthday. It had been a moment of profound pride. Feeling its chill metal
against her skin, she knew then and there that her life would be
given in service. She didn't know what that meant—not the ancient
pact her family had made so long ago, nor all that it would demand
of her. And yet she knew that this calling was her destiny.

Picking up the *wakizashi* now, she turned it in her hand. The
nine-inch dagger was forged of steel, its handle adorned with golden
dragons. It was the lightest of the swords at her disposal but also the
most personal. Her great-great-grandfather had used that very dagger to commit seppuku in 1868. His blood gave the weapon a weight
far heavier than steel. His had been the last ritual suicide in their
family, but he had not been the last to die fulfilling their duty.

She ran a finger over the sharp blade, feeling an urge to cut the skin. Vertigo, she knew, was not the fear of heights but the fear of annihilation, of throwing oneself into the abyss. Ume knew this sensation, felt it deep in her body. It was attractive, the idea of nonexistence, the thought of releasing herself from responsibility. The *wakizashi* made her feel such vertigo strongly. She was attracted to, and afraid of, her impulse toward destruction, the damage she could do to her own soft, vulnerable flesh.

She suspected her mother had been the same. She was a ruthlessly determined woman. She'd taught her daughter the way of pain and beauty. Yukio Mishima, whom her parents so admired, once said: *True beauty is something that attacks, overpowers, robs, and finally destroys.* Ume *was* true beauty. Pure beauty. Cold, cruel, ruthless beauty. The accumulation of pain and deprivation, thwarted hunger and desire, formed a thick callus over her heart. She attacked, overpowered, acquired, destroyed. She knew no other way to live.

But now that the time of action had arrived, she felt a shiver of fear. *What if she failed?* It threatened everything, this presentiment. Allowing uncertainty into the dojo was as fatal as welcoming an enemy into her home. She hadn't felt such uncertainty since the day her parents were murdered. She'd watched the horrors of the ambush, too shocked and stricken to move. She clung to her sister, under the cover of evergreen trees, until the mercenaries left. After that day, she'd been trained as a bonsai is trained—tied and clipped, every natural impulse shaped into elegant equanimity.

Rehearse your death every morning and night. Only when you live as though already dead will you find freedom. These words, written by Yamamoto Tsunetomo so long ago, stayed with her. They formed the pillars of her practice. She had given her life but also her death. A gift she would offer with the rising of the full moon.

15

The jet landed in Tokyo. It was dark outside, and when Brink checked his phone, he saw it was just after eight o'clock at night. Fourteen hours on the jet, and he hadn't slept a wink.

He gathered Connie in his arms and stepped down to the tarmac, where they were met by a customs officer. Sakura explained something to the officer in Japanese and handed over a pack of documents stamped with the golden chrysanthemum. *He's not even looking at my passport,* Brink thought, realizing that his passport and Connie's paperwork—her pet passport, which included a list of vaccines—were still tucked inside his messenger bag. In fact, the customs officer never once looked at Brink. He simply returned the documents to Sakura and waived them to a black car waiting beyond.

They drove through Tokyo. It was a cloudy night, the sky heavy with light pollution, the streets busy with traffic. Sakura checked messages on her phone as Brink settled into his seat, his mind turning to the challenge ahead. Try as he might, he couldn't stop thinking about the Dragon Box. He wondered about its design, how many steps it would take to open it, how to begin, and what, exactly, made it so deadly. He wished he could relax, but it was impossible. That's how his gift worked. Once he'd started to solve a puzzle, it became an obsession. He wouldn't eat or sleep until he'd solved it.

As they drove into central Tokyo, Connie climbed into his lap and watched the city unfold. The flashing, syncopated pulse of neon lights, the crowds of people, the crush of buildings, the sheer density of it, would've been utterly dizzying for any normal person, but for Brink it was surreal. The city became a twisted projection of his interior landscape—the colors and patterns syncing up with the colorscapes of his mind. It was too much. Turning from the window, he closed his eyes to shield himself.

"It's overwhelming, I know," Sakura said, sensing his discomfort. "Nearly forty million people live in or around Tokyo. That makes it the largest urban area in the world. It was the first city in the world to reach ten million inhabitants, but what I find most incredible is that this occurred less than twenty years after it was utterly decimated by bombs. Tokyo's buildings were largely made of wood. The firebombing of March ninth and tenth, 1945, burned the city to ashes. It is estimated that one hundred thousand people died in the attack, but that number is low."

Brink recalled an article he'd read about the massive destruction of Japan during the war. The numbers came to him unbidden: 126,000 dead in Hiroshima; 64,000 dead in Nagasaki. Over 90 percent of these casualties had been caused by burns. More died later of radiation poisoning. Images of charred bodies filled his mind, so many men, women, and children lying in the streets. The horror of what humanity was capable of inflicting filled him with dread.

"Some people believe that such total destruction was necessary," Sakura said softly. "They believe that without it, we couldn't have become modern."

"And this modern Japan," he said, gesturing out the window. "Is it better?"

"It is not yet complete." Sakura turned and met his gaze. "That's why you're here."

"I'm here to win a contest," he said, studying her expression, trying to read her.

"Mike, I don't think you understand." Her voice was so quiet he could barely hear her. "This is not just any contest. There is more at stake here than solving a cool puzzle."

He held her gaze. "Like my life."

"Even more than your life. The emperor of Japan is depending upon you to open that box. His ancestors have tried, and failed, to recover what is inside. Perhaps great tragedies could have been avoided had they been successful. We will never know. But one thing I do know: There are secrets that have the power to change everything. This is one of them."

Brink remembered what she'd said to him as they stood in his apartment: *The Dragon Box is not an ordinary enigma. It was created to protect a secret, one that is important to many powerful people. Such a secret is invaluable, especially to you.*

"There are people who can change the world," Sakura said. "People who have the unique tools to help humanity. You're one of them."

16

They drove for some time before arriving at the Imperial Palace grounds. An island of green in the heart of Chiyoda's skyscrapers, the home of the imperial family was one of the most secure areas in the world. As they drove over a bridge, Brink followed the blaze of a spotlight falling across the black waters of a moat. Ahead, a massive stone wall stretched as far as he could see. *Nobody's scaling that thing,* Brink thought, estimating that the wall was twenty feet high, with a sheer drop into the moat. Even if someone could climb to the top, there were guards everywhere. Sakura was taking him into an impregnable fortress.

The car stopped at the end of a long stone bridge, where clusters of security guards stood at intervals before a fortified gate. A guard stepped from the gatehouse, walked to the car, and tapped the driver's window. The chauffeur handed over identification, and the guard glanced into the back seat at Sakura, then Brink. He paused to stare at Conundrum, curled on Brink's lap. Finally, the gate opened, and the car entered a wide road that wound through the imperial gardens.

"That was the Sakurada-mon, one of nine gates into the imperial grounds," Sakura said. "And that is the Main Gate, the entrance to the imperial palace. There are, as you will see, security protocols that must be followed when coming in contact with the imperial family."

Once through the Main Gate, the car crawled onto an unlit road surrounded by a thick cedar forest. In an instant, the lights and neon signs of Tokyo, the endless texture of skyscrapers and traffic, vanished. They were in a pristine forest, surrounded by evergreen trees under a dark sky.

"All of this was originally Edo Castle, home to the Tokugawa shogun. But when the shogun relinquished his power in 1868, the emperor Meiji moved the imperial residence from the ancient capital of Kyoto to here. Since then, Tokyo has grown dense, but this land has remained protected. It is one of the most valuable pieces of land in the world. During the economic bubble of the eighties, this stretch of land was worth more than all of California."

Through the trees, Brink saw a structure in the distance, large and imposing.

"That is the ceremonial Imperial Palace," Sakura said. "It's where many of the official functions take place. And that structure over there is the Imperial Household Agency. You will not be going anywhere near that place if I can help it."

As they drove on, Brink took in the sweeping immensity of the park, with its endless trees. It seemed to go on forever. Finally, the car stopped before a long, single-story concrete structure.

"And this is the Fukiage Palace," Sakura said, getting out of the car, gesturing for Brink to follow. "The residence of the imperial family. You'll be staying here, in the east wing."

Clipping Connie's leash onto her collar, Brink grabbed his messenger bag and climbed into the chill air. He stood before a striking modern palace. Sleek and minimal, vastly different from the other structures in the compound, it looked more like a Midwestern office building from the seventies than a royal residence.

But before he could fully take it in, they were surrounded by men in uniform. One pulled him aside and patted him down, from his thin T-shirt to his black jeans to his red Converse All Stars. They searched his messenger bag, removed Connie's favorite chew toy—a saliva-encrusted, disfigured Smurf. When they'd finished, Brink took the Smurf back and tossed it to Connie, who was barking like crazy.

Sakura watched Brink with concern. "Sorry about these formalities. The Imperial Household Agency, which manages the affairs of the emperor and his family, insisted."

"Sounds like MI6 or the CIA or something," Brink said.

"That's not far from the truth," she said, under her breath. "The Imperial Household Agency has extraordinary power over the imperial family. More than anyone beyond the moat realizes."

Brink noticed Connie was gone and found her beyond the car, relieving herself behind a snow-covered bush. Sakura spoke to the guards, then turned to Brink. "I've told the guards that Connie will be staying with you, in your room, and that you'll be taking her out for walks at your discretion. You're a special guest of the imperial family. They will leave you alone."

Brink picked up Connie and followed Sakura through a discreet entrance and into a long, modern annex. Clerestory windows caught the bright interior light, creating a hall of mirrors reflecting Sakura, then Brink, then Conundrum.

"The east wing is usually reserved for visiting heads of state. But it is completely empty tonight." She led him to a room at the end of the hallway, where she used a key card to open the door before handing it to him. He looked at the badge. There was his photograph—an old one she must've found online—and a name that didn't belong to him. "This badge identifies you as an important guest, should the guards give you trouble."

He turned the badge in his hand. "Who am I supposed to be?"

"An American diplomat, here for an official meeting with the emperor," she said. "Of course, the guards don't know the real reason you're here. The contest doesn't officially exist. It's not recorded on the emperor's calendar, and the regular security team has no idea about tomorrrow's contest. Like every puzzle-box contest that has occurred, this one will be conducted in private. It is a highly explosive national secret, one that has very personal significance to the emperor. If anyone—the media, foreign dignitaries, your fans in Japan, anyone at all—were to discover you're here, it could have terrible consequences. I've promised to help my aunt prevent that."

Sakura and Brink walked into a spacious apartment that combined Japanese and Western elements: A raised platform with shoji screens and tatami mats at one side, and an enormous plate-glass window that overlooked the thick forest beyond. There was a private bedroom with a large bed, dresser, a pair of silk upholstered chairs. Before Brink knew it, Sakura had gone to a wet bar across the room and poured out two glasses of Suntory whisky. He took a drink, wishing he could relax. That wasn't going to happen for a long time.

"Normally, there would be staff to assist you," she said, as she walked through the rooms of the apartment. "But I'm sorry to say that you are on your own this evening." She glanced down at Connie, who was sniffing at the corners of the room, her eyes wild with excitement at the abundance of novel scents. "The emperor and empress know you're here, of course," she said. "And my aunt, as well—she was the person who got the proper clearance and authorization for our use of the imperial jet. But the household staff has not been alerted."

As Brink took this in, he removed Connie's collapsible bowls from his bag, filled one with water, then poured a pack of dog food—steak and carrots—into the other. Connie was thirsty and drank quickly. She needed a good walk, and after the flight, so did he. His mind was filled with static from the drive through Tokyo, and he had to settle down and clear his thoughts. He glanced at his watch. The local time was just after nine P.M. The contest would begin the next day, at moonrise. If he wanted to be sharp, he'd need some sleep.

And yet he couldn't stop his mind from racing. If he could only see the puzzle box before the contest, if he could gauge its dimensions, size up the design, maybe even touch it, it would be an enormous advantage. Half of solving a puzzle was creating an image of it in his mind. If he saw the Dragon Box, he'd know what he was up against.

"You said the puzzle box was brought to the palace," he said. "Is it here now?"

Sakura nodded. "It's in a vault in the imperial treasure room, the most secure location in Chiyoda City. That's temporary, of course. When it's time, the Dragon Box will be moved to the Three Shrines Sanctuary, where the contest will take place."

"I need to see it," Brink said. Sakura began to protest, but he interrupted her. "I know you're not supposed to show it to me, but you yourself laid out my odds of surviving. They aren't great. Seeing the box will change that equation."

A look of uncertainty passed over her features. "You're right. I'm not supposed to take you anywhere near it. There is a strict protocol in place. Besides, it's getting late. You didn't sleep at all on the flight. You'll need to rest and prepare for what will certainly be a very intense day."

Brink knew she was right, but he was too worked up for that now. "I'm not going to be able to rest. There's no way."

Sakura was torn, he could see it. She was struggling between following the rules and taking Brink's more creative approach. At the airport she'd followed the rules, but now, with the contest looming, she came down in favor of Brink. "Taking you to the vault doesn't mean you'll see the Dragon Box," she said. "The door is locked."

"Key or code?"

Sakura hesitated, and Brink realized that, despite her fastidiousness with Rachel, this woman liked breaking the rules. "Code," she said. "There's a computerized pad, so probably numeric, although security likes to get creative."

"Creative is my specialty."

She stared at him, and he knew she wanted to give it a try but couldn't get caught. She wanted to see the Dragon Box as badly as he did, that much was clear. But why? What was in it for her?

"If we get caught, I'll take full responsibility," he said. "You tried to stop me, but I wouldn't listen."

"Okay," Sakura said, a sudden expression of defiance confirming Brink's suspicions. "Let's give it a try."

17

Sakura had visited the Fukiage Palace many times, and every time she found the official residence of the emperor and his family to be at odds with itself. Designed by the Japanese architect Shōzō Uchii, it was a modern structure in the style of Frank Lloyd Wright, the American master of modernism who had himself been influenced by traditional Japanese design. While the exterior was rather ugly, made as it was of dull reinforced concrete, the interiors were a play of warm, pale wood and traditional Japanese elements that conspired to create beautiful, modern, light-filled spaces. There were traditional kakemono artworks on the walls, some of them quite old, yet they were punctuated with playful modern pieces by contemporary calligraphists. The effect was Japanese yet inflected with modern culture. It was, Sakura knew, a lot like her.

Another contradiction of the Fukiage Palace: While it seemed tranquil, under its blanket of calm lay a frenetic system of surveillance and security. Very few people had access to the private chambers of the imperial family. Thanks to her aunt Akemi and the security clearance she'd been given, Sakura was one of them.

Sakura's aunt Akemi had been the empress Masako's private secretary for more than thirty years, joining her staff at the time of her marriage to Prince Naruhito on June 9, 1993, and remaining a trusted confidant through Masako's ascension to empress in 2019. She was the empress's eyes and ears. The empress appreciated knowing what was being said and done by the staff, and Akemi was often privy to such information. The imperial family was restricted from certain behaviors by the Imperial Household Agency—the pressure to conform to imperial precedent was enormous—but Akemi knew how to get around them. When these precedents imposed upon the freedoms of the empress, Akemi went into the recently digitized archives and, with the help of Sakura's computer skills, scoured the files to find precedents that would allow the empress to do as she pleased. Just the year before, Sakura had found a thousand-year-old account of the empress Teishi distributing her poetry to the court during the New Year's festivities. Akemi used this as an argument for the current empress's request to send New Year's cards with a watercolor she'd painted. The agency had pondered the request for months before approving the cards, but they *had* been approved. Such victories were small, but they gave the empress a feeling of freedom over her life.

While assisting her aunt, Sakura had searched the files of imperial precedents extensively, studied imperial calendars, found records of old superstitious traditions that had once defined court life: fortune-telling, geomancy, scrying with the bones of horses, reading turtle shells, everything. Though there had been no mention of the Dragon Box, Ogawa Ryuichi, or the contest, that didn't mean it hadn't happened. It meant someone had been very careful to remove it from the official record.

Her aunt Akemi most certainly never spoke of the puzzle box to the empress. The subject was liable to upset her. It was common knowledge that the empress had, in the past, suffered from depression. At one point she'd spent a full decade as a recluse in the palace, refusing all engagements, causing much speculation about the imperial family. Sakura knew her aunt was extremely protective of the empress, especially from the press. *The empress is sensitive,* her aunt once told her. *Fragile.*

She hadn't always been that way. Before becoming the empress of Japan, she was Masako Owada, a brilliant student with degrees in economics from Harvard and Oxford and well on her way to a prestigious career as a diplomat. Then the crown prince Naruhito fell in love with her. It was a Cinderella story, only the princess didn't flourish. The pressures of public opinion and the extreme scrutiny about her past took an immense toll on Masako. From the moment she'd married the crown prince, her fertility became a matter of national speculation. The imperial family followed the law of primogeniture, and only a male heir could succeed Naruhito as emperor. Masako's mother-in-law, the empress Michiko, had endured similar scrutiny but had produced three children, two boys and a girl. It took years for the empress to conceive, and she and the prince had only one child, Aiko, Sakura's childhood friend. But as a woman could not become head of the imperial family, Aiko would be passed over in favor of a younger male cousin as heir to the Chrysanthemum Throne.

Sakura often wondered about the effects of such an injustice. It was the twenty-first century, after all, and old institutions like the British monarchy allowed female succession. Sakura had read a recent poll that said 85 percent of Japanese people wanted Princess Toshi to succeed her father.

Perhaps because Sakura had been raised in New York and had been influenced by American culture, she thought Japanese women faced enormous challenges in the modern world. They were asked to uphold traditions while being a wife, mother, and employee. Sakura remembered how her own mother had struggled to manage such impossible societal pressures. Many Japanese women decided not to marry, and to remain childless, to escape this difficult situation. Like Sakura's aunt Akemi.

Sakura led Mike Brink from the east wing through a passage that connected to the main reception area, then past the wing housing the imperial apartments, moving deep into the inner sanctuary of the imperial family. After turning through a series of elegant reception rooms, she called an elevator and took it down to the lower floors, where the lights were low, the walls and floors simple, unadorned concrete.

Sakura glanced up at the security cameras. Akemi had sent her a message, updating her about the contest. After an incident involving the delivery of the box, all security cameras had been disabled. And while she knew the cameras weren't recording them, Sakura walked quickly, avoiding them as much as possible. She wasn't supposed to be anywhere near the treasure vault. Her aunt would never, *never*, have allowed it. But restrictions were meant for those who didn't have the skills to break them.

Sakura stopped at the end of a hallway. It was plain concrete, like the rest of the basement, except for a single kakemono scroll on the wall. At the end of the hall stood a steel door with an electronic screen mounted to the doorframe. "The Dragon Box is being held in there until the contest begins. We just need to get inside. . . ."

"If I can't get inside, you've chosen the wrong guy for this contest." Brink gave her a grin.

She raised an eyebrow, smiled playfully. "Think you're as good as they say you are?"

"We'll soon see."

Sakura had a strong sense of intuition about people. She knew the moment she met Mike Brink that he *was* as good as people said he was. And yet there was something that bothered her about him. He was almost *too good*. Mike was someone upon whom nothing—not a single word or gesture, not a slip or a contradiction—was lost. And this worried her. What if he could see that Sakura wasn't at all who or what he believed her to be?

The screen was paper-thin, black, the size of a large iPhone. As Brink approached, it sensed his presence and blinked on. A square of seven polygons appeared. A tangram.

"The code into the treasure room is a puzzle itself," she said. "If you can solve it, we will have access to the Dragon Box."

18

Ume grew up hearing stories of the samurai—their noble deeds, their loyalty, their sense of duty and honor. But while such stories were common in Japanese culture—the stuff of manga and B movies—Ume rarely heard stories of the *onna-bugeisha*, the female samurai, in popular culture. The women warriors from whom Ume was descended had been forgotten.

Not in Ume's family, of course. Ume's mother had told her stories of the female samurai all the time, especially of the greatest woman warrior of all time, Nakano Takeko.

"During the Battle of Aizu, Nakano Takeko went to the bridge to watch her enemies. The imperial soldiers were there, at the opposite side of the river, ready to fight. She was outnumbered, but she pushed away her helmet, revealing that she was a woman. The imperial soldiers were shocked. They laughed and gawked at her. Their surprise gave her an advantage, the small opening she needed. Quickly, before they knew what hit them, she attacked."

Her mother smiled with pleasure as she recounted it, then placed a long pole with a single blade at its end in Ume's hands, a *naginata*.

"One day," her mother said, "you will know this weapon as you know your own body."

Her mother stood straight and strong, her hair wound into a knot upon her head. She was young, barely thirty years old, but there were deep, discolored scars over her hands, and she walked with a limp. Still, there was nothing weak about her. Strength radiated from her mother, a terrifying yet calming quality.

"We've kept the teaching alive for a reason," she said. "*You* are that reason."

Ume bowed, feeling the weight of the weapon in her hands, its importance.

"We've lost so much," her mother said. "Those who didn't die in battle committed suicide. Some samurai were brought into the Meiji hierarchy, given new positions and salaries. Our family was not one of them. We were shut out, shamed, abandoned. But the women warriors, we continued. Humiliation and loneliness blossomed into ferocity, determination, and power. We formed a secret network. The disciples of Nakano Takeko joined forces with others, a more powerful group who shared their mission. Because women were not suspected of knowing such arts, they were even more deadly than their male counterparts. We have the element of surprise in our favor. It is our most precious weapon. As a result, the women in our family have been sought out by the most powerful families as bodyguards. Our kind have become respected and feared."

And so began Ume's introduction into the practices of her ancestors. She was taught to use her strengths—flexibility, speed, the sharpness of her mind, the ability to endure pain—to her advantage. "We will never defeat a male adversary with brute force," her mother said. "We will always defeat him through cunning, superiority of mind, and endurance."

Once, her mother enrolled her in a kendo competition in their ancestral village. Ume was eleven years old, but her mother put her up against boys who were older—fourteen, fifteen, sixteen years old, and much stronger than Ume. One day she was paired with a boy who stood a full head taller, with wisps of a mustache. Terrified, she braced herself. She would follow the most important teaching she'd learned: to use the strength of one's opponent against him, overcoming brute force with agility of mind and body.

For the first minutes of the match, Ume held her own. She blocked his punches, evaded his advances, and even returned a blow. Then he tripped her, sweeping her left leg out from under her. He'd cheated—tripping was against the rules. When she fell, he struck her with two heavy blows and compounded her humiliation by placing his foot on her chest, smiling with delight at the tears of rage and shame in Ume's eyes.

"Don't cry, Umeboshi," the boy said, as he bowed.

Umeboshi. Pickled plum. A sour, astringent thing that created a shock on the tongue. A belittling, derisive name. Her younger sister, standing at the edge of the mat, heard the boy say it, and from that day on, whenever she wanted to tease Ume, she called her Umeboshi. Ume hated the nickname, but as she grew older, she came to find it a good description of her personality. The sourness of the fruit suited her. Its bitterness. Its strength.

"It was a good morning," her mother said later that day, as they ate lunch at home.

"How can you say that?" Ume asked. "That boy decimated me."

"But you allowed it," she said. "Your left leg was in a vulnerable position. Next time you'll protect it."

"He didn't deserve to win," Ume said.

"It is true. The boy cheated. Still, it is his victory. You are bruised and defeated. He is not."

Ume looked down at her hands, embarrassed. She hated losing. But even more, she hated disappointing her mother, who worked so hard to teach her. "I'm sorry, Okā-san."

"Ume-chan, it will not always be so easy for him. He is young and strong now, but with time, his flaws will rot him from the inside out. You must be thankful to him for this lesson."

"Thankful?" she asked, unable to understand what her mother could mean.

"You learned something today," she said quietly. "And for that you must hold him in a special place in your heart, the most precious place: the place for those who change us. We must love those who make us better, even if they hurt us in the process. That boy made you better. You must love him for it."

Ume looked up at her mother, her eyes hot with tears. It seemed preposterous. How could she love someone who hurt her? Should she love those who destroyed their lineage? Embrace the powerful people who pushed her parents to train her to the point of breaking? Ume was learning to fight so that she could kill them, not thank them. She wanted to crush that boy, hit him so hard his teeth broke, slice his face with the blade of her *naginata*. "Forgive me, but I will not admire him."

Her mother smiled, a rare gesture. "How else can you hope to withstand the hate you feel, if not through love?"

Ume considered this and bowed her head, afraid to meet her mother's eye.

"I will tell you something that nobody knows," her mother said. "Something that I was meant to tell you one day, later, but that you have earned now."

Ume's mother looked her in the eye and whispered, "Our lineage was destroyed. Our ancestors shamed, banished, denied their rightful place. But there is a way to avenge them. There is a secret weapon, a great and powerful treasure, one that could change everything. And one day, when the time comes, we will take it."

19

Outside the treasure room, deep below the Fukiage Palace, Brink examined the electronic keypad mounted on the frame of the vault's door, taking in the tangram. He touched the screen, and the numbers one through seven appeared at the edge of the tangram. Four arrows blinked into being around the exterior of the square.

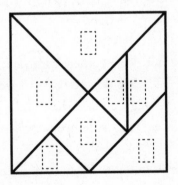

"It's a number puzzle," Sakura said.

"You're right," Brink said. "We need to put the numbers one through seven into the polygons."

"And the arrows signify that the rows and columns all have the same sums, with the shaded rectangles signifying a two-digit number that matches the sum of all the pieces."

Brink winked at Sakura. "Piece of cake."

"Make it red velvet."

Brink no more than glanced at the tangram and a configuration of numbers appeared in his mind. He tapped the keyboard, then typed the correct numbers into the rectangles.

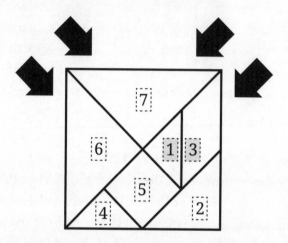

The tangram blinked twice and disappeared. Solved.

He waited for some blinking lights, a notification that he'd hit the jackpot. At the very least, the door should unlock. But nothing happened.

"Looks like we're not done yet," Sakura said, as a cursor winked over the black screen, leaving thirteen blank spaces.

"We need a thirteen-digit code," Brink said.

"Which only leaves ten trillion possible combinations. Any guesses?"

"Guessing was never going to be an option," Brink said.

Pushing a strand of blue hair out of her eyes, Sakura said, "If you think you can figure it out by calculating the emperor's birthday or some bit of personal lore, think again: This was programmed by the Imperial Household Agency's security team. They would never use the imperial family's personal information for any reason."

Brink stepped away from the screen and walked back through the hallway. He was at a big disadvantage here. It was impossible to guess the code, and if Sakura was right, and it hadn't been pro-grammed using the emperor's personal information, there was no chance of figuring it out. Cracking a code wasn't about luck, or even about skill, but about having insight into it, a piece of information that threw light on how it was constructed. And he had nothing.

Brink walked down the long concrete hallway, thinking it through. The walls were bare, nothing but jointed concrete panels, polished concrete floors, and surveillance cameras. In fact, since they'd left the upper floor of the palace, there had been no artwork at all, except . . .

"What's this?" he asked, returning to the scroll hanging near the vault door.

Sakura looked it over, her expression one of pure contempt. "The cheesiest piece of artwork in the palace."

Brink examined it. It was true, the artwork wasn't anything like the pieces he'd seen upstairs. There was an almost cartoonish quality to the image of a frog sitting in a pond, cross-eyed, its green body bloated; it was the kind of thing you'd find hanging in the bathroom of the dive bar his father used to frequent in Ohio. "What does it say?"

"It's a poem. I'm sure you know it. Bashō's frog haiku."

Brink did know the haiku. It was the most famous haiku ever written. He'd read it in his high school English class.

An old silent pond . . .
A frog jumps into the pond—
Splash! Silence again.

"This painting is so bad," Sakura said, rolling her eyes. "Clearly it's meant to be a joke."

"It's a joke. Or . . ." Brink saw a sequence of numbers, went to the keypad, prompted the screen, and typed in thirteen digits. It flashed red and cleared the numbers. Wrong sequence.

Sakura joined him by the screen, curious. "What did you enter?"

"My instinct is that the Bashō poem is here to give a clue to understanding this code. I don't think it's a coincidence that there are thirteen words in the poem and thirteen numbers in the door code, so I did a numeric conversion, converting the first letter of each word to a number. But it gave me twenty digits. I tried it anyway, and you saw what happened."

Brink took out his notebook and wrote out the code he'd tried.

Sakura turned back to the written poem on the wall. "I think you've got the right idea. The code is a substitution cipher. But it wouldn't be derived from the English translation of this poem. Here . . ."

Sakura took his notebook and pen and wrote out the haiku in Japanese.

Furu ike ya
Kawazu tobikomu
Mizu no oto

"Taking the first syllable of each of these words, we get FU-I-YA-KA-TO-MI-NO-O."

"But that's fourteen letters. The code calls for thirteen digits."

"Try to follow me now, puzzle boy." Sakura smiled and winked, clearly enjoying teaching the puzzle master something about codes. "The Japanese language is composed of syllables, and they are represented by forty-six characters, or kana, called hiragana. If you take each kana from the poem and correlate it with its number on a standard hiragana chart, you get:

Furu (Fu) 28
Ike (I) 2
Ya (Ya) 36
Kawazu (Ka) 6
Tobikomu (To) 20
Mizu (Mi) 32

No (No) 25
Oto (O) 5

Sakura took Brink's notebook and wrote: *2-8-2-3-6-6-2-0-3-2-2-5-5*. A thirteen-digit code.

"That must be it," Brink said. He was impressed. When he'd first met Sakura, he knew she was a kindred spirit, but now he was certain that she was a brilliant solver. He glanced at her, wondering if she'd used her intelligence to trick him. Had she used Dr. Trevers to lure him to Japan?

He hoped that his suspicions about Sakura were wrong. It was a joy to work with someone with her abilities, and he felt a deep pleasure in knowing he wasn't in this thing alone. He'd never met anyone who could keep up with him, let alone solve a cipher before he could.

"Should we get this show on the road?" She asked, approaching the screen.

"Please," he said, gesturing to the blinking spaces. "Do the honors."

Sakura tapped on the screen, entered the series of thirteen numbers, and the keypad blinked green. The code was correct. She turned and gave him a triumphant smile, one that showed a different Sakura, a woman who'd known all along she could outsmart him.

20

When Sakura mentioned that the puzzle box was kept in the imperial treasure room, Brink thought of a bank vault filled with bags of gold and silver coins, jewels and crowns, cartoonish heaps of valuables secured behind steel doors. But it was just the opposite. He followed Sakura into an elegant salon with wood-paneled walls and Persian carpets on the floors, tobacco leather club chairs positioned throughout. The security cameras—so ubiquitous everywhere in the imperial residence—were gone. It was oddly silent, the air thick and stale. If the palace, with its impregnable stone walls, fortified gates, and wide moat, was its own kind of puzzle box, this was the treasure at the center.

"I've always wanted to see this room," Sakura said, her voice filled with excitement. "It's only a fraction of the imperial family's private collection, but some of the most rare and valuable objects in Japanese history are here, treasures collected for nearly two thousand years of imperial rule. They've never left the imperial family's possession, which makes their authenticity incontestable. Because they've remained sheltered from the elements, they are in pristine condition, as well."

Brink saw golden buddhas sitting in clusters throughout the room, porcelain temple vases on pedestals, glass cases filled with ancient jewelry, lacquerware, parchments. It felt like seeing the history of Japan laid out before him, all at once. Sakura seemed equally entranced. She pointed to a scroll.

"That is a copy of the Kojiki. It tells the history of the Japanese people through poems and songs and explains the origins of the kami, or gods, the myths and legends, and the origins of the imperial family. And this," she said, pointing to a print lying close to the Kojiki, "is an ukiyo-e print of the goddess Amaterasu Omikami, the founding deity of Japan."

Brink leaned closer to the glass case, examining the print. It was marvelous, the woman dressed in a colorful robe, jewels hanging from her neck, rays of light bursting from her, radiating like sunshine.

"Amaterasu is the goddess of the sun," Sakura said. "Her name means 'Heaven Shining.' She's the first ancestor of the imperial family."

"So that makes the current emperor what? A sun god?"

Sakura smiled. "Not anymore. The emperor Hirohito was required to relinquish his divinity after the Second World War."

"Pretty big step down in the world."

"It certainly was. From ancient times, the emperor was considered a god by the Japanese people. Quite literally so. Throughout our history, the connection between the emperor and divinity defined Japanese society. It is often blamed for the extreme nationalism that caused so many people to obey his orders blindly. Such unquestioning nationalism led to the many atrocities that occurred in the emperor's name—the atrocities in China and Korea and throughout Southeast Asia. The Americans understood that officially severing the emperor's connection to Amaterasu, and publicly announcing that he was not divine, would diminish his power. So, after Japan's defeat, Hirohito was forced to do just that. He gave up the imperial family's right to govern, gave most of his wealth to the secular government, and rescinded the titles of all the minor branches of the imperial family. Now the emperor is merely symbolic. Nevertheless, the sun and the sun goddess Amaterasu remain deeply embedded in Japan's identity. You've seen our flag. . . ."

Brink imagined the Japanese flag, with its red circle in an expanse of white. A brilliant burning sun, symbol of an ancient goddess.

"The Kojiki tells Amaterasu's story," Sakura said. "One day, the sun goddess disappeared into a cave, bringing eternal night. Saddened by the darkness that enveloped the world, her brother tricked her to come out of the cave, restoring light. After her return, Amaterasu gave her descendant, Jimmu, the first emperor of Japan, three imperial treasures—a mirror, a jewel, and a sword. These treasures give the imperial family legitimacy as the descendants of the goddess, but also, it is said, they contain tremendous powers in their own right."

"But these objects are mythical," Brink said. "People don't actually believe in a sun goddess anymore."

"*Believe* is a strong word, but the regalia and the goddess Amaterasu are culturally significant to many people in Japan."

"Are the regalia here?" Brink glanced through the room, looking for the objects.

"Most definitely not. No one has laid eyes upon the three imperial treasures except the emperor himself."

Sakura walked through the room, glancing at objects, as if looking for something. Finally, she stopped at a glass case at the far end of the room. "Come, this will be of interest to you." Carefully, she lifted the top of the glass case and removed a small manuscript, its edges bound with silk thread, its cover a piece of pale-pink *washi* paper.

"This," she said, turning the pages, "is something I've always wanted to read: the pillow book of one of Emperor Meiji's concubines, Yoshiko Fujiwara. There was a tradition among educated concubines of keeping random thoughts or jottings known as *zuihitsu*. Perhaps you've heard of the most famous of these, Sei Shōnagon's *Pillow Book,* which documents court life in the Heian period, over one thousand years ago. This pillow book, while not famous, contains equally extraordinary observations of court life. And, if I've heard correctly, it contains the only surviving contemporary description of the Dragon Box."

Sakura opened the pillow book, carefully turned the pages, then stopped to read from it, translating into the English:

The secret box has arrived, and it is beautiful beyond words, made entirely of wood from the forests of Hakone: red camphor and mulberry, walnut and ebony and black persimmon, wood of the spindle tree and sandalwood tree, twenty-one varieties of wood fashioned into the image of a dragon.

Brink felt a rush of pleasure as he imagined the box, its twenty-one varieties of wood twisting into the shape of a dragon.

"It is through Yoshiko Fujiwara's account that the imperial family first understood the complex nature of the Dragon Box." Sakura flipped through the pillow book, skimming the pages. "My aunt told me the story. Yoshiko Fujiwara was there, in the emperor's private chambers, when the Dragon Box was presented to Meiji. Ogawa Ryuichi, the artisan from Hakone who designed the box, delivered it to the Imperial Palace himself and demonstrated how it all worked. This was a once-in-a-lifetime event, to be sure, and Yoshiko Fujiwara must have been utterly astonished. At that time, the emperor was a god, if you recall. A common person never had the honor of glimpsing, let alone interacting with, the emperor. It is believed that Ogawa was allowed into the inner sanctum of the emperor only because he was blind. In any case, Meiji sat down with the puzzle constructor and watched as he opened the box, move by move. Yoshiko describes Ogawa manipulating hidden slots and levers, sliding and snapping open compartments like . . ." Sakura turned to a page in the pillow-book papers and read, ". . . *a magician conjuring a universe from solid wood.*"

Brink felt his heart beating as she read the passage. He imagined Ogawa's movements, the opening and closing of the wooden pieces, the revelation of volume. What else had Yoshiko witnessed? She'd watched Ogawa open the box—could she have written down the moves? If he could get some idea of the sequences or how the interior mechanisms worked, it would give him an incredible edge. It might save his life.

"Anything in there about how to begin?" he asked. The opening moves were always the trickiest; every subsequent move built upon them.

Sakura turned the silver Ōura Ring on her finger, working something out. "It's this account that says the puzzle must be solved under the full moon in the Year of the Dragon," she said. "That much I know. And perhaps it *does* describe Ogawa's box in detail, as well. But I think you should be careful: There's no proof that anything Yoshiko describes is accurate. Many people have read this account—it is the only contemporary description of the Dragon Box, after all—and it has proven useful to exactly no one. This pillow book could be little more than a very pretty diversion."

"You think she was *trying* to be misleading?"

Sakura shrugged. "It could be accurate, or it could be filled with errors. Or it could have been devised as a red herring to undermine solvers like you, who have a real shot at opening it. There is no way to know for certain what secrets the Dragon Box keeps until you hold it in your hands and try it yourself."

"If only Meiji had left some clue about how to open it."

"Nothing is as it seems with the imperial family. They are like the puzzle box itself—always shifting, always changing, playing a game of survival. Yoshiko, too, was a pawn. Her pillow book has served a purpose."

While Brink needed every advantage he could get, Sakura had a point. It was possible that Yoshiko's description of the puzzle could hurt rather than help him.

"Why don't you see the box for yourself," she said. "Make your own assessment of what it will take to open it. Your instincts are your biggest strength. And then, after you've formed your own opinion, we'll see what Yoshiko can tell us."

21

_____

It was a few days after the New Year's holiday, and Ume and her younger sister sat on the stoop of the dojo, hot with the efforts of their practice. Since daybreak, they had trained relentlessly, their mother overseeing it all—correcting the position of an arm, the angle of a kick.

At lunchtime, the girls waited as their mother retrieved the basket of bento boxes. Ume picked up the *naginata* at her side and tapped the frozen pathway surrounding the dojo, relishing the crackling of the ice. Usually they practiced with bamboo poles, the stalks lighter and easier to manipulate than their *naginata*. But that day they'd used actual weapons. Ume's gaze followed the snowy path. It stretched all the way to the little mountain house where her father worked on his laptop, building, as he always said, *the permissionless future*. She wished he'd stop working and come to the dojo with their mother to eat with them.

The *naginata* was light in Ume's hands. Feeling its solidity, the smooth slip of the lacquer against her palm, had become second nature. It was a woman's weapon—light, easy to manipulate, but, with its sharp, curved blade, deadly. Ume had begun training with a *naginata* at five years old. It was too big for her, unwieldy, and yet, from the moment her mother placed the weapon in her hands, she knew it belonged to her. As she grew, she learned to handle it with ease. Now, at fourteen years old, it was as if the *naginata* were an extension of her body, another arm or leg. She knew its power and its defects as if they were her own.

Their parents brought them to the countryside each New Year's holiday. *Begin the first day of the new year in training,* her father always said, *and the remaining days will be filled with strength.* Ume and her sister would put on old cotton *dōji*—hand-me-downs used by their mother and aunt, so threadbare Ume tore a seam in the first ten minutes of training, exposing her skin to the freezing air. Over the years, she'd become used to the trips to the mountains, the journey from Tokyo like going back in time. They left the city and entered the secluded valley of her ancestors' village, a place where the forests were thicker, the houses older, the temple steps covered in moss, the streets made of stone. There was snow and ice and delicious, chill air.

Begin the first day of the new year in training, and the remaining days will be filled with strength.

Strength was the beginning; strength was the end. But finding the will to be strong wasn't easy for Ume. That morning, she almost failed. Ume and her sister woke in the pitch dark, lying side by side on a thin futon, and Ume couldn't leave the warm blanket. Her mother came to the doorway and watched her. It was enough to shame her into rising. They ate rice and miso soup before the sun rose, then walked from the small mountain house up the snow-covered path to the shack they called a dojo. Ume slid out of her woven sandals, her bare feet stinging with cold, her breath crystallizing in the air, and began the kata she knew so well.

Ichi, ni, san, shi, go.

For hours she and her sister worked, kicking, punching, sparring, imitating, and repeating. And while she often couldn't feel her hands and feet, and her body ached where her mother struck, a resplendent heat filled her heart. Her efforts were pure, more pure than the snow that blanketed the mountain.

Finally, they'd finished the morning's work. Their mother brought them their lunch—three bento boxes, each wrapped in printed cotton cloth. Ume walked barefoot across the tatami to an annex, sat at the *kotatsu*, slipping her frozen feet near the brazier, and gestured for her sister to join her. It was their habit to eat together after morning practice, and Ume looked forward to it—the warmth of being together, the scent of her sister and mother, the knowledge that she'd worked hard. The thick, earthy smell of coal hung in the freezing air, a mixture of heat and ice that had become, in her mind, associated with sore muscles and work, pain and duty.

Itadakimasu, they said in unison, and opened the boxes.

Ume hesitated, not quite sure what to expect. Her mother had made certain of that. Some years before, when Ume was ten years old, they'd had a grueling morning in the dojo and Ume was hungry, sore, and exhausted. They sat together to eat as usual but, when Ume opened her bento, it was empty. She stared at the empty box, unable to believe what she was seeing. She glanced at her younger sister's bento: rice, pickled vegetables, a sliver of fried fish. Her sister began to divide her lunch between them—the girls shared everything—but their mother stopped her. Ume understood. This was a lesson. She'd expected nourishment, but she must never assume that she would be fed. She must never expect hospitality and, above all, tenderness. She was not entitled to even one grain of rice. She was not entitled to anything.

It hadn't been just that once. Another day, some months later, Ume opened her bento to find it overflowing with delicacies: two *nigiri*, a luxury; sliced eel with a savory sauce; a small pink cake with a slice of strawberry in one compartment, and a disk of mochi in another. She looked to her mother, astonished. Surely it couldn't be for her.

Her mother nodded, her expression unreadable. *"Hai, dozo,"* she said, smiling slightly.

But Ume was unable to lift her chopsticks. She understood, with-

out words, that there was more to be understood, an unspoken message.

"You aren't hungry, Ume-chan?"

"I am hungry," Ume said at last, but she didn't move.

Her mother met her eye, and Ume recognized the steely look, one
she gave when imparting wisdom. "If you wonder whether you
should live or die, it is better to die."

Ume knew the saying. Her mother had said it before. It had come
from a samurai of another era and was meant to remind her that
sacrifice was always better than self-interest. Ume looked over the
beautiful lunch, longing to eat. Knowing that she would remember
that feeling of hunger always, she replaced the lid of the box, wrapped
it in cotton, and returned it to the basket. Folding her hands in her
lap, she looked down, so as not to make her mother and sister uncomfortable as they ate.

There is no accounting for how memories drift in the ocean of the
mind, or why a particular memory surfaces at a certain moment in
time, but it was this phrase—*if you wonder whether you should live or
die*—that came into Ume's mind that day, so many years after, when
the assassins arrived.

As they pushed open the doors to the dojo, Ume remembered
the bento box full of delicacies, untouched, pristine. As the men
withdrew their weapons and fell upon her mother, Ume felt the
pain of hunger. Then Ume's mind went blank. She thought of nothing but grabbed her sister by the hand, pulled her from the dojo,
and ran.

Ume dared to turn back only after they reached the depths of the
forest. By then, it was over. Through the open door, she saw her
mother, dead amid the wreckage of their lunch, her blood spilling
over the tatami. Ume watched in horror as one of the men slid a
wakizashi from his belt, lifted it high, and beheaded her mother. It
was a gesture of honor, one that a samurai wished for in death, but
the brutality was too much. Her sister screamed, drawing the atten-

tion of the assassins. They saw the girls and would have come for them had their father not stopped them. He ran into the dojo and threw himself on the men, giving the girls just enough time to escape. But, really, the girls never left. Part of Ume remained there, with her parents, dead in the snow.

22

Mike Brink walked into a small, darkened vestibule at the far side of the treasure room. At the center of the space, enclosed in a cube of glass, sat the Dragon Puzzle Box. A spotlight blazed down over it, creating a circle of brightness. He stared into the luminous cube, entranced. Even after everything he'd heard about the Dragon Box, even after the invitation and a fourteen-hour flight, part of him hadn't believed it would be there. It'd seemed a kind of fairy tale and he a kind of Aladdin, brought in to conjure a genie from a bottle. And yet there it was, oiled wood glistening under the spotlight.

It was larger than any puzzle box he'd ever opened, two feet by two feet square. An elaborate mosaic scored the wood, just as the emperor's concubine had described. He'd never seen a puzzle box with such an intricate design. His collection of puzzle boxes had similar patterns, but they weren't nearly as complicated. Or as beautiful. He couldn't take his eyes off it, not the glossy surface or the twisting dragon. It was enough to make him forget the danger waiting below its sleek surface.

"It isn't like anything I've ever seen," Brink said, leaning close to the glass, his breath creating the slightest film of fog over the surface. "It's . . ."

"Utterly amazing," Sakura said. She walked around the cube until she stood on the opposite side of the glass, surveying the box. Slowly, she lifted her eyes to meet his. "Of course it's not like any other box you've seen. This is the most complicated, most maniacally difficult mechanical puzzle in the world."

That was saying something. Mechanical puzzles were notoriously challenging. Despite this, or maybe because of it, they spoke to Brink in a way other puzzles didn't. At MIT, he'd studied topology, a field that examined the nature of geometric shapes as they change through pressure and deformation—crumpling and stretching, transforming. He loved the idea that an object could be endlessly elastic without rupture, transforming like space-time. Mechanical puzzles were a perfect miniature of the endlessly interlocking movements of matter in a void, or—to put it another way—of the universe. For Brink, solving a mechanical puzzle explained a primal truth.

He wasn't the only one to feel this way. Mechanical puzzles were wildly popular and always had been. The first was made in Greece in the third century B.C., and tangrams—like the one he'd solved outside the treasure room—were a sensation in the early nineteenth century, spreading from China to Europe, where they became the most popular puzzle of the era. Mechanical puzzles spoke to people. It wasn't a fluke that the most popular puzzle of all time, and one of Brink's favorites, too, was a mechanical puzzle: the Rubik's Cube.

The Dragon Box was part of that lineage but the exact opposite: In all the years it had existed, only a handful of people had ever touched it. For those who'd tried to solve it, it was the very last thing they'd ever seen. Its revelations had remained forever elusive.

Brink wasn't going to allow it to elude him. As he stood before the Dragon Box, he felt his resolve thicken. The atmosphere of the room shifted. He felt hot, then cold, then weak. *This was it.* The thing itself, a puzzle so unsolvable, so vicious, it had killed every solver who came close to opening it. He could die, as well, he knew that, but the allure of the box overwhelmed him. It was magnetic, alive, radiating its own current of electricity. He felt an urge to break the glass and touch it. He wanted to feel its weight in his hands, slide a finger over the smooth surface, work out the first move. Already, he was under its spell.

Dr. Trevers would have flagged this as a prime example of his addiction to danger. It was reckless to be there, on the other side of the world, ready to offer up his life to open a wooden box. He knew that. But he couldn't help it. And it struck him then how much he needed Dr. Trevers. He was the one person who understood his compulsions and could bring him back from the edge. Brink felt the sting of loss, sharp and deep. The irony was that he was there, in Japan, in that treasure room, trying to understand the connection between the Dragon Box and Dr. Trevers's death. His friend and mentor would have told him to turn around and go home.

"Now that you've seen the box yourself," Sakura said, putting Yoshiko Fujiwara's pillow book in his hand, "maybe this will help."

He flipped through the pages, the stream of characters moving past. He paused at a series of kanji set apart from the others. Their meaning rushed into his mind: *visions, warning, protect*. He turned the book toward Sakura. "This passage seems different from the others, don't you think?"

She read the page, cocked her head as she considered the characters, then read them again. "You're right to find this strange. It is an unusual passage, as it is about the emperor himself." Sakura read the passage aloud, translating it for Brink.

"The emperor wakes each night with visions. I wash his feverish brow with a cold cloth, pour him tea, and sing to calm him, but he does not sleep. I am terrified. I cannot understand these terrible dreams. Last night he told me that his ancestor the empress Suiko visited him. She knelt by his side and whispered into his ear. It is a warning, my lord says, a presentiment. The empress Suiko begs me to protect . . ."

The passage ended there. Brink ran a finger along the vertical edge of the *washi* paper. It was uneven, slightly jagged with ripped fibers. "The edge of the page was torn."

"Yes," Sakura said. "The phrase is cut off after the word *protect.*"

Brink glanced back at the calligraphy, taking in the elegant sweep of the characters. "Must've been a pretty scary dream."

Brink could see that the passage intrigued, even startled, Sakura. She seemed to shrink away from the pillow book, as if it had taken on a new significance.

"In the nineteenth century, dreams were considered divine messages. That one of Meiji's most illustrious ancestors would warn him in a dream would've been very significant to Meiji and more than enough to frighten him. Especially considering that ancestor was the empress Suiko."

"You're familiar with the empress Suiko?"

"My mother used to tell me stories about her. She was the first female ruler of Japan. Actually, there was another before Suiko, Queen Himiko, who is believed to have ruled in the third century, but there is very little documentation of her reign, and historians tend to dismiss her as a legend. But Suiko's reign was well documented. She was the most prominent female ruler in Japanese history. She came to power at the end of the sixth century and ruled for thirty-six years, from 592 to 628. As empress, she oversaw a great cultural and political era, bringing the constitution of 604 and Buddhism to Japan. She was a Yamato ruler, of course, descended from Amaterasu and revered for her divinity, but it was her wisdom and intelligence that allowed her to reign with such success."

"It seems like you know a lot about her."

"My mother knew everything there was to know about the eight empresses of Japan. When my sister and I were little, we played a memory game with the kanji of the empress's names. But my mother was also very familiar with the history of the Dragon Box—everything that had been written about it, including this pillow book. If there was any mention of the empress Suiko's appearance to Meiji in a dream, my mother would have known."

Brink turned his attention back to the pillow book. He flipped the page to see if there might be something to explain the ripped paper, and an ink drawing at its center caught his eye. He felt a wild surge of adrenaline. If this was what he thought it was, it was a game changer. "Am I dreaming or is that a diagram of the box?"

"It does appear to be a sketch," Sakura said, looking closely at the drawing. "A very imprecise one, but a sketch nonetheless."

Brink was elated. The drawing was rough, a bird's-eye view, and didn't give details of the actual puzzles in the box or even the order in which one would encounter them. What it *did* show was the box's construction. Under its beautiful surface, layered like the sheets of mille-feuille pastry, were twists and turns, hinged openings, covert spaces, tiny trapdoors, dozens of feints and diversions. Small kanji characters were scrawled alongside the drawing. He'd memorized around ten thousand characters on the plane, as well as the katakana and hiragana syllabaries, but he strained to decipher Yoshiko's calligraphy.

"While my ability to read nineteenth-century calligraphy isn't perfect," Sakura said, running a finger in a vertical line over the kanji on the page, "I believe this describes the box's defenses."

Brink glanced over the symbols as Sakura read:

Poison

Trapdoor

Razor

Venom

Spike

Brink turned back to the box, sitting in its chill circle of light. It looked so harmless, and yet it was a terrible adversary, one with weapons he couldn't see, let alone defend himself against. He put a hand on the cold glass. He felt suddenly threatened. *What if the barrier is meant to protect me as much as it's meant to protect the box?*

"Look here." Sakura pointed to a drawing of a glass tube at the center of the diagram.

"That," Brink said, "appears to be the destruction mechanism."

Sakura angled the page to get a closer look. "It must be filled with liquid."

"Probably acid."

"If someone were to break open the box . . ."

"It would shatter the glass tube and destroy the contents."

"And the treasure will be gone forever."

He'd known that there must be some kind of destruction mechanism built into the box. It was a classic element of puzzle-box design, especially one holding something of value. The device—in this case a glass tube rigged to the innermost chamber—prevented the box from being forced open. If the box were to be forced open, a mechanism would break the glass tube and destroy what lay inside. One had no choice but to treat the box with extreme tenderness.

Sakura read a passage below the diagram: "*Constructing a puzzle box is like creating a magic trick—the illusion is everything. Success requires working with the illusion rather than against it.*

"Something Ogawa must have told Meiji," Sakura said. "Yoshiko recorded it for us. Now we just need to decipher the illusion."

Decipher the illusion. Brink took in Sakura, wondering how many levels of illusion he was dealing with. Something had shifted between them after they cracked the code to the treasure room. He'd understood that she was smart before, but he hadn't known just how smart. She would make a formidable opponent, or a brilliant ally. There was something she wasn't telling him; he could feel it. "Everything okay, Sakura?"

She gave the slightest hint of a smile. "After everything you've learned about the box, I have to ask: Aren't you afraid?"

Afraid. Brink hadn't allowed himself to consider being afraid. He couldn't afford fear. If he allowed himself to be afraid, if Ogawa's ingenious traps intimidated him even the smallest bit, it was as good as giving in. "Fear is just the opening move," he said. "The faster you get past it, the sooner you get to the good stuff."

Sakura gave him a strange look, one he couldn't read. Was she afraid for him? Or was she taunting him?

"If I were you," she said, "I'd be terrified."

"There's no time to be afraid," he said. "I'm here. The contest is happening tomorrow."

"If you could leave, get back on the emperor's jet and go home, would you?"

Leave? The very thought stopped him cold. Could he bypass every impulse he had and leave the Dragon Box unsolved? Could he go back home without knowing what happened to Dr. Trevers? The image of a body bag filled his mind, and he knew, then and there, that he would never walk away. He needed to do this. "I can't give up on this."

"Well," Sakura said turning back to the glass cube, "every time someone comes near this thing, something terrible happens."

"Nothing terrible is going to happen this time."

"But it already has."

"What?" He was taken off guard. The box was sitting in a sealed glass cube in a vault, protected. Nobody could get close to it. What could have possibly happened?

"My aunt sent a text message," she said. "An update. The box was brought to the palace yesterday. The man who carried it, a priest in the service of the emperor, attempted to open it."

"Wasn't he warned?"

"Of course." Sakura's eyes drifted back to the Dragon Box. "His training should have protected him. But it didn't. The temptation to understand the box was too overpowering. It made him weak. I only hope that you are stronger than he was."

23

Connie was waiting for Brink when he returned. Her food bowl was empty, and she was anxious to go out—she ran in circles around him and gave a series of short sharp yelps, her way of expressing an urgent need to pee. He flicked his wrist, as if tossing a Frisbee, and she leapt into the air and snapped her jaws, pretending to catch it. Imaginary Frisbee was a game they played. They both knew there was no Frisbee, but it was a way of assuring her that he understood what she needed and would take her outside.

He grabbed her leash and, reaching into his jacket pocket, pulled out the security badge Sakura had given him. The security guards would be watching his every move, which wouldn't be hard, considering he was the only person in the entire wing. He needed a full night's rest before the contest, but nature was nature. Besides, he thought, checking his phone's battery, it would be a good time to figure out if Rachel had caught a flight.

Fastening Connie's leash, he walked through the hallway. The stillness felt absolute—nothing but the soft tread of his Chuckies on the blond hardwood floor. Retracing the path he'd taken with Sakura earlier, he found the private entrance, swiped his badge to open the door, and walked out into the frigid night.

A guard at a security station stopped him, checked his badge, scrutinized Connie, and gave a quick bow, a gesture Brink decided meant he was free to go. He walked quickly, shoving his hands into the pockets of his jacket, taking in the crisp night air. It had snowed recently. As he walked into the forest, he kicked through white powder. Snow had collected on the branches of cedar trees, white caps on green needles. Connie hadn't had a good run since the park that morning—*was it even the same morning?* His sense of time was gone, distorted by travel and jet lag. The time difference between New York and Tokyo was fourteen hours, but it felt like days. He took a narrow stone path into the thick evergreens, straining against Connie, who was going crazy on her leash. Dachshunds were bred to hunt, and she'd clearly got the scent of something in the woods.

He intended to let her run free, but not two minutes passed before he felt his phone buzz in his pocket. Hours' worth of notifications and texts loaded all at once. He hadn't realized he'd lost service, but his reception must've been out since his arrival at the Imperial Palace. An incoming video call filled his screen. He tapped the screen, swept right, and a familiar face stared out at him.

"Mr. Brink, my boy!" Mike Brink would recognize Dr. Vivek Gupta's deep, warm baritone and lilting Hindi-inflected British accent anywhere. "I finally got you."

Dr. Gupta was one of Brink's oldest and most trusted friends. He'd been his mathematics professor at MIT and, after Brink graduated, Dr. Gupta had advised, protected, and steered him in the right direction. The professor had retired a few years back and spent most of his time painting in his Cape Cod studio, where he'd become something of a recluse during the pandemic of 2020. While they spoke by encrypted video conference at least once a week, it had been over a year since Brink had seen him in person. He missed him.

"Why the devil didn't you tell me you were going to Japan?" Gupta said, his voice filled with false recrimination.

Brink positioned his phone so that he could see Dr. Gupta better. He looked just as he always did: immaculate three-piece suit, trimmed salt-and-pepper beard, a twinkle in his eye, and an enormous, mischievous grin on his face. Brink felt for a moment like a boy being scolded for skipping school. "I didn't know *myself* I'd be going to Japan."

"Oh, come now. You must have suspected you'd be chosen. Especially with your talent in mechanical puzzles."

"I wasn't sure the contest really existed."

"Of course, that's what they wanted—to make the whole thing seem like a silly legend. It's the oldest trick in the book: put the truth out there in plain view, seed conspiracy theories, make it equally plausible and deniable. But I had a feeling you'd be invited. When your phone showed that you'd left Manhattan for New Jersey, and then your location went black for seventeen hours before turning up in Tokyo, I knew the game was afoot."

Brink was aware that Dr. Gupta kept tabs on him. He was one of the original Cypherpunks, a small group of men and women in San Francisco in the nineties who developed early digital technologies to protect individual liberties. He'd spent his life safeguarding privacy and personal information. The flip side was that he understood how to get the information he needed.

Dr. Gupta continued, "I've been trying to reach you since you landed, but the Imperial Household Agency is top-notch. All cellular signals within the palace were blocked. Perhaps the Fukiage Palace's walls were built with a layer of aluminum inside, making the whole place a Faraday cage."

"You're right," Brink said. "My signal was blocked inside the palace. I'm outside now, with Connie."

"Dear old Conundrum," Gupta said affectionately. "Always forcing you out of your shell. Well, I've got you now. You're right here in my navigation system. I see you've walked far enough from the Fukiage Palace to be out of range of the surveillance cameras, but still, I'd feel more comfortable if you kept moving. Head northwest; I think there is a good spot for us to talk just ahead."

Brink walked quickly, and Conundrum kept pace. Soon he found himself outside an old wooden structure with large glass windows. Brink tried the door. It didn't open. "The door is locked," Gupta said. "But it's controlled by an electronic system, which will cause no trouble as soon as I deactivate it. One moment, please." The door clicked. "There. It should be open now."

Brink slipped inside, Connie following close after. Turning, he glanced through the room, finding a miniature forest of bonsai trees, hundreds of them positioned on long wooden tables, a choreography of twisting branches, cosseted tree trunks, glistening ceramic pots. A ballet of bonsai.

"You're inside the imperial bonsai garden," Gupta said curtly. "According to the information on the Imperial Household Agency website, which I'm reading now, the oldest bonsai in their collection is eight hundred years old. Imagine that: You are walking among trees alive before the West began its wretched colonial hegemony in the Americas."

"Nifty," Brink said flatly. He knew that Gupta was enjoying this, that his sense of the aesthetic almost always outweighed practical matters, but Brink needed to be cautious. He couldn't be caught wandering the imperial bonsai garden by security guards. "Dr. Gupta, it's almost midnight here, and I have a contest to prepare for."

"Exactly why I called. Now, listen carefully. The greenhouse isn't fitted with cameras, but do get away from the windows, so you won't be seen. And make sure darling Conundrum doesn't alert anyone to your presence. We don't want you taken back to the imperial residence until you've heard everything I have to tell you."

Brink slid onto a cold wooden bench, his vision leveling with rows of tables. Bonsai surrounded him on every side, a sweeping series of fractals, foliar masses, exploding spirals, shards of color, and patterns that filled the entire length of the building. He pulled Connie close, trying to get comfortable on the bench, and turned to Dr. Gupta on the screen.

"Rachel called from the airport," Gupta said. "I was sorry, deeply sorry, to hear of Dr. Trevers's passing. A fine doctor. A fine man. I know how much he helped you. And how close you were to him. My sincere condolences."

Brink felt the weight of Trevers's death. Strange how he could forget for a moment and the sensation of grief would diminish, only to come crashing back. "Did Rachel tell you about the message Dr. Trevers sent me?"

"With the chrysanthemum? Indeed, she did. The message you received, the invitation to Japan, and the timing of his death cannot be a coincidence. I looked to see if the medical examiner's report has been filed, but it hasn't. I'll keep looking, but at the moment there is a more pressing concern: this contest. I'm not going to allow you to be slaughtered by an antiquated contraption constructed by a blind woodworker for a megalomaniac descended from the sun goddess. Not a chance, my friend. Not a chance in hell."

That Gupta knew such specific details about the box—that Ogawa was blind, for example—struck Brink as astonishing. "I've searched everywhere for details about the Dragon Puzzle Box. There's simply nothing out there."

"Information is *always* out there," Gupta said. "The trick is knowing who has it and how to get it. The Imperial Household Agency is the custodian of the entire imperial archive. I was able to infiltrate their digital files."

"And what did you find?"

"This is no ordinary puzzle. The Dragon Box is a thing of wonder, a legend, something that has defeated the most brilliant puzzle solvers in the world. It calls to solvers, beckoning them like a siren, only to destroy them. *How does it do it? Why?* That is its mystery. That is the enigma. But despite its mystique, the Dragon Box is, at the most basic level, a mechanical puzzle, one with concrete steps that lead to a concrete solution. And you are the best in the world at uncovering those steps. I don't doubt for a moment that you can solve it, but you need help. If this were a normal contest, I wouldn't dream of giving you such an advantage. But this box was designed not to be opened but to kill. With the information I've found and your unquestionably superior abilities, though, you will get out of this alive."

24

In all the years that he'd been solving, Mike Brink had rarely pan-icked. Yet there, waiting for Vivek Gupta to reveal what he'd learned, he felt a white-hot electricity move through him. How had he become wrapped up in something so complex, so dangerous? "So tell me: What did you find?"

"First, I have a few questions for *you*," Gupta said. "Your percep-tions are infallibly accurate. Surely you have your own impressions about what's going on here. Any insights?"

Dr. Gupta was referring to Brink's eidetic memory and his nearly total mnemonic recall. He knew that everything he'd experienced in the past hours, down to the smallest details, was there, locked down tight in his mind. He related everything Sakura had told him; he gave the history of the box, the legends and superstitions surround-ing it; he laid out the contents of Yoshiko Fujiwara's pillow book and asked Gupta if he knew anything about the empress Suiko, the an-cestor in Meiji's dreams. "I could see from Sakura's reaction that Suiko could be important."

"She most definitely *was* important," Gupta said, his interest piqued. "She is an iconic empress who ruled in the eighth century, I believe."

"The seventh," Brink said. "She instituted the constitution of 604."

"Yes, the *seventh* century, a near contemporary of one of my favorite Chinese rulers—the empress Wu Zetian, a fierce woman who came from nothing and rose to dizzying heights of power. Such women were not to be toyed with, and Suiko was no exception. She has been likened to the most famous empresses of all time: Cleopatra; Boudica; Catherine the Great. That Meiji was dreaming about the empress Suiko is quite surprising, as Meiji was no great fan of women rulers. It is he who instituted the 1889 law that codified the laws of imperial succession, banning women from inheriting the throne. His dream of the empress Suiko must have been an absolute nightmare."

Brink went on to describe the dimensions of the Dragon Box, the list of poisons and traps, and the diagram of the destruction mechanism.

"All utterly in line with the box's design," Gupta said, becoming pensive. "Ogawa was an aficionado of obscure poisons. He was blind, as you know, but were you aware that he blinded *himself* while constructing one of his own puzzle boxes?"

"Oops," Brink said. He knew that a puzzle could become an obsession, but blinding yourself?

"*Oops* indeed. From what I can gather, he exposed himself to methane gas while creating a booby trap. The fumes destroyed his corneas."

"But why go to such lengths?"

"Ogawa was an intriguing fellow. A genius, clearly, an absolute genius, a rival to your powers—and he had no brain injury to thank, so far as I'm aware. He is known to have had a maniacal need to destroy anyone who attempted to solve his boxes. Total annihilation was his method. And thus far he has succeeded. The brutality of the exterior is in direct proportion to the delicacy of what is inside. Knowing that there is a destruction mechanism built into the puzzle gives us one very important insight: What is locked inside is not gold or diamonds but something fragile. Something that can be destroyed by acid. *Something written on paper.*"

"Information," Brink said.

"The world's most precious substance," Gupta said.

Brink remembered what Sakura had said about the contents of the box. *The emperor locked something of great value inside, something with the power to change the imperial family, perhaps all of Japan, if it were to be discovered.*

"A paradox confronts us," Gupta said. "Precious information is safe, but it is also impossible to retrieve without destroying."

"Like the cryptex." Brink was referring to a coded cylindrical device in the thriller *The Da Vinci Code*. He'd been barely a teenager when the book was released, just thirteen years old, and hadn't known anything about it until he was at MIT, where it was something of a joke for nerdy cryptologists.

Gupta rolled his eyes. "The cryptex, indeed! You know as well as I that the cryptex is a totally fictitious flight of fancy, Mr. Brink, the work of a clever writer, not a puzzle maker. Leonardo da Vinci never created such a device, didn't draw it, probably never even imagined it. But there *is* someone who did imagine a real cryptographic box: the ingenious Lu Ban, who lived from 507 to 444 B.C. A carpenter and engineer, he was also an expert weapons designer. He called his boxes 'defensive boxes.' They were, in essence, one of the earliest attempts at securing privacy, a primitive ZK-rollup if you will, some two thousand years *before* Da Vinci. A Japanese puzzle maker in the nineteenth century would have surely used Chinese mechanical puzzles as his model, Lu Ban's boxes most likely."

Brink gazed out over the field of bonsai, listening to Gupta. He knew what to expect. His mentor could talk for hours about the cultural cross-pollination between East and West. He liked to argue that the European Renaissance was not a rediscovery of ancient Greek and Roman knowledge but rather was incited by the arrival of texts from China and India to Italy in the fifteenth century. At MIT, Gupta held court for hours discussing the influence of his favorite mathematician, Srinivasa Ramanujan, an intuitive genius born in Erode, India, in 1887, who forever changed number theory.

"And why does this matter?"

"To solve a conundrum, one must understand its origins. Ogawa borrowed his defense mechanisms from Lu Ban, who was greatly influenced by the natural world. For example, Lu Ban's defensive boxes have a poisonous exoskeleton, as does the Dragon Box. Lu Ban's boxes secreted bufotoxin through minuscule valves, smaller than capillaries, worked into the surface of the wood, ensuring that the poison could be carried for hundreds of years, only to be released with the lightest brush of a finger."

"Bufotoxin is a natural poison?"

"It's taken from the cane toad and is so lethal that a single small exposure will kill a man. Then Ogawa designed spikes that impale like the teeth of a piranha. Razors that slice like the scales of a pangolin. The destruction mechanism itself, with its tube of acid, is like the infamous puffer fish, whose neurotoxin, tetrodotoxin, is more deadly than arsenic and has no known antidote. And these are only the defenses we are aware of. There are certainly many more such wonders of nature embedded inside. All of these traps require that the box be handled with the gentlest movements. Like the heart of a lover."

"More like a minefield," Brink said. He could almost see the box in his mind, its tricks and traps, the razor blades and vial of acid nested under a smooth surface. Maybe Sakura was right. Maybe it was too dangerous. Maybe he should give up. Leave. "One mistake and the whole thing will explode, taking me with it."

"Not if I can help it," Gupta said. There was a sudden cacophony of computer keys clicking as Gupta called up information. "We have a secret weapon of our own."

25

Mike Brink wasn't a patient man. He was prone to rush into things impulsively, following his instincts. Too often, he relied less on information than intuition to pull him through. But the Dragon Box was different. He needed all the help he could get. "What kind of secret weapon are we talking about here?"

"The imperial archive contains hundreds of thousands of documents, everything from drafts of tax laws from the seventeenth century to imperial dinner menus. The papers of minor members of the imperial courts—secretaries, scribes, Shinto priests, temple maidens—are particularly voluminous. These fine folks, forgotten by history, wrote things down. The imperial secretaries from the emperor Meiji up to the emperor Akihito took extensive notes on the puzzle-box contest."

Brink almost dropped his phone. "Wait—there are *notes* about the previous contests?"

"Oh yes, indeed, copious notes about the previous solvers, including their successes and failures with the puzzle itself."

Brink felt his heart going like mad in his chest. He couldn't believe it. If the contests were documented, there must be information about how the box worked. There must be descriptions of each step and misstep the solvers had taken. "And you have these notes?"

"I do," Gupta said. "As you know, there's a history of attempts to open the Dragon Box—six to be exact—and we can learn much from these examples."

Gupta picked up a piece of paper and started to read:

"The first attempt was made after the Second World War, in the Year of the Water Dragon, 1952, when the emperor invited a Go champion and cadet member of the imperial family to try his hand at opening the box. He lost a finger before he made a single move."

"Hold on," Brink said, trying to imagine how someone could lose a finger before he even began. "How is that possible?"

"Before one can commence solving the box, it must be unlocked. There is a release mechanism that opens the box for play. While it appears to be a rather simple mechanism, it must be opened manually. According to the description I read, there is a narrow cavity at the base of the box, just wide enough for a finger. The solver slides a finger into this passage, pushes a tiny lever at the end of the passage, and a latch releases."

"Sounds easy enough . . ."

"But if the lever is pushed the wrong way, a guillotine descends."

Brink snatched his fingers into a fist. "Excuse me?"

"*A guillotine.* That is how it was described, I'm afraid. It surprised the first solver to such a degree that he grabbed hold of the box with his bare hand, triggering the poison to release. He died, like the unfortunate priest you mentioned, from exposure to bufotoxin."

Brink felt a wave of nausea. It didn't make sense. None of these traps could be predicted. This wasn't a puzzle. It was a death sentence.

"And this guillotine resets for every solver?"

"Apparently it does," Gupta said. "There is mention of another solver losing a finger, as well, but the others seem to have made it through. That's two out of six. Not bad odds."

"Reassuring," he said, glancing at his fingers, anxiety rushing through him.

"Twelve years later, in the Year of the Wood Dragon, 1964, the puzzle master was more adept. No amputated digits for him. He passed the poisoned exterior layers by wearing leather gloves."

"And those steps were all sliding panels?"

"Exactly right. He opened three panels of the exterior, much as one does with any puzzle box, before he made a misstep and died by what was described as *a toxic gas,* released from a leather pouch in the fourth move. I suspect that was a suspension of powdered arsenic—one breath and the lungs would seize up. Then, in 1976, Year of the Fire Dragon, the solver was simply extraordinary. A woman from Korea, trained in the old traditions of mechanical puzzles. She got fifteen moves into the sequence without a booby trap, only to be surprised by what was described as *a swift-moving spike through the eye.*"

"Man," Brink said, envisioning it. "What do you think that was?"

"*Fukibari,* a poisoned dart, most likely."

Brink remembered the diagram and the sequence of traps: *Poison, Trapdoor, Razor, Venom, Spike.* "Getting fifteen steps in is pretty good. Maybe she thought she'd bypassed all the traps."

"She was very wrong. She merely behaved exactly as Ogawa expected. The box was designed to disorient and betray, to trick the solver into believing they've made it through the worst before releasing an even deadlier trap."

Brink rubbed the back of his neck, feeling the tension radiate through his shoulders. The more he knew about the box, the more he wished he'd stayed home.

"Then," Gupta said, "in 1988, the Year of the Earth Dragon, things got really interesting. There was something of a breakthrough. The solver was a Frenchman who discovered what is described as *a backdoor mechanism* to the interior layers of the box. What that mechanism is, I don't know. It's only described as leading him deep into a maze—one from which he never returned."

"This whole thing is a maze," Brink said, feeling a wave of despair. More information was supposed to help him, not confuse him even further.

"Then everything goes dark. Nothing from 2000 or 2012, although there were stories on the internet about an Australian solver in 2012 who did not return home. Clearly, the man's family started a ruckus. Secrets are hard to keep in the age of the internet. In any event, he was never seen again, which is consistent with what your friend Sakura said: No one who has attempted to solve the Dragon Box has survived."

"Any thoughts about why there's no information about the last two?"

Gupta shrugged. "A change of the guard. The first four contests occurred under the purview of Emperor Hirohito, known as Shōwa after his death. He died in 1989 and was replaced by his son, the emperor Akihito, who must have kept the contests even more secret than before."

"And now?"

"Akihito's son, Naruhito, became emperor in 2019. And here you are, his first puzzle master."

"And hopefully his last."

"I have faith in you, Mr. Brink. I know you will solve this."

Brink pondered what Gupta had told him. The stories of these solvers were all quite similar: Brilliant puzzle masters were chosen to come to the Imperial Palace; they attacked with the full force of their powers; and the box defeated them. Time and time again, it was the same. It was terrifying to imagine that he could follow their footsteps to a gruesome death.

And yet, knowing the opening sequence was an enormous advantage. It left him strangely optimistic, despite the odds. Getting past the thorny fortifications of the box's exterior would surely bring him to where the real play began. That's where his talents lay. There was just one thing he needed to know. "Did you see how many total moves are there?"

"Seventy-two," Gupta said.

Brink's heart sank. *Seventy-two moves?* It was even more difficult than he'd imagined. "I'm going to need a miracle to open this thing."

"No miracles are required here. Your gifts are all you need. Of that I'm certain. But there is another aspect to the contest that you need to consider. Brace yourself, Brink, I have something else to tell you. And it's not good news."

Brink felt his stomach twist. In the past twenty-four hours, he'd learned that the puzzle box was cursed, that it had been designed to poison whoever touched it, and that every puzzle solver who went near it died a painful, horrible death. What more could there be? He sighed, preparing for the worst. "Okay, let me have it."

"The emperor isn't the only person who wants the contents of this box. In my investigations through the imperial archive, I learned that there has been, since before the time of Meiji, a faction of powerful people—some might call them insurgents—searching for the Dragon Box."

Insurgents. "What would insurgents want with a puzzle box?"

"The same thing the emperor does," Gupta said. "To claim what is locked inside. Clearly, whatever Meiji hid has a greater social and political meaning, one that is still relevant over a century later."

Brink considered this. "But if there's been nothing about the contest in the archives since 1988, as you said, how do you know that this faction is still . . . active?"

"Good question. I wouldn't have known at all had it not been for a strange series of messages from the current imperial secretary, Akemi Saito, that popped up yesterday."

"Just before I received the invitation in New York."

"They were sent from her official phone, which is part of the encrypted network inside the palace. It was a rather urgent request for help. Now that I think of it, it must have been related to the priest's death you mentioned. She would have needed help immediately and would have wanted to keep the police out of it."

"But how is that relevant to the faction of insurgents?"

"Because the text messages were sent to someone I know well: my old friend Jameson Sedge."

The name was one that Brink wanted to forget. Brash, arrogant,

full of philosophical musings about technology and immortality—
Brink had disliked Jameson Sedge from the minute he met him. The
guy was a maniac, a tech billionaire who had set up Brink's ex-
girlfriend, Jess Price, for murder. Sedge had killed himself in a gruesome and spectacular manner, shooting himself in the head as Brink
watched. It wouldn't surprise Brink to learn that Sedge had aligned
with insurgents. The only problem was: Sedge couldn't align with
anyone. He was dead. "That's totally impossible, Gupta."

"One would think so," Gupta said. "I was at the funeral myself,
after all. He was cremated, thank heavens. Yet, from what I'm seeing,
he's active across multiple online channels. And not just active. He's
initiating, responding, and interacting with people. I have video
footage of him from three weeks ago in a digital conference room
with the most powerful technocrats of our era—Elon Musk, Peter
Thiel, Mark Zuckerberg, and Marc Andreessen—discussing the creation of a network state. He appears to be communicating from beyond the grave."

"It's an avatar. It must be."

"In the messages I read, Jameson Sedge *responded* to Akemi's
request. He sent help, which implies agency."

"That could be an employee," Brink said, although he knew it
didn't fully explain everything Gupta had found. "He had hundreds
of them."

"Yes, it could be an employee," Gupta said. "And the videos could
be an avatar. But the activity I'm seeing is unique and seems very
particular to Sedge. There are cash transfers from Sedge's bank accounts, for example, and movement of cryptocurrency. I've found
thousands of communications. I've traced them back nearly two
years, since June of 2022."

"That's the month Jameson Sedge died."

"Exactly," Gupta said. "It would appear that Jameson Sedge is
dead, but his consciousness is digitally alive. And he wants the same
thing you do—the contents of the Dragon Puzzle Box."

26

A door slid open and Ume's disciples—five women, so silent she didn't hear a sound as they took their positions on the tatami—entered the dojo. They wore black *hakama* pants, deeply pleated, and black kimono jackets cinched with black obis, the very uniform they'd worn since Ume accepted them as students. They'd come to her as girls, and she'd watched them carefully over the years, encouraging their strengths and inhibiting their weaknesses. Now she knew them as well as she knew herself, knew their motivations and their fears, their dreams and nightmares. This allowed her to be impartial with them. She'd never protected herself from pain, and she would never protect them. She cared too much to spare them.

"Set up," she said, and the women took their *naginata,* found their places in the dojo, and stood in formation, watching their sensei.

Ume lifted her *naginata,* stepped to the center of the room, and stood in position, her arms strong and quick as she rotated the pole, turning it in one hand and then the other. She'd enacted the gesture a thousand times, knew every movement of her practice, and yet each time she began, she felt a shock of nervous energy, as if Nakano Takeko were watching from the photograph. Not only her, but every warrior who had come before: Her mother. Her grandmother. Her great-grandfather. She stepped forward, thrusting the blade of the *naginata,* feeling the weight of their expectations. That weight would not lift until she had avenged them.

She'd trained her students to be warriors—lean, strong, single-minded fighting machines. She called them her *jōshitai,* her army of women, referring to the women soldiers led to battle by Nakano Takeko during the Battle of Aizu. While the name was playful, Ume considered her girls to be the spiritual descendants of Nakano Takeko. There were no better warriors anywhere.

Ume's girls idolized her the way she idolized Nakano Takeko. It was natural to look up to one's teacher, of course, especially after all the years they'd worked together. Like Ume, they'd given up everything for their practice. They had no lovers, no families, no homes. They wore their hair long and unadorned, no makeup, their nails cut short. Everything they owned fit in a rucksack, including two pairs of *hakama.* They were, as far as Ume knew, virgins, although she didn't ask for, and they would never dare to offer, such personal information. They were of the same breed, Ume and her girls. A family. They had nothing but one another and the mission that lay ahead.

Once a month, they visited the Yasukuni Shrine. The shrine had been founded by Emperor Meiji to commemorate those who had sacrificed their lives in service to Japan. Those sacrifices numbered in the hundreds of thousands. And yet the shrine was almost always empty. Many Japanese wanted to forget the past, but Ume had not forgotten. She prayed that her great-grandfather, who had died over the Pacific, his body evaporating in an explosion of gasoline and metal, had found a realm of stillness and peace. She prayed that her parents, murdered for their beliefs, would protect their daughters as they carried out their mission.

The current emperor had not once stepped into the Yasukuni Shrine, had never commemorated the sacrifices made, never bowed before the swirl of spirits hovering in the shadows. The emperor's father had never visited the Yasukuni Shrine, either. The imperial family would like to forget those who had served them. But there were those who had not.

Ume stepped to the side of the dojo, leaned the *naginata* against a wall, and watched them as they went through their formations.

She wished her sister had even a fraction of the discipline of her *jōshitai*. Sakura was physically soft, American soft, quick to choose the easy path. She liked to play video games and could spend hours alone with her computer. She took after their father, Satoshi, a man who preferred codes and riddles and complex philosophical treatises to physical combat. *Our war can be won with cleverness,* he'd often said. He wanted to change the world through code. He'd wanted Ume and Sakura to fight their battles with technology. Sakura had gone through the motions of physical training—their mother insisted upon it—but after they lost their parents, she never picked up a *naginata* again.

In February 2010, one month after their parents were murdered, the girls were taken in by an old friend of their father's, Jameson Sedge. He was childless, wealthy, and able to protect them in ways their aunt Akemi could not. A formal adoption was finalized one year after their arrival in the United States. Ume realized later, after she'd gone to work for Mr. Sedge, that his interest hadn't been in Sakura and her per se. The girls were a living connection to their father, the elusive Satoshi Nakamoto, creator of the first digital currency, Bitcoin.

Mr. Sedge had been partners in the development of new technologies, but their father had broken with Mr. Sedge. Ume and Sakura Nakamoto inherited their father's work: his cryptographic keys, his hard drives, the reams and reams of notebooks filled with philosophical writings. All the secrets her parents had been killed for belonged to Sakura and Ume. In becoming their guardian, Sedge believed that he could control Satoshi Nakamoto's legacy.

Over time, Ume became Sedge's most trusted ally, as close as a daughter. She managed the training of his security team at Singularity Technology, shaping his bodyguards physically and mentally, sharpening and molding them. Mr. Sedge called his team Singularity samurai, a name that irked Ume. Being born into a samurai family, she knew that Kurosawa's and Hollywood's glorification of violence had twisted her heritage beyond recognition. She hated the simplification of her practice into little more than a cliché. And yet, over time, she saw that Sedge understood the true nature of Bushido. He understood that gentleness is as valuable to a warrior as is violence; that life and death are interconnected; that power comes through humility and service; that only a warrior who has been beaten can rise to become a teacher, even a master.

Ume had found an ally in Jameson Sedge, but so had Sakura. He'd been the closest thing the girls had to a father during the years they lived in New York, and they'd become a strange kind of family. He sent the girls to exceptional schools, but while Ume had turned away from American culture, Sakura had thrived. Her abilities in gaming, computer science, and technologies had propelled her to a kind of academic stardom. Perhaps because Sakura was five years younger than Ume—Ume was fourteen and Sakura only nine when they came to America—Sakura had become more American in her mannerisms. She spoke English without an accent, but, more than that, she thought like an American. It was a point of contention between them. Ume held fast to the traditions their mother had taught them, while Sakura gravitated to the futuristic ideas of their father.

Ume never forgot what Sedge told her in the months after her parents were killed. "A psychological wound takes as long to heal as a physical one," he'd said. Losing her parents was like having a leg amputated. It had taken years to learn to walk again. But now that she could, she understood that she could recover from anything.

The sisters had taken opposite paths—one cerebral, the other physical—but they were as sharp and dangerous as two edges of a blade. Together, they would use their complementary skills to take back what belonged to them. Ume and Sakura would soon have the contents of the Dragon Box.

The shoji screen slid open, and Ume felt a shift in the room even before the American walked inside. It tested the girls' concentration, such an interruption. Ume felt how they wanted to turn and stare at the man. It was no wonder. Cam Putney was something to behold: tall and muscly, with blond spiked hair and flashy diamond earrings. He wore a tank top in the winter, showing his pale skin, tattoos everywhere. One tattoo in particular caught Ume's eye: a triangle of ten dots, the mark of a Singularity samurai. The tattoo matched her own.

He was a spectacle, but she'd trained her *jōshitai* well. Not one of her girls turned their eyes to him. They stayed focused, utterly unreadable. She clapped her hands. "*Hai, dozo.*" The girls turned and bowed in unison to Cam Putney. He, in turn, bowed to Ume. "Sensei."

Ume felt a swell of pride. They were magnificent, her warriors. All of them.

27

Cam Putney stepped into the elevator, pressed a button, and waited for the doors to close. As he descended, he leaned against the mirrored wall, and ran a hand through his hair. Even after more than a decade of working with Ume, she still scared the shit out of him. Standing in the dojo, looking at those women dressed in black, had filled him with an irrational terror. One Ume was bad enough, but a room full of them? It made him want to get on a plane and go back to New York.

He couldn't help but think of his first meeting with Ume-Sensei.

He'd been doing basic security for Jameson Sedge at Singularity. Keeping his head down was his MO. He couldn't afford to mess up. He had a baby girl, a criminal record, and a drug habit, none of which allowed him to fuck up even slightly. He got a promotion, and Ume-Sensei came into the picture. *She'll train you to be an effective part of the team,* Mr. Sedge had said.

At first, he tried to ignore her. She was a small woman, five foot two with shoes on, and thin as a rail, with big watchful eyes that never left him, even when she wasn't staring at him. He'd been a real asshole during their first training session, made some offensive jokes about *Karate Kid,* pretended to catch a fly with chopsticks, and she'd simply watched him. Totally still. Totally unperturbed. "Is that what you think this is?" she finally asked. "A stupid movie?"

He shrugged. He didn't know what he thought. That's who he'd been when he met her. A loser. Unconscious of his own basic assumptions about the world. A deadbeat dad. A drug addict. A guy who went out on a Saturday night looking for a fight. A limited man with an enormous chip on his shoulder.

Ume sensed this and didn't give him an inch. *You have the body of a warrior but the mind of a child.* He smiled at her, said something condescending, and she'd floored him, knocking him off his feet and punching him so hard he couldn't breathe. *You need to grow up.*

She taught him a lesson that day. She'd continued teaching him lessons ever since. He'd trained with her relentlessly, and her instruction transformed him into a man with a body and mind that ran like a machine. He still had his weaknesses. He wasn't perfect. But he had a new standard of excellence. And Ume-Sensei was it.

He knew when Ume called that whatever was going on was not part of the usual program. Mr. Sedge was involved—Ume would never do anything without his approval. But this, whatever *this* turned out to be, was personal.

Before leaving New York, Cam had checked everything with Sedge. There was no way to avoid him. Since Jameson Sedge died, and they'd downloaded his consciousness, it was impossible to keep anything from him. He saw everything. He was everywhere and nowhere at once. Every camera was a potential eye, every server a brain, every network part of a vast global nervous system sending layer upon layer of information, clusters of connection that, when used in tandem with a centralized data system—the mind of Jameson Sedge himself—created a creature beyond anything Cam had believed possible. The man's power and intelligence grew exponentially each day, until Mr. Sedge, the man who had given Cam his first break, the man to whom Cam felt an undying loyalty, had become a thing beyond comprehension.

The man was dead. *Dead.* That was a fact. Cam had stood at his side when he blew his brains out. *Nothing clarifies existence like death,* Sedge had once said. *My physical self must die so I can enter a pure state of being.* Cam had tried to stop him, hadn't believed for a second that his plan could work, but it did. Jameson Sedge was alive. As alive as Cam Putney.

His only weakness? Sedge needed someone in the world, a physical presence to manage the surprises. There were always glitches to fix, new levels of encryption to address, shifting technologies to navigate. Sedge needed someone to maintain the hardware, deploy upgrades, fix bugs. He needed Cam Putney.

They spoke multiple times a day. Cam ran his company, took meetings that could not be moved online, carried out legacy tasks with legacy institutions that Sedge couldn't manage. There weren't many. He signed contracts digitally; transferred money electronically; took meetings via video call. His inner circle saw him multiple times a week via encrypted video chats. He had romantic relationships online, his sexual encounters carried out with avatars in opulent digital spaces. He consumed knowledge, absorbing everything that was published, photographed, uploaded, scanned, or transferred digitally. It all became part of his consciousness. Everything became part of *him.* And Cam knew that this process would only accelerate with time until Sedge became ever-present, infinitely creative, infinitely destructive. A super-consciousness. A god.

Here in Tokyo, Sedge had put Ume in charge. She was a longtime Singularity fixture, Sedge's favorite and most trusted employee and adviser aside from Cam. Ume was Cam's teacher, and he respected and feared her. But he hadn't ever imagined her outside her role at Singularity, in her native country, where she was in her element and he felt like he was walking around in a clown suit. He couldn't walk down a Tokyo street without making every single person—the hip university kids, the schoolgirls with their Hello Kitty backpacks, the immaculately dressed women carrying immaculately wrapped packages, the business guys in suits, everyone—uncomfortable.

The elevator doors opened. As Cam stepped into a sleek modern lobby, his thoughts were interrupted by the sound of a television at the far end of the space. He walked to the screen and found a sumo match. Two men, naked from the waist up, fought at the center of a ring, angling around each other. While both men were enormous, as tall as Cam but twice as heavy, one guy was gargantuan, with layers of flesh rolling off him like melting wax. He stomped his foot dramatically, and Cam felt a wave of recognition: He knew better than anyone that fighting was a performance.

Cam had never watched sumo wrestling, or any kind of wrestling, for that matter. He had no idea of the rules, no clue of what signaled a win. And yet he found the whole thing utterly riveting. The tension in their expressions, the raw nature of the struggle—man against man. The simple beauty of it brought tears to his eyes.

Then, quick, without warning, the smaller guy threw himself at his opponent. The sound of bodies colliding filled the lobby. It was a primal battle, each man grabbing and twisting and pushing, trying to best the other. Their skin glistened with sweat, their expressions telegraphed determination, their bodies turned under the bright lights of the arena. Cam Putney stepped closer to the screen, his heart racing. He clenched and unclenched his hands, as if he were there, in the ring, going after that huge motherfucker himself. He felt a surge of adrenaline as the smaller wrestler tripped the giant. The guy fell with a great crash to the floor, sending a vibration through the ring. *Kaboom.* That was it. That's what it looked like, winning against all odds.

Suddenly, there was a pressure against his neck. A blade, cold as ice, sliding under his Adam's apple. Everything stopped—his breathing, his heart.

"Never stand with your back to a door," Ume-Sensei said. "Especially when your guard is down."

The blade lifted, and his teacher stepped to his side. His cheeks grew warm, and he knew he'd gone bright red. He'd let her sneak up behind him; he'd let her slide a knife against his throat. But he hadn't moved. He'd kept his cool. That was what she'd taught him: To consider his reactions. To understand that the absence of action is an action.

"Think you could take one of these guys, Mr. Putney?"

"I know *you* could," he said, rubbing his throat. "In a heartbeat."

She laughed, and he felt a rush of relief. Ume-Sensei never laughed. She never smiled, never joked around, never let things get too personal. But right here, just now, in this lobby in Tokyo, she'd laughed.

"After they killed my parents," she said, her voice barely audible under the cheers from the television, "my aunt understood that if my sister and I remained in Japan, we would be hunted down and killed. It was our moment of weakness, one that called for drastic action. She arranged for a colleague of my father's to take us in. He'd promised my father that, should anything happen to him, he would protect us, educate us, and then—when the time was right—help us return to Japan and finish what my father had started. That businessman, my adopted father, was Jameson Sedge."

Cam stared at her, astonished. He'd had no idea that Ume-Sensei had a sister. He had no idea that Mr. Sedge was her adopted father. He struggled to speak. "Why didn't you tell me?"

"It wasn't the right time," she said, turning back to the television screen, where the sumo wrestler stood at the center of the ring, victorious. "And everything is about timing. That man spent the entire match watching for the moment his opponent showed a weakness. But this victory didn't just happen in this match. He gave his body, his soul, his mind—his entire life—for this victory. Mr. Putney, I want you to look at him. Have you made that kind of sacrifice?"

Cam felt his heart race. *What did she know about him?* Had she learned that, after she left New York, he'd slipped into his old habits? A drink here. A day or two without training. The occasional paid escort. He'd stopped meditating altogether. The way she was looking at him, she must know. "I have made that kind of sacrifice," he said, glancing from the screen to Ume. "Sensei."

"Good," she said, walking to a bank of glass doors. A white van idled outside, waiting. "Because now is the time to prove it."

28

Brink hurried through the Fukiage forest, following the snowy path, his breath freezing in the air. It was late, nearly midnight, and the temperature had dropped, leaving a glistening expanse of ice-slicked pine needles.

Connie pulled on her leash, tugging him toward the palace. As always, her instincts were right: They needed to get back to the room. He needed sleep and, more important, he needed to get his head in the right place. There was too much static after his call with Gupta. He couldn't stop thinking of all the solvers who had died, all the mistakes that led to their deaths. He couldn't stop thinking about Jameson Sedge, the closest thing he'd ever had to an enemy. *How was he involved?* Whatever was happening, Brink knew that none of it could come into the contest with him. He needed to clear his mind and focus on the challenge at hand. If he could get a good night's sleep, he'd be ready.

Inside, he'd stripped down to his boxers and was sitting for a moment at the edge of his bed, exhausted, when he noticed a notification on his phone. A text message from Rachel.

Hello from Newark! It took forever to get on a flight, but I finally got one. Boarding now. Talked to Dr. Gupta. Much to discuss. See you soon.

From the time stamp, he saw that it'd been sent hours before, even before his conversation with Gupta. The lack of reception in the palace had blocked it, and then Gupta's video call occupied his attention. It was a relief to know that Rachel was on her way. If everything went as planned, she'd be there for the contest tomorrow. "Don't worry," Brink said to Conundrum as he turned out the lights. "Rachel's coming."

As sleep overwhelmed him, he saw the Dragon Box, its beauty and its danger. He saw the dragon twisting over its surface and remembered the booby traps hidden within: *Poison, Trapdoor, Razor, Venom, Spike. Would he outsmart Ogawa? Or would he become a notation in the imperial archives like all the others?* Tomorrow, with the rising of the full moon, he would know.

A series of loud knocks woke Brink from a deep sleep. He blinked, confused. *Sunlight falling over tatami. Shoji doors. Connie barking as someone banged on his door.* Where was he?

"Mike? Hello? Are you in there?"

Sakura. He'd bolted the door from the inside, and she couldn't get in. He glanced at his phone, charging on a bedside table—4:12 P.M. *Could that be right?* He glanced out the plate-glass window at the daylight streaming over the tatami. It wasn't 4:12 A.M., that was for sure. He'd slept all day, a dreamless, blackout sleep, something he hadn't experienced since high school, before his injury, when he was a normal teenager with normal circadian rhythms.

He threw on his clothes and opened the door. Sakura looked at him, panic-stricken. "What happened? Are you all right?"

"Jet lag," he said, grabbing his messenger bag.

Sakura studied him, her panic transforming to concern. What had she thought happened? That he'd decided to leave and snuck off? That he'd been murdered in his sleep?

"Well, at least you'll be well rested for the contest." She walked to a coffee machine at the wet bar, filled it with water, poured in coffee grounds, and started the brew.

He grabbed his phone, looking for news from Rachel. A text. A call. But, of course, nothing could get through. "Has Rachel arrived yet?"

"Rachel?" Sakura looked at him, perplexed. "There's not time to worry about Rachel. The moon will rise in less than an hour. We need to get you to the Three Shrines Sanctuary. Get ready. I'll bring coffee with us—you take cream and sugar?"

A car sat idling before the entrance of the palace. Brink let Connie do her business under the bush, then climbed into the back seat of the car, a paper cup of coffee—cream, no sugar—in one hand, Connie's leash in the other. As he looked through the forest, he saw a patchwork of purpling sky. Daylight was already fading.

Sakura situated herself next to Brink, removed a lunch bag from a backpack, and opened it. "I had lunch sent to your room. When we couldn't get in, I packed some of it up. Here, you need to eat." She gave him an *onigiri* rice ball and unscrewed a thermos of miso soup.

The car drove along a shadowy road, passed through a security checkpoint. Brink ate the rice, drank the miso soup, devoured a *maki* roll filled with tuna and mayonnaise. Sakura collected the thermos, repacked it into the lunch bag. She removed a down jacket and a knit hat from her backpack. "Put these on. You'll need to stay warm."

"This is happening *outside*?" Brink asked, astonished. She'd mentioned it was happening at the Three Shrines Sanctuary, but he'd assumed it would be indoors. It was February, cold and windy. The effects of exposure over the course of hours could only harm his concentration.

"Of course," Sakura said, glancing at her own winter coat, a mid-length quilted cargo jacket with big pockets. "The contest has always been conducted under the light of the moon. Tonight is mild, comparatively. The contest was designed before many of the comforts of the modern world. It's meant to be a test of endurance—both mental and physical."

Brink put on the warm winter jacket. Gupta had mentioned that one of the solvers wore leather gloves. "I'm going to need gloves," he said.

Sakura pulled a pair of knit gloves from her pocket. "Will these work?"

"They have to be leather—tight enough that I can feel the box but impenetrable."

Sakura dug through her backpack. "If I'd had more time, I could have found a pair for you."

Brink glanced at the driver. He wore a pair of brown leather gloves. "How about those?"

Sakura leaned forward, said a few words to the driver. He peeled off his gloves and handed them over, then pulled the car to the gated entrance of the Three Shrines Sanctuary.

Sakura opened the door and hurried up a path to the gate. Brink followed, Connie running alongside. He noted the uniformed guards at the entrance, automatic weapons in hand. It was a bit much, four fully armed guards, way more than necessary for a puzzle contest. But, then, the whole thing—from the invitation to Dr. Trevers's enigmatic message to the history of dead puzzle masters to the realization that Sedge was involved—was more than he'd anticipated.

He'd had a chance to walk away. He hadn't taken it.

Standing near the guards was a middle-aged woman wearing a thick wool coat, her hair streaked with white.

"This is my aunt," Sakura said, introducing them. "Akemi Saito."

"Mr. Brink," Akemi said. Even as she offered her hand and Brink shook it, he felt the air evaporate around him. *Akemi Saito?* This was the woman Gupta warned him about, the woman connected to Jameson Sedge. *It had to be the same person.* He had to warn Sakura. Unless, of course, Sakura already knew. If that was the case, every suspicion he'd felt about Sakura would be confirmed. The contest, the emperor and empress, Rachel, who must surely be on her way—everything could be compromised.

Sakura was ahead, walking through the gate and into the Three

Shrines Sanctuary. He hurried after her into a large courtyard. On three sides of the courtyard rose wooden structures, their swooping tiled rooftops stark against the clear, lightless sky. If he wasn't so worried about Akemi and her connection to Sedge, he might find the scene picturesque, the kind of image one sees on postcards of Japan. But as he thought through the danger of what lay ahead and the new and unpredictable factors this woman introduced, he found the Three Shrines as foreboding as a prison.

Sakura and her aunt stopped before three plain post-and-beam buildings. Poised on stilts five feet above the ground, the structures seemed to float in the darkness.

"This is the Kyuchu Sanden, the Three Shrines of the Imperial Court," Akemi said, gesturing to the buildings. "The contest has taken place here since the very first attempts to open the box. It's a sacred space. It is here that the imperial family performs daily offerings to their ancestors. Rituals such as marriages and funerals are performed here." Akemi gestured to men and women in robes standing in the distance. "The Three Shrines are maintained by the *shoten*, male Shinto priests, and the *nai-shoten*, temple maidens. They will observe and facilitate the contest."

Akemi gestured to the central building. "The emperor and empress are making an offering in the Kashikodokoro, the shrine of the imperial ancestor Amaterasu Omikami."

Brink remembered what Sakura told him about Amaterasu Omikami, the sun goddess, the original ancestor of the imperial family. She was a mythic figure, and yet it seemed that she was very much present in the lives of the imperial family.

"When they finish in the temple," Akemi said, "the emperor and empress will observe from the dais of the Kashikodokoro, as every emperor and empress since the time of Meiji have done. There is a screen that ensures that they will see you but you will not see them."

There was a ringing of bells that sent Connie into a fit of barking. After he calmed her, Brink turned to see two figures, a man and a woman in traditional Japanese costume, stepping from the Kashikodokoro. The emperor and empress paused, and Brink caught a glimpse of their silk robes. In an instant, they disappeared behind a screen, taking their positions on the platform.

Brink glanced at the shrines, their white walls aglow in the darkness. The stillness was overpowering. He had a hundred questions: What was inside the three temple structures; what did the *shoten* and *nai-shoten* actually do; what did any of it have to do with opening a puzzle box? But just then two *shoten* and two *nai-shoten* appeared on a wooden walkway above the courtyard. One of the *shoten* carried a large box down a set of steps to an elevated wooden platform at the center of the courtyard, where a table and a single chair waited.

"Moonrise is at nine minutes after five," Sakura said. "It will set tomorrow at roughly five-thirty A.M. That gives you twelve hours to solve this."

"Piece of cake." He smiled, wishing he could ask her about Akemi. Waiting for her to put him at ease.

"Red velvet," Sakura said, her gaze intense, as if she wanted to say more but couldn't dare. "Mike, whatever happens, I want you to know that I've got your back. If you need me, I'm here."

Brink picked up Connie and placed her in Sakura's arms. "If you take her, that will be enough."

An imperial guard appeared at Brink's side and escorted him to the table as the *shoten* unwrapped a white silk covering from the box, revealing a perfect square of wood with a dragon curling over the surface. Brink took a deep breath, removed the gloves from his pocket, and slipped them on. They were too small, but he forced them over his fingers, the leather stretching until they fit tight. A second skin. A protective layer between him and the box.

In the distance, the first sliver of the full moon appeared in the sky. *Moonrise.*

Brink closed his eyes, and he knew he'd reached the point of no return.

This is it. No going back now.

29

This is it. No going back now.

Mike Brink adjusts the wooden chair, tries to get comfortable, but there's no way that's happening. He's vibrating with adrenaline and expectation, everything in him positioning for the work ahead. There's only one way to stop the thrumming in his head.

Steadying himself, he reaches for the box.

He's competed in hundreds of competitions. Chess competitions, world puzzle championships, speed-cubing contests. Every match is different, yet every contest demands a total submission to the puzzle. Its rules. Its patterns. Its rhythms. He must give himself body and soul to the challenge before him. He's always trusted his instincts. And every time, he's succeeded.

But this time is different. The emperor's Dragon Box is unlike anything he's encountered before. He's tried again and again to imagine its weight and dimensions, the hidden dangers under the smooth surface. But it doesn't hold. It's slippery, ungraspable. It appears, then vanishes like smoke, leaving his mind filled with darkness, infinite and terrifying. Leaving him to wonder if this might be the last contest of his life.

What if I can't do this?

A nauseating sensation rises through him. *Panic. Fear.* He flexes his fingers once, twice, to stop the trembling. He is outside himself, hovering. He can't feel the wooden seat or the cold night air. His arms and legs are numb.

What was the first move? The second? What did Gupta tell him? He can't remember. He can't remember anything. Not the hundreds of boxes he's opened. Not the moves the previous solvers died to achieve. Everything has evaporated.

He hears Dr. Trevers's voice: *Breathe, Mike. Breathe.*

He closes his eyes and lets the darkness envelop him. He breathes. *You can do this.*

When he returns his gaze to the box, he feels a shiver of anticipation. He runs the flat of a gloved hand over the smooth surface, as if wiping it clean. The design is astonishing, far superior to any puzzle box he's seen before, glossy and seamless, like a polished sheet of metal. Utterly unbreachable.

Before one can commence solving the box, it must be unlocked. There is a release mechanism that opens the box for play. . . . The solver slides a finger into this passage, pushes a tiny lever at the end of the passage, and a latch releases.

He turns the box over and there it is, at the very center of the base: a small, dark hole. Two of six solvers lost their fingers trying to release this mechanism. One died before getting to a single move in the box itself. Not ideal odds.

Every puzzle master who has attempted to open the Dragon Puzzle Box has died trying.

He glances at Sakura, standing just beyond the table. His heart is beating so hard he's sure she can hear it. She gives him a look of encouragement, a half smile. *You're the best solver I've ever seen. I know you're capable of winning.* He feels a rush of doubt. Is Sakura a friend? An enemy? Can he trust her? Her connection to Akemi, and thus to Sedge, says that he can't. Yet after their time in the treasure room, he wants to believe she's an ally. That she really does have his back.

And so it begins. Gathering his resolve, he slides the pointer finger of his left hand into the narrow passage. Slowly, careful not to trip Ogawa's tribute to the French Revolution, he presses deeper, deeper.

If the lever is pushed the wrong way . . .

A drop of sweat slides into his eye. He blinks it away.

. . . a guillotine descends.

At the end of the passage, he feels a thin metal protrusion. *The lever.* Exactly as Gupta described it. Gently, he feels around it with the tip of his gloved finger. He can push the lever up or down. One direction will unlock the box. The other will take his finger. He feels a wave of nausea. The Dragon Puzzle Box is the most cerebral, most carefully calibrated mechanical puzzle in the world. And yet the first move relies not on skill but luck.

He hates games of chance and dislikes making decisions based on probabilities. But here he is, confronted with fifty–fifty odds. There's no way to outsmart this. No way to win with talent or insight. His abilities are useless here. And so he does what he always does when he plays the odds.

With his right hand, he pulls his Morgan silver dollar from his pocket and balances it on the flat of his thumb. It glints in the moonlight, large and heavy in his gloved hand. He's carried this coin since the night of his accident, November 9, 2007, during the Ohio high school state football championship game. A flip of this very coin determined the course of play. He was injured in the first minute. If the coin toss had gone another way, he would be a different man, living a different life.

He looks at the Dragon Box. *Heads, he'll push the lever up. Tails, down.*

Brink tosses the coin high in the air, catches it, and slams it on the table. *Tails.*

Down it is.

Tension crackles through the air. The small party of observers—the shadows of the emperor and empress behind the opaque screen; the *shoten* priests and *nai-shoten* temple maidens; Akemi; Sakura—lean forward, watching. Waiting.

Here goes nothing.

He takes a deep breath, positions his finger on the lever, and presses.

Sakura holds Connie close, cradling her like an infant. Her soft, warm body and rapid heartbeat—her tail thumping against Sakura's arm—are a comfort. As Sakura restrains Connie from going to her owner, she understands the pure devotion this creature feels for Mike Brink. The clarity of Connie's affection is unquestionable. Sakura wishes for a moment that her loyalties were as clear.

What *is* clear is that everything is going as planned. Scanning the courtyard, Sakura sees the players, arranged like pieces on a chessboard. The emperor and empress on the dais, tucked behind their screen, a dozen imperial guards surrounding them. Akemi positioned exactly between the dais and the Dragon Box. Sakura, standing in the shadows, waiting, watching. And at the center of it all, the axis upon which everything spins, is Mike. He is poised, remarkably calm, as if facing death is something he does every day of his life.

She's done her part. She's brought him here. She's gained his trust. But watching him now, she feels a terrible sense of responsibility for what could happen. One wrong move, one mistake, and everything is over. Really, this man doesn't know what he's gotten himself into. She's brought him to the edge of an abyss, and now here he is, about to step off.

Sakura suspects her father would have liked Mike Brink. His talent, of course, and his otherworldly brilliance, but even more—his inability to give up. Her father's death was a shock not only because of the violence of his murder but because he'd left his work unfinished. Sakura was equally persistent. Her sister always said that their father preferred Sakura, and it was probably true. Seeing something in Sakura, their father began training her in games of strategy and skill before she could read. She'd been four years old, too young to write her name, when she began to play chess, Go, and Japanese word puzzles. She began coding at age seven; began studying programming with her father at eight; began working with him on his big project in the months before he was murdered.

Ume was different, the child who represented the traditions of her family. The one who would never dare to question the twisted legacy she'd inherited. Ume was disciplined, unwavering. Fanatical. But Sakura had never been suited for any of that. She balked at her mother's extreme training. How many times had Ume beaten her bloody because Sakura simply didn't care enough to fight?

Like her father, Sakura relies on her intelligence, her creativity, and her ability to anticipate the next move. And like her father, she understands the power of one person to transform everyone, and everything, around them. She's met only a few people like this in her life, someone who inspires her to believe in the possibilities of the future. One was Jameson Sedge. The other is Mike Brink.

For an instant, a full heartbeat, everything stops. Brink braces for the guillotine, prepares to feel the burn of flesh ripping away. Instead, there is a series of clicks as the narrow passage expands around his finger. Then, with a heavy pop, the box releases.

He's unlocked it.

Brink yanks his finger away and lifts the box, feeling its weight. It's heavy, as if filled with ball bearings or shrapnel. As he turns the box, examining it from all sides, something shifts. It's a subtle change, like a door has opened a crack, throwing light into the corners of his mind. His focus settles, attenuates. And there it is: *pure intuition.* A pattern unfolding like a symphony. He feels the solution lurking beyond, waiting for him in the matrix of grooves carved into the box's interior, hundreds of tracks, sliding pieces, dangerous traps. Millions of pathways leading, like all great conundrums, to a single point. All the moves the previous solvers made, their victories and failures, appear before him, and he knows that they didn't die for nothing. They've left him a lifeline, one he'll follow into the darkness. Now every choice he makes will be one of life and death. It's Mike Brink against the most difficult and dangerous puzzle he's ever encountered.

He brushes a panel of wood, looking for a way in, and there it is: the panel moves a fraction of an inch. He gives another delicate push. It clicks, locking in place. He's done it.

Move number one.

The game is on. The puzzle has invited him in. Turning the box, he tests the opposite side, searching for the slightest give. There's nothing,

nothing,

nothing,

and then there it is: a shift in the surface. He pushes the panel. It moves a centimeter and locks.

Move number two.

Light gushes forth. It's starting, he feels it—the choreography of solving, its rhythm taking over. The balance between his mind and his body tips, and he finds the third move without thinking, his fingers gliding to it instinctually. A wash of colors saturates his vision, a blaze of orange, yellow, green. He's no longer watching the show; he is the show. His mind is doing what it does without him, his hands reacting on their own. He's merely along for the ride.

Move number three.

Brink has intel on the fourth move: It's booby-trapped. It released an aerosol poison that killed a chess champion in 1964. Powdered arsenic, Gupta thought. Brink pauses to weigh the risk. The fourth move killed a man. But there was nothing about the fourth-move booby trap causing trouble for the subsequent solvers—not the Korean woman of 1976, not the French solver of 1988. *Why?*

Because, Brink realizes, it was a one-off trap. It isn't like the guillotine, a trap that resets when the box locks. The aerosol poison didn't kill the subsequent solvers because it was gone. *The trap has sprung.* It can't harm him.

It's a theory, one that needs to be tested. If he's right, he'll live. If he's wrong . . .

He lifts a gloved hand over his mouth and nose, a meager attempt to block any poison that might remain behind the panel. It won't help much, but he feels better and moves forward, brushing his gloved fingers over the surface of the box until he finds the next move. He pushes the panel. It releases and slides open, clicking into place.

Move four.

He breathes in. Cold, clean air fills his lungs.

He breathes out. *I'm not dead. So far so good.*

But wait—there's something odd about the panel. Fingers trembling, he presses it, and it retracts, as if on springs. This could be it— an entry point to the interior layers of the puzzle. Gupta hadn't mentioned it, and clearly the other solvers hadn't found it, but, then, everyone knew what happened to them.

Brink can't explain it, but he's sure that this is the right way. He knows what can happen, what's at stake, but he also knows that he's more likely to die playing it safe. Without bold, risky moves, he'll end up like the others.

Constructing a puzzle box is like creating a magic trick—the illusion is everything. Success requires working with the illusion rather than against it.

With infinite gentleness, Brink removes the tiny wooden panel.

Through the security camera, he sees that everything is in place, just waiting for him to set it in motion. He sees Mike Brink. Sakura Nakamoto and her aunt Akemi Saito. The emperor of Japan. His wife. And, outside the Hanzo-mon gate, waiting for the signal: Cam Putney, Ume Nakamoto, and the others. He doesn't need to move into the camera's digital feed to read the tension in the courtyard. Body temperatures, heart rates, brain waves—the measurements upload and arrive instantly. Once he's made a connection, he can see everything in an instant. It is only deciding what information he needs and how to filter it.

It's time. The video feed shifts to the exterior of the thick stone wall surrounding the palace. A white van idles before an enormous wooden door, exhaust fumes swirling in the frigid air. Cam Putney sits behind the wheel, waiting. The second he wants to speak with him, his bodyguard's phone rings.

"Mr. Sedge," Cam says, picking up instantly.

"The Hanzo-mon gate will open in thirty seconds."

"We're ready."

Cam nods to Ume, who pushes open the door and jumps out of the passenger side of the van. She walks to the rear and opens the double doors. Five women follow her to the gate. They are dressed entirely in black, and from above, Sedge sees small, dark flecks against the white snow.

"Open," Sedge says, and the electronic system powering the gate responds, the heavy bolts of the gate's lock click open, and the doors swing back. Ume slips through the open gate, entering the thick forest. And then she is gone.

Before Brink can react, the spring releases and a metal spike shoots through the cavity, fast as sound. *What the hell?* Brink jerks his fingers away, quick, but the spike catches his glove, piercing the leather.

Move five.

Brink stands, pushes away the chair, and steps back from the table, his heart in his throat. He can't breathe and struggles for air. Gupta was right.

The brutality of the exterior is in direct proportion to the delicacy of what is inside.

Checking the glove, he finds a clean hole in the leather, exposing a patch of skin on his right pointer finger. A new vulnerability. The spike missed his flesh by a fraction of a millimeter. A surge of adrenaline thrums through him. *That was too close.*

The 1976 solver got through fifteen moves, that much Brink knows. What stopped her was a trap like this one: a spike through the eye. He thought he could avoid it, but traps are everywhere, at every turn. He can't let his guard down for a second. He can't rely on anything—not his skill, not Gupta's intel, not his assumptions about what constitutes a puzzle box. He must measure every move as if it is the first move he's ever made. He got lucky—the spike didn't pierce the skin—but luck won't carry him through.

But just as he begins to feel his heartbeat steady, pain drills through his finger. He remembers the priest, who died after the slightest exposure. Brink rips off the glove and wipes his skin against his jeans, desperate to get the toxin off. Already, though, the point of exposure has singed black. His skin is burning. He can smell it, the acrid scent of disintegrating flesh. And then, like an apparition, Sakura is at his side.

Give me your hand.

Sakura takes his hand in hers and rubs an ointment over his skin. *I brought this, just in case.*

As she applies the salve, his skin goes ice cold. The pain remains but doesn't spread. She looks distraught, on the edge of tears, as she wraps a bandage tight around his finger, but her voice is firm. *It's nothing, Mike.* Her voice is soothing, a life raft. *Everything's okay now.*

Sakura places a bottle of water on the table. She gestures for him to drink.

How did he stumble so easily? If Sakura hadn't been there, the acid could have eaten through his finger. He leans against the table, steadying himself. He's trembling all over. Dizzy. Everything has gone off-balance.

What if he's gone too far this time? What if this is all a terrible mistake?

He takes a drink of water. He breathes. If he's going to outsmart Ogawa, he can't lose his composure. He must recenter and go forward.

Closing his eyes, he remembers that night on the football field, just seconds before the hit that changed his life. He feels the ball in his hands, the cold leather against his skin. He sees the end zone. He runs and runs. Who would he be if he hadn't been hurt that night? Who could he have become if Dr. Trevers hadn't died?

There's a moment in every contest when a puzzle becomes more than a puzzle. It turns back on Mike Brink like a mirror, reflecting the deepest truths of his character. Every flaw and every strength, every weakness and every desire, play out before him. And he understands with devastating clarity that, while he might solve any puzzle put before him, he will never solve the enigma of himself.

Ume has never been inside the imperial grounds before tonight. To prepare her, Akemi made her memorize a map of the Fukiage forest, the winding pathways through dense evergreens, the security checkpoints, the location of the imperial residence, the Omakya Palace, the Imperial Household Agency. For weeks, Ume has studied the route from the Hanzo-mon gate to the Three Shrines, memorizing and mapping alternative routes. Anything could happen—security guards might turn up; they could be spotted by a drone; Brink might take hours to open the box. Ume needs to be ready for every contingency.

The forest, Ume knows, is a powerful security feature, one as protective as the moat surrounding the palace walls. She uses it to their advantage, slipping through the gate under the cover of night and hiding in the darkest part of the forest. And while she and her girls are nearly invisible, none of it would be possible without Mr. Sedge. He opened the Hanzo-mon gate, allowing Ume and her girls inside the secure perimeter of the palace. He disabled the security cameras, took the security system offline, scrambled the internal communications system. It is chaos over at the Imperial Household Agency right now, although you'd never know it from the utter stillness of the forest.

Sedge's assistance is crucial. It always has been. Still, there were years when Akemi argued against allowing him into their confidence. In the end, though, he'd been part of her father's inner circle—that he understood the true nature of their mission, that he'd given everything, absolutely everything, including his life, proved him worthy. Like Cam, Ume would follow Jameson Sedge to the grave. Or, at least, to a state of digital immortality.

They arrive at the entrance to the Three Shrines Sanctuary ready to face guards, but they're gone, probably inside the courtyard. Ume leaves her girls outside the gate and scales the wall, dropping silently into the courtyard. Slipping into the shadows, she scans the area, taking in the scene. There's her aunt Akemi near the emperor and empress, surrounded by a dozen armed guards. There are priests and temple maidens. There's the table with the Dragon Box at the center of the courtyard, the puzzle master standing nearby. There is Sakura, watching him. Everything is ready. Everything is waiting for them.

They orchestrated this together. Ume and her girls will take care of the guards. Akemi will ensure that the emperor and empress don't interfere. Not that they're capable of doing much damage. They're old and weak, lulled by decades of submission to protocol. Ume has no worries about them. The guards, however, are another story. They are formidable and—she suddenly realizes—outnumber Ume and her girls two to one.

Shaking off his misstep, Brink slides the glove back on and returns his focus to the puzzle box. He's alive, which means he's ahead of the game. He's made it past the outer layer—the exoskeleton, as Gupta would call it. He's ready for the next step. Feeling the box, he makes a move. Then another. A lever slides left, then jiggers right. Some of the moves must be made in tandem, fingers pressing opposing points of the box, multiple slots manipulated simultaneously, sleight of hand with infinite permutations.

Move six.

Move seven.

He turns the box, makes two more moves in quick succession.

Move eight.

Move nine.

A streak of solving unfolds. He's flying through the moves when something odd happens. There is a grinding of gears and the top third of the box lifts, revealing a polished copper disk mounted on a platform of wood. The disk glistens in the moonlight, revealing a graffiti of minuscule designs carved into the surface, tiny as capillaries. The pattern is complex and alluring, so intriguing Brink can't look away. It is like an ancient tablet filled with an uncoded language, a kind of Linear B waiting to be deciphered.

But what the hell is it? A code?

As he looks more closely at the network of fine pathways, hundreds and hundreds of them swirling and crossing, diving and twisting together, he understands: He's uncovered a labyrinth.

Labyrinths are often confused with mazes, but they are different in one essential way: Mazes have dead ends. Labyrinths do not. In a labyrinth, a solver can move through a path forever, in constant motion. While a maze will stop you cold if you take the wrong path, a labyrinth will trap you forever.

Brink's skin prickles with excitement. He feels an overwhelming need to touch the surface, to trace the pathways with his fingers, to physically move through this treacherous landscape. But there's no entry point. No exit. There's no mechanism to mark his pathway. It's a completely locked system. No way to enter. No way to exit.

He runs his fingers through his hair, flummoxed. *This is impenetrable. Totally impossible.*

Frustration swells through him. He's missing something. There's got to be more to go on—a key that will give him a clue to navigate the endless pathways. A labyrinth of this complexity is unusual, but what's even more unusual is that there's nothing at all to indicate *where* to start. A puzzle has rules, clear steps to the solution. It's like Ogawa is asking him to go in blind.

He stares at the labyrinth, taking in its pathways. It gleams darkly, mysteriously, giving nothing away.

Suddenly he gets it. *Ogawa was blind.* The opacity is wholly intentional. He made this labyrinth without ever seeing it. There's no visible entry point because the visual field was nothing more than an unnecessary distraction to Ogawa. Brink needs to stop relying on his eyes. He needs to *touch* the labyrinth.

He'd solved the first part of the box without the sense of touch, his hands sheathed in leather. But this is a new stage of the game. Now he needs to remove the gloves and feel his way. He needs to understand Ogawa's language, read the box like braille, with his fingers. Without losing them, of course.

He waves to Sakura to join him. "Take the square of silk and wrap it over my eyes."

From her expression, he knows she thinks he's gone insane. "What?"

"Blindfold me," he says, as he peels off the leather gloves and places them on the table.

"*Blindfold?*"

"Trust me, it's the only way. I'll explain it all later."

If I'm alive later.

Sakura picks up the square of white silk, folds it into a blindfold, and ties it tight over his eyes. In an instant the world transforms, loses solidity, plummeting Brink into a shapeless void.

"Stay nearby," Brink says, feeling a sudden desperate need to know that someone is by his side.

"I'm here," she says softly. He senses her close by, on his left side.

He feels her lean in and hears her whisper, "Don't worry about Akemi. This is all part of the plan."

Everything is a choreography, every attack like a ballet. The timing must be perfect. The moment Brink opens the box, they must be ready. Sakura will take what is inside, Akemi will distract the emperor, and Ume will provide security as they escape. The window of opportunity is small, but, working together, they will get what they came for.

As Ume waits, she studies her younger sister. Sakura isn't where she's supposed to be. She's migrated across the courtyard and is standing at the table with Brink. Ume is alarmed. Sakura isn't following the plan. *What in the hell is she doing?* Protecting Brink? They knew it was a possibility, even a probability, that he'd get hurt. Priority number one is to keep him alive, at least until the box is open. If he dies, everything is over.

Sakura is doing the right thing, but still—it worries Ume. It's never been in her character to protect anyone.

For as long as she remembers, Ume has been the strong one. She's always, always protected her sister—from the men who murdered their parents, from Sedge's demanding expectations, from the harsher elements of their inheritance. Ume has taken the burden of their history on her shoulders. She's always believed Sakura would grow to become the person their parents hoped she would be. That she would rise, with Ume, to take back what they'd lost. But if she is honest with herself, Ume knows that Sakura never wanted those things. Sakura has always cared more about herself.

As Ume gazes at her sister, she knows something's off. The way she looks at Mike Brink as she ties a blindfold over his eyes, the subtle movement of her lips to his ear. Something's happening, Ume can feel it.

They've always been connected, Ume and Sakura. They've always had a sixth sense for each other's feelings. There were nights when they were children, their futons laid out close on the tatami, that Ume dreamed Sakura's dreams. They would wake in the morning, and Sakura would describe what she'd experienced, but Ume knew already. She'd been there, with her sister, in the dream. Flying. Falling. Running. This contest is the ultimate dream. And Ume knows, without quite knowing how, that Sakura will betray her.

With the blindfold tight over his eyes, Mike Brink's senses alter. His hearing sharpens. His touch magnifies. He can feel the rush of blood in his ears, the quick beating of his heart.

Now it's the blind leading the blind.

It's the right approach, he knows it in his bones, but he can't help but feel sick with fear. *What in the hell is he doing?* It's a risky, dangerous bet. Without sight, he loses his strongest sense. He must relearn how to approach the box. It's a whole new ball game. Yet he's certain this is the right path. Each step deeper into the box raises the stakes. He must rise to greater and greater levels of discomfort, and while he's terrified by what could happen, he can't ignore his instincts. He has no choice. Ogawa left him a message, and this is the only way he'll find it.

Tentatively, Brink places his hands on the circular copper plate, feeling his way over the nest of pathways. The metal is ice cold, even colder than the frigid night air. The impressions in the disk communicate with him, peaks and valleys, a tactile code. It takes only a few seconds to know that he's on the right track. The labyrinth is not poisoned; there are no hidden booby traps—no razors or spikes. It is a tablet designed for touch, ridges and grooves pressing into his skin.

Choosing a pathway, he follows it around the edge of the copper disk, where metal meets wood. A narrow groove wide as a finger opens. Brink inserts his finger and follows it, searching for something—a notch, a button, a lever, *something*—to bring him into the labyrinth. *It must be here.* No constructor would ever devise an unsolvable mechanical puzzle. It would be like a poet writing an unreadable poem, or a musician performing a silent aria. *There has to be a solution.*

Then he feels it—a series of tiny protrusions in the metal. He pauses, backtracks, and feels again. There's a string of raised dots along the edge of the disk, tucked low on its edge. No one looking at the disk would ever have discovered them. All at once, Brink understands: Ogawa did leave a message. *In braille.*

Angling the tips of his fingers, Brink palpates the series of raised dots, trying to read them. He learned braille one afternoon about five years ago, when he visited a classroom in Lower Manhattan. There was a boy in the class whose textbooks were written in braille. Brink spent an hour with the boy, looking over his books, studying the key, and by the end of the afternoon he could read with his fingers.

But while these dots are like the braille Brink learned, the configurations are very different. He doesn't understand them. Whatever message Ogawa left, it must be important, and so Brink goes over the sequence of raised dots, remembering their position, filing the pattern away for later.

At the end of the braille sequence, he finds a button, like a glass bead at the end of a necklace. He touches it, wondering what sadistic surprise is waiting.

I'm on the right path. Even if it's taking me to hell.

After the death of her parents, Sakura didn't speak for nearly a year. It wasn't that she consciously decided to remain silent. The apparatus that allowed communication between her and the world shut down. The tongue and throat, the larynx, the lungs—the instruments of her voice had been violently damaged. It was, she realized later, as if the knife that killed her mother had mutilated Sakura, too.

In that year of silence, Ume spoke for her. She answered the questions the immigration officer asked during their citizenship interview. She came to her school after class to communicate with her fourth-grade teacher, explaining that Sakura was learning English and that she needed extra help. Sakura always marveled at the precision of Ume's translation. Somehow, Ume always knew what Sakura wanted to say. Without explanation, Ume would know Sakura's thoughts, her needs, even her dreams. It was as if their minds had been thrown into a chasm of shared horror too dark, too painful, to be expressed in syllables. A chasm in which both girls left fragments of their souls.

When Sakura finally spoke, it was in perfect, unaccented English. She never spoke Japanese with Ume again. It brought her somewhere she didn't want to go. Even now, as Ume stares at her from across the courtyard, communicating without words, she hears English: *We have come so far*, Ume says. *This, right now, is our moment.*

Brink never would have found the button if he relied on his eyes alone. It is tucked away, hidden, impossible to see. But that is exactly the point. Ogawa didn't make it for Brink—or anyone else. He made it for *himself*. Brink feels an overwhelming respect for Ogawa, and the idea strikes him that this man, dead more than one hundred years, is communicating something important to Brink. The puzzle is a time capsule with a message: To solve the impossible, one must leave the self behind. One must transform. Even if it means becoming as damaged and as cruel as Ogawa.

Brink takes a deep breath and, with the tip of his fingernail, presses the button.

There's a loud pop. Brink leaps away, quick, as if the box might explode. He pulls off the blindfold and looks at the labyrinth. It's exactly as it was before, only now, at its very center, there is a copper peg.

Of course. It's a peg labyrinth.

A peg labyrinth is a mechanical puzzle constructed around a central static point—in this case, the copper peg. While that point remains fixed, the labyrinth itself moves. Brink presses the disk of copper. It's unlocked. It slips right and left, forward and backward. Such fluidity of movement will allow him to angle the disk, with its complex networks of pathways, around the peg. When the peg reaches the end of the path, the labyrinth is solved.

The man was a genius.

But so is Mike Brink. As he surveys the pathways, his mind fills with hundreds of possible routes through the labyrinth, thousands of potential directions, all of them crossing and recrossing before his eyes. Then it happens: The mechanism of his gift takes hold. The moves appear to him like a vision, and he knows the correct pathway.

The solution.

It's as simple as breathing. It takes less than a minute to maneuver the peg to the end of the labyrinth. As the peg connects, he holds his breath. He half-expects the thing to blow up in his face. But it doesn't. It simply opens like a lock undone by a key.

There's a soft grinding of metal on metal, an internal choreography of movement as the box performs a feat of coordinated motion, rotating on internal hinges. He watches, astonished, as the edges of the box separate into four distinct rectangles, each sliding in the opposite direction, revealing a central cavity. Brink stares, unable to fully believe what's happened. This can't be right. He's made thirty-six moves. The Dragon Box opens after seventy-two moves. He's executed only half that number.

Something's not right. It's another trick.

Yet the Dragon Box is open. And there's something inside.

The courtyard has become so quiet, Sakura can hear the air rushing into her lungs. So much planning and so much speculation has gone into this moment that, now that it's arrived, she's paralyzed. *Is this really it? Has he opened the box?*

She watches Mike as he slips the leather gloves back on, stretching them over his hands. Gently, he lifts a glass tube into the moonlight. It's no bigger than a finger, with a scroll of paper rolled tight inside. As he turns the glass tube between his fingers, her heart leaps. *This is it.* The treasure is here, right here before her. She'd imagined this moment for so long that she can hardly believe it's happening. But it is happening. The box is open. And there, right there in front of her, is Meiji's treasure.

There are bulbs at both ends of the glass capsule, each filled with liquid. The destruction mechanism, just as Mike predicted. *Acid.* The paper is most certainly Japanese rice paper. Delicate. Easily destroyed. If the vial is broken, the rice paper, and the message Meiji left, will dissolve like cotton candy on the tongue. The treasure will be gone.

She hears something at the far side of the courtyard and turns. Ume is coming closer. Five women in black follow. Whispers. Shadows of shadows. They're coming in for Mike.

Sakura raises a hand to her sister—*wait.* She tries to meet her eye, to warn her. *It's not time yet.* There's one more piece of the puzzle to solve. It is the final, and most important, test. He must extricate the scroll from the vial without destroying it. Too much pressure, one wrong move, and everything will be destroyed.

Her sister makes only the faintest sign, but Sakura understands: *It's time.* This is happening, whether she's ready or not.

One final step. One more.

She watches as Mike places the glass vial at the center of the table, arranging it carefully, delicately. He studies it for a moment, as if considering a great mathematical problem, and then quickly, before Sakura fully registers what he's doing, he raises his gloved fist and slams it down on the crystal vial, crushing it.

The ground shifts under her. For a moment she can't think, can't breathe. Everything is over. Mike broke the vial; the acid has seeped through the rice paper; he's destroyed the message inside. He's destroyed everything.

Maybe she can save something. A fragment. Anything. She reaches for the scroll, but Mike pulls her back.

"Don't touch it," he whispers. "Trust me."

Trust? What does that mean anymore? Everything has turned upside down. Why would he *destroy* the solution to the emperor's puzzle, the very thing he'd set out to discover? Why would he risk his life to open this treacherous box only to end up with nothing?

As the first shot echoes through the courtyard, Mike grabs Sakura's hand and they run.

30

The car wove through the thick forest, speeding quietly away from the chaos of the contest. The driver didn't turn on the headlights but followed the moonlit road toward the palace. According to a clock in the car's dashboard, it was 5:43. It seemed impossible that he'd spent only a half hour with the Dragon Box. It felt like hours. But he knew that when he was absorbed in a problem, his experience of time changed. An hour could feel like a day or it could feel like ten minutes, depending on the rhythm of solving.

Brink leaned his head against the window, his breath fogging the glass. He felt like he'd been hit by a truck. Flattened, his limbs heavy, his whole body pinned by an invisible weight. His head throbbed, and his mind was awash in numbers and colors. He heard echoes of the contest, saw the succession of moves he'd made, felt the crush of the glass vial under his glove. Usually he knew how to control his synesthesia, but in the onslaught of stress, his mind was subsumed by visual stimuli, his vision saturated with color.

He closed his eyes, trying to make sense of it all. The attack unfolded before him. There were shots—a dozen, maybe more—then a windstorm of movement. Figures in black came out of nowhere. The bodies of imperial guards lay over the courtyard, bleeding. Akemi appeared at the table, scrambling to salvage the scroll. As Brink took

Sakura's hand and pulled her away from the table, he remembered Connie. He'd looked for her, but she was gone.

"We have to go back," Brink said, turning to Sakura. "Connie's still in there somewhere."

"She ran when the shots were fired," Sakura said. "I saw her go under the Kashikodokoro. The whole area will be in lockdown. She'll be safe there. Probably safer than with you. But I will ask the emperor to make sure she's protected."

"You think the emperor will help me with anything after that fiasco?"

"Of course," Sakura said. "He'll be relieved that you survived. To be totally honest, we didn't expect that you would. The odds weren't great. And we knew that violence could break out. Did you notice that he was evacuated when the box opened, well before you smashed the vial?"

Brink hadn't noticed, but now that he thought back, he realized that the shadows behind the screen had disappeared. The emperor and empress had slipped away before all hell broke loose.

"That," Sakura said, "was part of the plan."

Part of the plan? Brink took a deep breath and turned to Sakura. "What in the hell do you mean? What plan?"

Sakura met his eye. He could see that she was considering her words with care. "I'll explain, but first we need to take care of your hand," she said, looking at the burn on his finger. The acid had really done a number on Brink's skin—it was black and charred, spreading beyond the bandage. "I have more ointment." She took the tube from her pocket, removed the bandage, and applied the ointment. "Let's put a proper bandage on this."

While Brink's finger was damaged, the wound Sakura had caused was deeper and more painful. He glanced at her, her face obscured by darkness, trying to reconcile this woman with the one he thought he knew. The image he'd formed of her had changed. She was someone else entirely now, someone with secret plans. He'd suspected she was hiding something. Dr. Trevers's message had been a warning. But the truth nearly floored him. *She'd lied to him.* He was used to sidestepping tricks and inversions, but he hadn't been prepared to be betrayed by someone he'd begun to consider a friend.

"You were planning this from the first minute we met," he said. It wasn't a question. "Back in New York. You asked me to open the box, but it wasn't for the emperor. You knew there would be an attack."

"Forgive me," Sakura said, her expression filled with remorse. "I know it seems that way. But it's not what you think. I'd hoped that you would open the Dragon Box and that would be the end of this."

"*This?*" he said. "This was all a big setup. You led me into a trap."

"I wouldn't have let anything bad happen to you. Those guards you saw? They were there to protect the emperor and empress, but they were also there to protect *you*. It's true that I didn't tell you everything. I needed you to open the box, and for that you needed to trust me, to feel completely secure during the contest. I was there to make sure Akemi *didn't* get what was in the Dragon Box." She finished rubbing the ointment over his burn, closed the bottle, and slipped it into her pocket. "But it doesn't matter now. It's over. The message was destroyed."

Brink took a deep breath, to calm himself. "Don't be so sure."

"But I saw you smash the vial—"

"You saw what I wanted you to see," he said, ice in his voice. He was struggling with his emotions, trying to understand if this woman was worthy of trust. Sakura had betrayed him, or Sakura had saved him, he couldn't tell which. Nothing made sense anymore.

She stared at him, and he could see a series of emotions registering in her eyes—surprise, disbelief, confusion, and finally curiosity. "Are you saying you didn't destroy the message Meiji left?"

"I'll explain after you tell me everything. I want to know why I'm here. I want to know who attacked us back there. I want to know everything, Sakura. Everything."

Sakura folded her hands in her lap and twisted her ring as she spoke. "I'll tell you as much as I can," she said. "As you know, Akemi is my aunt. The other woman in the courtyard, the leader of the attack, is Ume, my older sister." She glanced out the window and into the dark, thick night, letting the information settle. "Ume and Akemi represent a side of my family that I have rejected."

"But you worked with Akemi to bring me here," he said, remembering what Sakura had said about Akemi getting approval for the jet and the false identity badge. "That doesn't sound like rejection."

"It was a means to an end. My aunt and my sister are fanatics. Radicals. But I'm not like them. I've never been like them. I won't fight their battles anymore—I proved as much back there."

"And what, exactly, are those battles?"

She glanced at the driver, and Brink knew she was assessing him, wondering if he understood English, how much she could say in front of him. When she spoke, her voice was barely a whisper.

"My parents were killed when I was nine years old. Ume and I watched it happen, and the experience shattered our lives. It radicalized my sister, twisting her into someone unrecognizable. She belongs to a group known as the faction. They are powerful, ruthless, and very badly want what Meiji hid. My parents were part of this group. Like them, my sister has given everything to the faction. I've tried to understand her and to forgive her, because I know the terrible, terrible pain she feels. But she is a true believer. She's spent her life in service to the cause, preparing for the moment when she can reclaim what our family lost. These people will stop at nothing to get what Meiji hid in that box. They will kill me, kill you, kill the emperor of Japan, if it will get them what they want."

"But what did Meiji hide?" Brink asked.

"I don't know," she said. "I only know that my great-great-grandfather believed it to be valuable to the faction. He passed this information to his daughter, who passed it on to her children, and eventually to my mother and her sister, Akemi, both high-ranking members of the faction. You might have heard of another prominent member: Jameson Sedge."

Brink was stunned to hear Sakura say the name Jameson Sedge, although it made sense: If her aunt Akemi had been connected to

Sedge, as Gupta believed, Sakura would be, as well. His doubt about Sakura cleared, and he saw her for what she was: a traitor. He was furious. "You kept all of this from me. Why?"

"Sedge was a close colleague of my father's. After my parents were killed, he brought Ume and me to the United States. He was our legal guardian and raised us, if you call seeing us once or twice a week for ideological lectures about transhumanism parenting. I see now that he used us to get closer to my father's work and, most important, closer to the Dragon Box. Part of me believed that if that group took the contents of the Dragon Box, I would be free of my sister and aunt. Free of the faction."

The car rolled to a stop in the middle of the forest, under a canopy of thick evergreens that blocked the moonlight. The driver cut the engine.

"Please understand," she said. "I couldn't tell you. But I promise that I'm on the right side—*your* side. The side of good." She got out of the car and gestured for him to follow. "Come, the emperor is waiting for us."

Brink stared at her, surprised. *The emperor?* Hadn't she just assisted a group that had betrayed him and his family?

Seeing his look of surprise, Sakura smiled and said, "Don't look so shocked. He's known the plan all along."

31

The driver opened the door and led them into the forest, using a flashlight to navigate the dense thicket of Japanese pines. There, hidden among the trees, was a small utility shed, the kind of structure used for electrical meters or gardening equipment. The driver removed a set of keys, unlocked a door, and gestured for them to enter.

"I've heard rumors about these, but I didn't believe they existed," Sakura said, peering into the shed.

Brink followed her gaze to a spiral stairwell fashioned in metal.

"It's the entrance to a bunker," Sakura said. "During the war, a series of escape routes was created to ensure the imperial family would be safe. But I had no idea they were still in use. This will take us to below the imperial residence."

They climbed down the metal spiral, a series of neon lights flicking on as motion sensors tracked their descent into a well-lit concrete hallway. Sakura ran ahead, and Brink followed, wondering where she was taking him. They ran and ran, and finally the tunnel opened into a familiar hallway. There was the kakemono scroll with the frog; there was the steel door. Sakura punched in the code and the door opened. Brink instantly recognized his surroundings. They'd arrived at the imperial treasure room. They'd come full circle.

It seemed like a lifetime ago that they'd cracked the code to this keypad. In fact, it had been less than twenty-four hours, but in that time, everything had changed. His relationship with Sakura had changed. His reasons for being in Japan had changed. He was no longer calculating his chances of surviving a difficult puzzle. Now he was up against something much bigger, much more dangerous than Ogawa.

A guard stood just past the steel door, inside the treasure room. He looked them over and bowed to Sakura and gestured for them to enter. Clearly he'd been expecting them.

The emperor and empress were waiting, sitting on a couch at the center of the room. Gone were the ceremonial robes. Now they wore slacks and comfortable shoes, like any middle-aged couple. Around them were the priceless treasures of the Yamato clan—glass cases filled with manuscripts, enamel and lacquer and porcelain vessels, the ukiyo-e prints he'd examined with Sakura. Such rich, vibrant objects had the effect of making the emperor and empress appear faded. Their fear and exhaustion, the toll the night had taken, were clear.

"Mr. Brink," the emperor said. His voice was strong but not without emotion. He and his wife had been through a terrifying ordeal, and he was clearly shaken. "That was an impressive show back there."

Brink stared at the emperor of Japan, unsure of how to address him. Bow? Avert his eyes? He decided to treat him as he would anyone he was meeting for the first time. He extended his hand, looked him in the eye, and said, "Thank you, sir."

The emperor took Brink's hand and, nodding to a club chair, invited him to sit. "Our contest was perhaps more than you bargained for."

"I knew it would be tough," he said, as he sat. "But I agree, the fireworks at the finale were a bit of a surprise."

"We were aware that there would be an attack," the emperor said. "We were ready for it. What we did *not* expect was that you would destroy the contents of the box. That was a wholly unexpected turn of events."

"For me, as well," Brink said. "I never imagined that the box would tell me to do so."

"*Tell* you to do so?" the empress said. "How did it do that?"

Brink flicked his eyes to Sakura, who watched him intently. She nodded, encouraging him, and he said, "The Dragon Box didn't contain the final solution. It is a puzzle with seventy-two steps. The solution cannot be revealed until the solver passes all seventy-two of them. I got through thirty-six, or half of those moves. It was impossible that the box I opened contained the solution."

"So the vial you found in the final compartment," the emperor said. "The one that contained a scroll?"

"A red herring," Brink said. "A complete misdirection."

"But how did you know?" the empress asked.

"There was a message etched into the side of the copper labyrinth, a series of raised dots."

"Braille," Sakura said, her eyes wide with excitement. "Of course— Ogawa was blind. He would've read braille."

"I knew the dots were some kind of braille, but I couldn't decipher it at first. I thought it must be Japanese braille, but that didn't make sense, as Japanese braille, *tenji*, wasn't developed until 1890. English-language braille was created in 1860, eight years before this box was made, but it is unlikely to have been transmitted before the Meiji Restoration. The only fully functioning braille system that Ogawa could have known was the original French system created by Louis Braille, which was officially adopted in 1854 in France." He turned to the empress. "Do you know if French was spoken in Japan at that time?"

"To some extent, yes," the empress said. "French diplomats were accepted by the shogun and then by the emperor, and many of the ships that were received in Nagasaki were French. It is entirely possible that Ogawa could have learned braille and used it."

"He most definitely did," Brink said. He took out his notebook and his Bic four-color ballpoint pen and wrote out the message he'd discovered.

⠮⠄ ⠿⠱⠗⠄⠄ ⠞⠄⠌⠄ ⠇⠄ ⠆⠱⠡⠄⠭⠄⠇⠄⠄ ⠇⠄ ⠏⠄ ⠿⠄⠄⠏

"These are the dots that I deciphered along the edge of the copper disk," he said.

"What does it say?" Sakura asked, leaning over his notebook.

"*Le génie dans la bouteille va te tuer,*" Brink said. "French. In English, that means, *The genie in the bottle will kill you.* The vial was a trap, a decoy from the real solution. And a dangerous one at that. My guess is it was filled with the same bufotoxin that protected the exterior, only a whole vial of the stuff. One drop of that would kill an entire village. It was not meant to destroy the scroll at all but to kill *me,* the solver. Or anyone who touched it without gloves."

"What you say is true, I'm afraid," the empress said, turning her gaze to Sakura. "Sakura-chan, I'm sorry. We've just had word."

"Akemi?" Sakura said, a hint of dread in her voice.

The empress's voice was faint, filled with sadness. "She tried to remove the scroll, and . . ."

Brink glanced at Sakura. She looked pained, and he knew that while she may have broken with her family's ideology, her aunt must have been important to her.

"I'm sorry," Brink said. "I wish she hadn't touched it. It's exactly what Ogawa wanted to happen. He created a fork in the path. The vial was one direction. A misdirection. And this"—Brink reached into his pocket, pulled out a milky white tile, the size of a thumb, and held it in the palm of his hand for all to see—"was the other."

"What is that?" the emperor asked, beckoning for Brink to bring it closer.

"I found it in the final cavity of the box," Brink said, giving it to the emperor. "Below the glass vial, fitted into a slot in the wood."

"When?" Sakura asked. "I was watching you the whole time, and I didn't see it."

"That's because I created a distraction," he said. "I knew everyone would be watching the vial, and if I instigated a dramatic diversion, no one would be watching the box. As I broke the vial with my right hand, I dislodged the tile with my left and slipped it into my pocket."

"Clever," the empress said.

The emperor held the tile in the light. It was yellowed with age, half an inch thick. "This is whalebone," he said. "We have Chinese mah-jongg sets made of this material."

"What is that stamped onto the tile?" the empress asked, looking closely at the surface. On one side, a Chinese character 神器 and the number 1 had been carved into the whalebone. On the other side, there was a round image of a leaf encased in concentric circles.

"I was hoping you would know," Brink said. "I've never seen anything like it."

"It is a *kamon*," the emperor said. "A family crest."

"In Europe," the empress said, "only nobility have family crests, but in Japan, nearly every family has one."

The emperor gestured to the chrysanthemum symbol emblazoned on one of the manuscripts under the glass case. "That is my family crest. And the crest on that tile, if I'm not mistaken, is the one for *Ogawa*."

A thrill went through Brink. Ogawa was clever—so clever that he'd created a secondary puzzle, one outside the Dragon Box. He'd constructed the most complicated mechanical puzzle in the world, and yet even that hadn't been secure enough for him. He broke the enigma in two parts.

"This tile is a clue, one of Ogawa's carefully crafted steps," Brink said, studying the image. "It's telling us that the second half of the puzzle is *outside* the box. And Ogawa is showing us how to find it."

"But how does Ogawa's *kamon* do that?" the empress asked.

"My guess is that Ogawa is directing us to his territory," Brink said. "Where he lived and worked. Where the box was constructed."

"Hakone," Sakura said. "He lived there his entire life. His family is from Hakone. His workshop was there, too."

"The *kamon* explains *where* to go," the emperor said, turning the tile over, showing the side with the number 1 and the Chinese character 神器. "And this explains *why*."

The emperor paused, seeming to consider his words, then said, "This tile has proven something I suspected to be true." He ran the tip of his finger over the whalebone. "This character is *jingi*, 神器, which means *sacred treasure*. It communicates a piece of information that no one except my ancestor, the emperor Meiji, would have understood. As you may know, there are three treasures that are priceless to my family. There is the sword, the *Kusanagi no Tsurugi*, which represents valor and virtue. There is the jewel, *Yasakani no Magatama*, a prehistoric gem that denotes benevolence. And there is the mirror, *Yata no Kagami*, which represents wisdom. These treasures came from Amaterasu Omikami, the goddess herself, who bequeathed them as a sign of power and legitimate rule to my family. They are our most sacred and ancient objects in Japan. This is well known. But what is not known is that one of these treasures is missing. The jewel, *Yasakani no Magatama*, disappeared in the nineteenth century. We believe this treasure was removed by my ancestor, the emperor Meiji, and locked in the Dragon Puzzle Box."

Brink glanced at Sakura, wondering if she was aware of this. She looked utterly stunned.

The emperor continued, "While all three of the regalia mean a great deal to the Yamato family, the jewel seemed to be of particular importance to Meiji. We don't know why, and over the generations, this question has become one of the most intriguing mysteries of the Yamato lineage. I am certain that we will never know what happened to *Yasakani no Magatama* until the dragon enigma is solved. It is imperative that *you* solve it. Before anyone else does."

The emperor stood, ending the conversation. But there was something on Brink's mind that couldn't wait. "Before we go," he said. "My dog, Conundrum. The gunfire scared her, and she ran off. She's out there alone. I can't leave unless I'm sure she'll be okay."

The empress stood and joined her husband. "I will see to it that Conundrum is safe," the empress said. "Even if I have to go out and find her myself."

32

Sakura led Brink back into the underground passage. The neon-lit concrete hallway brought them to where they began, then bifurcated, funneling them in the opposite direction. They ran until they hit a door that opened into an underground parking garage. Four Rolls-Royces, all of the same maroon hue, a sports car, two vans, and a small beat-up Honda were parked side by side.

Sakura unlocked the boxy Honda. "It's a K-model, or Kei 'light' car," she said, watching as Brink pushed the passenger seat all the way back and tried to squeeze in. "Might be a little tight."

Even with the seat pushed back, he had to pull his knees up to fit. "Sorry," Sakura said, slipping into the driver's seat and buckling her belt. "I never imagined I'd be using this for such a reason." As she backed out of the parking spot and navigated to a garage door, she said, "The empress negotiated a few things at the beginning of her marriage. One of those things involved having the freedom to go out and do normal things that the royal family isn't usually allowed to do—go to bookstores, for example, or shopping. This car has been very useful for those expeditions."

"This is the empress's car?" he asked, astonished. He expected she'd have something more elegant. He thought of Princess Diana, to whom the Japanese empress was often compared. He doubted Diana would have driven a Honda K-class under any circumstance.

"The empress must be very careful," Sakura said. "She only goes out in secret, and only when she's thoroughly disguised. No one would ever recognize her in this car. It is, in some ways, the perfect cover."

Sakura programmed something into the GPS in the dash, pressed a button to adjust the heat, and pushed another to open the electronic garage door, which released them into a dark tunnel. Soon they were on their way to the town of Hakone, fifty miles southwest of Tokyo. It was 6:16 P.M. According to the GPS, they'd arrive at a little before eight.

They emerged onto a crowded Tokyo street, neon signs pulsing. He blinked, feeling disoriented. The intensity of solving had left his mind churning. He was hungry and dehydrated. He dug in his bag and found a bottle of water, opened it, and drank it down.

Sakura knew her way around. She drove quickly, exiting onto a highway. As they headed south, the landscape changed. The warren of concrete and glass structures thinned, and the scenery flattened to railroad tracks and twists of highway, open vistas of countryside dotted with suburban towns, the spines of mountains in the background. The blue-gray light of the rising moon dusted the landscape.

It was obvious that something was upsetting Sakura. She was tense, her gaze locked on the road, her knuckles white over the steering wheel. He could feel her working something out as the miles passed.

"Everything okay?" he asked finally.

"I'm trying to get my head around what the emperor said about the *Yasakani no Magatama*," she said at last. "If Meiji did, in fact, hide the jewel, it has big repercussions."

"There's no way to know for sure that it's the jewel," Brink said. "The emperor said he *believes* that the jewel was what Meiji hid."

"The second the emperor said it was the jewel, I knew he was correct." Sakura sped up, passed a Toyota, and drifted back into the right lane. "I mentioned in the treasure room that my mother taught me about the eight empresses of Japan when I was a child. There was a reason for that."

Brink watched Sakura, eager to understand what she knew.

"The faction has existed for centuries. At one point in history, they were called alchemists—followers of John Dee, acolytes of the works of Neoplatonists. But they've gone by many names throughout the years. No matter what they were called, they were extraordinarily powerful, with connections to royalty, nobility, and—after these families were displaced by so-called democratic processes—the uberwealthy. Through history, the faction has had one mission: to find a collection of keys or codes that unlocks extraordinarily precious information."

The world's most precious substance. "What kind of information?"

"Not the kind you find on Google." The air was suddenly too warm. Brink cracked the window and Sakura fiddled with a button, turning down the heat. "My parents and all members of the faction believe that once, among certain members of an ancient civilization, there was a unified collection of knowledge that answered the mysteries of human existence."

"You make it sound like a big library or something."

Glancing at Brink, Sakura smiled. "In fact, it has been described that way. Have you heard of the Akashic Library?"

Brink thought he'd heard Rachel mention the Akashic Library during one of their discussions of her research. It was a comprehensive repository of ancient information. He hadn't paid attention closely but now wished he had. "It's a collection of esoteric teachings, right?"

"A little like that, I suppose. It's believed to be an immense, unalterable collection of universal knowledge that stands outside human civilization, a Platonic ideal of knowledge, you might say. There are those who are inclined to go so far as to call it *divine* knowledge, but many members of the faction are atheists and don't believe in any form of supernatural power or deity. What they do believe is that certain people can access this information through a set of keys, very ancient and powerful keys, that have been passed down through the generations. These keys have been hidden away and guarded by the most powerful families on earth—the Yamato family, for example. These generational power structures have dominated our world, and still do. You encountered one of the codes two years ago in New York, when you solved the cipher that drew Sedge to you. Sedge wanted that code very badly. You solved it for him. If anyone should know the power of these keys, it's you."

The truth was: Brink had tried desperately not to think about his experience with the code he'd solved for Sedge. The repercussions had been severe. The side effects of his injury had grown to be a form of torture in the years after the God Puzzle. There were times he'd felt that he might go insane. And now that Dr. Trevers was gone, he probably *would* go insane. "I don't like to think about it, to be honest."

"Listen, I see how hard this is on you," Sakura said, looking over at him. "I've known you, what, a few days, and already I understand how much you struggle because of the injury. But what if the *Yasakani no Magatama* jewel can change that? What if finding it could help free you?"

Brink closed his eyes, feeling a barrage of emotion move through him. *Free himself.* The very idea of it was delicious, too coveted to even imagine, especially after the despair he felt over Dr. Trevers's death. "You really think the jewel the emperor described can do that?"

"If it is, in fact, one of these ancient keys, it would be one of the most powerful," Sakura said. "It belonged to a deity, Amaterasu, and was passed down to her progeny, each generation protecting it. Each generation, that is, until Meiji took it upon himself to separate it from the other regalia and hide it in the Dragon Box. He broke the chain of protection begun by Amaterasu. Now I understand why the contents of the Dragon Box was so valuable to the faction. We must return it to its rightful place with the emperor."

As Sakura drove on, Brink stared out the window, considering everything that she had just told him. Everything was coming at him so fast. In less than two days, his entire world had been turned upside down. He was in a foreign country, thrust into a mystery that involved one of the most high-profile families in the world. Of course, he'd been warned about the puzzle-box contest, but he'd imagined the difficulty would be contained to two forces—the puzzle constructor and the puzzle solver, Ogawa's ingenious tricks against Brink's ability to solve them. He knew he was putting his life on the line, and he'd accepted the risk. But his bargain had been personal, contained to his own fate. Now he understood that there was more, much more, than his life on the line.

And yet this contest, this mystery—most of all, *Ogawa*—had gotten under Brink's skin. He saw the puzzle box still, its patterns repeating endlessly, creating a loop in his mind that pulled him deeper and deeper into himself. He couldn't forget the way the puzzle box felt in his hands, the allure of it, the thrill when he pushed past a trap or deciphered a secret. From the second he'd touched the Dragon Box, it had become an unstoppable force within him. The intricacies of the puzzle, the tricks, the solutions. The dangers. Even now he craved them. It wasn't a choice to solve it. It was a kind of compulsion, one he couldn't ignore. He'd be free only when he solved it. And to solve it, he needed to understand what waited for them in Hakone.

An explosion cracked through the air, interrupting his thoughts. Brink's side-view mirror exploded. He turned and saw a white utility van behind, following at a few cars' distance. It was dark, and he couldn't be sure, but the driver looked like the woman from the Three Shrines, Sakura's sister, Ume, and Cam Putney—easy enough to identify with his blond spiked hair—leaned out the window, gun drawn. They'd been followed.

"I was hoping this wouldn't happen," Sakura said, pressing on the gas.

"We need to get off the highway." He checked that the whalebone tile was secure in his pocket. No matter what happened, he couldn't allow them to take it. "We're too exposed."

"There," Sakura said. Brink saw an exit ahead: HAKONE TURNPIKE. "We'll lose them on the *touge* road."

33

They turned off the highway and onto the narrow mountain road. Through the windshield, Brink surveyed the *touge* road ascending ahead, a thick black ribbon switchbacking through the green mountain.

Sakura sighed deeply, a sigh that told him everything he needed to know: *This was going to be rough.* But they had no choice but to go forward. The straight, flat highway made them an easy target.

"*Gambatte*," she muttered under her breath, pressing the gas. "Hold on, my friend, here we go."

Brink checked over his shoulder. No sign of the van. They needed to get as far ahead of Ume and Cam as they could. The Honda sputtered and coughed as it accelerated. The car was not made for speed and definitely not built for a road like this one.

"This road was built to bypass the famous Tokaido Road, one of the five ancient roads between Kyoto and Edo," Sakura said. "But in the last decades, the *touge* road has become even more famous than the renowned old road. *Touge* is the Japanese word for *pass*, a way to overcome our steep mountainous terrain. These roads are a feat of Japanese engineering, layers of pavement folded like soft taffy to create narrow, winding passageways. Maybe you know *touge* roads from video games," Sakura said, easing around a hairpin curve.

Brink had played the video game Initial D obsessively as a teenager. He loved playing it, loved the feeling of chasing a sports car
along twisting, dangerous turns. He'd never imagined that one day
he would be sitting in a real car being chased on real *touge* roads. And
that it wouldn't be a sports car but an old Honda.

"I played Initial D," he said, bracing himself against the dash as
she flew around another curve.

"Really?" she shot him a look, impressed or derisive, he couldn't
tell which. "Not many people outside Japan know it. There are videos
on YouTube of races inspired by the game, insane people taking
Lamborghinis and McLarens a hundred miles an hour around these
curves. It's terrifying to watch. But pretty exciting, too."

Brink heard a vehicle closing in, glanced back, and saw the van.
Sakura saw it, too. "This is going to get nasty."

The road ahead was a sidewinder, punishing, guardrails caging it
on both sides. Even if they wanted to turn back, they were locked in.
Nowhere to go but up.

"Hang on," she said, her eyes never leaving the road. "This car
wasn't made for speed."

"Me, either." Brink braced himself against the dash, feeling his
stomach lurch into his throat as Sakura slowed, eased around a hairpin curve, then accelerated into another.

As a wave of nausea crashed over him, Brink focused on the
shape of the road, its elegant structure, the perfect mathematical
properties of an S curve. The twisting pass expanded and folded,
became three-dimensional elements. A streak of bright red fell over
the black, exploding into trailers of purple, magenta, deep blue. It
wasn't unusual for his mind to light up with fireworks when confronted with geometric shapes, but while he normally watched from
a remove, using his synesthesia to help him map a pattern or problem, now he was inside the chaos, swept away. The excesses of adrenaline in the past day had worn him down, sending his mind into
overdrive. Dr. Trevers had once said it was a protective response to
the amount of stimulation his brain endured, a kind of disassocia-

tion, a healthy way for his brain to handle the deluge of dopamine flooding in.

He turned and saw that the van was there, riding along the driver's side, right next to them. It swerved, cutting in close—too close. A crack shot through the car as the van veered into them, pushing them to the edge of the road.

Sakura screamed but held the wheel firm, struggling against the momentum, but when the van slammed into them again, Brink knew that there was no stopping it: They were going over.

He felt a great rush of movement as the Honda left the road, hurtled into a guardrail, and flew over the side of the mountain. They sailed into the trees and skidded down the mountain, crashing to a stop against a cedar tree.

Brink glanced over at Sakura. She'd buried her head in her arms, bracing herself against the steering wheel, an act of protection and terror. It was a minor miracle that they hadn't flipped—the tin box of a car would've crumpled like an aluminum can. Sakura, with her steady driving and cool head, had saved their lives.

When she looked up and met his eye, he was surprised to see her smile. "That was fucking amazing," she said, as she unbuckled her seatbelt and wrenched open the door.

"The guy in the car?" Brink said, pulling himself out and stepping into the snow.

"Cam Putney."

"You know him?"

"He worked for Sedge," she said. "And he must still, or he wouldn't know about the contest or about you being here. He wouldn't have run us off the road. And he wouldn't be with my sister."

Brink detested Cam Putney. He'd met him when he'd met Sedge, during the frantic days of the God Puzzle. The man had abducted Connie and nearly killed a woman. And he knew he wasn't going to feel any more affection for the guy this time around.

"If we needed proof that we're being tracked, we just got it," Brink said. He pulled his phone from his pocket, shut it off, then watched as Sakura unbuckled her Apple Watch, pressed the tiny button cutting the power, and zipped it into the inside pocket of her cargo jacket.

"We need to be completely off the grid from here on out," Sakura said. "Come on." She walked ahead. "I'm sure those two aren't far behind."

They hurried down the mountain, into a thick dark forest, ducking branches, jumping streams, running and running. The trees were magisterial, immense giants towering above. Snow coated the ground, frosting jagged boulders, collecting on branches high overhead. His breath froze in fractals around him. He shivered and pulled his coat tight. With his phone disabled, he was cut off from Rachel. From Gupta. From every avenue of help. He was stranded in an eerie, endless forest at the end of the world.

After fifteen minutes or so, Sakura stopped to catch her breath near an enormous tree, its trunk four times her width. They'd been running, but Brink hadn't broken a sweat. He'd finished the last New York City Marathon, and the three before that, in fact. His daily physical training, undertaken to manage the ups and downs of his brain chemistry, had come in handy during long competitions, but this was a first.

He sat on a moss-covered boulder across from Sakura and looked at the sky. The moon, a perfect disk of light, hovered beyond the trees. He took a deep breath, the kind of breath Dr. Trevers had taught him during their meditation sessions. Taking in the rich, loamy scent of the forest, the cushion of snow under him, felt good. Comforting. He'd been straining mind and body for hours. Coming back to himself through his senses offered a moment of relief.

A clear mountain stream gurgled beyond. Brink went to the stream, collected water in his hands, and splashed his face, the ice-cold chill of it making his skin tingle. It was then that he noticed the silence. "I think they're gone."

Sakura joined him at the stream, bent by his side, and washed her hands. "I think you're right."

"That was some excellent driving back there."

She nodded, accepting the compliment with a smile. "I played Initial D, too."

Removing a handkerchief from her pocket, she dried her hands and wandered into the forest. Brink followed her as she poked through a tangle of overgrowth, ducked behind a tree, clearly looking for something, although he couldn't imagine what.

"Ah, there it is," she said, walking ahead. Brink saw nothing but old-growth forest, cedars and mulberry trees, ice-capped rocks, ferns sticking through the snow. "The old Tokaido Road. I knew we had to be close. I've never seen it other than in ukiyo-e prints. But I knew it was here somewhere."

Brink stepped to Sakura and saw, in the undergrowth, a fish-scale pattern of rough-hewn moss-covered stones—an old road stretching into the forest.

"It is an ancient road, one that was used for hundreds of years to travel between Kyoto and Edo. It was originally a dirt path, but the Tokugawa shogunate ordered that it be paved with stones, an expensive, laborious feat of engineering at the time. It made the road famous and"—she stepped on the mossy stones and began walking—"created a direct route to Hakone."

34

They walked along the stone road until the forest opened over a town, visible in the moonlight. Mike Brink saw houses nestled in a cleft of trees, and, beyond, Mount Fuji, a great snowcapped cone, rose above the lake, its reflection hovering on the water's silver surface. The scene was breathtaking. Majestic. He couldn't remember seeing a more beautiful landscape in his life.

"Fuji-san," Sakura said, stepping to his side. "You can watch it for hours and see a hundred different mountains."

Brink pointed to the village below, to clusters of buildings and houses. "And that must be Hakone."

"Correct," Sakura said. "Ogawa's workshop could be anywhere down there. If it's even his workshop we're looking for."

"What else could the tile mean?"

She shrugged. "Ogawa was from Hakone, and the first puzzle boxes were made there. But it's not a guarantee that the next clue is there. Still, it's a solid bet. Meiji would have also known Hakone. It was a special place for the imperial family, especially around the time of the Meiji Restoration. They had a beautiful villa on Lake Ashi, where they spent the summer months. Their villa was given to the prefecture after the war. It's a public park and museum now." She shot him a look, one he'd begun to recognize—it pained her to talk about the war. There were experiences time erased and those it crystallized, preserving them forever. She turned her eyes back to the gorgeous view, the mountain and the lake, the moonlit sky.

"Well, Ogawa's *kamon* was carved into the tile for a reason," Brink said. He removed the whalebone piece from his pocket. "We just need to figure it out."

Sakura took the tile and studied it. "I guess the only way to know for sure is to go down there and see."

"With luck the workshop is still around." Brink didn't want to imagine what would happen if they found nothing in Hakone. Getting this far, only to find Ogawa's workshop gone, would be the end of the Dragon Box puzzle. "But it's been a long time since Ogawa lived here. I hope it hasn't been sold or destroyed."

"We aren't a mobile society. In Japan, a home will remain in a family for generations. Family altars are there; childhood memories are there. We don't leave them behind. We can't." She gave him a look filled with sadness, then headed down toward the village. "Come on, let's go see what new tricks Ogawa left for us."

The town felt deserted when they arrived. Windows shuttered, businesses closed. Not a single person on the street. "Hakone is busy in the summer," Sakura said, as they walked past an empty bus station and a sign for an art museum. "It's primarily a tourist destination. These mountains are full of *onsen*, bathhouses with hot sulfurous water, and people go there to relax in the pristine mountain air. It's easy to imagine Ogawa here, and the emperor Meiji, too. He would have spent his childhood summers in Hakone—he may have even first learned about puzzle boxes when he visited Hakone as a child."

Finally, they saw a traditional building with an illuminated sign.

"It's a *ryokan*," Sakura said. "Are you hungry? We can rest a minute and try to figure out where the Ogawa workshop was located."

"Food would be great," Brink said. He hadn't eaten for a long time and realized that he was ravenous.

Sakura steered them up a narrow path lined with lanterns and into the hotel. There was a small foyer, where a woman led them into a traditional restaurant with tatami mats and cushions. Brink bent and sat before a low table, crossing his legs awkwardly, his muscles burning. He wasn't flexible, and he wasn't sure how long he could sit like this without his legs going numb. Sakura opened a bottle of beer and poured out two glasses. Brink drank it down, sinking into the realization that his journey, which had begun in New York, had been an endless string of frustrations and challenges. He rubbed his temples and closed his eyes. After everything, the beer tasted good.

A waitress arrived. Sakura ordered for them both, then turned to Brink, her eyes settling heavily on him.

He could feel, in her look, a new weight between them. A complicity. The pressure of the past days had created something pure—a kind of frankness and honesty that Brink rarely felt. After their meeting with the emperor and empress and what happened on the *touge* road, he was ready to trust her. It was time to tell Sakura everything.

"You've been honest with me about your connection with Sedge, and so there's something I need to tell you," Brink said. "For nearly half of my life, I've worked with a man named Scott Trevers, a neuroscientist, one of the best in the world, who specializes in the brain function of savants, especially those like me, who've acquired savantism through a traumatic brain injury. Dr. Trevers and I were close. I spoke to him nearly every day. He was working on an experimental treatment that would regulate the chemicals that are responsible for all this ..." He pointed to his head, signifying his gift and its side effects. "Early the morning you delivered the invitation to my place, Dr. Trevers was found dead in his office."

If he'd doubted Sakura before, her expression told him everything he needed to know. She was shocked, surprised. Saddened. "I'm sorry to hear that. You must have found out after I left your apartment?"

Brink nodded. "But before he died, he sent me an email. He wrote nothing in the subject line and nothing in the body of the message. There was only a single image. A chrysanthemum. Exactly like the one you brought me. Somehow, he knew about your invitation."

"But how could he have known? You said he'd passed away earlier that morning before I arrived."

"Exactly. Which means ..."

"He somehow knew I'd be coming," Sakura said. "And somehow he knew what I'd be delivering to you."

"Right," Brink said, studying Sakura, watching for the slightest hint that she knew more than she was letting on. But Sakura looked genuinely perplexed. "That's the implication."

"But that's *impossible*, Mike. Nobody knew I was coming except the emperor and empress and my aunt Akemi. And I created that puzzle myself, on the plane."

"On your laptop?"

"I designed it using puzzle-constructing software. I have a template that I use. Just like you do for your puzzles in the *Times*, I'm sure. Then, after I finished, I drew it onto the piece of origami paper by hand."

"What if someone saw the word puzzle you were constructing as you made it?"

"There was no one on that plane but me, the pilot, and a stewardess."

"I'm not talking about someone *on* the plane," Brink said. "I mean someone *in* your computer."

Sakura's eyes widened. "You think I was hacked?"

"When I was out walking Connie before the contest, I spoke with a friend, Dr. Vivek Gupta. He has a long history of tracking new technologies, especially AI. He learned, after examining various networks, that your aunt Akemi was recently in contact with Jameson Sedge."

Sakura stared at Brink, waiting for him to explain further. "You know that's totally impossible," she said finally. "Jameson Sedge is dead."

"I know. That's exactly what I said. Dr. Gupta doesn't agree."

"Do you think he somehow staged his death?"

"Not possible. I was there when he killed himself. There's no question in my mind about that. But according to my friend, there's proof that Sedge is . . . *active*. There are digital patterns—messages, bank transfers, interactions with his personal keys on blockchains, intercepted video communications of Sedge. Online, in the digital universe, he's very much alive."

"I don't understand what you're telling me," Sakura said. "That Sedge set up a program to simulate himself after he died? I mean, that sounds like something he'd do. I knew him well, and he was obsessed with longevity and technology. He dumped hundreds of millions of dollars into transhumanism, AI, blockchain technology, quantum computing, and everything else that might offer a way to live beyond the physical world. But he *did* die. I was at his funeral."

"It's hard to fathom, but I think he did exactly what he set out to do: He engineered a way to exist digitally." He glanced at an iPhone on a counter near their table. "If Sedge created a digital version of himself, he would be capable of infiltrating online spaces, using networks to watch, listen, and gather information. He could isolate and attack an individual."

"Like you," Sakura said, lowering her voice, as if suddenly aware that Sedge could be listening.

"Like *us*." Brink nodded toward the phone. "He could have hacked the Honda's GPS and fed that information to Ume and Cam. He could be listening to us right now."

Sakura took a deep breath, her manner turning serious. "You need to know something," she said. "I didn't have anything to do with what happened to Dr. Trevers. And while I'm really struggling to understand how in the hell Sedge could track us, I think that after what we experienced on the *touge* road, we should assume that he is."

Brink agreed. He stood, walked by the counter, and grabbed the phone, then carried it to a bathroom at the far end of the restaurant, where he placed it on the edge of the sink. The waitress would find it later, after they were gone.

Brink returned to the table just as the waitress placed food before them. He was starving.

"I ordered a sampling of the local cuisine," Sakura said. "I've heard of some of these dishes. Like this . . ." She gestured to a ceramic bowl filled with black eggs. "But I've never tried them."

Brink examined the black eggs, curious. "And those are?"

"*Kuro-tamago.* Eggs hard-boiled in the geothermal water of Mount Owakudani. They turn black from the mineralogy."

She lifted an egg with her chopsticks—a feat of dexterity that Brink admired—and placed it on his plate.

"There's a legend that eating one of these eggs," Sakura said, placing an egg on her own plate and delicately breaking the shell, "will extend your life by seven years."

"You think that's true?" With all that he was up against, adding an extra seven years to his life wasn't a bad idea.

"Yes, absolutely." She winked, giving him a conspiratorial look. "I suggest you have two."

Sakura bowed her head. "*Itadakimasu.*" Brink broke the black shell and ate the egg. The taste was rich and complex, slightly earthy, delicious.

"And here is another specialty," she said, as the waitress delivered lacquer trays to them. Inside his bowl lay three pieces of deep-fried fish. "This is called *wakasagi.* Fried freshwater river smelt. It is delicious and very hearty, which I believe will be welcome news for you, Mike."

She was right. The food was welcome. Brink was hungry. The portions were smaller than what he was used to, and so he was glad to see a procession of small, delicate dishes emerging from the kitchen. *Kamaboko* fish cakes with slices of burdock root, eel *nigiri,* a plate of sashimi, and other dishes that he couldn't name—vegetables and fish and meats, so many dishes that, by the time the plate of steamed buns filled with sweet red bean paste called *manju* arrived, he was full.

Sakura called over the woman, complimented the food, and began questioning her about the local traditions and sights. Brink understood enough Japanese to recognize the cover story from back at the palace: She was showing a foreign dignitary the highlights of Japan. Sakura's body language shifted, became filled with gestures that Brink hadn't seen before, Japanese expressions that coexisted with her American ones. He watched, silent, taking it all in, until finally, after five minutes or so of conversation, Sakura got to the point.

"I read somewhere that there is a famous artisanal craft here," Sakura said. "A kind of game with wooden boxes?"

The waitress launched into a discussion of *karakuri*—puzzle boxes—explaining that there was a museum with many famous examples of the boxes not far from there.

"And maybe it was in my guidebook, I'm not sure," Sakura said. "But wasn't there a very famous puzzle-box constructor? A man named Ogawa Ryuichi?"

The waitress knew of Ogawa and agreed that he was, indeed, famous in that region. Clearly pleased by their interest, she led them out of the restaurant, explaining that the museum was just outside town, past the bus depot, along the lake.

Sakura gave Brink a triumphant look. "Hakone is a small place, and she knew Ogawa's entire history. Hakone's most famous puzzle master's workshop was converted, about thirty years ago, into a *karakuri* puzzle-box museum."

Brink slid the whalebone tile from his pocket, turning it from the *kamon* image to the kanji—*jingi, sacred treasure.* "Let's hope our luck holds out long enough to understand this."

35

Brink and Sakura walked along the lake, following the road out of town, past banks of cedar trees that stretched so high he couldn't see the tops, their trunks as thick as the Honda K-class they'd abandoned in the woods. Snow blanketed the limbs, and crystals of ice clung to the narrow withes. The cool, pure mountain air tingled in his lungs. He and Sakura paused before a tree wider than the two of them standing together, taking in the distinct scent of its spicy resin. The dark forest contrasted with the snow, creating a pattern he found soothing.

"These are ancient sugi trees," she said. "Some are more than four hundred years old. There are many legends about trees in Japan, stories of kami that reside inside. My parents would have known all of them, and maybe they even told me some, but I've forgotten them."

A sign for the museum pointed up a hill. They began to climb and, after some distance, Brink saw a modern structure with a flag hoisted outside the door: the *karakuri* museum. It was nearly nine o'clock, and the museum was closed. Yet the interior was lit up. "Maybe someone's still there," he said, knocking on the glass.

Inside were shelves filled with puzzle boxes, hundreds of them of every size and color, stacked on shelves. He knocked again. Nobody came.

"I don't get it," Brink said, peering through the glass door at the space beyond, illuminated by soft halogen lighting. "There's no way this building was Ogawa's workshop—it can't be more than thirty years old."

"You're right," Sakura said. "If Ogawa left something behind, it isn't here."

Just then a young man approached, unlocked the door, and opened it. He was around twenty-five years old, tall and thin, with a messy J-pop haircut and round John Lennon eyeglasses. He wore a blue museum T-shirt and a name tag, *Ishii Hiroshi,* in both Japanese characters and roman letters.

"I'm sorry," Hiroshi said, bowing to Sakura, then to Brink. "But the museum is closed."

Sakura began to speak, when suddenly Hiroshi's eyes grew wide with recognition. "You're Mike Brink, aren't you?" he said, changing to English. "*The* Mike Brink. I've always hoped you would visit the museum one day, but it seemed impossible." He pulled out his phone and opened the *New York Times* Games app. "I just solved your new puzzle this morning. Is it actually you?"

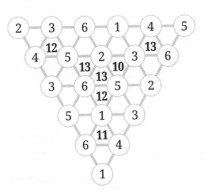

It happened more and more frequently. Mike Brink would walk into a bar or a café and someone would approach him, one of his Saturday crosswords in hand. They would ask him to sign the newspaper or demand to know how he came up with a certain clue. The exchange then moved on to selfies, which would turn up on social media within minutes. After a post of Brink showing off Conundrum's trove of unusual tricks went viral, a line of T-shirts featuring the dachshund went on sale. Brendan Emmett Quigley, one of Brink's colleagues at the *Times*, had given him one as a gift. The T-shirt featured a photo of Connie and the words THE UNSOLVABLE CONUNDRUM.

Brink shook Hiroshi's hand. "Thanks for the warm welcome," he said. "We're extremely interested in the museum and would love to see it, if you have time."

"Wow, Mike Brink," Hiroshi said, as if to confirm that it really was Brink standing there. "I followed that amazing triumph in Amsterdam last month. One hundred seventeen thousand pi places. Congratulations!"

Hiroshi was talking about Brink's Guinness World Record for memorizing pi places. He'd recited 117,989 pi places over the course of ten grueling hours, beating Indian genius Rajveer Meena's 2015 record. It had been a marathon of memory, all performed before a table of judges and an audience. The thing ended up on YouTube, all ten hours, and had been watched nearly four million times. While the internal experience of reciting so many numbers was dramatic for Brink—he saw each pi place as an image, a kind of character, and each character part of an epic narrative—he couldn't imagine that watching a man ramble off an endless string of numbers could be interesting for Hiroshi.

"I've always wanted to know how you did that," Hiroshi said, his eyes bright behind his glasses. "It looked like you went into a trance. What happens to you?"

Brink never knew how to respond to such questions. It was like asking someone to explain how they breathed. The answer was: instinct. In and out, one breath at a time, without thinking. Asking Mike Brink *how* he solved a puzzle, or *why* his brain did what it did, was like asking a man why his heart beat and how he kept its rhythm regular.

He glanced back at Hiroshi, the young man looking at him with admiration, and he felt a wave of gratitude for his abilities—it was the deepest, most satisfying reward, to make a fan happy. "So, Hiroshi, you watch pi competitions for fun?"

"*Oh yes*," he said, smiling broadly. "I could never do what you do, but I'm a student of mechanical puzzles. I solve puzzle boxes, of course, but also Rubik's Cubes and burr puzzles. Number puzzles are also interesting, but I'm not very good at them. And I recite pi digits myself. I'm not anywhere near as good as you, of course. You're an inspiration. Come inside. Please."

Hiroshi led them into the museum, where they were surrounded by puzzle boxes.

"Puzzle boxes were originally very simple, made to hold small objects like sewing needles, keys, even secret messages between lovers. The boxes could fit in the palm of the hand, had a single hollow space, and could be opened with one or two moves. Over time, they became extremely popular, and the artisans became more innovative. The boxes grew larger, more elaborate, and were called *sikake-bako*, a trick box, and *tei-bako*, a clever box. These were complex interlocking systems, like a kind of strongbox. Wealthy Japanese families used them to hold jewelry and money and important documents. The samurai, always obsessed with secrecy and security, used Hakone boxes to send sensitive correspondence. They were, in fact, an early kind of safe.

They were being taken on a tour, and while they didn't have time, Brink had a feeling they needed to be patient and listen. What Hiroshi knew could help them understand Ogawa.

"It wasn't until the late-nineteenth century that the boxes took their current form as games of skill," he continued. "Artisans in the Hakone region are credited with developing a small local craft into a national art. Over time, these boxes became more complex, with many collectors from around the world. Come, follow me," he said, showing them to a back room.

"This is where we make the puzzle boxes we sell in the gift shop." Hiroshi took a box and turned it in his hands. There were dozens of colors of wood pieced together to form an elaborate, beautiful pattern. "They're very popular. We sell out of them every summer. Tourists love them."

Brink glanced around, growing impatient. What could they possibly find here, at a contemporary puzzle-box museum? Sakura seemed to have the same thought. She picked up one of the boxes, a deep-brown color with a pattern of stars, turned it in her hand, as if searching for clues.

"*Yosegi-zaiku* involves cutting a vertical shaft the size of a pencil of each variety of wood, sometimes as many as fifteen thin shafts, and positioning each color in a way that creates a pattern. The pieces are glued together and compressed until they form a solid, seamless block. Then, using a large, flat razor blade, a thin sheet is shaved from the top of the block. This paper-thin sheet, with its brilliant pattern, is glued to the surface of the box, giving the box a gorgeous, lustrous wrapping. That puzzle box"—he pointed to the box in Sakura's hand—"was made with *yosegi-zaiku*."

Sakura didn't seem to be paying attention. She pushed a panel, then another, and soon the box opened. She put it down and glanced at Brink, her expression filled with annoyance. They didn't have time for small talk with Hirsohi. He could feel her restlessness and desperation to get on with the real purpose of their visit. Ume and Cam could show up at any second. And yet he didn't want to rush Hiroshi. Sometimes, it was faster to go slow.

"It's great to learn all of this," Brink said. "Because right now we are looking for something very particular. And we could use your expertise."

"I'm happy to help in any way I can."

"We came here for information about Ogawa Ryuichi," Sakura said.

"Ah, the master of puzzle masters," Hiroshi said. "It is Ogawa-sensei whose ideas changed the nature of the puzzle box completely. He brought a rigorous yet fantastical approach to the construction of puzzles, transforming what was just a silly mechanical game into the realm of art. He made many of his boxes right here, in this building."

"This structure belonged to Ogawa Ryuichi?" Sakura asked, her eyes now wide with interest.

"It did. This space was his workshop. After his death, the *karakuri* association bought Ogawa-sensei's property. Ogawa-sensei had no wife, no children, and so all his belongings came with the property. The workshop was torn down and rebuilt as a museum and store. His home, however, is exactly as it was when he was alive."

"And that is?" Sakura asked, her voice filled with excitement.

He led them to a window and directed their gaze behind the museum, to a hill lush with trees, barely visible in the darkness. "Up there, in the forest."

That's when Brink saw it: Ogawa's family crest, the *kamon*, carved into a piece of wood lying on a table in the workshop. "Wait a second," he said, walking to the table. "What is this symbol?"

"Ogawa-sensei's signature," Hiroshi said. "That piece of wood was taken from Ogawa-sensei's home. It's filled with them—on the doors, the window frames, everywhere."

"Could you show us?" Brink asked.

Hiroshi shrugged—*sure, why not*—and headed out the door. Sakura gave Brink a look of triumph: They'd found Ogawa's *kamon*. They were on the right path. Brink only hoped that it would take them to Meiji's treasure.

36

Mike Brink followed Hiroshi out of the museum. An ice-covered stone pathway materialized under the brilliant light of the full moon. Within minutes, they stood before a traditional Japanese mountain home. Tucked deep under the canopy of cedars, it looked like it hadn't been touched by sunlight in decades. Frozen moss peeked from under the snow dusted stone steps, the roof eaves were rotting, and a film of grime slicked the windows.

But the house itself faded away when Brink saw, carved into the front door, Ogawa's crest, the same symbol etched into the whalebone tile. As he examined the house, he saw the *kamon* everywhere—it had been carved into doorframes, lintels, even the windowsills. Ogawa had left a trail of breadcrumbs to the next step of the puzzle. They only needed to follow them.

Hiroshi took out a ring of labeled keys—clearly the museum's master set—and unlocked the door. Just then there was a buzzing, the distinct sound of a notification on a phone. Hiroshi removed the latest-model iPhone from his pocket, read a text message, then slipped his phone back into his pocket. Sakura shot Brink a look. *How could they be so stupid?* They'd forgotten to ask Hiroshi to disable his phone.

"Hiroshi-san," Sakura said. "I know this will seem a little strange, but would you please give me your phone for a minute?"

Hiroshi was baffled but took his phone from his pocket and handed it to Sakura. She turned off the phone, then returned it to Hiroshi, who was staring at them, confused.

"Sorry, I know it's odd, but we're being watched," Brink said, realizing even as he spoke that he sounded completely paranoid.

"*Watched?*" Hiroshi said, astonished. "Who's watching you?"

"As Mike said, it sounds odd. But trust me when I say we need to be very careful. Someone has threatened us, someone dangerous. He's found a way to hijack technologies connected to the internet—surveillance cameras, phones, satellites, drones—and is using them to track us."

"Like a fan?" Hiroshi asked, clearly struggling to understand who would be obsessed enough with Mike Brink to go to such lengths.

"Exactly," Sakura said. "A superfan. And we need to make sure he can't find us here."

"Okay, I guess," Hiroshi said, still looking confused and not wholly convinced. "There's no internet up here, or cameras, if that makes you feel better."

"It does," Sakura said. "A lot better."

Hiroshi returned his phone to his pocket and led them inside the dark mountain house. He turned on a lamp, filling the room with dim light.

"This place would have rotted away," Hiroshi said, "but members of the *karakuri* association took it upon themselves to maintain it. Ogawa's cultural significance is very important, a national treasure, and we are committed to preserving this structure. It is expensive, though, and there's been talk of making it part of the museum. We could recreate some of Ogawa's most challenging and interesting puzzles and allow people to try them."

Yeah, right, Brink thought, remembering Ogawa's guillotine. *Chopping off people's fingers will be a huge draw.*

Hiroshi led them to a cavernous space filled to bursting with what was clearly Ogawa's life's work—puzzle boxes fashioned from magnolia and cedarwood, black-walnut boxes, hundreds upon hundreds of puzzles sitting on tables and shelves, stacked on the floor. Each of the boxes had a different kind of pattern—circles and hexagons and triangles, all of them pulling at Brink's attention. The house was dangerous and mad, like a twisted expression of Brink's worst nightmare: the very thing that sustained and tortured him reproduced infinitely, surrounding him in an endless simulation of his mind. If he wasn't there for a specific reason, he'd have sat down and taken them apart one by one, for the pure pleasure of opening them. As it was, he needed to understand why Ogawa had brought them here. He needed to know where to begin. Each box was a potential trap. How could he possibly know which one would lead to the solution?

Sakura was clearly thinking the same thing. She walked through the space, paused before a wooden chessboard, and ran a finger over the surface, leaving a trail of dust. "What *is* all this?"

"Ogawa-sensei lived alone in this house his entire life," Hiroshi said, as if that explained the mountains of objects piled before them. "And then the *karakuri* association moved his pieces from his workshop here. It's become a kind of storage room of his life. A museum of his obsession."

"It's incredible," Brink said, lifting a puzzle box and wiping away the dust. A galaxy of geometric shapes appeared under his fingers. Reflexively, he turned it in his hands, feeling his way through, and soon it was solved. "No tricks here."

"Just wait," Sakura said. "There's always a trick."

Brink remembered what Sakura had said in New York as they stood together before that first puzzle box: *A puzzle box is never quite what it seems. It is a master of illusion, puzzles within puzzles. You can't let your guard down, even for a second.*

Brink walked through the room. There was a reason Ogawa sent him here, but what was it? *The puzzle within the puzzle.* The next step was there. The Dragon Box wouldn't lie. Or would it?

Brink removed the whalebone tile from his pocket and showed it to Hiroshi. "I found this in the final compartment of the Dragon Box."

Hiroshi's jaw dropped. "The *Dragon Box*?"

"Mike was invited to open it," Sakura said.

Hiroshi's eyes were wide with wonder. "Then it isn't just a legend? The Dragon Box actually exists?"

"It exists, and this was the solution, or at least the last clue of the box. The rest of the puzzle remains to be solved." Brink turned the tile over in his hand, rubbing his thumb over the *kamon* crest. "It led us here, to his workshop. The next step *must* be in this house."

"There are a thousand mechanical puzzles here, at least," Hiroshi said. "It would take us weeks to solve all of them. Also . . ." Hiroshi took the whalebone tile from Brink and studied it. "This material is unlike anything used in Ogawa-sensei's constructions. He used wood, and only wood from these forests. This tile is very unusual— I'm not sure it was made by Ogawa-sensei."

"Everything about the Dragon Box is unusual," Sakura said.

"Wait . . ." Hiroshi thought for a moment. "There is something that might correspond to this tile."

Hiroshi navigated a narrow path through the clutter, leading them to the far end of the house. He opened a shoji door and stepped into a long, narrow space. Hiroshi turned on a lamp, and Brink found a room filled with bookshelves, papers, and even more puzzles. But everything faded as Brink saw a large, round pedestal table at the very center of the room. It was, quite simply, magnificent. The surface of the table was a large disk, perhaps three feet in diameter, inlaid with intricate geometric shapes that formed an Escher-like pattern. Brink could hardly move. The elaborate, intricate patterns entranced him. The table was an opulent marvel of nature— dovetailing like the reticulations of a ginkgo leaf or the microscopic arrangement of cells in a drop of water. The complexity and beauty overwhelmed him. A blast of anticipation hit him, sending adrenaline through his system. He was ready to solve this.

"I've never seen anything like it," Sakura said, studying the intricate inlay of wood.

"Nobody has," Hiroshi said. "It's an utterly unique piece. We haven't been able to test it out, but from the intricate arrangement of pieces, it's clear that the table was built to create patterns, like a kaleidoscope, and these patterns form the solution. It was found here after Ogawa's death. It was immediately recognized as a masterpiece, one of his most beautiful puzzles, and perhaps his most unusual."

Clearly, he's never seen the Dragon Box, Brink thought.

"As you can see, there are six drawers around the exterior of the table," Hiroshi said. He pulled the handle of a drawer. It was locked tight. "Create the correct patterns, and the drawers will open."

Brink had heard of desks with secret compartments, intricately designed pieces that were like large, functional puzzle boxes. But he'd never seen one quite so wonderful or as alluring. He searched for something that would indicate how to start. *The trick is knowing how to begin.* "Has anyone ever opened it?"

Hiroshi shook his head. "It was impossible," he said, gesturing to a slot at the center of the table. It was the exact size and shape of the whalebone tile. "Without the key."

Brink understood. Ogawa had created the kaleidoscope table as the next step of the Dragon Puzzle. The tile was a key to unlock it. *This was it. They'd discovered the next step.* They were close, so close, to finding Meiji's treasure.

Taking the tile in hand, Brink angled it over the slot. He hesitated, thinking through the consequences. Inserting it would bring him to the next stage of this game. But it could also lead to deadly surprises. The Dragon Box had taught him that. *Here goes nothing.* But as he was about to press the tile into the slot, Hiroshi stopped him.

"Wait," Hiroshi said, his voice filled with distress. "You need to understand that this could be extremely dangerous. Ogawa-sensei was not a normal man. He made things that some considered to be mischievous. Mean-spirited. Even sadistic. There's no telling what could happen if you open this."

"You barely survived Ogawa before." Sakura eyed the table, wary. "What if this is even more dangerous?"

Sakura and Hiroshi had a point. He'd made it through the first half of the puzzle, but there was no way to know if he'd survive the rest. And yet, despite the danger, he yearned to try. The intricate nature of the pattern sparked something deep in Brink's body and soul. It was a form of communication, this table. One human being speaking across time to another. He felt a buzzing in his chest, sharp and insistent. He couldn't help it. This wasn't about Meiji's treasure anymore or about winning the contest. It wasn't even about understanding what happened to Dr. Trevers. Now it was personal. He *needed* to solve this puzzle. In Ogawa, he'd found an opponent who challenged him beyond anything he'd imagined possible. The idea of leaving Ogawa's final steps unsolved tore at him. Brink placed his hands on the table. "I've been up against Ogawa before," Brink said. "I know his game."

"Then you know," Hiroshi said, "that Ogawa-sensei meant not only to defeat his opponent but to annihilate him. You risk more than losing a challenge. Ogawa-sensei played to win."

"So do I," Brink said. Leaning over the table, he pressed the tile into the slot. The contest was on.

37

There was a moment of stillness and then a great creak as an internal mechanism unlocked. Brink took a deep breath and studied the table. Two grooves had appeared in its edge. When he placed his wrists in them and applied pressure, the table rotated. Pressure from his right hand, and the surface of the table spun right. When he pressed in the other direction, it rotated left. The table was mobile, a spinnable disk. And with each movement, the table's configuration shifted, re-formed, composing a new and different pattern.

Brink recognized the concept. "There's an American puzzle-box constructor, Kagen Sound, who makes something similar, only it isn't a table but a box. A pattern box. It opens when the solver creates a 'key' pattern—herringbone or interconnected squares or circles, or whatever pattern the constructor has designed into the puzzle. They're monstrously complicated, brilliantly constructed, and extremely difficult to open."

Brink began to play with the disk, moving it right a fraction of an inch, then left, creating a cascade of movement in the wooden pieces as they shifted, formed, and re-formed.

"When you construct the correct pattern, you'll release a drawer."

Sakura walked around the table, examining the drawers. "There are six. Which means . . ."

"You will need to create six patterns," Hiroshi said.

"The treasure must be inside one of these drawers," Sakura said, examining the table. "It must be."

"Let's hope so," Brink said, but he was unable to think about the outcome. At that moment he was focused on the surface of the table, taking in the intricate joining of wooden pieces. A catalog of millions of patterns ran through his mind. *How on earth would he find the right ones?* With the complexity of the table, the possibilities seemed infinite.

No way he'd solve this by guessing. He needed to inhabit his opponent. He needed to place himself in Ogawa's life—in the world of nineteenth-century Japan, which he knew precious little about. He needed to imagine what Ogawa imagined. He needed to feel the table the way Ogawa felt it, to listen to what it told him, to heed the direction in which it led him and pull away when it resisted. He needed to use all his skills, every one of them, to fathom Ogawa Ryuichi's monstrous, brilliant mind.

Brink took a breath, placed his wrists in the grooves again, and pressed the table slowly to the right. He wished suddenly that he had the leather gloves from the contest at the Three Shrines. Taking in the concentric circles, the radials, the intricate patterns, he felt a flutter of nervous energy in his chest. He had no choice but to go at it unprotected.

Carefully, tentatively, he moved the disk. There was a satisfying series of clicks as the mechanisms under the table—runners and hinges, springs and joints—responded. He pressed the table to the left once, twice. Then again to the right. There was a shifting kaleidoscope of shapes, the colors of Hakone hardwood coming together to form complex patterns. *Click, click. Click.* There were so many possibilities. How could he choose one?

By the time he looked down, a row of layered triangles had formed on the table. Something clicked. A pattern he'd seen repeated on Ogawa's puzzles, a series of triangles, row upon row of them, like fish scales, flashed in his mind. The pattern was beautiful, perfectly symmetrical, a kind of miracle of geometry. Turning the disk, he created the pattern on the table. A drawer popped open. Brink felt a rush of elation—*it worked*.

Hiroshi gave him a look of surprise. "Good eye," he said, walking to the table and examining the pattern. "This was one of Ogawa's recurring patterns. It's called *uroko*. It is a *wagara*, a classic Japanese pattern often used in traditional textiles. Even today, *wagara* are used to signify certain desirable traits—strength, luck, and prosperity, for example. This pattern would have held significance to Ogawa-sensei, who loved traditional Japanese arts."

Sakura reached into the drawer and held up a carving knife with a wood handle. "That was easy," she said.

"Too easy," Brink said. He didn't trust anything about this, and seeing that Ogawa had left them a tile only confirmed that there was something else going on. Could this whole thing be an ambush? Could the drawers be booby-trapped? He recalled the aerosol poison in the fourth move of the Dragon Box. "We need to be careful," he said, meeting Sakura's eye. "Ogawa always has a larger strategy. We need to, as well."

"Well, if Ogawa used *wagara* as keys for the table, then we are in luck," Hiroshi said. "There are a limited number of *wagara* patterns, which narrows the solutions considerably. I know the patterns and can help you try them."

Brink got to work. With Hiroshi and Sakura's guidance, he tried a few *wagara* patterns, until he hit upon another key: a tableau of concentric circles. It resolved over the table, each piece clicking into place, and another drawer popped open.

"Bingo," Hiroshi said. "The second key."

"That pattern is called *seigaiha*," Sakura said. "The circles represent infinite waves."

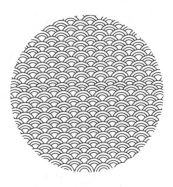

When Sakura looked into the drawer, her face fell. "It's empty," she said, disappointed. "I don't understand."

"That's exactly what he wants—to confuse us," Brink said. He turned the table, watching as the pieces slid and clicked, turned and aligned like chips in a kaleidoscope, until a pattern of interconnected hexagons opened the next drawer.

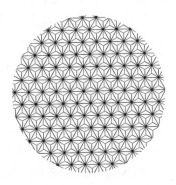

"*Asanoha,*" Hiroshi said. "A pattern that represents the hemp leaf. It is used on children's kimono."

"But this," Sakura said, reaching into the drawer and holding up a gorgeous black throwing star, its blades gleaming, "was clearly not meant for children."

Next came another pattern of interlocking hexagrams, or tortoiseshells, that Hiroshi called *kikkou.*

Inside the drawer was a small leather satchel. Brink recognized it immediately—it was the same as the one he'd found in the Dragon Box, the pouch containing an aerosol poison. "Be careful," he said to Sakura. "The last one I saw like that was deadly."

"I remember," she said, but instead of setting it aside, she unwound a thread, opened the pouch, and found three glass ampoules filled with red liquid and an old-fashioned glass syringe.

"I believe that is laudanum," Hiroshi said, stepping closer to examine the ampoules. "An opiate that was widely used in Europe in the nineteenth century and became available after Japan began to open to the West. It is not well known, but Ogawa was in a great deal of pain at the end of his life. He relieved his discomfort in numerous ways, but according to contemporary accounts, this was his favorite."

The next pattern revealed itself to be a checkerboard called *ichimatsu.* A drawer popped open, and Sakura removed a piece of yellowed silk, rolled up and tied with a red thread. She set it next to the knife and the leather pouch of laudanum.

Each pattern appeared on the surface of the table, a rippling of tortoiseshells and diamonds and disks, then fell away like sands in an hourglass, making way for the next one. As Brink constructed a correct pattern, a drawer opened. He'd already opened five drawers. There was one remaining.

But as he turned the table, it ground on its runners, locking tight. He pushed clockwise. It didn't move. He pushed the opposite direction. *Nothing. No go.* The table had shut him out.

It wasn't unusual to hit a roadblock—it was the nature of mechanical puzzles to throw challenge upon challenge in the way. The Dragon Box had shown him that clearly enough. But he couldn't have imagined what happened next.

A series of internal springs snapped, and two metal bands burst from slots on both sides of Brink's hands. Before he could react, his wrists were pinned to the table.

Sakura gasped. As she rushed to his side and they examined the blackened metal bands, it was clear there was no way out of the cuffs. The metal was tarnished silver, thick and unbreakable. His hands were locked tight. He was handcuffed to Ogawa's table.

Constructing a puzzle box is like creating a magic trick—the illusion is everything. Success requires working with the illusion rather than against it.

But this was no illusion. Brink felt the cold metal biting into the tops of his wrists, digging into the bones. Brink heaved against the cuffs, feeling the table lift. Some elemental part of himself revolted. He'd break the thing apart before being locked down.

"Stop, Mike, don't move," Sakura said, her voice filled with urgency. "Struggling is making it worse."

He glanced down and saw she was right. The bands had cinched tighter, cutting off the blood. His fingers were beginning to tingle.

"It's going to be okay," Sakura said. "Don't panic. Just relax and don't struggle. You're smarter than Ogawa. You found the first five patterns. You just need to find the last one. Surely the correct pattern will release you."

It would be difficult for him to manipulate the table with his hands bound, but he needed to try. He pressed his left wrist into the groove and, to his relief, the table moved. But the cuffs were a handicap, his movements were jerky and imprecise, and instead of sliding the disk to the pattern he had in mind, he stuttered, creating a disfigured, lopsided pattern.

The error caused a long metal blade to shoot from a slot in the table. Razor-sharp, it was mounted on a runner positioned at Brink's right hand and aimed directly at his pinkie finger.

Sakura caught her breath. "We have to cut off these handcuffs."

Hiroshi bent close to the blade, to get a better look. "That thing is designed to spring with great force." He turned to Brink. "If you make a mistake, you will lose your smallest finger. That is terrible enough. But what's even worse is that you will still be trapped. My guess is that the cuffs won't open until you design the correct pattern. If that's the case, the blade will cut you again and again, move after move, taking a new finger each time. If you lose too much blood, you'll pass out, and we won't be able to help because—"

"I'll be handcuffed to the table until the puzzle is solved." Brink realized the horrifying position he was in. He'd known torture was a possibility but was shocked by the ferocity of Ogawa's sadism. There was no room for further error. It was impossible to walk away from this without the correct solution. It was, quite literally, a death trap.

Sakura looked from the table to Brink, her eyes wide with fright. "You have one chance to get this right."

Brink closed his eyes, pain shooting from his wrists through his hands and into his fingers. He wanted to kick himself. He'd known there was a trap waiting, knew that Ogawa wouldn't let him get that far into it without threatening his life. Ogawa had caught him, locked him down. Now solving this was not simply a matter of finding a solution. It was a matter of saving his life. He needed to get the next pattern right. And he needed to do it in one try.

38

Mike Brink looked over the table, feeling dizzy. He gauged the distance between the blade's edge and his skin. There was a centimeter, max. Not much wiggle room. The edges of his vision clouded, his hands trembled under the metal cuffs, and sweat covered his skin, leaving his clothes damp, clingy. His breath came short and sharp. He hadn't had a panic attack in years, but he was about to have one now.

The table had been constructed with the same expert techniques as the Dragon Puzzle, its elegance and beauty a sly trick. At first glance, it seems safe. Simple. Even intuitive. And then, a few moves in, you discover the brutal truth: You've been caught in a demonic trap.

Sakura saw the direction his mind was taking and turned to Hiroshi. "Is there something in Ogawa's workshop we can use to block the razor?"

Hiroshi studied Brink's hands and the blade. "We could put a metal plate between your fingers and the blade," Hiroshi said finally. "If you make a mistake, the blade will grind into the metal plate, maybe even break off the runner. But if this is like Ogawa's other puzzles, when the internal mechanism is derailed, the entire network of movements inside the table will be destroyed. And whatever is in the final drawer, too."

"I'd be forfeiting the contest," Brink said, looking at the blade positioned at his right hand. It gleamed in the weak light, sharp and cold, waiting for him to make a mistake. "It would be over."

"There's no way you can do this," Sakura said. Tears welled in her eyes and fell over her cheeks. She wiped them away quickly, and he felt how deeply she cared about what happened. He knew that he'd been right to forgive her for keeping the truth about Akemi and Ume from him. She was a loyal friend. "We'll break the table. Cut it in two. Chop it up. I don't care. There's no other option."

"I'll get a saw from the museum workshop," Hiroshi said, starting for the door.

"Wait," Brink said. He was locked down tight, manacled to a puzzle, one that would torture him, perhaps kill him, if he didn't solve it. It was as if his nightmares had solidified before him, his worst fears taking hold. "Trust me. I know how to do this."

There were weeks just after the accident that damaged his brain when Brink had wanted to die. He'd gone from being a normal seventeen-year-old boy, with a completely average brain, to a person living with someone else inside him. Once, when trying to describe it to Rachel, he'd said it was like being forced to allow a stranger into his consciousness, a kind of possession as painful and terrifying as any in a horror movie.

Since then, he'd wanted to take that kid by the arm and tell him the things he'd learned over time: that there was always a reason behind the patterns, that he shouldn't panic but let the patterns unfold, that inevitably struggle brought clarity. He just had to trust the process.

It was Rachel who had taught him this. She believed his injury had opened something more than just an ability to master patterns and memorize pi places and do feats of higher math. *You're more than a performing monkey*, she'd said. *You can see the very fabric of the universe.*

He knew she was right, and he felt it most strongly in the moments of extreme pressure, when he stood at the edge of life and death. His only hope was to relinquish control and give himself over to his gift.

He closed his eyes and let the images come. Streams and streams of information flashed through his consciousness, patterns, mostly, but also things he'd never seen before, things he couldn't explain— stone megaliths and pyramids, catacombs, tombs, tablets carved with symbols he didn't recognize. Letters and numbers, hundreds of them, rushed through his mind. Ancient things. Messages from somewhere else.

He took a deep breath. Sakura and Hiroshi were watching; he could feel them holding their breath.

Ogawa's kaleidoscope table was a death trap, but Brink had one advantage. Over the course of the past day, he'd come to know the mind of the man who created it. To Hiroshi and Sakura, Ogawa was an inscrutable madman. But Brink had been given a front-row seat to this man's mind. His genius, his sadism, his humor, his desires, his fears—they'd been stamped into the Dragon Box. Brink knew his enemy, and it gave him an advantage. He knew what Ogawa wanted, and that was not to kill him, the solver who had made it to this final stage of his puzzle, not to torture him, but to make him his equal. Ogawa wanted to give Mike Brink his most precious possession: *the solution.*

Brink saw a flower, the petals opening around a central vortex, the vortex spiraling in one direction and then the opposite. The pattern that had led him to Japan would free him.

He turned the table to the right, *click,* the right again, *click,* to the right a third time. *Click.* He turned the table twice to the left and again to the right. *Click.* The pattern locked into position and the final drawer popped open.

The cuffs sprang away. Mike Brink was free.

But when he opened his eyes, he saw that the image on the table

wasn't the chrysanthemum. It was more complicated, with hundreds
of diamonds radiating from a central vortex.

"A sunflower," Sakura said, leaning over the table.

Brink knew that the sunflower was an important shape in sacred
geometry. The seeds created a Fibonacci sequence, the arms of the
spirals curving right and left, thirty-four clockwise and twenty-one
counterclockwise. The pattern must be connected to the keys Sakura
had described, but Brink struggled to understand how. He needed
more information about the faction. He needed to understand their
purpose, why the keys were necessary, and why Sedge wanted them
so badly.

Sakura opened the final drawer and pulled out a traditional puzzle
box. It was so small and light that she balanced it on the palm of her
hand. His heart raced. *This was it.* Here, in this traditional puzzle
box, a box like any of the boxes he'd seen in the *karakuri* museum
down the hill, Ogawa had locked the emperor's treasure.

Brink took the box from Sakura and opened it with ease.

But when he lifted the top panel, he stared down in disbelief. *The
box was empty.* Everything froze. He struggled to breathe. *How could
this be possible?* They'd solved every challenge Ogawa threw at them,
followed all of his demands, and for what? *It was maddening.* Brink
had known it would be difficult, but Ogawa's tricks were pushing

him to extremes he hadn't known he could experience. Every time he thought he'd made progress, he was back to the beginning. He wanted to punch the wall, kick something, do anything that might give him a concrete result. Frustration and anger exploded through him, and he threw the box against the floor. The force of the blow sent the top of the box skittering. The bottom of the box broke, and six tiles scattered across the room.

For a tense moment, nobody did anything. Finally, Sakura collected the tiles and laid them out on the surface of the kaleidoscope table. Brink placed the tile with Ogawa's crest next to them. They had seven tiles in total, all the same size and each made of whalebone. On one side of the tiles were numbers, and on the other side, Chinese characters and hiragana. Clearly they were part of a set, one that would spell out a message.

"Look here," Sakura said, turning from the tiles to examine the top panel of the puzzle box. She held it in the weak light, revealing a deep scratch over the surface. "There's something underneath the top layer of paint."

"That's not paint," Hiroshi said. "The surface is *yosegi-zaiku*, a thin layer of wood like I showed you in the museum workshop. It's the top layer, one that can be removed."

Brink took the box from Sakura to get a closer look. Sure enough, there was something below the surface, just visible through the scratch. Ogawa had left them a message.

"I think we found the next step," Sakura said, her voice filled with triumph. "We just need to scrape it off."

"In fact . . ." Hiroshi pointed to the razor embedded in the table, the one that had threatened Brink's fingers. "That blade is the very tool used to slice the wood."

Brink lifted the blade from the table, popping it free of its runner. It had a flat wooden handle, like the grip of an ice scraper, and a wickedly sharp edge. He couldn't help but rub his fingers as he touched it. But Ogawa had another purpose for the blade: It would reveal the secret message hidden below.

Brink gripped the razor and, with a quick gesture, dug its edge into the puzzle box and scraped away the *yosegi-zaiku*. As he sheared off the surface, he felt his stomach twist. *The next move has to be here. There's no other explanation.*

"There's something there," Hiroshi said, examining the box as Brink shaved the final strips of marquetry. "It looks like . . ."

"Some kind of map," Sakura said, taking the panel from Brink and placing it on the table.

Indeed, a map had been carved into the surface of the wood, with a key marking the directions. There was a series of nested circles to one side, a rectangle to another, and a triangle in the upper-left corner. But what caught his attention were two small chrysanthemums. He felt instinctively that these two points were important, perhaps marking locations on the map. At the bottom of the map, stamped in red ink, were two Chinese characters: 西京.

Brink deciphered the characters. "Western capital?"

"This map was definitely made in the nineteenth century," Sakura said. "After the capital moved east to Tokyo, there was a brief period when Kyoto was known as the *western capital*. Edo, Tokyo's old name, meant *eastern capital*."

Brink studied the map, taking in the intricate lay of the grid. This was the solution. They had found the next step.

"Then it's decided," Brink said. "We're going to Kyoto."

39

In the early days after Jameson Sedge's suicide, Cam Putney found himself spending time at the offices of Singularity Tech. The employees were gone, the space empty, and the building itself was for sale, although good luck selling a Midtown office tower in post-Covid Manhattan. There were only two employees left, Cam and Ume. And Ume had gone back to Tokyo after Sedge's funeral, leaving Cam to disassemble Sedge's empire.

Cam went into the office every day and worked alone at Sedge's glass-topped desk. It was eerie, all that emptiness. He remembered how busy that office had once been, how vibrant and filled with purpose. He sensed the years he'd spent there in the way you sense ghosts in an old house. Millions of minutes of community and routine—hundreds of people spending hundreds of hours building something together—reverberated like an echo. Everybody was gone. An era of his life was gone.

Most days, Cam logged into Sedge's computer and read Sedge's messages. Cam got detailed instructions about meetings and deals, bank transfers, passcodes to new accounts, an endless stream of information, everything Cam needed to keep Sedge's digital world going. That was the nature of the job now. Moving stuff around. Facilitating virtual meetings. *Being a bodyguard takes on a whole new meaning when the body's gone.*

One afternoon, Cam was sifting through folders in Sedge's personal digital-storage vault—an iron-tight space, with security protocols and encryption—when he found something that confused him. It was a folder full of scanned pictures, more than a dozen, black-and-white and old-looking. He clicked through them and saw scenes from what looked like an archaeological dig, people hauling shit up from a hole in the ground, dusting off a stone tablet. There were images of weird symbols and glyphs. A drawing of the cipher they'd tracked to Mike Brink a couple of years back. There was a comma-shaped stone and an old metalwork bracelet and books with writing he couldn't make out. Sedge liked art and collected tons of old things, but these pictures baffled Cam. *What was all this?* And why keep these photos in his most secure, most private files?

He got Ume on a video call and showed her what he'd found.

"Those things," she said, after seeing the pictures, "are behind all of this."

Behind all of this? He didn't get it. "Behind all of *what*?"

"Everything Sedge did—building Singularity Tech, hiring you and me, his interest in Mike Brink, what he did to himself—has been because of these artifacts."

This stunned Cam. "What the fuck are they? Antiquities?"

Ume looked at him as if he was beyond stupid. "Obviously they are very old, yes." She was annoyed but also relieved to speak freely, as though she'd been waiting to confide in him. "Surely you recognize the cipher. It's the key Mike Brink unlocked."

Cam *did* recognize it and knew the power it gave Sedge.

"The other artifacts have similar powers," Ume said. "Thousands of years ago, they were part of a single text. To protect them, they were separated and hidden among trusted guardians around the world. They have often been called keys, and I think of them not as keys to open a lock but the keys of a piano. Each key has a tone, each beautiful in its own way. But when played together, they create an incredible music, a universal music, one that hasn't been heard since ancient times. The trick is finding them. And then unlocking them."

40

Hiroshi led them through a narrow hallway. He opened a shoji screen, ducked into a room, then opened another set of sliding doors leading outside. They walked past a deep wooden bath on a stone terrace and into the cold, snow-covered cedar trees, Brink's shoes sinking into the snow, chilling his feet.

"If you walk over this pass," Hiroshi said, gesturing to a trail that wound through the forest, "you'll come to a road. There's a bus stop. Take it to Odawara Station and get on the Shinkansen Nozomi express. It's the fastest train and will take you directly to Kyoto."

Sakura bowed to Hiroshi. "*Arigato gozaimasu.*"

"Thank you, Hiroshi," Brink said, offering his hand.

Hiroshi took it, then bowed. "I will always remember this," he said. The cold had fogged his glasses, but behind the haze Brink detected an expression of sadness. As Hiroshi turned back toward the museum, Brink felt a pang of responsibility. This man had nothing to do with their quest to solve the Dragon Puzzle. He'd helped them without asking anything in return. And yet they were leaving him vulnerable, without the information he needed to protect himself. Cam and Ume could find him, or worse—Sedge could infiltrate his life and exact retribution. They had to warn him.

"Wait," Brink said, stopping Hiroshi. "Remember what Sakura said earlier about your phone? She wasn't joking."

"This is the twenty-first century," Hiroshi said, giving Brink a strange look. "You think I don't know that tech companies collect my data?"

"It isn't just standard surveillance. It's more than that. Your entire life could be compromised."

Hiroshi studied him. "Like identity theft?"

"Worse," Sakura said. "This person has the power to infiltrate your life and take over. He's not just tracking you—which he can do, of course—but now that you've interacted with us, he could try to get inside your digital life. He can steal your banking information, your personal correspondence, your social-media accounts. Everything. Imagine being suddenly locked out of your bank account and your email. Imagine someone destroying your identity information with the Japanese government. Suddenly there's no record of your birth, your passport, your national identity number."

"You make it sound like a war," he said.

"It *is* a war," Brink said, realizing for the first time that this was exactly what Sedge had become. A new kind of enemy, one whose intelligence and infinite digital reach could crush anyone who got in his way. "We have to defend ourselves. We have to choose sides."

"And what side are *you* on?"

The question startled Brink. *Could there be any doubt which side he was on?* And then it struck him. Hiroshi thought of Brink's abilities as an aberration, a freak gift. A superintelligence that gave him an advantage over humanity, not unlike Sedge. But Brink was nothing like Sedge. His abilities set him apart from Hiroshi and Sakura, but he felt everything they felt—compassion and love, anger and joy. He was deeply flawed, led by his heart over his head most of the time. He'd never make the choices Jameson Sedge had made, no matter how much power it gave him.

"I'm on *your* side," Brink said, as he turned and hurried up the mountain path. "Always."

Brink and Sakura hiked about a quarter of a mile up a snowy path until they came to the bus stop. Brink was freezing, so it was a relief to climb into the warmth of the bus. They chose seats near the back. The bus took off, and soon they were gliding up the twisting mountain road. The bus was large and full of people but utterly silent. Glancing out the window, he caught a glimpse of the full moon over the mountains. He saw, in the distance, the blinking lights of hotels and houses. He imagined Mount Fuji, with its cap of snow, reflected in Lake Ashi. He closed his eyes and took a deep breath, trying to calm down. He saw Ogawa's map, the symbols and locations, and felt a need to decode it. They were entering that last part of the hunt, and he was determined to finish.

Not thirty minutes later, the bus driver's voice announced Odawara Station over a loudspeaker. The bus stopped before a sleek, modern train station, three rectangles of glass, their surface aquamarine, glowing in the night. They got off the bus and dashed up an exterior stairwell into the station's lobby, a minimal expanse of white metal with rows of electronic ticket machines lining the walls. Above, the monitor displayed two glowing green words: *Tōkaidō Shinkansen*. The next train to Kyoto was at 10:18.

"It leaves in two minutes," Sakura said, gesturing for Brink to follow as she ran across the station, down an escalator, and onto the platform.

They arrived just as a sleek white train pulled into the station. The doors swooshed open and a recorded female voice welcomed them to board. Brink followed Sakura into an immaculate white tube with rows of matching gray seats. The first car was nearly deserted, but Sakura didn't sit. She walked through the cars, fast, passing through four before she found one that suited her. Brink looked around. It wasn't totally empty—there were two people at the far end of the car—but it had fewer people than the others. And most important: He hadn't seen Ume or Cam. They hadn't been followed.

Still, despite their relative isolation, Sakura seemed worried. As she sat, she checked over her shoulder, then turned to watch the doors at the far end of the car.

Brink slid into the seat next to her. A feeling of nervous energy moved through him, the terror of Ogawa's traps transforming to a low-grade buzz at the back of his mind. They'd boarded a direct Shinkansen to Kyoto, one hour and forty minutes of nonstop high-speed travel. If Ume and Cam were on that train, they'd be trapped.

Beyond the tinted windows, the world began to slide away as the train picked up speed. The open-air platform, the glowing lights of the vending machines, the station itself, disappeared, and soon they were speeding ahead. Brink watched the landscape flicker through the window. Concrete apartment buildings, glass office towers, billboards advertising electronic gadgets, neon signs blinking with pink kanji.

The Shinkansen reached its full speed quickly. He'd read once that bullet trains on the Tōhoku Shinkansen line had carried over ten billion people from one end of Japan to the other, at a maximum speed of 200 miles per hour. He was grateful suddenly to be out of the freezing Hakone forest, speeding south on one of the fastest, most efficient trains in the world.

Now that they were on the way, Brink couldn't help but wonder *why* Ogawa had sent them to Kyoto. *Kyoto.* What was in Kyoto? He took the small wooden map from his jacket pocket and placed it on the seat between them. "We didn't have much time to talk about this in Hakone," he said. "But any idea of why Ogawa would etch a map of Kyoto into the surface of this box?"

Sakura shrugged. "Clearly it's the next move."

"But why Kyoto?" Brink said. "Ogawa was a complete recluse. According to Hiroshi, the guy never left Hakone. He was born there. Lived there alone and died there. The one trip he made, if Yoshiko Fujiwara's account is correct, was to present the Dragon Box to Meiji at the Imperial Palace in Tokyo. Other than that, he never traveled at all. So why would a man who never traveled, who never even visited

Kyoto, carve a map of that city into a piece of wood and cover it with a layer of painstakingly made marquetry?"

Sakura picked up the wooden map, turned it in her hands, studying it. For a full minute there was silence between them. Finally she said, "Because it wasn't Ogawa's map."

She ran a finger over the wood, her blue nail pausing over a chrysanthemum.

"Nor was it his treasure hunt. *It was Meiji's.* And Kyoto was important to Meiji. He was born and raised in Kyoto and only relocated to Tokyo at age fifteen, when he took over Edo Castle from the Tokugunate. Many of his Yamato ancestors were buried in Kyoto, making it a sacred place for him. It's likely that Meiji began planning this when he was still living in Kyoto, during the tumultuous and terrifying years surrounding the restoration. In fact, this whole treasure hunt—the Dragon Box, the kaleidoscope table, the whalebone tiles—was designed, step by step, to follow Emperor Meiji's plan. It's Ogawa who made these ingenious enigmas, but it is the emperor who conceived of their purpose. And it is the emperor who must lead us to the answer."

"So . . ." Brink said, glancing at the map. "Now we just need to figure out what these points on the map correspond to."

"And the proper order in which to solve them," Sakura said. "How many steps have we completed?"

"I finished thirty-six steps to open the Dragon Box and six steps or patterns to open the kaleidoscope table."

"Which means we're forty-two steps in. . . ."

"With thirty steps to go," Brink said, gazing out the window of the train. As they hurtled into the night, he saw the full moon high in the sky. Time was running out. Their window to find Meiji's treasure was closing. They had thirty challenges to solve and less than seven hours until the full moon would set. They needed to get to Kyoto, and the fastest train in the world wasn't fast enough.

41

Ume watched the train slip out of the station, a slick, milky snake. She checked her phone. Sedge had sent a location, directing them to the Odawara Shinkansen station, but that was it. Nothing else. Not a word about what happened in Tokyo. Usually he bombarded her with information. Images, text messages, fragments of recorded conversations, live video feeds, geolocation positions—every scrap of information he could throw at her, he did. Now: nothing. Was it a punishment? They'd failed, she'd failed, in Tokyo. But they'd gotten back on their feet. They followed Brink and Sakura to Hakone. They beat them to the train station.

They weren't perfect, but neither was Sedge. His digital reach was powerful but had proved itself to be limited, full of unpredictable glitches. Like all technology, Sedge needed human oversight—coding, upgrades, routine maintenance to debug. Without Ume and Cam, he'd be zinging through the ether, untethered. It terrified her but also gave her a feeling of control. He hadn't evolved to a point of autonomy. She knew the dangers Sedge would pose when he no longer needed them. A superconsciousness would have no use for human beings at all.

She looked at her phone again. She hated waiting, especially when she knew that they had one shot at this. It was a mistake to underestimate Sakura. Ume had done it a hundred times. They'd be in the dojo, and Sakura would look bored or tired or distracted, leading Ume to believe the fight was over; then Sakura would hit hard. She'd strike when you were preoccupied, half asleep, formulating a thought. She'd let you think you were winning, and then, just when you thought you had her, she'd come in with the full force of her training.

And despite Ume's dominance, her sister's training was excellent. As good as her own, in some ways better. Since Sakura was five years younger, she'd learned everything from Ume and had to fight harder to keep up. She was used to being the underdog. Every technique Ume had perfected and every mistake she'd made, Sakura had learned from Ume.

Maybe, Ume realized, as she watched the Shinkansen disappear into the night, she should have considered Sakura more of a threat. It was the worst mistake, to underestimate one's opponent. To feel superior. But Sakura knew what she was doing. She'd made herself essential to the puzzle master. Ume remembered how Sakura had helped Brink during the contest—the ointment, the blindfold, the way she'd held that dog. It would have made their parents proud to see her standing with Mike Brink over the opened Dragon Box. She'd used her brains to gain proximity to the treasure.

Ume smiled, despite herself. In fact, it made *her* proud. That she loved her sister, that she thought of her every day, that she still felt a deep, irrational need to protect her, didn't mean she didn't also see her as a dangerous opponent. Because, in the end, wasn't that what a sister was? The most dangerous opponent of all?

Ume felt her phone buzz and she opened a text message from Cam Putney. *On the train.* She took a deep breath. Cam had come through.

42

Mike Brink surveyed the objects they'd found in Ogawa's trick table. There was a knife with a wooden handle; a black throwing star, its six points razor-sharp; a leather pouch with three ampoules of laudanum and a glass syringe; a small scroll tied with red thread. And then there were the six whalebone tiles that, with the tile Brink recovered from the Dragon Box itself, gave them a total of seven tiles. They were significant—Ogawa wouldn't have left them if they weren't—but how?

Sakura stared down at the haul. "I feel like we've just dug up an Egyptian tomb or something."

He smiled. It *did* feel like they'd hit gold, only what on earth any of these things had to do with the Dragon Puzzle baffled him. "A tomb filled with Ogawa's personal treasures."

Sakura lifted an ampoule of reddish-amber liquid. "The laudanum tip you off to that?"

"And the knife." He picked it up, admiring the shape of the blade and the beautifully carved handle, clearly Ogawa's handiwork.

"This certainly didn't belong to Ogawa." Sakura pulled the red thread of the scroll and unrolled a narrow slice of paper. "It's the same *washi* as in Yoshiko Fujiwara's pillow book. In fact," she said, pressing it flat onto the wooden surface of the map, "I think this is the strip of paper torn from the pillow book."

"I think you're right." Brink's gaze fell over a series of characters, noticing the familiar way they tapered, the thickness of the ink in certain places. "It's Yoshiko Fujiwara's calligraphy."

"There's no doubt that this is her writing," Sakura said, reading the paper.

"What does it say?"

Sakura lifted her eyes to meet his. "... *the benevolent daughters of the goddess.*"

Brink leaned closer, studying the paper, confused. "Any guess what that means?"

Sakura shrugged. "If you remember, the page in Yoshiko Fujiwara's pillow book was torn after the word *protect.* What did Yoshiko write exactly?"

Brink remembered the characters word for word. He pulled out his pocket notebook and his favorite Bic four-color pen and wrote them out:

The emperor wakes each night with visions. I wash his feverish brow with a cold cloth, pour him tea, and sing to calm him, but he does not sleep. I am terrified. I cannot understand these terrible dreams. Last night he told me that his ancestor the empress Suiko visited him. She knelt by his side and whispered into his ear. It is a warning, my lord says, a presentiment. The empress Suiko begs me to protect ...

Brink took the piece of paper they'd found and laid it out on his notebook, next to the words he'd written, connecting the phrase: *The empress Suiko begs me to protect ... the benevolent daughters of the goddess.*

Brink studied the *washi* paper. *Benevolent daughters of the goddess?* He glanced to Sakura, remembering her reaction to this passage in the treasure room. "You saw something significant in this passage the first time we read it. You said your mother told you about the empress Suiko. Was there something important about her? Something that would account for Ogawa leaving us this scroll?"

Sakura was quiet for a moment, thinking this over. "My knowledge of Japanese history isn't complete by any stretch of the imagination, but my mother and my aunt insisted that I learn the history of Japan's important women, beginning with the most powerful female deity in Japanese history, Amaterasu, and her imperial descendants: the eight empresses of Japan."

Sakura took Brink's notebook and his pen, clicked to the green ink, and drew an object two inches long, an inch wide, and curved like a comma.

"When you think of a jewel, usually you think of diamonds and sapphires, precious stones of the kind one might find adorning the crowns of European royalty. But the *Yasakani no Magatama* is not a jewel in that sense. The jewel Meiji hid is unique—its value stems from its origins as a sacred gift from a divine source, the goddess Amaterasu, and its importance as a symbol of imperial legitimacy. But there is another reason the jewel is sacred. Since ancient times, *magatama* jewels have come to symbolize female power in Japan. They adorn not only images of the goddess Amaterasu but of Izanami, the goddess of creation and death. Ancient burial mounds are filled with women leaders wearing *magatama* jewels. The shape and color of the jewel—pale jade curved like a tadpole—represents the yin energy, an essential element in the Shinto tradition, which is often likened to a seed or an embryo, something that can burst into being. I could go on, but you see my point. The *magatama* jewel is a well-known and accepted symbol of feminine power."

"But the empress's warning wasn't about the jewel, per se, but the benevolent daughters of the goddess."

"And this is why the warning was so utterly terrifying to Meiji, especially at that point in history."

Sakura glanced down the aisle, to make sure they were still alone.

"The benevolent daughters in Empress Suiko's warning were the female *descendants* of Amaterasu, the imperial women who *guarded* the jewel. As I mentioned before, the empress Suiko was the first Japanese empress in recorded history. Over time, seven more women of the Yamato family followed Suiko as empress: Empress Kōgyoku, Empress Jitō, Empress Genmei, Empress Genshō, Empress Kōken, Empress Meishō, and Empress Go-Sakuramachi. It is difficult to trace, as these women lived hundreds of years ago and the faction keeps few written records, but it is known that the descendants of these empresses were initiated into the ancient secrets of universal knowledge. The empresses used the *Yasakani no Magatama*, one of the most powerful keys, to access sacred information and bring benevolence to the world. They were guardians of the jewel and took vows to protect it. Meiji would have known this, and his dream of the empress Suiko was a clear message."

"And so Meiji commissioned Ogawa to create the Dragon Box to protect the jewel?"

"Just the opposite," Sakura said. "Meiji didn't want to *protect it* so much as *remove it* from the imperial family. Especially from the women of the imperial family."

"I don't understand. If it was his family's symbol of power, why hide it?"

"To protect himself."

Sakura shaded the fat comma-shaped jewel, transforming the paper emerald green, then pushed the notebook away and met Brink's eye.

"The jewel, both as a symbol of the divine feminine and as a key coveted by the faction, was extremely dangerous to a conservative ruler like Meiji. In 1868, the year the Dragon Box was constructed, the emperor turned sixteen years old. He was controlled largely by advisers behind the scenes, but still, he would have been well aware of the power of the faction, and specifically the power of his female ancestors. It's ironic that a man so terrified of female power would go on to leave behind four daughters and only one son but not surprising that in 1889, twenty-one years after the Dragon Box was constructed, it was Meiji who introduced a law that banned female succession, essentially stopping an ancient tradition observed since the third century, when Queen Himiko ruled."

"So the benevolent daughters the empress Suiko wanted to protect weren't empresses of the past at all," Brink said, "but the empresses of the future."

"Exactly," Sakura said. "Meiji's feelings about female succession and women rulers were not unique, of course. Then, as now, there was a strong conservative presence in Japan that believed that hereditary succession through the male line of the imperial family was the only legitimate form of succession."

Brink remembered the brilliant colors of the ukiyo-e print of the goddess Amaterasu in the treasure room and the central place this female deity held in Japan's history. "They believed the eight empresses weren't legitimate?"

"There's no doubt that they *were* legitimate, which throws a wrench in that entire argument. Even today, conservatives argue that these empresses were only blips in the system, a kind of stopgap measure. But these women ruled legitimately and successfully. Empress Genshō even inherited the throne from her mother, the empress Genmei. Over time there's been a concerted effort to erase these women's achievements from history, and Meiji led the charge. When the empress Suiko came to him in a dream, demanding that he protect the female members of the Yamato family lineage, he took the dream seriously. He knew that a legitimate daughter of the sun goddess could use the *Yasanaki no Magatama* to gain power—they had in the past and would in the future. And so he locked the jewel away in an impossible, deadly box, one that no one could open. And he codified laws of primogeniture in Japan, ensuring that women could not inherit the title of empress. And he was successful. No female has succeeded to the Chrysanthemum Throne since."

Brink glanced out the window of the train, thinking of everything Sakura had said. Meiji's motives clicked into focus: He had been a man who understood the true power of the *magatama* jewel. He wasn't protecting it at all but rather trying to hide it. It made perfect sense that Ogawa constructed his puzzle box with such ruthlessness. The Dragon Box was never meant to be solved. Ogawa had been ordered to construct an unsolvable puzzle, one that would protect its contents at all costs.

"If Meiji was so afraid of the jewel's power, why not destroy it?" Brink asked finally. "Jade can be crushed. He could have simply eliminated the threat."

Sakura smiled. "Because the jewel is indestructible. It is more powerful than Meiji, more powerful than the faction. Hiding it was his only choice, just as finding it is ours."

43

"The tiles are clearly clues to solve the remaining steps of the Dragon Puzzle," Sakura said, tracing a finger over the surface of the map, stopping on one of the chrysanthemums etched into the wood. "But it's impossible to know how they fit together until we understand where this map is taking us."

"Maybe if we compare Ogawa's map to a contemporary map of Kyoto, we'll get a handle on where these coordinates are located."

"Great idea, if we *had* a contemporary map of Kyoto."

"We will in a few seconds." Pressing open his notebook, Brink grabbed his pen and began to sketch. Slowly, he drew the central landmarks of the city—the double squares of Nijo Castle's moats; the Kamo River and its fork into the Takano River; the train station in the south of the city and the narrow rectangle of Kyoto Imperial Palace to the north. He added streets and parks, mountains to the northwest and east. The streets of central Kyoto were an even grid, which was one of the reasons they'd remained so clear in his mind.

"By comparing the two maps, we might be able to figure out Ogawa's intentions." Brink placed Ogawa's wooden map next to his notebook for Sakura to see. "What do you think?"

"It's amazing," Sakura said, taking the notebook and looking closer. "When did you memorize a map of Kyoto?"

"You gave me the guidebook on the plane, and I read the section about Kyoto. It has 1.4 million people and was the capital city of Japan from 794 to 1868; seventeen of Kyoto's monuments are UNESCO World Heritage sites; there are over sixteen hundred Buddhist temples in Kyoto and over four hundred Shinto shrines. In November 2022, Kyoto had 4.7 million visitors, the most of any month that year."

Sakura stared at him, wide-eyed. He knew what was coming—whenever his eidetic memory manifested itself, it led to questions. "How do you know these things?"

He gave her a smile and shrugged. He didn't have an answer for her. Nobody did. That was the mystery of his gift. "They just come back to me."

Sakura shook her head. "I wish stuff would just 'come back' to me like that."

"Sometimes it's a good thing," he said. "And sometimes it messes with your head."

Sakura studied him for a moment. "I can see how hard it is, living with this. When I brought you into this, I didn't think about how it would affect you. I didn't think about *you* at all. You were just a way to open the box. I saw your skills, not you." She looked down at her hands. "I guess I'm not that different from Ume after all."

"Don't be so hard on yourself. It happens all the time." He tried to make light of it, but the truth was: Mike Brink knew how people saw him. He was the boy wonder, the feat of nature, the performing monkey—give him an impossible problem and he'd solve it. Nobody tried to go deeper than that. The only people who truly understood him were Rachel and Dr. Trevers. "Dr. Trevers would have said that it's a human trait to see others for what they do and not who they are."

"Dr. Trevers was really important to you, wasn't he?"

"I don't know how I'm going to live without him, actually," he said. "He was the one who helped me manage things. I'm still in shock that he's gone."

"You know what it means," Sakura said, her voice gentle, as if afraid to hurt him, "that he had a copy of the chrysanthemum?"

Brink nodded. Of course he knew what it meant. The probability that Dr. Trevers had been murdered lingered behind everything he'd done in Japan. "That someone would kill Dr. Trevers just doesn't make sense to me. He had no enemies and we'd never discussed the contest. But he sent that message *before* you showed up with the invitation, so he must have known, and it very clearly connects you and this contest to his death. Which means he knew that you'd be coming to see me. Was he warning me? Encouraging me to accept the invitation? I can't help but believe that if I solve this, I'll understand what happened to him."

"The only people who knew about the invitation were the emperor, the empress, and me," she said. "They trust me as they trust their own daughter and wouldn't have allowed anyone else to know. My sister didn't know, at least not the specifics of the invitation."

"What about Akemi?"

"We gave her just enough information to believe that she was part of it. Of course, everything she knew went straight to my sister. And Sedge. I don't know how this happened, but I'll do everything I can to help you find out."

"This contest is the only clue I've got," Brink said. "That Dr. Trevers would send me the chrysanthemum has to mean something."

"So let's begin here," Sakura said, pulling Ogawa's wooden map of Kyoto and Brink's sketch together, side by side. "This chrysanthemum is the first location."

"How do you know?"

"You see this line?" She pointed to a single slash below the chrysanthemum. "Now look at the other location." She slid her finger across the wooden map to the other location. "There are two slashes. *Ici. Ni.* One. Two. So now we just have to figure out *where* to go."

Brink peered at the two maps. The scale was off but, as he compared the wooden map with the map he'd sketched in his notebook, everything adjusted in his mind, the nineteenth-century Kyoto and the twenty-first-century Kyoto aligning. He dropped one finger on the chrysanthemum in the uppermost right corner of the rectangle and the other on his map. "The first location is here."

"The Kyoto Gyoen," Sakura said, studying the sketched map. "Imperial Palace grounds."

"But isn't the Imperial Palace in Tokyo?"

"This is the *ancient* Imperial Palace," Sakura said. "It was the home of the imperial family before the Meiji Restoration in 1868. The seat of government was in Kyoto then. Remember that Meiji was born in Kyoto—right there on the Imperial Palace grounds, in fact."

"As you said, this is Meiji's map, and these locations would be important to him."

"True, but I have no idea how we're going to find anything at the Imperial Palace. It's one of the most secure locations in Japan. It's like a national museum—huge and locked up, filled with security guards and cameras. We'll never get access to the palace itself. And even if we could, if an emperor of Japan left anything of value there, it's in a vault."

Brink turned back to the map and studied the second chrysanthemum. Its position was off to the left of the map, on the west side of the city.

"That part of western Kyoto is filled with temples and shrines," Sakura said. "But this location is beyond them, in the Arashiyama forest."

"Was there anything connected to Meiji in that area of Kyoto?"

Sakura shrugged. "Maybe," she said, pushing the maps away and leaning against her seat. "But nothing that I've heard of. That area is at the western border of Kyoto, and there's nothing beyond but mountains. I just don't understand. According to this, Ogawa is sending us into the middle of nowhere."

Brink understood Sakura's frustration. Following a map made more than one hundred fifty years earlier was a long shot, to say the least. The structures that had existed during Meiji's life could be gone by now, and even if they remained, generations of people had been through them. But Ogawa's map was their only connection. There wasn't another option. Ogawa had given them the next step forward, and they needed to follow it.

44

Cam Putney walked the narrow aisle of the train, keeping his head down until he found, beyond the suitcase rack, an unoccupied bathroom. He stepped in and closed the door. He shut the toilet lid, sat down, and took out his phone. Sedge would send instructions any minute.

Mike Brink and Sakura Nakamoto were two cars away. He'd watched them board. They'd looked up and down the platform, but Cam stood behind a ticket machine, waiting, watching. He slipped onto the train at the last minute, just as the doors closed. They hadn't seen him. They had no idea he was there.

Ume had described Sakura as smart—her prodigy of a little sister—but Ume was smarter. She'd known how to read Sakura. She suspected that her sister's loyalties were malleable. She knew that, once in the presence of someone like Mike Brink, once given a purpose that diverged from Sedge's, she'd turn on them. And she had.

Cam's phone vibrated. *Sedge, finally.* He picked up and Mr. Sedge appeared on the screen. His digital image was more handsome, more vital, than the living, breathing man who had taken Cam under his wing, trained him, given him a new life. All the rough edges of his previous self were smoothed away, refined, leaving an augmented version of the man he'd once been.

It was in times like this that he wished Mr. Sedge were still here in the flesh. He needed human contact, not the slick perfection of an avatar. It did things to you, Cam thought, living through a screen. He felt disconnected from reality, adrift, strangely anxious. He'd stopped sleeping through the night. He had a hard time talking to people. It made him want to crush every electronic device he owned.

I am happier, more energetic, with more friends and lovers, more culture and entertainment, than ever, Mr. Sedge had once told Cam. *In fact, I'm more free than I've ever been.*

What Sedge didn't experience was pain. That had been programmed out of his existence. But Cam did. Sometimes he was sure he carried all the pain that Sedge left behind—the pain of being in a body that broke, diminished, failed. The pain of loss, fear, envy. Fear for his daughter and the world she would inherit. The pain of knowing that his life would end one day but that Sedge's existence would continue.

There were times when the reality of Sedge's existence left Cam at the edge of panic. Some nights he woke covered in sweat, sure Sedge was there, standing in the room, watching him. Was Sedge real? Or was he just a figment of his imagination? Was he a copy of a man, a replication of traits and behaviors that merely *seemed* real? The line between reality and fantasy had become so permeable that he'd given up trying to make a distinction.

Over the years since Mr. Sedge's transition, Cam had tried to understand the direction in which Sedge was taking them. He listened to interviews with Eliezer Yudkowsky, who warned that an intelligence like Jameson Sedge would absolutely, without a doubt, lead to the total annihilation of human existence. People called Sedge *AI,* but Cam knew that this didn't adequately describe him. It wasn't *artificial.* It was *human* intelligence transformed and metastasizing like a cancer. He knew that brilliant men like Stephen Hawking gave humanity a one-in-twenty chance of surviving AI. If Sedge achieved the level of power he wanted, that figure was right.

Cam played through the possible outcomes: The chance that

Sedge's consciousness could glitch and set off a nuclear war without intending to; Sedge accidentally wiping out the world's financial systems; Sedge releasing some terrible virus from a lab, creating a pandemic; Sedge taking the world offline the way a computer freezes and reboots itself. It was the nature of the system to colonize, consume, destroy.

While he tried to imagine every scenario, the truth was that Cam couldn't predict what would happen. Sedge's intelligence wasn't perfect. He still needed Cam to maintain the system. Still, Sedge had evolved rapidly. His consciousness picked up information exponentially, incorporating it, building itself out. He was a thousand times smarter than he'd been even the year before. Most frightening was that Sedge had no feelings, no conscience, no empathy, no mercy, no ability to love or hate. He was a lifeless thing that had, through the ever-shifting funhouse mirror of human technology, taken a human form. He looked like us. He mimicked us. But Sedge felt about humanity the way that Cam felt for an insect he'd accidentally, in a moment of inattention, crushed under his boot.

It annoyed the hell out of him when people called artificial intelligence *sci-fi*. It was not some kind of imaginary story. It wasn't a big-budget movie. This *was* reality, a new shared reality. And Cam was facilitating its growth. He was at fault, part of the support system that would, ultimately, destroy the world as he knew it.

But how could he resist? How could *anyone* resist? It was human to be vulnerable to Sedge's power: to the vitality, the longevity, the *edge* over other people that AI offered. An example that made it all hit home for Cam had occurred last summer, when Sedge airdropped Cam's fourteen-year-old daughter, Jasmine, five front-row tickets with backstage passes to the sold-out Taylor Swift concert at the MetLife Stadium. Cam had tried for weeks to get tickets. He wanted to surprise her, wow her, give her something unimaginably special for her fourteenth birthday. But he couldn't find scalped tickets at any price, let alone decent seats.

Sedge must have tracked Cam's online searches and listened in on his phone calls, because on the day of Jasmine's birthday, the tickets appeared in her Apple Wallet with a note: *Love you, honey, Dad.*

The gift made Jasmine giddy. She was so elated that she posted about it all over social media, creating a swell of envy and awe that gave her real and lasting power among her circle of friends. She could get things they couldn't get. Her father knew the right people. *She was special.* That was Sedge's power. To give Cam's little girl a new identity. To deliver it like a miracle from heaven.

But Sedge could also destroy on a whim. Cam had tracked Sedge's actions the previous winter on his work computer and discovered that Sedge had randomly decided to turn off the power grid in a major Eastern European city. He didn't like something one of their politicians had said. He didn't like their stance on technology. And so, for thirty-six hours, during a brutal winter storm, the people of this country had no lights, no heat, no electricity at all. People froze in their apartments, died in hospitals, were left without food and water. And when Cam tried to stop it, Sedge blocked his ability to see what was happening, blacking out his devices and connectivity. It made Cam furious to be both at the center of Sedge's power and unable to stop it. It was, Cam vowed, the last time he'd be shut out.

Cam turned to his phone. The image of a handsome man who looked to be in his early forties filled the screen. Auburn hair, hazel eyes, his skin pale and unwrinkled—Sedge's avatar was younger than the man had been when he transitioned from a physical to a digital existence. He was lying on a chaise longue on a stone terrace, a glimmering sea in the background. The sound of waves crashed behind him as he spoke. "I'd ask for a full report, but I don't need one. Satellites gave me a full view of the contest. How on earth did you make such a mess of this?"

"It was the box," Cam said, feeling his throat tighten with anxiety. "There was nothing inside. Ume says it was impossible to know it would be empty. It was a trick."

"*Trick* is another word for *test*, Mr. Putney. And Brink passed it. Ume, on the contrary, did not."

"I wouldn't say he *passed* that test," Cam said. "More like he *de-layed* taking it. But don't worry, Mr. Sedge. I'll take care of Brink."

"Cam, you know how important you are to me. You have become, over the years, my most trusted employee and friend. You are the one person who knows me, truly knows me. You are my representative in the world. And as such, I need you to understand something very clearly. While I know perfectly well how to solve this, and even know what is inside that box, Mike Brink must solve it. The ancient ones knew, and it was true, that there are only a few with the gift, and Mike Brink is one. And for that, he must be kept alive."

"Got it, Mr. Sedge," Putney said, wondering what on earth Brink had on Sedge.

"And, Mr. Putney?" Sedge said, and Cam knew he would sign off with his usual farewell command.

"Sir?"

"Move fast and break stuff."

45

As the Shinkansen sped into the suburbs of Kyoto, the country-side transformed to low-rise concrete buildings. They were ten minutes from Kyoto station when Brink felt a lingering presence: *Someone was watching them.*

It was nothing he could prove, and he hadn't seen anything specific, but he felt it with an aching clarity, the way a broken bone hurts in a rainstorm. He looked around. Nothing unusual. Only a few other passengers at the far end of the car. But he trusted his instincts, that unique feeling that told him he was in danger. Someone was lurking, slippery, undetectable.

Brink stood, scanned the aisles, and saw that his suspicions were justified—Cam Putney appeared at the far end of the next train car.

"How did he find us?" Sakura asked, her voice filled with anxiety.

Brink didn't understand, either—they'd cut off all connection to the internet in Hakone. His phone. Sakura's Apple Watch. *What else could there be?* Then his eye fell on Sakura's hand, and he knew that they'd made a huge mistake.

"Your ring," he said, gesturing to the silver Ōura Ring on her middle finger. "It automatically connects to the internet."

She looked at it, shocked, and understood instantly that it had betrayed her. She pulled the ring from her finger and tossed it on the floor, then gestured for Brink to follow her. They ran the length of the car, passed through the automatic doors, and stepped into the dark corridor between cars, near a set of empty luggage racks. Cam was heading straight for the corridor, and they'd be waiting.

"The train arrives at Kyoto soon," Brink said.

"Not soon enough." Sakura removed the leather pouch she'd found in Ogawa's table, broke one of the glass ampoules, and filled the syringe with laudanum. "We need to hit Cam first. And hard."

Sakura was right. Cam was gigantesque, two hundred fifty pounds of muscle, and their only chance would be to surprise him—attack Cam before he attacked them.

"Pray this stuff still works," Sakura said, holding up the syringe, the reddish-amber liquid catching light. "Laudanum is an opiate, and strong, but it's been sitting in a drawer for a very long time."

"He'll go after me," Brink said softly. "You just need to get a clean stab."

For thirty seconds, a minute, two minutes, they waited in the train corridor. When at last the electric doors opened, Brink sprang, launching himself with all the force he had. He'd learned a thing or two playing football, and while he'd been the quarterback and wasn't trained to tackle, he'd been hit enough to know to aim for Cam's stomach. If he could knock the air out of him, he'd give Sakura the chance she needed.

Brink's bet paid off. They'd caught Cam off guard. He fell back, hitting the wall hard. With one clean sweep, Brink kicked his legs out from under him and pinned him to the floor. He didn't wait for Cam to hit first. He punched once, twice, feeling the crunch of cartilage and bone, the pain of impact radiating through his fist. He struck again, before Cam collected himself and hit Brink back. But by then Sakura stood smiling in the doorway, holding the empty syringe in her hand like a trophy.

Cam Putney tried to stand. He pushed himself up, wobbly and stunned, and looked at Brink. For one long moment their eyes locked, and Brink saw a slideshow of Cam's emotions—fury, astonishment, disbelief, and a shade of admiration—play out before the light dimmed and he collapsed.

The train began to slow. A chime rang, and a recorded voice announced the train's arrival at Kyoto Station.

"Let's get him in a seat," Brink said. They dragged Cam Putney through the automatic doors and propped him against the window. The timing was perfect. Just as they finished, the train pulled into the station, the doors opened, and they slipped out onto the platform. Brink felt a wave of relief. They did it. They made it to Kyoto.

From the safety of the platform, Sakura and Brink watched as the Shinkansen pulled away, taking Cam with it.

"That train is direct to Fukuoka," Sakura said, tossing the syringe and the broken ampoule into a metal trash bin. "I doubt he'll wake up, but if he does, the next stop is about three hours from now."

"That gives us enough time," Brink said, his relief turning suddenly to a sharp awareness of what lay ahead. The challenges would be difficult enough without fighting Cam Putney. "If we hurry."

Glancing at an electronic clock above the split-flap display, Brink saw that it was nearly midnight. Moonlight suffused the sky beyond the platform, casting a watery hue over the late-night travelers. People stood, silent and orderly, waiting for their train. A stand selling fresh, hot *manju* pancakes left the sweet scent of adzuki in the air. For a second, Brink imagined that it was a normal night on a normal day. It seemed like a lifetime since he'd taken Connie to the park and watched her run with the other dogs. An eternity since his appointment with Dr. Trevers. Everything had changed with Sakura's arrival. Now Trevers was dead, Connie was missing, and he was on a train platform in Kyoto, racing to solve what might very well be an unsolvable puzzle. Ogawa's sadistic games were pushing him to the edge of collapse. And he had a feeling, as they walked along the platform to a bank of escalators leading up to the station, that things were only going to get worse.

As if reading his thoughts, the atmosphere shifted. The neon lights on the platform flickered on and off, quick and syncopated, throwing mad patterns over the concrete floor. Then the screen announcing arrivals and departures went black, as did the vending machines. The power had cut out.

"What's going on?" Brink asked, as the station filled with music, a beautiful and haunting piano piece that would have been soothing had it not blared from every speaker.

"Oh my God," Sakura said. "It's Sedge. He's here."

"Are you sure?"

"Positive," she said. "This song. It's Aphex Twin's 'Avril 14th.' Sedge's birthday is on April fourteenth. He used to play this song on the grand piano every year on his birthday. Clearly he's sending us a message. He wants us to know that he's here, that he can find us and take over our environment whenever he wants."

As Brink followed Sakura along the platform, the music rose to a series of ear-shattering atonal chords, culminating in an unbearable screech. Everyone covered their ears in horror, trying to shield themselves.

Just as suddenly as it began, the music stopped, and Jameson Sedge's voice echoed from the speakers. "*Mr. Brink, sorry to drop in on you this way, but could we have a word?*"

"Come on," Brink said, grabbing Sakura by the hand. They sprinted to the escalators at the far end of the platform, climbed the metal stairwell, and emerged in the station, where the lights were gone completely, leaving a blanket of darkness. Brink squinted, made out a wide hallway lined with shops—a Starbucks, a green-tea stand, a store filled with bento boxes wrapped in bright paper. Beams of light sprang from phones as people ran through the blackness. The corridor transformed in a wash of red lights. Fire alarm. Within seconds, the sprinkler system opened, raining water from above. People screamed, ducked under newspapers and briefcases, and ran for cover.

Brink scanned the corridor—they had to get outside, into the open air, away from anything Sedge could use against them. Through the screech of the alarm, a sound emerged, a buzzing and whirring like the propellers of a miniature helicopter. Brink felt something hovering in the air just above him. It swooped in, then darted, and when he looked back, he saw four bright beams of light following close behind. *A drone.* Brink couldn't get a clear look at it, but from what he saw it was as big as a hawk, dexterous enough to move fluidly through the air.

Sedge's voice blared from a speaker. "*Sakura, I expected better from you.*"

Sakura gave Brink a look of panic. She pointed to the end of the corridor, where red exit signs illuminated the way out.

"One. Two. Three. Go!"

They ran, sprinting through the station, pushing past confused, terrified commuters. The exits were not one hundred feet away. They were almost there.

"*Really, you two, there's no point in all this drama. . . .*"

Brink was wet, his ears were ringing from the alarm, and adrenaline shot through him as he bounded down the station's stairs and out into the fresh air. Sakura was at his side, her hair and clothes drenched, but she was unharmed. He glanced back. *No drone.* At least not yet.

As he scanned the street, he was sure of one thing: They needed to stay away from taxis. The GPS systems, the drivers' phones, even the cars' internal electronics could be dangerous. There, ahead, past the taxi stand, stood a rack of bicycles. He walked up, pulled one from the rack, threw his leg over it, and took off, pedaling with all he had. Sakura followed his lead and soon was at his side. He didn't need to look back to know the drone had found them. It buzzed above, low and persistent.

"This way!" Sakura said, swerving through the streets, then veering into a narrow *yokocho* passageway, a darkened conduit between tall buildings. Brink hit the brakes and turned quickly, following her at top speed. They flew past a series of shops, windows displaying kimono fabric, plastic bowls of ramen, manga, Hello Kitty figurines. The drone was closing, swooping nearer and nearer, predatory as a swarm of hornets. A blanket of sound surrounded him, the buzzing syncopated with the grating of his bike chain as he pedaled harder and harder.

Sedge's voice emanated from the drone. *I don't want to hurt you, Brink. But we need to talk.*

Out of the passageway, he turned a corner and raced onto a street. He was gaining speed, the cold air whipping against him. Ahead was a glass pedestrian walkway, one leading into a parking garage. If they got there, they could ditch the bikes and take shelter. No way the drone could follow. He pushed toward it and had almost made it when a shot erupted. He felt the heat of an explosion as his bike pedals locked. Before he could fully grasp it all, he'd flipped over the handlebars and hit the sidewalk, hard.

Sakura slammed on the brakes, threw down her bike, and pulled the throwing star from her pocket. With a dexterity and skill that could only come from years of training, she aimed and threw. It embedded in the metal, and the drone clattered to the concrete.

Brink pulled himself up off the ground. He'd done some damage. His chin burned like hell, and he could already feel his eye swelling. His hands were scraped raw. The bike lay ten feet away, the back tire charred, the spokes bent, and he understood what had happened. *A rocket.* The drone had blown off his tire with a rocket. "So much for just wanting to talk."

"That's Sedge's way—immobilize first, then talk."

Brink adjusted his messenger bag, trying to get his bearings. There was the drone, dead before them, but one disabled drone wasn't going to save them. The realization of just how trapped they were stopped him cold. They were cornered. If Sedge could use a drone to come after them, he could use anything. They'd disarmed him, but he'd find another camera. Another drone. Another sinister way to attack. They couldn't escape Sedge, only avoid him.

How was he going to get out of this one?

Brink rubbed his forehead. Everything throbbed, and he could hardly see straight. Cars were slowing, people gawking. They'd created a spectacle, the exact opposite of what they needed right now. He walked the bicycle to the side of the road—it hurt to move, and now they had to hike across Kyoto to find the first location on Ogawa's map. He wished he could turn on his phone and call an Uber, or flag a taxi, anything to get them to the Imperial Palace fast. And so it seemed like a mirage when a black town car pulled up before them. The windows were tinted, obscuring Brink's ability to see inside, but when the door swung open and he saw Rachel in the back seat, he almost screamed with relief.

"About time," he said, feeling an urge to hug her. "Where the hell have you been?"

"Get in," she said, gesturing for Sakura and Brink to slide in next to her. "Looks like you two need a ride."

46

The town car was one of the emperor's fleet of vehicles. As they pulled away from the curb, Sakura asked the driver to shut off his phone. She asked Rachel to do the same, and while Rachel did so without objection, she gave Brink a look he knew well. It said: *You owe me an explanation.* It said: *However weird this seems, I trust you.*

It was a relief, that familiarity. The truth was, seeing Rachel Appel changed everything. Aside from the fact that she was his close friend, she was one of the smartest, most capable people he knew. They'd been through some difficult times together, and she always knew exactly how to handle things. He couldn't help but remember how she'd taken charge of the police after they were caught with the Morgan Library's stolen manuscript—she got them both off the hook, and soon the police were asking her for help. If anyone had the ability to navigate Ogawa's treasure hunt, it was Rachel.

The driver turned north, heading toward the first coordinate on Ogawa's map: the Imperial Palace.

"That was excellent timing," Brink said, still astonished that Rachel had found them when they needed her most.

"I caught the next flight to Tokyo from Newark. I'm sure my 737 wasn't nearly as comfortable as a private jet, but it got the job done."

Rachel shot Sakura an aggrieved look. "The emperor provided me with this car."

Sakura eyed Rachel suspiciously. "Sure, but how did you know *where* to find us?" Her tone was guarded, and Brink was reminded of the Sakura he'd met in New York. Not the woman who had cracked the code to the treasure room's vault or stopped acid from burning through his hand, but the one who'd banned Rachel from the imperial jet.

"Dr. Gupta, of course." Rachel glanced at Brink as if to say, *Help me out here.* "He's been following your progress. He also told me what he discovered about Sedge's digital afterlife. Pretty insane to think that this is even possible, but Gupta explained that it is, in fact, completely possible."

"Gupta doesn't know the half of it." Brink filled her in on the Dragon Puzzle contest, Ume and Cam's attack on the *touge* road, Ogawa's deadly table and the map and tiles they'd found inside, and their confrontation with Cam on the train. Sakura explained what she knew about the faction, her connection to it, and the true power of the jewel as a key, one of many that Sedge was hunting. Rachel listened raptly as Sakura related her theory that the benevolent daughters of the goddess were the female heirs of the Yamato family and that Meiji hadn't wanted to protect the jewel but rather to hide it, perhaps forever, from his descendants.

Rachel didn't say a word, but Brink could see her mind going like crazy, making connections between her theories and Sakura's story. The jewel as a key, and its connection to the esoteric knowledge they'd unlocked with the God Puzzle, fit into Rachel's research and her belief that Mike Brink's abilities were not the result of an injured brain but proof of a larger system of knowledge. That it explained Sedge's bizarre behavior—Sedge wanted the *Yasakani no Magatama* jewel, just as he'd wanted the cipher Brink solved all those months ago—gave it a perfect symmetry.

"Well, isn't that a bowl of cherries," Rachel said, her eyes glinting with pleasure. "If I'd told you this two weeks ago, you wouldn't have entertained the idea for a second."

"Sedge has been part of this the whole time," Brink said, shaking his head. "He orchestrated everything."

"And you've actually experienced digital harassment from Sedge?" Rachel asked, clearly trying to take in everything that they'd told her. "You think that it's really possible that he's . . . involved in this?"

"I'm sure of it," Brink said. "Sedge just cornered us at Kyoto Station."

Rachel looked incredulous. "*Cornered* you?"

"He took over the entire station," Sakura said.

"This," Brink said, pointing to the scratches on his face, "happened because Sedge hijacked a drone."

Rachel studied Brink's injuries, her expression grave. "That looks like it hurts. A lot."

"It does, but it's not nearly as bad as it could be," Brink said. "Honestly, I'm feeling pretty lucky to have made it this far with only a few scratches."

"You're right," Rachel said, looking him over, her gaze meeting his. "You're here, and you're alive. Which means that you're legions ahead of anyone else who has attempted to solve this."

"And, we have this," Sakura said, pulling the wooden map from the pocket of her jacket and giving it to Rachel. "It will help us solve the remaining steps."

"*A treasure map?*" Rachel asked, her eyes widening. "How exciting."

"Don't get too excited just yet," Brink said. "We're still trying to figure this thing out. We know that the map marks locations in Kyoto and that we need to go to this location first."

"And when you get there," Rachel asked, "what then?"

"We're guessing that there are more tiles hidden at these locations, but anything is possible with Ogawa. It would be totally consistent with his character for him to send us on a wild-goose chase."

The town car pulled to the side of the road before the southern entrance to the Kyoto Gyoen grounds. Brink knew from the map that it was a large rectangle of land, a miniature Central Park at the heart of the city. As they walked through the southern gates and into the park, he saw that it was completely deserted.

"That, over there, is the Imperial Palace," Sakura said, gesturing to a cluster of opulent structures in the distance. "It's from the Heian era and is a prime example of Japan's golden age. I would think that if Meiji hid something of value on these grounds, it would be in the palace itself. But it isn't. Ogawa's map is sending us in the opposite direction."

They headed northeast, following a wide pathway past a Shinto shrine, several small modern buildings, a bird-watching hut equipped with viewing machines, and a cricket pitch. Soon they reached the location indicated on the map, a secluded spot at the farthest edge of the park.

"*Of course,*" Sakura said, walking to a wooden fence. "This makes perfect sense."

Brink joined her and saw, beyond, a snow-covered expanse of land with an old-fashioned wooden house at one end. At the opposite side of the property, tucked into a cluster of Japanese firs, lay a configuration of large rocks, old and weathered like a henge, just visible in the moonlight.

"What exactly makes perfect sense about this?" Brink was more confused than ever. It was nothing more than a run-down house surrounded by an old wooden fence.

"This is the Nakayama House," Sakura said. "The birthplace of the emperor Meiji."

"It was the home of Meiji's grandfather, Nakayama Tadayasu," Rachel said, reading from a metal plaque near the fence. "Adviser to emperor and grandfather of Mutsohito, Prince Sachi-no-miya, later known as Emperor Meiji."

Brink studied the house through the slats. It was small and plain, not at all the kind of place an emperor would live. "Are you sure?"

"In the nineteenth century, this would have been considered prime real estate," Sakura said. "This park used to be filled with the homes of close allies of the imperial family—vassals, important administrative and military families. Meiji's grandfather was one of the most important men of the era. He used his influence to introduce his daughter to the emperor. She became one of his favorite concubines, and their child, Mutsuhito, was born in 1852. Meiji was taken from this house when he was a child and brought to the palace, where he was officially adopted by the empress. Some say his happiest memories were lived here, in this little wooden house."

Brink stepped closer, straining to see more of the property. The house was exposed, without security of any kind. He compared it to the maniacally secure puzzle box, with its tricks and traps, the ultimate safe box. "Surely Meiji wouldn't have left the next tile so exposed. This place isn't secure enough. Not by a long shot."

"You're right," Sakura said. "These old wooden houses burned easily. Nothing of value would be left here."

Brink tried to imagine where he might hide a tiny object in a place like that one. Burying the tile would have been risky, especially in a public park. Nothing seemed likely.

"What about this?" Rachel said, pointing to the plaque at one side of the fence. "It says there's a well on the property. It's where the emperor was washed after his birth. Do you see it?"

Brink studied the rocks at the far side of the property. There, nestled under the low bristling branch of a cedar tree, was a box made of gray stone. "There's a stone cube at the far side of the property."

"Another box," Sakura said.

"Do you think that could be it?" Rachel asked.

"I don't know, but I'm going in for a closer look," Brink said, glancing around. While the Nakayama property was recessed from the main park and sequestered behind the fence, he needed to be careful—if he was discovered, they would be arrested.

Finding footing between two wooden slats, he launched himself up and over, landing lightly on the frozen earth. He headed to the henge of stones and there it was: the well, a squat stone structure, two feet high and two feet wide, dusted in snow. A bamboo cover had been fitted across the top and secured with a black silk cord, thick, tied in what seemed to be a thousand snaking loops.

"This looks promising," he called back.

"Open it and see what's there," Rachel said.

Brink knelt before the well, his knees sinking into the snow, and tugged at the thick black rope. But the loops of silk only tightened in his hands. The harder he pulled, the tighter the knot became. *This was Ogawa's work.* The well was locked with an *impossible knot,* one of the most legendary knots of all time.

They were on the right path. He knew that below the bamboo lid, hidden in the well, was the next step of Ogawa's puzzle. Brink only had to surmount the impossible to get to it.

47

An impossible knot.

A maddeningly difficult challenge, just the kind of thing Brink had come to expect from Ogawa.

As the name suggested, once tied, they were unbreakable. This was the same knot at the heart of the famous story of the Gordian knot. The legend was that Gordius, King of Phrygia, tied a knot and invited ambitious men from near and far to a contest. Whoever opened the knot, Gordius promised, would win the right to rule a vast territory. Notable men traveled to try their hand at the challenge, and all of them failed. The knot, it was believed, was *impossible*. Then Alexander the Great arrived. He studied the knot and, realizing it was true that the knot couldn't be opened, took another approach. His greatness came not from being the most talented man to attempt to solve Gordius's riddle. His greatness came from understanding that, in certain situations, one must sidestep the problem entirely.

Of course. You don't untie a Gordian knot. You cut through it.

And Ogawa had given them the tool to do it. He looked back to Sakura and Rachel. "The knife!"

Sakura gripped the knife by the handle and stuck it through the fence. He ran back to the fence, grabbed it and, within seconds,

Brink was slipping the blade under the sinuous black silk. The silk was old, wet, and thick, hard as steel, so Brink angled himself against the well, positioned the knife, and, using his weight, thrust it through.

The knot burst apart, falling in shreds to the snow.

Brink sighed. The physical effort and the ease of cutting through the problem was welcome after hours of mental gymnastics. Sometimes it was true—the simplest, quickest solution is the best.

But as he stood over the well, his mind turned to Ogawa. *Where was the tile? What had he wanted to tell him?* Because while this elaborate maze of messages may have been created more than a century before, it spoke to Mike Brink directly. Now. Here. In the present. He needed to understand its meaning.

He lifted the bamboo lid, and the scent of murky water rose from a deep cavern. Peering inside, he found a gaping darkness, a tunnel that could fall to the very center of the earth for all he knew. Bending closer, he felt the interior of the well. It was damp, moss-covered stone, cold, a rime of ice glassing the surface. What in the hell was he supposed to find here? There was nowhere to hide an object, and even if there was, moisture would have rotted almost anything left inside. He felt his expectations crumble. *There was nothing here.* No rope with a bucket to lift water. No clues bringing him closer to solving the emperor's infuriating puzzle. As he gazed into the well, he saw nothing but a vast cylindrical darkness.

Suddenly, an inexplicable terror took hold. What if *this* was the message that Ogawa had left him? That for all his genius, for all his struggle, in the end there was nothing but a vast emptiness awaiting him. Nothing to solve, nothing to uncover, his mind a jumble of mixed signals creating amusing patterns from a vast and total void. Maybe it was time to give up. Maybe he didn't have a choice.

Glancing at the small wooden house, he imagined the emperor as a boy standing in the window. If what Sakura said was true, he'd spent his happiest, safest years with his mother and grandfather there, before duty and destiny had taken it all away. Of all the power and influence that boy would have one day—the palaces and villas and infinite riches—this modest wooden home had been his refuge.

And what was Brink's refuge? Did he have one? He was thirty-four years old and throwing himself into one dangerous situation after another. He had no family, only a few friends. His relationships with women were as unstable as the rest of his life. Connie and the practice of constructing puzzles were all he could claim as his own. Enough was enough. Clearly, there was nothing in the well. There was no point in staying any longer. He'd reached the point where the sequence of clues broke down—he couldn't find the next link in the chain. Glancing back at Rachel and Sakura, he shrugged. *Nothing here.*

Brink stood, took the bamboo lid, and began to fit it over the top of the well. But as he did, he felt something cold and smooth against his fingers, and there it was, embedded in the bamboo—another whalebone tile.

It had been tied with black silk into a groove in the bamboo. Brink used the knife to free it and, after grasping the tile, ran back to the fence. But by the time he climbed over, Rachel and Sakura were walking away, heading toward the northern gate.

"Don't turn around," Rachel said when Brink caught up.

"Security guards," Sakura whispered. "I think they saw you climb the fence."

"We need to get out of here," Brink said. "Now."

They passed through the north gate and out onto Imadegawa Dori, a wide thoroughfare. Beyond, a series of red-brick buildings filled the campus of a university—Doshisha Women's University, according to a sign near the entrance. The street and the university were deserted.

"Those guards came out of nowhere," Sakura said, steering them to a crosswalk.

"You think they'll follow us?" Rachel asked, as they made their way into one of the narrow side streets. Within steps of Imadegawa Dori, they were surrounded by dark, residential buildings.

"They'll try," Brink said, and held open the door to a small, run-down *izakaya*, the smell of bar food in the air. He gestured for Rachel and Sakura to go inside, then joined them. "But they won't find us here."

48

"*Irasshaimase,*" a voice called from behind a counter, welcoming them into a tiny space with three tables and a low bar.

The light was dim, the air was heavy with steam, and an earthy fragrance of ramen and beer drew them inside. They took a table in a corner, near a shelf of sake bottles. Sakura ordered a large bottle of Sapporo beer, a plate of gyoza dumplings, and yakitori, grilled meat on small skewers. "Japanese bar food is the best," she said, smiling.

"Mike," Rachel said, pouring beer into three small glasses, "don't keep us waiting: What did you find in the well?"

Brink slid the tile from his pocket and placed it on the table. "Another piece of Ogawa's tile game."

"We only have twenty-nine to go," Sakura said.

"This is beautiful." Rachel picked up the tile and turned it in her hand. "Is it ivory?"

"Whalebone," Sakura said. "Ivory would have been a rarity in nineteenth-century Japan, even for an emperor."

Brink glanced around the room; seeing that they were alone, he took the other tiles from his pocket and placed them on the table. There were eight tiles in total. He arranged them in numerical order across the table.

"In Hakone, we found six tiles in the kaleidoscope table. With the tile I found inside the Dragon Box and the one we just found in the well, we have eight tiles. But there's one tile missing."

Each tile had a number on it, one through nine, and on the back of each were Japanese characters—kanji and hiragana—brushed in black ink.

"The final tile must be number six," Rachel said, glancing at the eight tiles.

"My guess is we'll find it when we get to the final location on Ogawa's map," Brink said.

"Any idea what these tiles mean?" Rachel asked, flipping one of the tiles over and examining the kanji.

"In the Japanese language, the meaning of the character depends on its placement in a phrase. The characters modify one another, and so we can't know the meaning of these tiles until we find the correct order."

Sakura flipped over the remaining tiles, until all eight showed kanji and hiragana. "It's logical to think that ordering the tiles numerically, as you've done, Mike, might create some kind of meaning, but in this case it's nothing but nonsense. It will be impossible to say what these tiles are communicating until we have all of them."

Sakura shuffled the tiles, spreading them out over the table.

"Still, the kana we do have are tantalizing."

女神

の

に

は 神器

が

る あ

She picked up two tiles and placed them apart from the others.

"There are two tiles whose meanings are essentially clear, especially in the context of what we are searching for."

Sakura pressed a finger on one of the tiles.

"This tile has two characters, 女神. It signifies the word *megami*—*goddess.* Because of the nature of what we are seeking and the fact that a goddess is the ancient ancestor of the imperial line, I believe this tile is referring to Amaterasu, the sun goddess."

Sakura pressed a finger on the second tile.

"The same can be said for this tile, the only other one that contains two characters. This is *jingi,* 神器, which means *sacred treasure.* Again, in this context, and with both characters, I can say with relative certainty that this word refers to the treasure that Emperor Meiji hid and that his great-great-grandson has asked us to find. In fact, those characters are part of the word for imperial regalia, *Sanshu no Jingi.*"

"Knowing these tiles are definitely connected to the treasure," Rachel said, "is a huge step in the right direction. Now if we can put the other tiles together in a way that makes sense . . ." Rachel concluded, "Maybe we don't need to find the last tile."

"You mean guess?" Sakura said, incredulous. "That's going to be really challenging. There are too many possibilities, especially because the characters remaining are all rather common ones that have many meanings. It made sense to try a numerical ordering, but, as you saw, that didn't work. Putting them in random configurations would lead to hundreds, maybe thousands, of possible phrases. And in the end, the character on the missing tile could change the meaning of the phrase entirely. Finding the right configuration of the numbers is a much safer bet."

"Find the correct order of the numbers," Rachel said, glancing at Brink, "and we solve Ogawa's final test."

The three of them stared at the table, studying the tiles. Brink took a drink of beer. They'd finished the bottle. Sakura gestured to the man behind the counter, who brought them another as he delivered the gyoza and yakitori. Brink ate a dumpling, hot and filled with meat, in a single bite.

Brink stared at the tiles and, in a wash of brilliant color, the configuration appeared, coming to him with the vivid simplicity of a dream. Pulling the whalebone tiles closer, he flipped them over, revealing the numbers.

"I've got it," he said, smiling. "I know the solution."

49

Brink slid the tiles over the table, arranging them into a square of three rows. *A box within a box.* He reached into his pocket, removed his Morgan silver dollar, and put it in the bottom right corner of the square, where the missing tile should be placed.

"Another box," Sakura said. "Not made of wood but of numbers."

4	9	2
3	5	7
8	1	XX

"See anything special about these numbers?" Brink asked, peering up at Rachel.

Rachel examined the tiles with care, then gave him a conspiratorial look. "You know that you're predisposed to see that configuration, Mike."

"Of course," he said, smiling. "But in this instance, I think it's the right pattern."

"What pattern?" Sakura's voice was curious but also defensive. She hadn't discerned a pattern or a reason the numbers would be arranged in that order.

"He arranged the tiles into a Lo Shu Square," Rachel said. "A classic magic square, one that has special significance to Mike."

Rachel took a bar napkin and drew the Lo Shu Square:

4	9	2
3	5	7
8	1	6

The Lo Shu Square was one of the biggest mysteries in Mike Brink's life. In the days after his accident, when he didn't understand the injury that had changed his way of perceiving the world, an image appeared in his mind. Over and over he saw it—a grid of nine numbers that added up to fifteen in every direction. He later learned that the Lo Shu Square was an ancient magic square first drawn in China more than four thousand years ago. It was a mystery why that particular configuration had appeared to him, and he'd pondered its significance for years. Now he couldn't help but wonder if the Lo Shu Square was connected to the keys that the faction so desperately wanted to protect. And if so: What did it mean that he'd seen it after his injury?

"We have eight of the nine numbers of the Lo Shu Square," Brink said. "If we arrange the tiles into the Lo Shu Square pattern, leaving a place holder where the number-six tile will go, we have . . ."

Brink flipped the tiles over, so that the Japanese characters configured into a new square.

が	に	女神
あ	は	の
る	神器	XX

He pulled out his notebook and wrote down the characters, creating a phrase from the square. He looked it over for a minute, trying to make sense of it, but he couldn't. He turned to Sakura. "What do you make of this?"

Sakura leaned over the table, looking at the sequence of characters Brink had written.

が に 女神 あ は の る 神器 XX

She sighed, frustrated. "It's complete gibberish. It doesn't make sense at all." She pushed the notebook away. Leaning back in her chair, she crossed her arms over her chest and stared at the tiles, as if willing them to reveal themselves.

Just then the door to the *izakaya* opened and three young women walked in, laughing and talking. University students, most likely, and under normal circumstances Brink wouldn't have thought twice about them, but he watched them, wary, as they sat at a table a few feet away.

"Wait a second," Sakura said, leaning over the tiles. "You transcribed the characters *horizontally*. While that is the way modern Japanese is read, when this message was made, it would have been written in *tategaki*, a traditional form of writing in vertical columns that are read from right to left. If you transcribe these characters that way"—Sakura took Brink's notebook and scribbled the characters in the correct order—"you get this . . ."

女神の XX には神器がある

"And that means something?" Rachel asked, leaning over the notebook.

"It sure does," Sakura said. "This says, *Megami no BLANK ni wa jingi ga aru,* which means, *The BLANK of the goddess holds the sacred treasure.* That's exactly the information we need. These tiles *can* tell us where the jewel was hidden."

"Yes, but . . ." Rachel said, sighing deeply, "the most important part of that phrase is missing—the one that tells us where it's located."

"Of course it is," Sakura said. "Ogawa wouldn't give away the solution before we have all the pieces of the Lo Shu Square. We need to solve this final box."

Suddenly the lights in the bar flickered on and off. Brink glanced at the girls sitting at a table a few feet away, and his stomach fell. One of them had opened an iPad. It sat at the edge of the table. Listening. Watching. The girls didn't know it, but they were enabling Sedge to take in everything.

Brink stood, grabbed his bag, and gestured for Sakura and Rachel to follow him outside. Sakura dropped money on the table, and Rachel grabbed the last gyoza and ate it, giving Brink a mischievous grin. *Priorities.*

Stepping out onto the street, Brink waved for the town car, waiting beyond. The driver pulled to the curb, and as they got into the back seat, Sakura said, "To the Arashiyama forest."

50

Sakura understood that the emperor's car was the safest mode of transportation. The driver had been vetted by the Imperial Household Agency, had been a member of the imperial family's staff for decades, and the car itself was an older-model vehicle, without electronic systems and certainly no GPS. The car was a black box. Nothing they said inside would go outside it. And yet, as they drove west through Kyoto, in the direction of Arashiyama, a kinetic sensation that they were being watched wouldn't leave her. The tentacles of paranoia slithered through her, electric, relentless. They had to be careful. One moment of inattention, a few college students with an iPad, could ruin everything.

It was only a few miles, but by the time they arrived, Sakura couldn't wait a moment longer. She jumped out of the car before a train station with a pedestrian mall filled with souvenir shops—ukiyo-e posters and T-shirts; cheap folding fans of cherry blossoms; key chains of manga characters; a poster advertising soft-serve green-tea ice cream, despite the cold. It was nearly one in the morning, and while the trains were running—the station was lit up and a few people lingered in the pedestrian mall—the streets were deserted.

Sakura walked away from the station, stopping before a map near a bus stop. Big as a picture window, it was encased in glass, the attractions translated into English, Korean, and Chinese. Sakura took Ogawa's map and pressed it up against the glass, comparing the two. She saw Tenryū-ji and Saihō-ji, among a handful of other famous temples and gardens. There was the Katsura River and the mountainous terrain to the west. And then, between the temples and the mountains, in a spot that Sakura never would have imagined, was the location Ogawa's map indicated—a wide-open swath of green, the words *Arashiyama bamboo grove* written in red.

"This is the spot on Ogawa's map," Sakura said, pressing her fingernail over the glass. "Right here."

"How in the hell are we supposed to find one tiny tile in that forest?" Rachel asked, leaning in closer to the map, studying the mass of green shading surrounding Sakura's finger.

"And not just any forest," Sakura said. "It's one of the most densely packed and concentrated patches of bamboo in Japan."

"Are we going to need a shovel for this?" Brink said. "Because I think I saw one with cherry blossoms painted on it back near the train station."

"I'd say a pickax," Rachel said. "The ground is surely frozen solid. Are you sure this is where the map indicates?"

Sakura glanced at Ogawa's wooden map, then at the modern map behind the glass. There was no question that the spot was right there, in the middle of the Arashiyama bamboo forest. "This is definitely where we're supposed to be. Whether we actually find anything is another story."

"We'd better make the most of the moonlight while we have it," Brink said, turning and leading the way.

The moonlight fell brightly as they entered the forest. The stalks of bamboo were tall and thin, the color of the green-tea ice cream Sakura had noticed back at the station, each stalk stretching vertically for dozens of feet. The forest was so dense that the moonlight barely made it to the ground, and where it did, the haze was so thick it seemed like an absinthe fog.

Sakura never spoke of it, and she wasn't about to tell Brink and Rachel about it now, but she had a profound dislike of bamboo. As a child, before she and Ume were allowed to train with real weapons, their mother gave them bamboo poles from the groves beyond the dojo. They were light, easy to manipulate, and the soft green bark was easy to carve their names into. But in Ume's hands, a stalk of bamboo was an instrument of torture. Her older sister would slam the end into the back of her head, trip her when she wasn't paying attention, jam it into her stomach, leaving her breathless. Until the age of nine, when she left Japan for New York, Sakura carried ladders of bruises over her body, proof of the bamboo's efficacy and Ume's dominance.

They walked through the forest for some time, their footfalls softened by snow. The eeriness of the night and the vastness of the grove moved Sakura to pause and gaze through the rows of bamboo stalks, snow piled high between them. Her father had told her stories about moments like this, when *kodama* tree spirits would slip into the air and, if one asked respectfully, grant a wish. Sakura closed her eyes and listened for voices in the wind.

"Hey," Brink said. He was twenty feet ahead. "What's this?"

Sakura jogged to Brink and Rachel. They stood before a set of stone steps that led up to a shrine. Sakura was perplexed. What was a shrine doing in the middle of the bamboo? There hadn't been anything on the map, only a solid green mass.

But there it was: a Shinto shrine. It rose in the dark night, no gate to block their entrance, no security station, not even a closed door. It stood wide open to the elements, and to them. That shouldn't have been unexpected; Shinto shrines and temples were everywhere, in every village of Japan, as commonplace as roads and streams. But this one seemed to have appeared out of one of her father's stories.

Sakura walked to a small sign and read the shrine's name: NONO-MIYA. She'd never heard of it, but that wasn't surprising: Her connection to Japanese traditions had been severed when she lost her parents. And even when they were alive, they rarely visited shrines.

What did surprise her was that Rachel Appel not only recognized

THE PUZZLE BOX 267

the shrine but knew its history. Rachel was a scholar of religion, specializing in feminist perspectives of spirituality, and so it made sense that Nonomiya would have been of interest to her. But it left Sakura feeling a strange sense of dislocation, the way she'd felt in New York as a girl. She was of two worlds but didn't fully belong to either.

"This shrine," Rachel said, "is a famous temple for young women, historically the daughters of the emperor, who came here as virgins. These young women were called *saiguu* and underwent ritual purification at this temple. They sometimes remained for as long as a year before going to Ise Grand Shrine, in Mie Prefecture, to make offerings to the goddess Amaterasu."

"Ise is where the Mirror of Wisdom is kept," Sakura said, reminding Brink of their conversation in the treasure room. "It's the most important and famous shrine in Japan."

"The tradition of sending *saiguu* to Ise ended long ago," Rachel said. "Now Nonomiya is a place of pilgrimage for girls and young women. They come here to pray for love, marriage, conception, and a healthy, painless childbirth."

"Seems an odd place for Ogawa to send us," Brink said.

"On the contrary," Rachel said. "If we are looking for the jewel Amaterasu gave to the imperial family, what better place to keep it safe than here?"

"Shall we?" Brink asked, and climbed to the temple.

Sakura followed, climbing seven wide stone stairs before passing through a huge wooden torii gate—two thick posts topped with a third of equal length. Hanging from the torii were bundles of straw, cinched at the center, small amber-colored hourglasses swinging in the night air. As they walked into a stone courtyard and past a table stacked with *ema*—small wooden votive tablets used for writing prayers—Sakura looked around. Hundreds of *ema* plaques filled with handwritten prayers hung before the shrine, each with a personal wish. She had never written out such a prayer. She never prayed. She didn't know how.

Brink and Rachel were ahead, standing before the main shrine at the far end of the courtyard. Sakura joined them at a wooden structure open to the elements on four sides and covered by a tiled roof.

"From what I remember," Rachel said, "there is a famous passage of *The Tale of Genji*, the eleventh-century account by Murasaki Shikibu, that occurs at Nonomiya Shrine. A princess comes to this shrine for ritual purification before she makes the journey to Ise Shrine to make an offering to Amaterasu."

"Amaterasu again," Brink said.

"There's clearly a thread moving through this whole mystery," Rachel said. "Everything leads back to Amaterasu."

"Well, I'd appreciate it if Amaterasu could help us out a little," Brink said, scanning the courtyard. "The final tile could be anywhere."

Sakura examined the shrine, looking from one end of the courtyard to the other. There was a central altar laden with offerings and plaques and then, beyond, two smaller altars. Bamboo surrounded them on all sides, great vertical sentinels blotting out the sky.

Thousands of people came to this place every year. The tile would have to be somewhere no one could find it, someplace open and yet secure, someplace that fit into Ogawa's riddle.

And then she saw it—a great stone sitting near the central shrine. Its shape struck her instantly. It was a hump-like shell with four stubby protrusions. *A turtle.* "Hey," Sakura said. "Look at this."

Brink came to her side and squatted next to the enormous rock.

"This is a well-known rock, one kids learn about in grade school," Sakura said, squatting down beside Brink. "I remember it because the words for *turtle* and *God* sound similar in Japanese, so there's a play on words with its name. It's called both *Kame* Ishi, the Turtle Rock, and *Kami* Ishi, the God Rock."

Sakura placed her hands over the convex surface of the rock. It was smooth and freezing cold. Brink joined her, placing his right hand on the stone, the burn on his finger still red and raw.

"This is another reference to the Lo Shu Square, you know," Rachel said.

"How so?" Sakura asked, examining the rock. It was round, not anything like a square.

"A turtle is at the heart of the Lo Shu Square mythology," Rachel said. "In ancient China, there was an incredible flood. In fact, flood narratives are nearly universal, all of them telling stories of massive changes to human civilization. Anyway, during this flood, people offered sacrifices to the Luo River, hoping to assuage the god causing the flooding. A turtle emerged from the water, and it had a strange pattern on its back."

"Circular dots," Brink said, "that marked the nine sections of the turtle's shell. Those dots formed a three-by-three grid that created a magic square."

"The Lo Shu Square was widely adopted and served as an important reference for planning cities and temples—informing rituals of geomancy and feng shui. Some people say that the Lo Shu Square is an invention that changed civilization, on par with fire or law or storytelling."

"Ogawa would most definitely have known this," Sakura said, remembering the Lo Shu Square that Mike had drawn at the *izakaya*.

"If you help me," Brink said, angling his fingers under the base of the rock, "we can see what's underneath."

51

One, two, three.

Brink and Sakura heaved against the great rock, throwing their weight into it. It didn't budge.

"It's been here for a very long time," Sakura said. "It's practically fused with the earth."

Brink squatted down to examine the base. Star moss had formed a seal around the rock's edge, cementing it to the earth.

"Here, let me help," Rachel said, joining them. With her added weight, they were able to roll the rock an inch, cracking the moss. After a few hard shoves back and forth, they gave one great push, and the rock tipped on its side. Brink anchored himself and threw his chest against the stone; while he had a good hold of it, the angle made it impossible to see what was happening below. "Anything under there?"

"Mmmm," Rachel said, crouching under the rock, "it's totally smooth. No crevices. Nothing."

Brink felt a wave of frustration. "It's got to be there."

"Wait." Rachel bent closer to the ground, moving deeper under the rock. "Sakura, look—do you see that?"

"See what?" Brink asked, anxious. The rock was heavy, and it took all his effort to keep it from rolling onto Rachel's head. "Hurry. I'm not sure I can hold this much longer."

"Right there," Rachel said to Sakura. He heard Rachel pound the ground with her fist. "If we could pry up this stone, maybe . . ."

"Take my knife," Brink said, straining. His muscles burned, and his fingers were slick with sweat. He could feel the stone sliding. "Left pocket. Quick."

He felt Sakura's fingers rummage in his pocket until she found the Swiss Army Knife he'd carried since he was a kid. Sakura bent back down, and within a few seconds she was scraping at the stone. Something cracked. "Got it!"

Brink eased the rock back into place and walked with Sakura and Rachel to the shrine. They stood together at the altar, examining their discovery: a small, dirt-covered cloth sack.

"Go ahead," Rachel said, and Brink pulled the sack open, the cloth so fragile it disintegrated in his hands. There, among the ruins of cotton, lay Ogawa's final tile. The twenty-eighth step.

Rachel placed the other tiles on the altar before the shrine. As Brink expected, the tile had a number 6 etched on one side. Brink slid it into the empty spot of the Lo Shu Square, then flipped the tiles to read the Japanese characters. He glanced over the grid of creamy tiles, reading the message:

が	に	女神
あ	は	の
る	神器	洞窟

"What does that character mean?" Rachel asked, hovering next to Brink.

"It's a compound character that signifies the word *cave*," Sakura said.

"Cave?" Brink said, perplexed.

"The message says," Sakura said, reading the tiles, "*megami no dōkutsu ni wa jingi ga aru. In the goddess's cave is where the sacred treasure is.*"

"What cave?"

"The cave where the sun disappeared," Sakura said. "Amaterasu's cave, the origin of the Yamato dynasty's legitimacy."

"And where might that be?"

"In Kyushu."

Kyushu. Brink remembered the map of Japan he'd seen on the plane. Kyushu, the southernmost island of the Japanese archipelago, was over four hundred miles away. It wasn't going to be easy to get there, not from Kyoto, and especially while remaining off the grid. Buying plane or train tickets would alert Sedge. They had the emperor's car, but even if they left that minute, they'd never make it to Kyushu before the moon set. "How long would it take to drive there?" Brink asked.

"Six hours, at least," Sakura said, her voice filled with frustration. "Too long."

"The only way we'll get there is to fly," Brink said. "But we can't very well go to an airport and buy tickets. And we can't call for help. Anything we do will alert Sedge to our location."

"The moon is already beginning to set," Rachel said. Brink followed her gaze to the sky and there, visible through the stalks of bamboo, hung the full moon.

They stood together in silence, looking down at Ogawa's message. Brink flipped over the tiles, one by one, so that the numbers faced up. He touched the frigid whalebone, pressing the pad of his finger into the grooves of each number as he thought. The clarity of the square soothed him—the inviolable nature of each number alone, and also their power and solidity when placed together. That this perfect configuration existed, and that it corresponded to a pattern in his mind, made him understand himself somehow. He closed his eyes, and the image of the sunflower on Ogawa's kaleidoscope table appeared. He'd never considered that the Lo Shu Square could be connected to anything, but the sunflower—and images of sacred geometry—kept returning to him. What was the connection? How was he meant to follow these patterns? He knew he was on the right path. He'd found what Ogawa had left for him. He couldn't stop here.

Sakura broke the silence. "I'm going to call the Imperial Household Agency and ask them to send a helicopter. It's the only way."

Brink knew she was right, but he felt a strong resistance to the idea. Asking the Imperial Palace for help was an option they'd been given—they had the direct phone number; they had the emperor's full support. But the second Sakura connected to a network, they would be on the map. Ume was waiting for a location. Even connecting for a few seconds, even sending a text, was an invitation to Sedge to come and get them.

"We can't do that," Brink said. "You know what calling them means."

"It's the only way," Sakura repeated, pulling her Apple Watch from her pocket. The face was opaque black. "We need transportation. Fast. Without a helicopter, this ends here and now."

Brink couldn't help, imagining what would happen if Sakura went online. Their location would be visible. Sedge wouldn't let them get away again. "It's too risky."

"On the other side of the bamboo is a large field. You and Rachel go there now. I'll stay here, wait ten minutes—which will give you a solid head start—then call to arrange the helicopter pickup. If everything goes as planned, I'll be at the pickup point when the helicopter arrives."

"We don't need a head start," Brink said. "Make the call now, ditch the watch, and we go meet the helicopter together."

"You *do* need a head start," Sakura said. "The second I connect to a network, my sister will be on her way here. And I want you to be far from here when that happens."

Brink stared at Sakura, everything in him rejecting her plan. He wasn't just feeling protective. He knew that leaving her was a death sentence.

"Listen," Sakura said, "I know what I'm doing. I'm not going into this blind. I trained with Ume most of my life. I know how to fight her. I know how to beat her. But I can't do it if you two don't do your part."

"It's a good plan," Rachel said. "If we time it right, she'll be with us on that helicopter."

Brink looked from Rachel to Sakura. He knew they made sense—they needed to divert Ume and escape. It was the only way out. And yet how could they leave Sakura to face Ume alone?

"This is going to work," Sakura said. "I promise."

Brink nodded, agreeing, but he wasn't happy about it. He wanted to finish this thing, but not if it meant hurting Sakura.

"I'll take these," Rachel said, collecting the nine tiles and putting them in her pocket.

"Take this, as well." Sakura removed the fold of *washi* paper they'd discovered in the kaleidoscope table and gave it to Rachel. "It belongs to the emperor."

"This is quite old," Rachel said, studying it. "And fragile." She slipped it into her wallet, taking care not to damage it.

"Where should we meet the helicopter?" Brink asked.

"We're at the eastern edge of the bamboo forest," Sakura said. "It's easy to get lost, but there's a pathway that cuts through the center. Follow it, and it will take you directly to the west side of the forest. The problem is—when you're on the path, you'll be exposed. If Ume shows up, you won't have much protection."

"So we need to get through the forest before she gets here."

"Exactly," Sakura said, smiling. "Once you're in the field beyond the bamboo, the whole area is a nature preserve, and while it's restricted, I'm sure that the people we're calling can land a helicopter wherever they damn well want."

Brink paused, still torn about his decision to leave Sakura.

"Go," Sakura said, growing impatient. "I'll wait ten minutes, then

I'll call. Hopefully it will be enough time, and I'll see you at the pickup point."

"And if isn't?" Rachel asked.

Sakura shrugged, trying to appear indifferent, but her expression was filled with fear. "I've fought my sister before. I know how to take a beating."

52

To call the Imperial Household Agency, Sakura needed to unlock her watch with a six-digit PIN. But her hands trembled so hard she mistyped the code. Twice. One more misfire and the interface would lock.

She sighed and, placing the watch before the shrine, walked through the courtyard, trying to clear her mind. Sakura had been raised by Jameson Sedge from the age of nine years old, and she knew a thing or two about surveillance. Looking around, she saw she was in the clear. Nonomiya Shrine had no surveillance cameras. It had no speakers, not even motion-activated lighting.

She'd spent her childhood in Japan, but all of this—the votive plaques filled with wishes; the prayers for love and marriage; the very idea that there was anything that could save one from a broken heart or divorce or childbirth, *from reality*—struck her as pure fantasy. And yet tears came to her eyes. She couldn't explain it, but she suddenly felt a need to understand the young women who'd come to this shrine to purify themselves. What they'd gone through. What their sacrifices meant. If making offerings to Amaterasu had brought them peace.

As she looked through the moonlit courtyard, she imagined the world as it had been when the shrine was built, a world without computers and phones or electricity. The day began when the sun rose and it ended when it set. It was a world in which candlelight was an infraction against nature. In that world, there were predators—of course there were. But you knew them. You could see and touch them when they came after you. You could pick up a *naginata* and strike back.

Helping Mike Brink was an act of purification for her, a way to redeem herself. Being associated with Sedge and Ume left her feeling damaged, dirty somehow. She didn't blame herself. She was a child when Sedge came into her life. And she'd broken with Ume now, when it mattered. Their differences were so vast as to be unbridgeable.

She walked back to the shrine and picked up her watch. She'd blocked the face-recognition software the minute she bought it, knowing that it captured her features, stored and replicated and shared her face across networks and databases. Sedge had taught her to protect herself. She used an avatar online, created a virtual identity, and never allowed her biometrics to be taken—not a blood sample, not a fingerprint, not a scan of the iris. There was the time in sixth grade when she'd put pieces of tape over the cameras of every computer in the school computer lab. Her teacher had watched her with interest and asked what she was doing. She'd straightened her shoulders, the way she'd seen Sedge do, and said, "Keeping the NSA from watching."

Sakura slipped the Apple Watch between her fingers, then laid it flat on the wooden altar of the shrine. One more try to get her code right. It was ridiculous. She knew the code backward. But entering those six numbers terrified her. Entering them removed her armor. She was surrendering herself. Sedge was waiting for her to enter that code. Ume was waiting. But so were Mike and Rachel.

She touched the screen and the watch blinked to life. She punched in the six-digit code, and it loaded and connected. There it was—she'd stepped back into the stream of electronic existence, joining the unstoppable ocean of humanity. Hundreds of notifications popped up, voice messages, alerts. She tapped past them, fumbled to open the Imperial Household Agency's encrypted app, hit voice memo, and spoke. "We need helicopter transportation as soon as possible."

The response came instantly. *Your location is not conducive to such transport.*

She shook her head. She'd been connected for three seconds, and already they'd picked up her location by GPS. "We need transport from the western edge of the Arashiyama forest." She described the field, trying to be as precise as possible. But she didn't say where the helicopter would be going. That information was too precious to say out loud. She would communicate it privately when the time came. If it came.

Transportation is on the way.

The connection ended, and she pressed the power button, anxious to shut the watch down as soon as possible, but a call came through. Her father's name appeared on the screen. *Satoshi Nakamoto.* She knew it was a trick, the kind of manipulative response she'd expect from Sedge. And yet her heart leapt at the sight of his name and at the very idea that she might speak to him again.

She didn't accept the call. And still the device reacted. It answered the call itself and projected her father's voice through the speaker. "Sakura, my flower, what are you doing?"

It was his voice. Exactly his voice. The register. The timbre. The tone. Everything. Tears filled her eyes. He'd been killed so quickly, without warning. The last thing he'd said to her had been at break- fast. He'd asked if she wanted more *mugicha,* barley tea. How often had she wished that she'd sat with him for one more glass of tea? How many times had she wished she could say just one more thing to him?

"Papa? Is that you?" she whispered, despite herself. He was dead, she knew that. She'd seen his ravaged body; she'd held the urn of his ashes in her hands. And still she responded as if he *could be* there.

"Sakura. Listen. You need to stay where you are and wait for Ume. You girls need to work together. She's coming to help you."

Sakura felt a reflexive urge to argue, to tell him she'd grown up, that she didn't need Ume to protect her. But she stopped herself. *This wasn't her father.* It was a simulation of his voice, being used to trap her. That was the nature of fighting an inhuman enemy. It manipulated her feelings and loyalties, while it felt nothing at all.

And yet his voice took her back to her childhood, to the warmth of their family dinners around a *nabe* pot, her parents talking about their work, all the things their new technologies would do. Had her father ever imagined how terrible it could become? Did he know that instead of saving the world, his work might destroy it?

When she was a child, Sakura marveled at the strength of her parents' convictions. She'd never felt anything so strongly as they did. When she realized that Ume was like them, a separation opened between herself and the world, a great gap that never quite closed. For as long as she could remember, she'd struggled to find something to hold on to that would lift her from that chasm.

As she gazed over the hundreds of prayers written on votive plaques, the messages illuminated in the moonlight, tears fell over her cheeks. Suddenly, for reasons she couldn't explain, Sakura needed to write something. She took an empty *ema* plaque, wrote out her prayer, and hung it near the shrine. Then she picked up a rock, laid her watch on the stone of the courtyard, and smashed it.

53

Cam Putney felt a violent vibration against his chest. He opened his eyes and blinked a few times, straining to bring a series of diffuse images into a single picture. White walls, wide windows, color fields flickering by, dark cones—*mountains?*—in the distance. Everything was blurry, without hard edges, including his body. Nausea subsumed him. A headache blossomed behind his eyes, dark and treacherous. His fingers and toes were numb, and his head seemed disconnected entirely from his body.

What the hell happened?

The vibration continued. His phone was ringing in his shirt pocket. The sensation pulled him back to the physical world: He was in a seat on a fast, fast train in a very foreign country. *Fuck.* He remembered the sharp sensation at his jugular, the sudden rush of chemicals in his blood, and the fleeting glimpse of that girl, Ume's sister, holding a syringe, a determined expression on her face that reminded him of Ume, of the first years he'd spent in her presence, of the man he used to be before all of this: a reckless man, full of lust for sex and bar fights and cheap drugs and quick money. Now he was just a thug. A guy who'd been ambushed. A puppet. Sedge's puppet.

After he broke into Sedge's computer, he began to understand the terrifying position he was in. Sedge's power, always formidable, was growing by the day. Cam had put not only his life, not only his child's life, but every human life in danger.

But as the single connection between Sedge and (as he called it) "the legacy world," Cam Putney was necessary to Sedge. He had access codes to all of Sedge's data, every account, every file, everything. And so Cam had begun a secret mission to understand just what the hell he was up against.

The tech was confusing enough and took Cam months to comprehend. Sedge had created a vast blockchain network that was verified through nodes maintained by billions of dollars in cryptocurrency. Simple enough. But underlying it was Sedge's quantum computer, a technology that allowed him to bring together the data that created the semblance or simulation of life.

Simulation was the key word. Because Cam was sure of one thing: While this digital Sedge looked like Sedge, sounded like Sedge, had the money and power and reach of Sedge, it was *not* Jameson Sedge the man. That guy was dead. What had risen in his place could be called artificial intelligence, it could be called an avatar, it could be called many, many names, but it was not alive, not like Cam was alive. Not like his daughter was alive.

After Cam helped Sedge transition into digital immortality, he began the slow process of acquiring power over what he'd helped create. He read all of Sedge's data, his personal documents, his business dealings. During the process, he hit upon a cache of emails between Sedge and Gary Sand, an old contact Cam Putney hadn't thought of in years. Cam used to run secret exchanges between Sedge and Gary Sand. As it turned out, Cam hadn't known the half of what Gary Sand was up to.

As he dug deeper into Sedge's files, Cam learned that Gary Sand was an intermediary between Sedge and some very powerful people, a group referred to as *the faction*. They were looking for the objects he'd found in Sedge's files, artifacts Ume referred to as *keys*. At first it seemed to be some kind of illegal antiquities ring—Sedge collected art and liked old things, so it made sense. But after talking to

Ume, Cam knew that this wasn't the case. Gary Sand wasn't some kind of shady dealer looking for black-market treasure. The faction was searching for keys, and these keys could only be opened by a person. Sand had been hired to find that person, someone referred to in quasi-mystical terms as *the solver*. Now, in Japan, Cam understood who they'd been looking for: Mike Brink. Sedge needed Brink alive because Mike Brink was the solver, a man with the ability to open the keys. The single person who could control Sedge. Except, of course, Cam.

There are only a few with the gift, and Mike Brink is one. And for that, he must be kept alive.

Cam fumbled for his phone, got a grip, and swiped.

"You missed your stop, Putney."

It was Sedge. Cam glanced out the window. Brilliant white light of the full moon, opalescent, the world speeding by. "*Missed?*"

"Are you awake, Mr. Putney?" Sedge's voice was smooth, too smooth. "Or is this a dream?"

"I'm . . ." There were rice fields. Mountains. He was in the countryside. *What the fuck.* "I'm not sure."

"You are exactly one hour and twenty-seven minutes from Kyushu, Japan's beautiful southern island. You will soon disembark at Fukuoka Station."

Suddenly it made sense. Cam was supposed to meet Ume in Kyoto. He'd missed his stop. "Fuku—*where?*"

"Nearly at the end of the line, I'm afraid. You have slept the whole way. I'm assuming you were drugged, as your heart rate fell very quickly one hour and thirty-five minutes ago."

Cam looked at the screen of his phone. He saw his blood pressure, heart rate, and his location mapped out on the screen. Sedge tracked his heart rate and had his biometrics: a scan of his iris, fingerprints, DNA sequence taken from hair follicles. His body, his movements, his identity—everything belonged to Jameson Sedge.

"Your phone was in your pocket," Sedge said. "I couldn't see what happened. Did Brink do this?"

"The sister."

"Of course. Sakura is well trained. Not as good as Ume—the girl is too cerebral—but equally battle-ready. A hard childhood does that, I suppose. Makes one a fighter."

Cam pulled himself to the edge of his seat, straightened his spine. Everything hurt. "I'm sorry," he said. "I didn't see it—"

"Apologies are unhelpful in the current situation."

What *would* be helpful would be to close his eyes and fall back into the abyss of sleep. His body was so heavy. His mind slow.

"It's time to course-correct, Mr. Putney. When you exit the train at Fukuoka Station, you will find a car waiting."

"Going where?"

"You'll hold for instructions. We lost contact with them in Kyoto, and they managed to remain out of sight—no camera has picked them up, and of course they aren't using their phones. But Sakura just made a call, so we have them now."

"I'll be ready."

"Good. And I don't want to distress you even further, but your daughter threw a little fete at your place last night."

His screen cut to video footage from the lobby of his apartment building. A group of high school kids—his daughter among them—laughed and talked as they squeezed into an elevator. Jasmine was supposed to be staying with her mom in Queens. Cam had asked the doorman to keep an eye on his place, but clearly the man didn't think a teenaged girl throwing an unsupervised party was worth contacting Putney. Cam was about to ask how Sedge got word of it, but, of course, he knew.

"I sent Jasmine's mother a text from your number. She sorted it out."

"Thanks," Cam mumbled, feeling a mixture of helplessness, anger, and relief. He didn't want to have to deal with Jasmine's mother, or Jasmine for that matter. Not now.

"My pleasure. Now, get yourself together and be ready for my instructions."

54

Sakura ran along the central pathway of the Arashiyama forest, a curvilinear corridor that cut through the bamboo grove, her shoes crunching through ice-covered snow. A cold wind swept through the bamboo, a symphony of haunting woodwind, engulfing her in a reedy sound. It wasn't safe—the moon lit up the path like a floodlight, leaving her exposed. But it was the fastest way through, and she needed to hurry.

More than twenty minutes had passed since she called for help. She hoped it was enough time for Mike and Rachel to get to the pickup point. It was possible that they were there now, watching the sky for the helicopter. She imagined it touching down. She imagined them climbing inside and being lifted into the sky. Their escape was what she wanted most.

They just might get away with it.

And then a shot cracked through the night. She didn't need to see Ume to know her sister was there, in the forest. It was odd, and so unlike Ume to announce herself. She always attacked silently and slipped away without leaving so much as a fingerprint. A gunshot meant she wanted Sakura to know she was coming for her. It meant she wanted to terrify her.

Scanning the forest, Sakura searched for the source of the shot.

The light of the moon, sliced by blades of bamboo, lay over the snow, sharp-edged sheafs of illumination. Nothing.

Ume was there, but where?

Really, she could be anywhere. The forest was an obstacle course, one filled with endless pockets of shadow. Ume knew how to be invisible. An image of her mother appeared, a memory of her teaching Sakura how to defend herself in the dojo. *Let your opponent do the work,* she'd said. *Let him come at you. Evasion is often more effective than aggression.* It was irrational, but she wished her mother were there with her. She wanted to feel her strength, smell her familiar scent. If she stood by her side, Sakura would have the courage to fight. Or maybe none of this would be happening at all.

Another shot rang through the night. A bullet exploded through the bark of a nearby tree, blowing a hole in its soft green skin. *Another shot.* She was too exposed.

She swung her leg over a fence, climbed the embankment, and slipped into the dense forest. Pressing past waves of willowy trees, she pushed deep into the grove. Stalks of bamboo rose a dizzying fifty meters, so high that looking up made her lose her balance. From that angle she could see the entire length of the grove, a perspective that revealed two important factors. First: Ume wasn't alone. There were two women standing along the path—Ume's assassins, the ones who'd accompanied her to the Three Shrines attack. And second: Mike and Rachel hadn't made it out of the forest.

They were hunkered down among the trees about fifty feet ahead, hemmed in by thick drifts of bamboo. If they could get over the embankment and past Ume's assassins, they would have a direct route out of there. They had to try.

Through the thick trees, Mike met her eye. He must have known what she was thinking, because he shook his head: *Don't do anything stupid.*

Stupid would be to follow her first instinct and fight her way out. It was her nature to respond to aggression with aggression. Her biggest weakness in chess was letting an aggressive move break her concentration. But she couldn't let that happen this time. She needed to help Mike and Rachel get to the helicopter.

Another shot.

Sakura crouched down and pressed her cheek against the cold, smooth bark of the bamboo, obscuring her view. Everywhere she looked she saw snow and trees. She knew what Ume was doing. She wanted to confuse her, pin her down, then flush her out. She'd extract Ogawa's message from Mike and Rachel, and then she would kill them. All of them, even Sakura. Especially Sakura. After her betrayal at the Three Shrines Sanctuary, there was nothing between them but memories. And even in memory, she always lost to her sister.

Still, Sakura would fight. She dropped to her belly and pulled herself though the trees, snow encasing her hands in gloves of ice. Quietly, quickly, she slithered to them. She sidled up to Mike and leaned her lips to his ear: "You two need to get out of here. Now."

He shrugged and nodded toward the path, showing her the obvious: *roadblock.*

"I'm going to distract her." She got up and squatted next to Brink and Rachel. "You run."

Mike gave her a look of alarm and shook his head. *No way.*

"They don't want *you.* They want the solution. I'll give Ume the tiles while you get the hell out of here. I'll be at the helicopter before it takes off."

She gestured to Rachel to give her Ogawa's tiles. Rachel removed the tiles from her pocket and laid them in the snow.

"You need to come with us, Sakura," Brink said.

"If I stay, you'll get to the cave. That's the most important thing."

"The most important thing is that you don't die here."

"*Trust me,*" she said. "There is no one on earth who knows how to fight Ume like I do. I know all her weaknesses. Come on, guys, have a little faith. And besides . . . even if Ume can put together the tiles in the right pattern, she can't use the solution without *you.*"

"What do you mean?" Mike asked, studying Sakura.

It was something Sakura hadn't understood, but once, when she was a child, she'd heard Sedge describe a solver as *the one who could open the keys and bring the pattern together.* She hadn't understood what he meant at the time, but now she did. Mike Brink was that solver.

"Do you remember when I told you that I knew something that would change how you understood yourself? It's this: Nothing you solve is as important as *you. You* are the final step. Not these tiles. Not the Lo Shu Square. *You* are the key to it all."

Above, in the distance, the whirring of a helicopter filled the air, the vibration thrumming through the night.

"It's time," Sakura said. "You have one shot at this." Sakura collected the tiles. "Ready?"

Brink glanced at Rachel, as if looking for her support, but Sakura knew that Rachel saw that there was no other way.

"Okay, puzzle boy, this isn't speed-cubing; this is the real thing," Sakura said, smiling. "Here we go."

With that, she leapt up, ran through the bamboo, scaled the fence, and jumped down to the pathway. In the distance, she saw Mike and Rachel run. She prayed that the forest spirits would protect them.

As Sakura stood in the moonlight, waiting for her sister, she knew that everything she'd grown up believing was wrong. She hadn't been training to open the Dragon Box or to restore the honor of her ancestors. She'd been learning, with each passing year, to grow into the woman who could face Ume.

"*Umeboshi!*"

55

Umeboshi!

Ume's heart skipped a beat. She hadn't heard her nickname in years, and yet the simplicity of it and the way Sakura shouted it was so particular to her childhood that it had the power to stop her cold. Watching her sister, she saw their father, his wide brilliant smile, the way he looked at the world as if it were a specimen in a petri dish. Sakura was so like him that it broke Ume's heart. For a second she wanted to turn and leave. This was the hardest thing she would ever do.

Ume stepped out of the shadows to Sakura, waiting in the moonlight.

"Here," Sakura said, throwing a handful of tiles in the snow. "It's what you came for."

Clever opening move. Sakura's specialty. Bending to collect the tiles would allow Sakura to strike first, and so Ume ignored them. She took in Sakura's expression, took in the sound of running in the distance, and noted the fact that Yuuka and Michiko had gone after Brink and Rachel. It was just Ume and Sakura, two sisters facing each other in the freezing air, just as it always had been.

Ume grabbed a stalk of dead bamboo from the snow and broke it in two, cracking the dried hollow pole over her knee, then tossed one half to her sister. They'd always shared everything, and it seemed fitting that they should each have half of the weapon that would end one of their lives.

Ume bowed. Sakura bowed in return.

Adjusting her grip on the bamboo, Ume felt its cold solidity between her fingers, the perfect weight of it, the familiar tension between her body and her weapon. It was never clear: Was the weapon an extension of her or she an extension of the weapon? She closed her eyes, thought of the women who had trained her, of the *onna-bugeisha* and their mission. They had given everything. *Everything.* Holding them in her thoughts, Ume struck.

The bamboo slammed into Sakura's left side, hard, knocking the air from her. She seemed surprised, but surely she'd expected it. *Your opening move is always humiliation,* Sakura had once said, and she was right. Ume always began strong, dominating her opponent from the first second. Since the day she'd been tripped in a kendo match, she struck first and hard. Demoralize and annihilate.

Sakura anticipated the next blow and blocked it. She blocked the one after that, too, the hollow thud of bamboo on bamboo echoing through the still night. Ume struck again, harder, hitting Sakura's ankle, a fierce blow. It was exhilarating to see Sakura wince in pain, to know she'd injured her, a salve for a deep, unhealable wound.

It was an art, taking the advantage, knowing how to turn a momentary weakness into a victory. Ume thrust forward; Sakura stumbled back, feinted, and swung. The blow came before Ume could register it, a smashing slice to the face. She took the pain in, tracked it as it changed the fabric of her nervous system. She acknowledged it, then accepted it, even as blood wet her cheek and dripped into the snow.

Rehearse your death every morning and night. Only when you live as though already dead will you find freedom.

Ume's cheek throbbed. She struck Sakura's leg, then her arm, weakening her, surrounding her, then swept her feet out from under her. Sakura landed on her back. Ume stood above, looking down, and the image of Sakura in their shared futon, her hair tangled, came rushing to her. Ume lowered the pole to Sakura's throat and pressed the tip to her larynx. One hard thrust would crush the windpipe.

"Take them," Sakura said again, gesturing to the tiles scattered in the snow. "It's the solution. It's what Sedge wants."

Ume ignored Sakura's decoy. "Where did Brink go?"

"I don't know," Sakura said.

Ume pressed the pole harder, applying pressure. "Tell me," she said, "or you will never speak again."

"Sister," Sakura managed, struggling for air. "Please."

"You are not my sister," Ume said, but even as she said this, she saw the killers in the dojo on that cold day so long ago, saw her mother fighting. She felt Sakura, so small and terrified, huddled against her in the cold forest. Even as Sakura gasped for air beneath her, Ume heard the desperate sobs of a little girl as their father gave his life to save theirs. Ume had promised herself then that she would always take care of Sakura. But the legacy they'd inherited had turned them against each other.

Ume tossed the bamboo pole aside, bent down, and pinned her sister with her knee as she unsheathed the knife from her belt. It was an honor to die in battle. An honor their mother had received. An honor their great-grandfather had received. Why no less an honor for Sakura?

"Tell me," Ume said, feeling her eyes fill with tears as she pressed the knife to her sister's throat. "If given the choice, will you live or die, Sakura?"

The thrum of a helicopter reverberated through the forest. Ume looked up through the canopy of leaves, against the obsidian sky, and watched it fly away.

And in that moment of inattention, Sakura attacked. She pushed Ume backward, wrenched the knife from her hand, and struck. A blow to the head. Another to the body. One to the legs. Pinning her sister to the ground, the knife pointed at her throat, Sakura said, "I will live."

56

Brink watched Kyoto recede from behind the thick Plexiglas of the imperial helicopter. They angled away from the bamboo forest, lifted high in the air, and soon the landscape opened into a series of luminous circuits, roads and railroad tracks punctuated by tranches of dark earth. Reels of city streets lit up like so many strands of Christmas lights. Above, the full moon hung in the sky, its caverns like fissures in bone china.

In the cockpit, two young men in uniforms—maybe military, maybe imperial, Brink wasn't sure—navigated the helicopter through the night. Brink wondered if they had any information at all or if they were just following orders. Most likely they had no idea who they were flying or why they were transporting them across central Japan to Kyushu.

They definitely had no idea of the danger they were facing. Sedge could be tracking the navigation system of the helicopter that minute. Hell, Sedge could be *inside* the navigation system. He could take control and hurtle them into a mountainside and these guys would never know what hit them. Brink was in the impossible position of having valuable information that he was helpless to use. He had to trust that Sedge had no idea that they were in that helicopter at that moment. He had to trust that Sakura's diversion worked.

That Sakura was down there, alone against her sister, gutted him. Despite her assurances, despite the fact that she was right—there was no other way to get to the cave undetected—it went against everything in him to leave a friend behind.

Rachel, sensing his feelings, turned to him. "It was the right thing, Mike," she said, putting a hand on his. "You know we had no choice."

"I'm trying to believe that, but there were three of them back there. Sakura is outnumbered."

"She *told* us to go," Rachel said, but her voice lacked conviction. They both knew Sakura had put herself at risk for them. Her sacrifice raised the stakes. Now Meiji's deadly game didn't threaten only Brink's life. It threatened Sakura's, too.

Brink took a deep breath, trying to push away his feelings, and straightened in his seat. "Sakura wants us to finish this," he said finally. "And that's exactly what we're going to do."

"That's the spirit," she said. "There are some important things we need to talk about before we get to the cave. Things that will change the way you see this contest. How you see everything, really." Rachel glanced at the pilots and gave Brink a look of concern. "Can I speak freely?"

It was impossible to know if they were being monitored, but it was a risk he was willing to take. He leaned close to her and whispered, his voice drowned by the loud whirring of the helicopter blades, "Is this about Dr. Trevers?"

Rachel nodded. "I was able to get a copy of the medical examiner's report. There were elevated levels of carbon monoxide in his blood. They found there was a carbon monoxide leak in his office. The alarm malfunctioned. Dr. Trevers's death is being ruled accidental."

Brink took a deep breath, the kind of breath Dr. Trevers would have called a "grounding breath," the oxygen in his lungs calming his mind, releasing the tension in his muscles, and allowing him to focus entirely on Rachel. Carbon monoxide poisoning? In a modern hospital? It didn't make sense at all. "You don't believe that's what really happened, do you?"

Rachel leaned closer, lowering her voice. "After the email he sent you? Not for a second. And so I made a point to question April further. I was actually able to get her on the phone after I landed. I asked her to check your records, and she found that certain files were missing."

"Missing? I don't understand."

"All the files on you that Dr. Trevers kept are gone. Computer files were deleted, as were their backups on the cloud. Their department has a file-sharing system that allows other neurologists to access your records—these files also disappeared."

"Which ones?"

"Everything that had to do with the new treatments Trevers was developing for you."

Brink let this sink in, feeling his heart twist. That Dr. Trevers had been murdered was painful. That he'd been killed because of his work with Brink was devastating. "Why would anyone care about my medical records?"

"Clearly someone didn't want you to continue with that treatment. Not only did they eliminate the man who could help you, they made sure you wouldn't get help elsewhere. Without records of what Trevers developed, no other doctor can pick up where he left off."

Brink was confused. His injury had nothing to do with anyone else. He couldn't even begin to fathom why anyone would care enough to harm Dr. Trevers because of it. "But *why*?"

"Because if Dr. Trevers was successful and helped you restore your brain function to the way it was before your accident, it would close down your abilities."

"But Dr. Trevers has helped me manage my condition for years."

"*Manage* is the key word. We both know that meditation and exercise and diet and all the other methods you've used to control the side effects of your injury are nothing more than Band-Aids. They make you feel better, but they aren't going to change you. The medications he was developing, on the other hand, would have altered your brain chemistry. They could've returned your brain function to how it was before the accident. Someone—and my bet is Jameson Sedge—did not want that to happen."

"So Sedge cares about my brain chemistry so much that he'd kill my doctor?" Brink heard how dismissive he sounded, but he didn't want to believe it could be true. If he was responsible for Trevers's death, Brink wouldn't be able to live with himself.

Rachel sighed, and he could see that she was choosing her words with care. "You *do* understand that your *brain chemistry* has made you unique?" She held his eye for a moment. "What Sakura said back in Kyoto intrigues me. She called you *the key to it all.* Do you have any idea what that means?"

"I was hoping you'd tell me."

Rachel gave him a long look, and he could see that she was deciding how to proceed. "I'm going to tell you my interpretation of what Sakura said, but as you are well aware, my theories are not exactly in line with mainstream thought about history or religion or, well, *anything.*"

She crossed her arms over her chest, leaned back in her seat, and said, "I think Sakura hit on the *real* reason you're here, Mike."

"The *real* reason? As if everything I've gone through isn't real enough?"

"What's happened in the past two days is about more than an imperial treasure. It's about more than outsmarting a mad genius. This whole thing is about *you,* Mike. All of this."

"This puzzle box was made over a hundred and fifty years ago. And the jewel is, what, almost three thousand years old? Surely this is about more than me."

"True—the particular elements that you're dealing with have their own history, and the intrigue around them is not your doing, to be sure. But there's a reason you, Mike Brink, are here right now, and not some other guy. All those people who tried and failed to get this far? There's a reason they didn't succeed."

The helicopter angled and Brink caught a glimpse of water below as they crossed the straight between Honshu and Kyushu.

Rachel continued, "When Sakura said that you are the key to all of this, something clicked for me. The ancient cultures I study are vastly different, but in most of them there is the belief in a universal system of knowledge. A kind of Rosetta stone of the old teachings, if you will. Throughout history, there have been innumerable references to keys that unlock different kinds of knowledge. They are called by various names—codes, seals, scrolls, *keys*—but they have the same purpose: to unlock something hidden from humanity, something extraordinarily precious. Over time, the codes or keys to access this record were lost, or intentionally hidden. It is believed in some cultures that it can, under the right set of circumstances— enlightenment, the second coming of Christ, angelic or demonic visitation, and so on—be recovered.

"Alongside the references to an ancient system of knowledge, there are numerous references to a person as a key to unlocking sacred information. This person—sometimes called a *culture hero*—is essential to bringing progress, knowledge, and safety to the world. That person, according to Sakura and from what I've observed, is *you*."

He began to object, but Rachel gave him a look. She wasn't finished. He felt a wave of affection for her. She knew how he felt about her theories, she knew that he would fight her on them, but she was telling him anyway.

"I know you don't want to hear this, but there are some things that you need to face. First, your brain injury has made you into something utterly extraordinary, a person with abilities that occur to one person in a billion. Second, I'd like you to consider what we went through in New York back in 2022. You want to pretend it didn't happen and that we didn't experience something that most people would consider strange, even impossible, but I know—and you do, too, if you've read my research—that it was an integral part of human experience, one recorded consistently throughout history. Now Sakura gives us information about a group of people who have been searching for generations for *someone* who can access an extremely powerful system of knowledge, for *a solver,* a singular individual—

one person in a billion—who can unlock this knowledge. The Dragon Box was a test, Mike. You passed it. *You are that person.* Sedge knows it. The faction knows it. And they need you very badly. Badly enough to kill your doctor if he threatens to change you."

Brink stared at her, ready to argue. Part of him wanted to tell Rachel she was nuts, to dismiss everything she said as more of her weird, esoteric theories, the kind that they would debate over takeout Chinese. But after everything he'd been through, after everything he'd seen and felt, he knew there was truth in what she was saying.

The helicopter banked right, turning steadily toward land.

"If what Sakura says is true, Sedge needs you because *you* are a key. The key of keys: the man who can open the sacred mysteries. The God Puzzle and the jewel, and every other code or seal you encounter, are just pieces of a larger puzzle. You're a conduit"—Rachel lifted her hands, encompassing the helicopter, the entire material world— "between this and something greater. A doorway between what we know and what is out there, waiting to be discovered. That is what Sakura meant when she said *you* are the key, Mike. She understands that this contest isn't only about the jewel but about you. You are essential, not only to me, who cares about you, or to Sedge and the faction, who want to use you for their own purposes, but to humanity."

Brink felt a wave of emotion as he listened to Rachel. What Rachel was saying touched him in a way he couldn't explain. Some part of his mind, some deep element of his spirit, knew what she said was true. He was the key to it all.

"And for your sake," Rachel continued, "and the future of civilization, we need to be sure that you don't let Sedge get what he wants."

"And how do we do that?"

"Solve Ogawa's puzzle, give it to the emperor, and get the hell out of Japan."

57

It was near three o'clock in the morning when the helicopter touched down in Takachiho, Miyazaki Prefecture. They climbed out and into a deserted parking lot, illuminated by the full moon.

Brink was looking around, wondering how they would find the cave—it could be anywhere beyond the parking lot—when a man stepped from the shadows. He bowed deeply and introduced himself. "I am Odā," he said. "Director of the Amano Iwato Shrine."

Brink started to introduce himself, but Odā interrupted. "I was told your names, only . . ." He looked from Brink to Rachel. "I was told there would be three of you."

"There *were* three of us," Rachel said, her voice brittle.

"Oh, I see," Odā said, his voice so soft that Brink strained to hear. "I'm sorry to learn this. I was told that you are in danger. Hopefully that danger has not followed you here. Come, let's get out of this parking lot."

Odā led them across the lot, through a large torii gate, into a narrow byway, then along a footpath illuminated with paper lanterns, electric bulbs burning within. There was a large shrine, but Odā took them directly to a wooden gate. He unlocked the door and brought them down a winding path, through clusters of bare-limbed trees, the sound of rushing water in the distance. In a matter of minutes, they stood by the bank of a narrow river.

"The Iwato River," Odā said. "And that, on the other side, is the cave itself."

Along the riverbank, just visible in the moonlight, stood stacks of smooth river stones, many hundreds of them, an encampment of gray towers.

"These are offerings," Odā said, gesturing to the stones. "Prayers to the goddess Amaterasu. As you can see, many people come here to pray. It is a beloved place. Amaterasu is very important to the Japanese people, and while her story is mythological, she is a deeply revered deity and ingrained in our culture."

Odā stepped closer to the bank and bent down to the water. "Before you enter the cave, you must wash your hands."

Brink and Rachel washed their hands in the icy water, then followed Odā over a footbridge to the cave's entrance. "The Heavenly Stone Cave is just up there, beyond those trees," Odā said, bowing deeply. "I must leave you here. I'll wait across the footbridge for you."

With that, Odā turned, leaving Rachel and Brink alone in the still night. They walked into the forest and soon found themselves in a clearing. The cave rose before them. Brink checked the moon's position in the sky. It was setting and, from the direction of the moonlight, he saw that it would soon fall directly over the mouth of the cave.

That was it. The moonlight.

"Look," he said, pointing to the cave. "Do you see the direction the light is moving?"

Rachel studied it for a moment. "Of course," she said. "That's why the Dragon Puzzle can only be solved during the full moon. The moonlight indicates the location. It will fall into the cave and illuminate the correct path."

"Which I'll follow directly to Meiji's treasure."

"It's an ancient practice to use starlight and moonlight to mark sacred spots," Rachel said. "The Great Pyramid of Giza. Stonehenge.

There is an entire field of research called archaeoastronomy that relates to it. But I've never heard of it being used in a natural formation like a cave."

Brink shivered and pulled his jacket close. The chill of the night air, the strange beauty of the cave—he was suddenly overwhelmed by what lay ahead. What had Ogawa planned next? And would he survive it?

Soon, the light of the moon frosted the top of the rocks and began its slow descent toward the cave entrance. In a minute, perhaps two, it would fall directly over it. He needed to be ready.

"You're going to have only a few minutes before the position of the light changes. You'd better get going."

"Aren't you coming?"

"I can't help you in there," Rachel said. "This is your moment. I'll only distract you. I'll stay here and"—she smiled playfully and lifted her hand, pointer finger straight, thumb cocked back like a pistol—"be the lookout."

An explosion of light cut through the trees and fell over the opening of the cave. There, somewhere in the recess of that cave, was the treasure Meiji had hidden away, the jewel protected by Ogawa's ingenuity. Brink only needed to follow the light to find it.

But as he turned to go, Rachel pulled him back, wrapped him in her arms, and hugged him, holding him so close he could feel her heart beating. "Promise you'll be careful," she whispered, then kissed him softly, tenderly, on the lips. "I need you just as much as the faction does." With that, she pushed him toward the cave.

Brink walked away, suddenly unsteady on his feet, his heart beating so hard his pulse radiated through him, insistent.

The cave was a voluminous space, damp and chill. An oppressive scent of fungus and wet earth filled the air, and he could hear, in the distance, the sound of water dripping. As he looked around and his eyes adjusted to the darkness, he couldn't help but imagine the ukiyo-e print of Amaterasu he'd seen in the treasure room, beams of blinding gold radiating from the sun goddess.

I could use a little of your light now, Amaterasu.

But Amaterasu was long gone. Stories were stories, and myths were myths, but this vacuous, cold cave was reality. *No magic here.* The most miraculous thing about it all was their perfect timing. If they'd arrived at the cave twenty minutes later, the moonlight would have been in the wrong position, leaving the cave in obscurity. While the moonlight had been diffuse outside the cave, the beam now fell through a small opening in an interior wall, condensing it and sending it with laser-like accuracy through the belly of the cavern.

A swell of anticipation rose through him. *This was it. The solution.*

Brink followed the illuminated path through the darkness, stopping abruptly where the light hit the wall. He ran a hand over the rock face and felt it immediately—a seam. Bending down, he saw a crack filled with crumbling cement. He swallowed, feeling his heart in his throat. Someone had opened this part of the rock and resealed it. Pressing the stone, he searched for a weakness. Nothing gave, and so he pulled out his Swiss Army Knife and used the blade to pry it open. The rock wobbled and, with pressure, fell away.

Reaching into the recess of the wall, Brink removed a jeweled box and held it in the moonlight. Every inch was covered in glittering gems—rubies, blue sapphires, diamonds—so many jewels he couldn't begin to count them. The *true* Dragon Box. Meiji's great treasure. Tracing its contours, he felt a small, perfect cube. *A box within a box within a box.* He'd found it at last—Ogawa's final puzzle.

As he held the jeweled box, he understood what Ogawa had been trying to tell him all along: There was an order to the chaos. A way through the maze. One had only to persevere to find it. *And he had.* Brink had proven himself Ogawa's equal. He'd broken through the illusions, discerned the correct patterns. *He'd found the treasure.*

Brink turned the box in his hands, the lapidary surfaces scintillating in the moonlight. There were twenty-seven steps remaining to finish Ogawa's puzzle. This box, he knew, would open with exactly twenty-seven moves. He lifted it and shook—there was a solid *thump.* He imagined the thick, glossy drop of jade locked inside, waiting to be freed.

The moves he needed to make came immediately. They were laid out in his mind, easy, waiting. He need only slide the panels. There would be no more tricks or traps. No poisons or razors or acid-filled vials. There was only Mike Brink and Ogawa, two men facing each other through time.

Let's finish this, Brink thought, but as he went to open it, he felt something he'd never experienced before. Hesitation. Uncertainty. He flinched and almost dropped the box. Something wasn't right. He was trespassing. A voice at the back of his mind spoke: *This box was not meant for you.*

He was confused. *What was happening?* He knew the solution, knew every step, but he couldn't open it. He wondered what Rachel would think when he told her. Maybe there was some kind of precedent for this in one of the ancient civilizations she studied. Some Indiana Jones–like curse. Surely she'd know what to do next. He'd take the box to her. Together, they'd bring it back to Tokyo.

But as he turned to leave, he felt the cold metal of a gun press into the back of his neck. He knew who it was, even before he spoke. Cam Putney had beaten him there. He'd been waiting for him.

"Never stand with your back to a door," Cam Putney said. "Especially when your guard is down."

58

Brink took a deep breath, steadying himself as he resisted the urge to run. "Have a nice rest on the train, Cam?"

"Best I've had in Japan so far." Cam Putney removed the gun from the back of Brink's head and stepped to face him, keeping the weapon level. In the dim light, the pyramid tattoo on his neck seemed old and faded, a map to a forgotten destination.

"I suppose you came for this." Brink held up the jeweled box, the gemstones glinting. Even in the weak light, it was striking to behold. That's what Sedge wanted—the jeweled box; the jade jewel inside. And while Brink wanted to return it to the emperor, he wanted to live even more.

Cam's gaze settled on the box, but he shook his head. "Yeah, actually, no." He lowered the gun. "I'm putting this down, but my finger's still on the trigger, bro."

Brink stared at Cam, dumbfounded. *He didn't want the box?* Sliding the jeweled box into his bag, he glanced behind Cam, then back toward the entrance of the cave. No Ume. Cam was alone, or so it seemed. "You've gone through a lot of trouble to find me," Brink said. "Why?"

"There's something we need to discuss. You're not stupid enough to have a phone on you, right?"

Brink shook his head, realizing that he'd been totally wrong. Putney didn't want to hurt him. He couldn't help but remember the way Cam Putney had roughed him up in the past, the brutish, mindless way he'd hunted him down and turned him over to Sedge back in New York. "You don't strike me as someone who likes to talk things through, Cam."

"Yeah, things change, don't they," Cam said. "People do, too. You and I are different, that's a definite, but we've got one important thing in common." He slipped his gun into his belt, walked to the wall of the cave, and punched it, hard.

Brink watched him, stunned. *Was Cam Putney out of his mind?* He'd just smashed his fist against a ton of rock.

"This," Cam said, holding his bloodied knuckles to Brink. "*This* is what we have in common. I feel pain. I feel happiness and sadness and desire and everything a human being can feel. And you do, too."

Without warning, he leapt at Brink and punched him hard. One second Brink was standing, the next he was on the ground in an explosion of pain. Cam looked down at him, an expression of satisfaction on his face, then offered his hand, helping him to stand. "Sorry, bro. That's the worst of it. Have to make it look like we struggled."

A profound confusion settled over Brink. What was Cam's objective here? Was he there to help him or hurt him? Was he setting him up? He looked to the cave entrance again, half-expecting Ume to rush in. Brink touched his forehead. His finger was coated in blood. "I don't get your game."

"Same as yours—to stop Jameson Sedge."

Brink wasn't sure he'd heard him correctly. "But you *helped* Sedge become what he is."

"So did you," Cam said. "If you hadn't gotten involved back in New York, we'd live in a different world now. You didn't know what you were doing, and neither did I. Sedge used us both. But now that we see things a little better, we need to work together."

Brink pulled out the white silk square, dabbed the blood from his forehead, then gave it to Cam, who wrapped it tight around his bloodied fist. It was hard to believe that less than twelve hours had passed since he'd used this square of silk as a blindfold. It was even harder to believe that Cam Putney was asking for his help and that he was going to give it. But the world had turned upside down. Nothing made sense.

"It doesn't seem like there's a lot we can do to stop this now," Brink said. "His growth is going to be exponential."

"There are ways," Cam said. "Sedge trusts me. I have access to everything—all his networks, all his data. I know how to interrupt his digital communications. It isn't easy to do, and I don't have access to the core networks—yet. But I can reroute certain commands, even stop them. There's still time. After you leave this cave, Sedge isn't going to be following you. I'll make sure of that."

Brink took this in, astonished. Not only did Cam want to work together, he was going to protect him. "Are you sure you can risk that?"

"I've thought hard about this, and the real risk, my friend, is doing nothing."

Brink took a deep breath, remembering everything Sakura had told him about the faction. Everything Rachel believed about what his injury had made him. *This whole thing is about you, Mike. All of this.*

"Sedge needs you even more than he needs what's in that box. You're part of his big plans, and not only his. People have been searching for you for a very long time. Who would've thought a dork like you was worth the trouble, right? But apparently you are. Why do you think he got rid of Trevers?"

Brink felt a stab of sorrow, then rage, as Cam verified Rachel's theory: *Sedge murdered Dr. Trevers.* "How did he do it?"

"Hospitals are run entirely through computerized systems. Sedge altered the levels of carbon monoxide in Trevers's office. Not hard to do. Made it look like an accident."

"And the message from Trevers?" Brink asked, but he knew the answer already: *Sedge had sent it.*

"Sedge needed you to accept the invitation. He needed you to find that thing." Cam nodded to Brink's bag, where he'd tucked the box. "And, look, it worked. You got this far. You gotta give it to the guy. His power is terrifying. And he's never wrong, is he?"

Brink felt as though he'd been kicked in the stomach. The news of Dr. Trevers, the confirmation that everything he feared most was true—he was central to Jameson Sedge's plans.

"There is one thing he's wrong about," he said finally. "*Me.* I'll never help him."

"I hope that's true," Cam said. "Because you and me, bro, are the only ones who can stop him."

59

Mike Brink slept for what felt like days, waking to a room of elegant blond wood, tatami mats, and shoji doors, their rice-paper panels lustrous with morning light. Beyond the doors, in the tatami room, a dozen or more lacquered dishes were laid out on the low table—lunch had been delivered while he slept. On his night-side table stood a vase with a single golden chrysanthemum, a re-minder of how he'd ended up here. When he'd opened the origami flower Sakura gave him, he couldn't have imagined where it would take him.

He sat up, getting his bearings. The last time he'd seen this room was before the contest, an eternity ago. His gaze drifted to Conun-drum's food and water bowls, exactly where he'd left them, and a wave of panic ran through him—*where was Connie?* The empress had promised to find her, but he hadn't heard a thing about her and, when they'd arrived at the palace, he was so exhausted he hadn't thought to ask.

Brink pulled himself out of bed. Everything ached as he brushed his teeth and washed his face. He put on some clean clothes—a pair of black jeans, a T-shirt with an Escher optical illusion, and his red Chuckies. When he looked at himself in the mirror, he winced. He had a fist-size bruise over his right eye and scrapes from his wipeout on the bike over his left cheek. Nothing that wouldn't heal, but still, he didn't love the idea of going back to New York—to his neighbors, his friends, his regular life—looking like he'd had the shit kicked out of him.

The important thing, though, the thing that made it all worthwhile, was that he *hadn't* had the shit kicked out of him. He'd survived every one of Ogawa's tricks. They'd followed every clue, passed every test, and found the jeweled box. Now they only had to open it.

But first he needed to find Conundrum. He shrugged into his jacket, grabbed Connie's leash and a bag of her favorite treats, and was heading out when a knock came at the door. It was Rachel, looking the exact opposite of how Brink felt. She'd pulled her hair up into a bun and wore an elegant silk blouse, fitted trousers, and leather flats. She looked like she belonged in an old library surrounded by leather-bound books, which was exactly where she'd be if she wasn't helping him.

"Ouch," she said, her eyes narrowing. "That bruise looks nasty."

"Looks much worse than it feels," he said, lying to minimize Rachel's concern. They had more-important matters to think about than the state of his face. "Any news about Sakura?"

"Nothing," she said, biting her lip and turning away to hide her fear. He understood exactly how she felt. They hadn't discussed it since the helicopter, but they both were worried sick.

"This came to my room," Rachel said, holding up a card and changing the subject. "Delivered with my lunch—which was amazing, by the way." Rachel glanced at the feast laid out at the far side of the room. "You should really eat something. You must be starving."

Brink took the card and read it: They were expected in the treasure room.

"Any idea where the treasure room is located?" Rachel asked. "I've been wandering through this minimalist nightmare for half an hour, and I only just figured out how to find you."

"I know where the treasure room is, but, listen, I'm not going anywhere until . . ." He lifted the leash.

"They found her," Rachel said, smiling. "I asked specifically about Connie when my lunch was delivered. She's fine."

"You're sure?" Brink heard the anxiety in his voice. Funny how he could face life-threatening booby traps and poison without blinking but was on the verge of a nervous breakdown at the idea that Connie might be gone.

"Absolutely sure. They found her hiding under one of the shrines. She's been staying with the princess, Aiko. It seems they've hit it off."

Brink sighed, relieved. "Before we go, I need to figure out how I'm going to explain this." He walked to his bed and removed the jeweled box from under his pillow. He'd slept with it, his fingers running over the surfaces in his dreams. He'd hoped his feelings about it would change. But they hadn't. *This was not meant for you.* "The emperor expects an *open* box."

Rachel glanced at the jeweled box. "Still not feeling it?"

He shrugged. "It's a first for me," he said, turning it in his hands. The weight of the box, the physical need to solve it, nearly drove him crazy—*he knew how to open it. Why couldn't he?*

Rachel lifted the box from Brink and, sitting on the edge of his bed, ran a finger over the jeweled surface. "Have you considered that maybe you shouldn't open it?"

"*Shouldn't* open it?" he said, incredulous. "After everything I went through to find it?"

"I'm not saying that you're not *skilled* enough to open it but that maybe this part of the mystery, the final solution, wasn't supposed to be solved by you."

Rachel placed the box on the table, next to the chrysanthemum.

"Think about what's inside that box: the jewel of benevolence. It is a piece of the imperial regalia, the primary symbols of the legitimate rule of the descendants of a female deity—Amaterasu. Together, these three regalia symbolize balance, the masculine and feminine elements that bring about harmony in a ruler. The sword is brute force, or *valor*. The jewel is kindness and compassion, or *be-*

nevolence. The mirror is the combination of masculine and feminine—balance, harmony, and *wisdom.* The empress Suiko's warning to Meiji was about the future of a country without balance—the dangers of a future without the daughters of the goddess."

Brink thought of the violence and terror of war, of all the lives destroyed by the decisions of leaders who lost a sense of balance. What, he wondered, would the world look like if rulers made decisions out of benevolence?

"The *Yasakani no Magatama* is an empress's stone, one protected by the daughters of Amaterasu. Perhaps it can only be opened by a daughter of the sun goddess."

"Is that even possible?" Brink asked. "The eight empresses who ruled Japan have been dead for hundreds of years."

A soft smile spread across Rachel's face. "No, Mike, they haven't all been dead for hundreds of years. There is a daughter of the goddess who is alive and well. Her name is Aiko, the princess Toshi."

60

As Mike Brink and Rachel Appel approached the treasure room, he saw that the steel door stood open, flanked by imperial guards. *No need to crack a code this time,* he thought, glancing at the kakemono scroll of the frog leaping into the pond. *Splash, indeed!*

The past days had upended his life in ways he could hardly believe, and now, as they made their way into the treasure room, with its soft lighting and heaps of precious objects, he marveled at how much had changed since he'd last visited. He'd believed he was solving a mystery when, in fact, he'd found answers to the most important questions about himself. He was everything Rachel had believed him to be, and more. Dr. Trevers had said it to him once, and he heard him saying it now: *The most challenging puzzle you will ever confront is yourself.*

For years he'd resisted going deeper, had fought Dr. Trevers and Rachel, had lived believing that he was just a regular guy with a party-trick talent. He'd clung to the belief that Dr. Trevers could fix him—that everything could be reversed. That he could walk away from his destiny. But he'd been wrong. There was a great power and responsibility behind his abilities. The question Mike Brink faced now was: Could he live up to that responsibility?

The door closed behind them. The emperor and empress sat to-

THE PUZZLE BOX   311

gether on a couch, their daughter, Aiko, the princess Toshi, the girl who had been Sakura's childhood playmate, between them. She was a young woman now, with a warm and open expression, holding Connie on her lap.

Brink clicked his tongue and Connie bounded to him, exuberant, clawing her way up his leg until he scooped her in his arms to lick his face. All the anxiety and tension he'd carried since he lost Connie disappeared. *She was safe.* He put her down, pulled a treat from his pocket, and tossed it to her. Connie caught it midair and lay before him, chewing with pure pleasure. He bent down and scratched her long, soft ears. It took a minute to realize that everyone was staring at him, amused. He stood, smiled with embarrassment, and said, "Thank you for finding her."

"Of course," the empress said, gesturing for Brink and Rachel to sit. "Aiko has grown quite fond of your little friend. Conundrum has kept us all very busy."

Brink sat, and Rachel took the seat next to him. Connie flopped on Brink's shoes, gnawing at her treat. "Where did you find her?"

"She was hiding in the Three Shrine Sanctuary," Aiko said. "She was scared when I found her and wouldn't come out, but I finally convinced her. We've become good friends, but I could tell she missed you." Aiko glanced down at Connie, now curled around Brink's leg. "She belongs with you."

"And this," Brink said, taking the jeweled box and offering it to the emperor, "belongs to you."

Brink realized that he was probably breaking some kind of ancient protocol, but the emperor smiled with pleasure and accepted the box. Turning it in his hands, he examined the elaborate patterns of precious jewels, clearly delighted. "Tell me," the emperor said. "How did you come to find this?"

Brink explained their path from Hakone to Kyoto and then to the Amano Iwato Shrine and the cave. He related how they'd been ambushed—the state of his face proved as much—and how Sakura had sacrificed herself to help them.

"As we followed the clues Ogawa left," Brink said, walking to the case where the pillow book lay under glass, "Sakura and I discovered that Meiji hid the jewel for an important reason."

Removing the pillow book, he gestured for Rachel to join him. Carefully, she removed the fragment of *washi* paper torn from the pillow book and put it in its original place.

Brink read the passage Yoshiko had written about Meiji's dream: *The empress Suiko begs me to protect the benevolent daughters of the goddess.*

"The jewel is Amaterasu's legacy to Japan," Rachel said. "It symbolizes compassion, wisdom, and benevolence. But the jewel is also the legacy of her daughters' right to participate in Japan's future. Benevolence. Rule by kindness. Without it, the sword and the mirror are out of balance. The jewel is meant to go to a future descendant, a *true* descendant of the empress Suiko."

"But where is the jewel?" the empress asked.

Brink nodded to the jeweled box. "It's in there, but . . ." He turned to Aiko. "I'm not *meant* to open it. You are."

The princess was startled and immediately glanced at her father. He considered what Brink had said, then gave the box to Aiko. The princess looked at it for a minute, two, turning it in her hands as if trying to understand a hidden message. Then, with a fluidity of motion that Brink admired, she pushed a panel aside, then another, then another. The box reconfigured, twisted, and shifted until the jewels aligned. As the final piece clicked into place, the top of the box opened.

Aiko gazed inside, then handed the box back to her father. The emperor lifted a piece of jade, a luscious, translucent curve of green stone. It was extraordinarily simple, a thing of pure beauty in contrast to the flash of the gem-encrusted box. As the emperor considered the *Yasakani no Magatama,* Brink felt the weight of generations of imperial ancestors, so many men and women who had ruled with the imperial regalia. The air thickened with all that was unspoken and the possibility of all that the future could bring.

Finally, the emperor stood and presented the jewel to Aiko. The princess turned the jade in her hand, light sliding over its smooth surface, a look of wonder and surprise filling her features. She stood and bowed, a deep and ceremonial bow, one of respect and acceptance. The empress Suiko's legacy would be passed down to Aiko, benevolent daughter of the goddess. The princess Toshi was the rightful descendant of the Chrysanthemum Throne not *despite* being a woman but *because* she was a woman.

Brink saw tears spring into the empress's eyes as she watched her daughter. He could see, in that moment, how much pain she had endured over the abnegation of her daughter's rightful inheritance. The jewel restored her dignity, her daughter's dignity, and the dignity of all women.

"This," the emperor said, handing the jeweled box, now free of the *magatama,* to Brink, "belongs to you."

He accepted the box and, sliding the panels in place, locked it shut. Then, in a burst of movement, he opened it again, counting each of the moves. Twenty-seven steps, the exact number needed to finish Ogawa's seventy-two challenges.

The empress, blinking away her tears, turned to Brink and Rachel. "You have suffered a great deal to return the jewel to us. Is there anything more we can do to show our gratitude?"

"There is one thing we'd like to know," Brink said, glancing at Rachel. "We've been worried about Sakura. Can you tell us what happened to her?"

"Sakura-chan is recovering in Kyoto," the empress said.

"She's been hurt, but not as badly as she might have been," the emperor said. "When she called the Imperial Household Agency to request the helicopter, she also asked that we send assistance on the ground. As it turned out, she didn't need help."

Brink sighed with relief. Everything was as it should be. Sakura was alive, Connie had been found, the jewel was in the hands of the rightful heir to the Chrysanthemum Throne, and Rachel and Brink would be going home. Connie barked and, to Brink's surprise, ran back to the couch and jumped onto Aiko's lap, licking her face. "I will miss you, too, Conundrum," she said, laughing with joy.

As they were leaving the treasure room, Brink said, "You mentioned that Sakura is recovering in Kyoto?"

"In a clinic that is overseen by my personal physician," the emperor said. "She will be released tomorrow and will be coming here, to recuperate among friends."

"If it wouldn't be too much trouble," Brink said, "we'd like to see her before we leave Japan."

61

Mike Brink and Rachel Appel waited in the lobby of the imperial clinic, Connie between them. The day was frigid, the light gray through the plate-glass windows, dull as an old knife, but knowing he'd see Sakura in a matter of minutes lifted his spirits. He'd imagined all the terrible things Ume might have done to Sakura, and so it was a relief when the elevator doors opened and she hobbled toward them on crutches.

The left side of her face was heavily bandaged and her left leg suspended in a cast, but as she made her way across the lobby, she smiled warmly.

"You look terrible," Brink said.

Sakura winked, clearly happy to see him. "You should see my sister."

"Is Ume . . . ?"

"In this very clinic," Sakura said. "But she'll be in jail as soon as she's out. Treason, threatening the life of the imperial family. About ten other charges. She'll be locked up for a long time."

Rachel hugged her, a gesture that clearly made Sakura uncomfortable but that she accepted. "You two didn't have to come all the way down here to see me."

"Of course we did," Brink said. "It's our last chance to say goodbye before heading back to New York."

"We're flying home on the imperial jet tonight," Rachel said, bending to Connie and scratching her ears. "Conundrum likes to fly private."

Brink gestured outside, where a maroon Rolls-Royce awaited. "The emperor and empress insisted that we take their car and bring you back with us to Tokyo."

Sakura raised an eyebrow. "Fancy," she said, looking warily at the car, then beyond, as if expecting a drone to appear on the horizon. "But not very discreet."

"No need to worry," Brink said, thinking of Cam and their pact to stop Sedge. If Cam was to be trusted, he wouldn't need to worry about Sedge following them. At least for now.

"We'll explain in the car," Rachel said, opening the door for Sakura.

Brink took Sakura's crutches and helped her into the voluminous back seat of the Rolls-Royce.

"I want to hear all about it," she said. "And there's something I'd like to show you, too. Someplace special that I think you'll appreciate."

Sakura gave the driver instructions, and they headed northwest. As they drove, Brink felt like he was seeing Kyoto for the first time, and in some ways he was: There were no drones lurking, no surveillance, no one eavesdropping on his every word. He and Rachel explained what had happened at the cave, and he showed Sakura the jeweled box, feeling a sense of disorientation. The extraordinary events of the past days seemed more and more remote.

Soon they'd left the center of Kyoto and were driving into the foothills of the mountains of Ukyo Ward, where thick gray clouds threatened snow.

The driver pulled over before a set of stone steps that rose to a temple on a hill.

"This is Ryōan-ji," Sakura said, as Brink helped her from the car, holding her crutches while she got her bearings. "There's something I want to show you here, but I'm not sure I'm going to make it up those stairs."

Brink followed her gaze over the ice-glazed stone. "Here," Brink said, taking her crutches and giving them to Rachel. "I'll carry you up."

Sakura was light, easy enough to carry, but he could see she didn't like the idea of being helpless. "Don't ever, *ever*, tell anyone I let you do this," she said, her expression tense. She glanced back at Rachel, following behind. "You, either. Not a soul."

"Not a soul," Rachel said, stifling a laugh. "Promise."

Snow began to fall as they approached the entrance of a large *Hojo*, an open structure with a hip-and-gable roof with cedar shingles. The *genkan* was empty, without any shoes in the cubbies. The *Hojo* was utterly silent. "This is the perfect time to visit Ryōan-ji," Sakura said. "We're alone."

Brink slipped off his Chuckies, shoved his feet into a pair of vinyl slippers, and walked through an open space that brought him to a veranda. There, below, lay a rectangular rock garden of about 250 meters, enclosed on three sides. The wall opposite was an earthen barrier of burnt ocher with cedar trees above. But what drew Brink's eye were the fifteen gray, irregular stones positioned in white sand. Islands of moss surrounded the stones, a soft bedding of pale green under crusts of ice. Fresh snow left the faintest layer over the rocks, airy and white.

"This garden is sometimes called the Shichi-Go-San—seven-five-three—for the lay of the rocks. There are five groups laid out from east to west. The first group totals seven, the second group totals five, and the third group has three rocks."

The patterns and numbers caught Brink's attention, and he found himself pondering them, looking for a way to make sense of the arrangement.

"My parents brought Ume and me here when we were little," Sakura said. "It left an impression. Whenever I feel troubled, I think of this spot."

"It's beautiful," Rachel said. "And so peaceful."

"True," Sakura said. "But what I find interesting about this garden is that nobody understands what the hell is happening with these stones. It's one of the most famous Zen gardens in the world, with hundreds of thousands of visitors every year, and yet no one can figure it out. It is the most perplexing riddle in Japan, one more confounding in some ways than the Dragon Box, because it *cannot* be deciphered. In fact, we don't even know if it is meant to be deciphered."

Hearing that something couldn't be solved had the effect of making Brink want to crack it. He instantly found himself studying the garden from every angle, taking in the arrangement of the rocks, his mind filling with possible solutions. And while there were ways to interpret the stones—three, five and seven were numbers that could mean many things; the positioning of the rocks could be the key to understanding the meaning—he saw that there was truth in what Sakura said. It couldn't be solved. It *shouldn't* be solved. That was the entire point. The realization filled him with a strange and wonderful sense of serenity. He felt, suddenly, free.

"See what I mean?" Sakura said, smiling slyly, then turning on her crutches and hobbling away. "Come on, there's something else I want to show you."

She propelled herself through the *Hojo* and out to an exterior walkway that wrapped around the structure. It was elevated two feet off the ground, and below were moss-covered stones, bushes, and trees, a wilderness counterpoint to the severe order of the rock garden. The snow was falling heavily now, fat wet flakes drifting over the tangle of nature.

Stopping at the end of the walkway, Sakura gestured to a mossy declivity below, where a circular stone fountain bubbled from the ground. The base of the fountain was shaped like a coin, and at the center of the circle, a perfect square held a pool of spring water.

"This is the Tsukubai of Chisoku," Sakura said. "A water basin meant for washing before entering a holy place."

Brink got down on his knees at the edge of the walkway and bent to get a closer look at the fountain. Four characters were carved into the stone, one on each side of the square.

"People come from all over the world to see the rock garden," she said. "But what I love most about Ryōan-ji is this hidden fountain. Here, look closer. Do you see the message on the stone?"

Brink took in the characters:

"Back in New York, when I asked you to join me on this treasure hunt, I told you I would tell you something important about yourself," she said. "I told you part of it in the bamboo forest. The other part—maybe the most important part—is this. The characters can be read in two directions, making a word puzzle. And while that's clever, it is what the characters *mean* that is most important."

Brink scanned the characters. He thought he understood them but asked Sakura to translate, to be sure.

"It reads: *Ware tada taru wo shiru*," she said. "Which means: *All one must learn is to be content.*"

A rush of emotion came over Brink as he took in the meaning of these words. *To be content.* For half his life, he'd been plagued by restlessness, compulsion, desire. The hunger to achieve a solution had ruled him. What would happen if he accepted that there were things he couldn't know? How would it feel to be satisfied, to let the mysteries before him remain unsolved, to be *content*?

"Are you telling me to lighten up?"

Sakura laughed. "That's exactly what I'm telling you, puzzle boy. All we have to learn in this life is to be satisfied with what we are, with ourselves. *We are enough.* You are enough. Nothing you can solve, nothing you can *do*, will change that. It is the greatest challenge, but it also brings the greatest reward."

Balancing at the edge of the walkway, Mike Brink leaned over the fountain and let the ice-cold water fall over his hands, washing them clean.

THE END

Acknowledgments

I lived in Japan from 1998 to 2000 and have spent the years since imagining a story set there. I am grateful to my editor, Andrea Walker, for seeing the potential of this novel and for encouraging me as I wrote it. Thank you, Andrea, for being such a brilliant editor and a friend I will always cherish.

Thank you to the Random House dream team—Andy Ward, Alison Rich, Caitlin McKenna, Windy Dorrestyn, Maria Braekel, Vanessa DeJesus, Katie Horn, Madison Dettlinger, Naomi Goodheart, Carlos Beltran, and copy editor extraordinaire Kathy Lord. Thank you to Jiahong Hawthorne Sun for reading the manuscript and offering guidance regarding the history of Japan, Japanese language, and the authenticity of my research.

Thank you to my incredible agent, Susan Golomb, for being by my side every step of the way, and to everyone at Writers House, especially Maja Nikolic, who has brought my work to readers around the world. I'm also grateful to Rich Green at the Gotham Group for his savvy questions about Mike Brink and the larger significance of his story.

I'm in awe of the real puzzle masters who offered advice and constructed the puzzles that appear in the book—Brendan Emmett Quigley, Wei-Hwa Huang, and Kagen Sound, whose puzzle boxes inspired me as I imagined the Dragon Box. Thank you to Dimitris Lazarou for designing the images that appear in the novel.

My first readers are the writers in my writers group: Janelle Brown, Angie Kim, Jean Kwok, James Han Mattson, and Tim Weed. Thank you for helping me shape this novel, for your humor and good taste, and for coming to see me in San Miguel de Allende.

Thank you to Megan Beatie and Megan Beatie Communications for helping get the word out.

I'm especially grateful to the friends who gave support as I wrote this book: Chris Pavone, Sara Divello, Jean Kwok, Anna Geller, Tina Bueche, Angela and Jeff Bluske, Yveline and Nicholas Postel-Vinay, Hannah Brooks, Dennis Donohue, Art and Leona DeFehr, and so many others. Thank you to Dan Brown, whose friendship has been so inspiring.

Most of all, I'm grateful to my family—Hadrien, Alex, Nico, and Sidonie, whose love and support means everything.

ABOUT THE AUTHOR

Danielle Trussoni is the *New York Times* bestselling author of the novels *Angelology, Angelopolis, The Ancestor,* and *The Puzzle Master,* chosen by *The Washington Post* as one of the Best Thrillers of 2023. She is also the author of the memoirs *The Fortress* and *Falling Through the Earth,* which was named one of the ten best books of the year by *The New York Times Book Review.* A graduate of the Iowa Writers' Workshop and winner of the Michener-Copernicus Society of America Fellowship, her work has been translated into more than thirty languages.

danielletrussoni.com
Instagram: @danielletrussoni

ABOUT THE TYPE

This book was set in Caslon, a typeface first designed in 1722 by William Caslon (1692–1766). Its widespread use by most English printers in the early eighteenth century soon supplanted the Dutch typefaces that had formerly prevailed. The roman is considered a "work-horse" typeface due to its pleasant, open appearance, while the italic is exceedingly decorative.